WHITE ALERT

A PROSECUTION FORCE THRILLER

LOGAN RYLES

Severn River Publishing
SevernRiverBooks.com

ISBN: 978-1-64875-599-6 (Paperback)

ALSO BY LOGAN RYLES

The Prosecution Force Series

Brink of War

First Strike

Election Day

Failed State

Firestorm

White Alert

Nuclear Nation

The Reed Montgomery Series

Overwatch

Hunt to Kill

Total War

Smoke and Mirrors

Survivor

Death Cycle

Sundown

To find out more about Logan Ryles and his books, visit

severnriverbooks.com

For Mr. and Mrs. S...
Thanks for opening the door to a marvelous world.

1

Canada

Abdel Ibrahim escaped North America by the skin of his teeth.

The first part, fleeing the United States, had been surprisingly easy. After a near brush with death at the hands of a counter-terrorism strike team in St. Louis, Ibrahim made it to the Canadian border at Detroit/Windsor without incident. The Nissan Sentra he had pre-staged at a storage unit three miles from the site of his attack waited for him, unmolested. The trunk was loaded with supplies—food, a change of clothes. Basic medical essentials and lots of fresh water.

Most important of all was the fake Canadian passport that listed his name as Samuel Hassan, a sufficiently ethnic name as to match his appearance, but innocuous enough not to alert the prejudices of the border guards. The balance worked perfectly, and Ibrahim cleared the gate at Windsor without a snag. He made London, Ontario, by nightfall, and stopped at a ratty motel. He paid in cash. He watched the unfolding panic in the United States on the motel's outdated television set, then fell asleep with a SIG Sauer P320 at his side, loaded and chambered.

He should have kept driving, denying his exhaustion and keeping the Sentra running all through the night, pushing straight through to Quebec.

As it was, he departed the motel just before sunup, and the mistake almost cost him his life.

The Americans had moved more quickly than he'd anticipated. The law enforcement arm of Washington swung into action even before the bodies were finished dropping, and the FBI coordinated immediately with authorities in Mexico and Canada.

The Royal Canadian Mounted Police turned out to sweep the highways en mass. Every radio station carried bulletins concerning the missing terrorist. News websites and TV stations displayed his picture. The whole of North America was urged to be on the lookout for the FBI's most wanted man, and the Canadians in particular leaned into the hunt more aggressively than Ibrahim expected.

Halfway through the seven-and-a-half-hour trek between London and Montréal, the traffic stops began. The Ontario Provincial Police pulled cars over at random, their blinking blue and red lights dotting the emergency lane of Highway 401 every couple of miles. With each passing cruiser, Ibrahim's blood pressure rose a little higher. He kept the SIG pressed between his thigh and the Sentra's console, ready at any moment to resort to desperate measures.

When an OPP cruiser pulled directly behind him and switched its lights on, his heart leapt into his throat. He placed a hand around the SIG and kept driving, praying to Allah that the cruiser was coming for somebody other than him. As the cop closed in and other vehicles faded on all sides, Ibrahim knew his luck was up.

But as with all things concerning the fate of humanity, the smallest of rocks tumbling down a hillside can change the course of history. In this case, that falling rock took the form of an idiot in a race-red Chevrolet Corvette, blowing past the cop as though the cruiser were in reverse.

Ibrahim's blood pressure spiked again as the cop swerved into the left lane. The siren screamed to life. He laid on the gas and raced past Ibrahim in favor of the flashier prey.

And the world's most wanted terrorist drove on.

Ibrahim reached Montréal just after noon. He left the Sentra in a Provigo parking lot and walked the two miles to the Port of Montréal, where the Liberian flagged container ship *Cartova* rested at dock, just as she was supposed to.

Ibrahim was admitted without question. The captain had already been paid. He found a berth concealed inside a shipping container, and the vessel set sail that same afternoon without hitch, reaching the North Atlantic thirty-six hours later.

Ibrahim never left his hidden berth. He lay awake on his cot, breathing silent prayers to Allah. Imagining the terror he left behind. Savoring the terror he had yet to bring.

By the time the *Cartova* made dock, twenty-three days later, Ibrahim was refreshed. His body was strong. His mind razor sharp.

He was ready to unleash the next attack.

2

Guantánamo Bay Detention Camp
Guantánamo Bay Naval Base
Cuba

Four heavily armed U.S. Navy Masters-at-Arms escorted Reed Montgomery and Rufus "Turk" Turkman through a series of concrete hallways and reinforced steel doors, straight into the heart of the detention camp. Reed had experienced prisons before—in fact, he'd even been incarcerated for a time. The smells of harsh cleaning chemicals, body sweat, and damp concrete were all familiar to him.

But there was still something about Gitmo that felt overwhelmingly final. Like the last stop on a long rail line—a solid concrete box in the middle of absolutely nowhere. A place where men are forgotten, and where faces become nameless.

Circumstances aside, he couldn't ever imagine working here. One look into the eyes of the chief petty officer walking at his elbow, and Reed knew his feeling wasn't unique. Nobody wanted to be here. Not the captured. Not the captors. The detention camp at Guantánamo Bay was the ultimate poster child of the reality of war. The definition of a necessary evil, if there even was such a thing.

The MAs stopped at the end of a long hallway, where a steel door painted blue-gray was bolted shut. No window. No viewing port.

The CPO turned to Reed. "Do you want company?"

Reed glanced to Turk. The bigger man wore a look of restrained distaste on his face, as though he were about to clean a toilet, or change the diaper of his six-month-old daughter. Reed couldn't help but identify with the feeling, but there was no use putting off the inevitable. They had both flown through the night to be here—long hours aboard a CIA SAC jet flying through some of the worst turbulence Reed had ever experienced.

No part of this was fun. They might as well get it over with.

"We're good," Reed said. "Can he speak?"

The CPO snorted. "He's capable, if that's what you're asking."

Turk cocked an eyebrow. "He still hasn't spoken?"

"Not a peep. Not even when we put the gloves on him."

Reed tilted his head toward the door. The CPO lifted the latch while the other MAs stood back with hands on their sidearms. Everybody was a little jumpy. Reed pressed inside, unarmed save for his fists, and wrinkled his nose at the immediate stench.

Urine. Sweat. Vomit. The place smelled like a pigsty, but everything was uniquely human. As Turk cleared the door, the CPO flicked a switch, and harsh lights flooded across blank concrete.

The room was empty—or almost empty. Fifteen feet square, with a single metal chair situated right in the middle, just on top of a drain. Seated in that chair was a man with a black bag over his head, his hands and feet cuffed with a chain running between them. Another chain held his body to the chair, and the chair was bolted to the floor.

The Navy wasn't fooling around.

Reed stopped five feet from the guy and wrinkled his nose. The floor was stained with body fluids, the drain grate blackened by use. There were no other items in the room, but a closed closet door stood to one side. Reed could imagine what lay behind it—what tools of the trade the Central Intelligence Agency kept there. Those unspoken things which would be immediately denied before a congressional committee.

The man in the chair knew about those things, also. That much was obvious. He quaked as Reed and Turk entered, and a stream of urine ran across the seat of the chair and down his leg when the door clanged closed. The chains rattled around his chest, and Reed thought he detected a whimper.

But the man didn't speak. Not even a word.

Reed tilted his head, and Turk walked behind the chair to remove the bag. A brown face clouded by tangled black hair was revealed. An untrimmed beard and two black eyes. The CPO hadn't been kidding about the gloves—somebody had put the work on the prisoner. Somebody with a mean right hook, by the look of it. The guy's eyes were barely slits, and the left side of his face had taken the worst of the abuse.

But he stared Reed in the eye without blinking, raw hatred shining from the depths of a desperate soul.

Reed stood with his arms crossed, just staring. Unsure what to say or how to begin. This sort of thing wasn't his forte. He was an operator—a soldier. Not an investigator, and certainly not an interrogator. He didn't belong here. He hadn't wanted to come.

And yet he had, without argument. Not only because the CIA was failing to extract anything from the bound man in the chair, but because Reed was obsessed with this hunt. It consumed his mind day and night, keeping him awake and filling his dreams even when he did sleep.

The blast of fire. The wreckage of loss. The daughter who would never be.

The terrorist Abdel Ibrahim had taken half of Reed's soul. He would fly to any pit anywhere in the world to return the favor.

"Do you know who I am?" Reed said at last. It felt like a bad movie line even as it left his lips, but it was the first thing he could think to say. The prisoner didn't respond. He didn't blink.

"I'm a warrior," Reed said. "A man who works off the books, off the record. A soldier who carries the fight to the enemy, and uses unconventional methods to secure victory. I'm a shadow. A ghost. I don't exist on any paperwork. I don't play by the rules. In some ways, maybe a lot of ways, I'm the American version of you."

Reed's voice never rose above conversational volume as he spoke. He kept his arms crossed. The man didn't speak, but Reed could tell by the glint in his eye that he understood. At least a little.

"The difference, of course," Reed continued, "is that you lose, and I win. Always. Whether by technological advantage, or the weight of resources, or sheer volume of numbers, my side lands on top. Your side goes home in body bags. Five of your friends are already rotting as we speak. The two you sent to Philadelphia, two of the three you sent to St. Louis, and the guy we found you with. You're a lucky survivor . . . so far."

Another glint in the dark eyes. A slight curl of the lip. The man definitely spoke English.

Reed approached the chair and squatted. He placed both hands on his knees. He looked into the man's face at eye level. Reed didn't blink.

"There's two things you need to know," Reed said. "The first: we're going to catch Abdel Ibrahim. Whatever it takes, wherever he hides. I'll be given whatever resources and weaponry I require, and I will run him to the ground if it's the last thing I do. Because that's *what* I do. It's what I've always done, and I've never failed. Not once."

Reed let the threat linger. He waited. The prisoner's breath whistled through his teeth. He trembled a little.

"The second thing you need to know," Reed continued, "is that *you* get to decide how bloody our hunt becomes. I don't have to describe the cost of war. Not to you. You know what happens when bombs rain from the sky, when Marines storm cities. The longer my country searches for Ibrahim, the more bombs they will drop. The more of your people will be caught in the crossfire. It's simple math."

Again, Reed let the comment hang. He kept his hands on his knees. He stared until finally, the terrorist blinked.

"My government has sent me here as a last resort," Reed said. "If you don't talk to me, you won't have another opportunity, and you'll never leave this box. You'll remain here for the rest of your life while your homeland burns, and that will be on *you*. On your soul. Forever."

Reed stood slowly. He folded his arms again. The terrorist quaked a little.

"Tell me where Abdel Ibrahim is," Reed said.

The room went quiet save for the rasping breathing of the prisoner. Reed waited, willing to allow the slow drip of neurosis to wear away at the man's willpower. To beat him down with simple logic and pure hopelessness the way a trickle of water erodes a block wall. Slowly . . . over time.

Because with the strongest of men, that's the only way.

"You think you can threaten me with the blood of my people." The terrorist spoke in a rasp, dry lips adding a lisp as he sagged against the chains. Reed didn't move.

The man looked up, slowly. Bloodshot eyes gazed with pure vacancy at Reed. No heart. No soul. No life. Complete emptiness.

"There is nothing you can take that America has not taken before," the man said. "No number of bodies you can pile that will change your fate. You seek a man, but a man is only the tool. Your war is with Allah, and Allah will have the victory. He has never failed . . . *not once*."

Reed gritted his teeth. He sank to his knees again and placed one hand around the prisoner's exposed thigh. It was already purple with bruises. As Reed squeezed, the terrorist gasped. His lips parted. His eyes watered.

But he didn't look away.

"*Where is Abdel Ibrahim?*" Reed growled.

The man choked. Then he laughed, a heartless sound erupting out of a dry throat. Tears ran down his face, but the smile never broke. His swollen eyes never blinked.

He simply said: "I don't know."

Reed stood outside the compound and cupped his hand against the Caribbean breeze. The cigarette ignited under the jet flame of his lighter, and relieving nicotine flooded his lungs. It wasn't enough to take the raw edge off his nerves following a two-hour interrogation of the man chained to the chair.

But it certainly helped.

Turk appeared through the door next to him, scrubbing damp hands against his pants to wipe away the water from the hand sink. He looked battered and very tired—older than Reed had ever seen him. The bigger man said nothing as Reed shook out another cigarette and passed it to him. Turk lit up, and for a while the two smoked in silence while Navy MAs paced the fence line thirty yards away. The moon hung bright over Cuba, dark clouds gliding across its silver surface but failing to block its light.

It was a beautiful night—or it would have been, on another island. In another world.

"He's not gonna talk." Turk's east Tennessee drawl was toneless and flat. Not defeated, just absolute.

Reed grunted and sucked on his cigarette. He felt a slight tremor in his hands and looked down to see the tip of the smoke tremble. He blamed it on the breeze and knocked ashes over the concrete.

"He doesn't know anything anyway," Reed said. "This was a wasted trip."

"He might know where they prepped," Turk said. "He might know where Ibrahim sourced the VX—originally, I mean. Before the arms dealer. Or he might know how they blasted us with all those robocalls."

Reed contemplated, remembering the tens of thousands of automated calls that had blanketed America just prior to Ibrahim's unprecedented attacks. All the threats of violence and retribution. It was a technological masterpiece. A riddle the best technicians and investigators at the FBI and the NSA still couldn't unravel.

But the man in the prison block behind them wouldn't know the answer to that riddle. He wasn't a kingpin, or even a captain. He was a pawn. A front line soldier.

An *expendable*. Much like Reed.

"He doesn't know," Reed said.

Turk accepted the judgment with a grunt and a nod. Both men finished their cigarettes. Reed was already thinking about the rough flight back to Nashville. A few hours of sleep before he had to be up in the morning to look after his two-year-old son while his wife attended physical therapy, slowly learning to put her life back together after the monster known as Abdel Ibrahim had done everything in his power to rip it away.

"Did you mean it?" Turk said suddenly.

Reed glanced left. "What?"

"What you said in there, about guys like him and guys like us being the same. Do you really believe that?"

Reed locked eyes with Turk and saw something he hadn't before. A dark uncertainty. A question.

"Hell no," Reed said. "We're nothing like that thug."

Turk nodded slowly, and Reed stamped the cigarette out. Then both men turned for the tarmac, and the turbulent flight home.

3

Walter Reed National Military Medical Center
Bethesda, Maryland

President Maggie Trousdale lay perfectly still, her head cradled on a pillow, headphones clamped around her ears. New Orleans–style jazz played through the speakers, not quite loud enough to block out the irregular clacking, banging, and humming of the MRI machine, but enough to calm her strained nerves.

She didn't like enclosed places. She didn't like laying still. She wasn't a fan of loud noises, either. Who was? She kept her eyes closed and measured each breath, hands at her sides, ignoring the noise.

And ignoring the pain. It radiated from her midsection, not far above her pelvis. Right where her liver lay—right where an assassin's bullet had torn through her body like a freight train the previous November. There was a scar there the size of a tangerine, and there always would be. If she pressed on the spot, her mind would sometimes turn hot with terror. She would feel that awful sensation of crushing force and blazing pain all over again—the moment she toppled to the stage floor, right before everything went black.

It was like a nightmare playing right before her eyes, and sometimes it was an actual nightmare. Sometimes she would wake up in cold sweats, consumed by raw panic. Sometimes it hurt to breathe, hurt to walk, hurt to think.

But the pain erupting in her liver was new. It stood in stark contrast to a steady track of physical recovery, aided by half a dozen medications and supplements and enough physical therapy torment to call into question her Eighth Amendment protections against cruel and unusual punishment. The pain now was searing and sudden, ripping and persistent.

It restored real fear to her mind for the first time since she awoke in a Chicago hospital, clinging to life by a thread. It brought a repeat omen of doom to her mind that she couldn't ignore, no matter how hard she tried.

The promise that her recovery might be failing. That this fight may not be over.

Maggie breathed evenly and kept her eyes closed. She embraced the music, and the machine ground on.

In addition to providing 2.4 million square feet of sprawling clinical space, Walter Reed Medical Center featured a designated treatment facility exclusively reserved for the health, well-being, and recovery of the president of the United States. Besides all the usual hospital rooms and medical equipment necessary to manage any number of injuries or ailments, there was a presidential suite fully equipped for the leader of the Free World to live and work almost indefinitely. It was like a secondary White House, where the business of the nation could proceed while inconveniences such as gunshot wounds could be managed with minimal impact and maximum comfort.

The suite even included space for a presidential spouse, the White House chief of staff, and a conference room for cabinet meetings. It was the Cadillac experience, but after Maggie re-dressed and took a seat at the conference table, she sat alone. With the shades drawn and the morning sun blocked out, the room was dim. The dull hum of an air conditioner groaned from one wall, and the smooth leather of a high-backed chair supported Maggie's aching back.

While she waited for the doctor to bring her prognosis, she drank water flavored with an energy supplement, and gazed at an iPad displaying the day's headlines. None of them were good.

THE LAME DUCK PARADE CONTINUES. WHERE IS TROUSDALE?

SHE SOLD US ON ANTI-CORRUPTION . . . ONLY TO BE CORRUPTED HERSELF

SPIKING INFLATION, NATIONAL UNREST, AND A TERRORIST ON THE LOOSE

REPORT: INTERIM DIRECTOR OF THE CIA FLOUNDERS DURING CONFIRMATION HEARINGS

Maggie selected the last of the stories and scanned past an image of the interim director of the Central Intelligence Agency, Dr. Sarah Aimes, sitting before a panel of the Senate Select Committee on Intelligence. It was a confirmation hearing—Maggie had submitted Aimes's name to Congress after ousting Victor O'Brien six weeks prior. She expected Aimes to be confirmed quickly . . . because she had no reason to think otherwise.

But the tides of Washington were turning against the Trousdale administration. The glitz and glory of America's first female president—elected as an independent, no less—had worn off. Congress had once rolled over at her feet, largely because they didn't know what else to do. Now Maggie's lack of direct affiliation with either of the major political parties was less an agency and more a liability. She was taking fire from both sides, and in the wake of the largest terrorist attack in American history, the storm was growing.

A lance of pain shot through Maggie's gut, and she doubled over before she could stop herself. The iPad fell to the table, and she clamped her eyes shut. Hot fire raced up her spine and consumed her skull. It felt like a fist had closed around her liver and was clamping down with jagged fingernails. It was all she could do not to scream. She focused instead on breathing her way through it, one abbreviated gasp at a time.

By the time the door opened next to her, much of the pain had subsided, but Maggie sat sweating and limp against the desk. The news report gleamed from the iPad's screen, but she ignored it, guzzling water instead.

Dr. Cara Fletcher, the White House physician, took a seat next to her.

Another iPad rode in her hands. Her worn face was gray, her lips pressed into a tight line.

"How bad is it?" Maggie demanded.

Dr. Fletcher smoothed her scrub pants and set the iPad down. She offered a tight smile.

"I do have some good news, Madam President. Your surviving kidney seems to have adjusted perfectly to the increased demand. There are no indicators that—"

"I'm not here about my *kidney*, Doc. How is my *liver?*"

The shadow returned to the doctor's face. She pressed graying hair behind one ear and removed her glasses. Maggie waited, each passing second only reinforcing the prospect of doom.

"We'll need to run additional tests," Fletcher said. "But my initial prognosis is that your liver regeneration is failing. We marked strong progress through the spring, but development stalled over the summer. Now . . . it seems that we're losing ground."

"Losing ground? What does that mean? It's *shrinking?*"

"No—not shrinking. It's . . . well. Dying. That's the simplest way to put it."

Dying.

It may have been the simplest way to put it, but the word sent a shockwave through Maggie almost as abrupt as the assassin's bullet. She swallowed despite herself.

Dr. Fletcher replaced her glasses on her nose and read from the iPad.

"The headaches you're experiencing are likely a result of brain swelling. It's a side effect of liver failure. We also need to be concerned about infection, both bacterial and fungal. Blood sugar should be monitored. But most importantly . . ." Fletcher lowered the iPad. "Your stress level has to moderate. Immediately. Additional tests will confirm whether some other factor is at play, but my gut tells me that the regeneration failure is nothing more complex than overwork of the body. Too little sleep, too much work, and too much mental strain."

Maggie looked away. She sipped water, ignoring the grainy texture of the poorly mixed energy supplement, and trying to ignore Fletcher's comments along with it.

Oh, she hadn't been sleeping well. That was for sure. She'd been overworked, and she had certainly been stressed—more than she'd ever imagined was possible. It was day in, day out, an endless grind. One gut punch after another, after another . . . after another . . .

Maggie closed her eyes. The liver pain was starting again. She breathed through it.

"What are you telling me?" she said. "Am I dying?"

The answer wasn't as immediate as Maggie would have liked.

"You're not dying," Fletcher said. "Not presently. But the situation is very serious. We'll work through our options over the next couple of weeks, but I don't think we can depend on the regeneration resuming."

Maggie's eyes snapped open. "What does that mean?"

"It means you may need a transplant. In fact, you almost definitely will."

A transplant.

The prognosis hit Maggie harder than she expected. Since returning to office following her attempted assassination, Maggie had known her condition was serious, and her recovery would be slow. But she was *thirty-seven*. Still a young woman.

Too young for this.

"How soon?" Maggie asked flatly.

"That depends. If you can moderate your stress level and take better care of yourself, we may have a few weeks to work through options. But I must warn you, additional pressure could be deadly. We'll need to monitor your blood carefully against the risk of poisoning, and with brain swelling there's always the risk of a stroke. It's *imperative* that you take a step back from work. If it were up to me, you'd isolate yourself at Camp David for the foreseeable future."

The lame duck parade continues. Where is Trousdale?

The headline repeated in Maggie's mind, and she knew there was no chance she was headed to Camp David. No chance she could take a break. If anything, she needed to be working *harder* right now. To be more visible. To throttle the Senate and to ram this confirmation through by sheer force, if necessary. Sarah Aimes didn't need to be tied up in Senate hearings. She needed to be dragging the world's most wanted terrorist in by the hair before growing panic consumed the nation.

"Thank you for your time, Doctor. Please run your tests and advise my office. I'll get some rest."

Maggie got up and took her iPad. Doctor Fletcher opened her mouth to add further protest, but Maggie was already out the door. Already flanked by a pair of secret service agents, already headed back to the Beast for the nine-mile drive to the White House.

Because the president of the United States would be a dead duck before she allowed herself to be a lame duck.

4

The West Wing
The White House

The day closed with a blushing red and purple sunset fit for a watercolor painting, but with the pain in her gut and the reel of negative headlines flashing through her mind, Maggie barely noticed the view. She changed into royal blue sweats embroidered with the presidential seal before ordering her dinner to be brought into the Cabinet Room. It was a strangely calm place with the sprawling conference table empty, surrounded by high-backed chairs and lit by the sunset. Even when the door rocked open and Vice President Jordan Stratton stepped in, Maggie barely flinched. She was halfway through a bowl of Louisiana-style crawfish gumbo with white rice and French bread—not a meal Dr. Fletcher would have approved of, but Dr. Fletcher wasn't the commander in chief.

"There you are!" Stratton said. "I thought you'd disappeared."

Maggie grunted and continued with her meal, not even looking up. Stratton settled in next to her with a restrained sigh. He looked impeccable as always in a jet-black suit with a red power tie, his hair gelled and styled to frozen perfection. But if Maggie looked closely, she detected broader streaks of gray amid his natural black, and deeper lines around Stratton's weary eyes. His face sagged a little more.

He might have even put on a few pounds.

"Should you really be eating that?" Stratton poured himself a cup of coffee and stirred in a measure of creamer. Maggie endured a flash of gut pain while mopping her bread through the bottom of the bowl, soaking up the last delicious ounce of glorious roux.

She would never admit it, but the White House cooks rivaled the best chefs in New Orleans.

"If I want your opinion on my menu, I'll ask for it," she retorted.

Stratton clicked his tongue, setting the spoon down. "Testy, testy. Did somebody have a bad visit with the doctor?"

Maggie's gaze snapped sideways, momentary indignation crossing her face. Stratton held up a hand.

"It was on the travel log . . ."

Of course it was. Maggie was simply irritated that Stratton had checked.

"What did she say?" Stratton asked calmly.

Maggie finished the bread and pried a bit of rice from behind one tooth with her finger. It wasn't ladylike. She couldn't care less.

"All good," she said. "Just moving a little slower than we hoped."

Stratton nodded slowly. He didn't blink. He didn't say anything.

"What?" Maggie snapped.

"Nothing," Stratton said. "I was just thinking. It's been a busy month. Maybe you're due for a little R&R. A few days at Camp David."

Maggie's blood pressure spiked. Her gut pain spiked with it.

"I'll take a little R&R, *Jordan*, when I've got the carcass of a dead terrorist rotting on this table. Where is Aimes?"

Before Stratton could answer, the door at the end of the room burst open and Dr. Sarah Aimes appeared in the flesh. She wore a fetching navy blue pantsuit and carried a briefcase. Her hair was perfect, her face a little flushed but still bright. She was forty-four, and Maggie had no doubt that she could pick up a guy in any bar on the East Coast faster than her seven-years-younger president.

Figures.

"I apologize for being late, Madam President. It took some time to escape the Capitol."

Aimes settled into a chair across from Stratton. Maggie said nothing as she pushed her bowl away and slurped water. She wasn't in a mood to be cordial. She wasn't in a mood for anything except results.

"What happened, Sarah?"

The question was undercut by a razor edge, but Aimes maintained her composure, sitting straight-backed and resting her hands on the table.

"It's mostly Senator Roper, ma'am. I'm really not sure what his angle is, but my advisory team thinks he's making legal hay out of the confirmation hearings. CSPAN certainly isn't helping. I'm confident with another week we can reach confirmation—"

"I'm not asking about the hearings," Maggie cut her off. "I'm asking about Ibrahim. What's your update on *him?*"

Aimes took the cannonball in stride, snapping her briefcase open and withdrawing an iPad. She clicked it on and slid the device across the tabletop.

"U.S. Border Patrol obtained these images from the Detroit/Windsor border crossing. They're dated for the day of the attacks."

Maggie squinted at the screen. The pictures were grainy, shot in black-and-white. They depicted a car—some kind of import, she thought, maybe a Nissan—parked at a border crossing. The camera focused on the face of the man sitting behind the wheel as he spoke with the border guard.

As Maggie flicked through the images, the man's face rotated. He looked ahead. The car started forward. The camera caught a clear shot of his face.

"Is that him?" Maggie said. She couldn't be sure. It looked like Ibrahim . . . mostly. But something was off. His face was a little swollen. His nose too long, hair hanging down into his eyes.

"We think so," Aimes said. "He crossed the border at 9:52 p.m. local time. He used a Canadian passport which has since been determined to be fake—Samuel Hassan, of Toronto. We think he was probably wearing a disguise. Face putty and makeup."

"And that *worked?*" Maggie couldn't help herself.

"It seems so," Aimes's voice remained calm. "I've already reached out to CSIS. The Canadians are working every system they have to try to trace that car out of Windsor, but it's a big country and they don't have cameras everywhere. It could take some time."

"It's *already* taken time," Maggie said. "I've given you six weeks. I've got fifty-two hundred bodies in Baton Rouge and a country coming apart at the seams, and you can't even tell me how a bunch of third-world thugs obtained enough nerve agent to poison an entire city?"

Aimes didn't answer. She sat ramrod still, not blinking, breathing in deeply. Stratton filled the silence.

"I think what the president is asking is, what leads have you developed?"

Maggie flinched. She wanted to jack slap Stratton, but it wasn't the time.

"We are making progress, Madam President. I can assure you of that. I dispatched a specialty team to Guantánamo Bay yesterday to interview our captured witness. I'm optimistic they will uncover something. We're also working our networks all across the Middle East and Eastern Europe. We already know the VX was obtained from a Ukrainian arms dealer named Oleksiy Melnyk—"

"Have you talked to him?" Maggie pressed.

"He's dead."

"How do you know he sold Ibrahim the VX?"

"We had a source. A third party who—"

"Have you talked to *them?*"

Aimes went quiet. The first hint of discomfort crossed her perfectly poised face. "No ma'am," she said at last. "He's . . . gone missing."

Boiling pain erupted in Maggie's torso. She blinked it back and fixated on her now empty bowl, working simply to not scream. To not let the bottled frustration and rage out.

It wasn't supposed to be this way. She was supposed to be a lioness. A warrior. A fearless leader who piloted America straight into calm seas and fair skies. Instead she felt like a cat chasing its tail—a cat on fire, in a house on fire, in a city on fire. Without a drop of water or a fireman in sight.

Every time she closed her eyes, she saw Baton Rouge. The thousands of news cameras that swarmed the city to report on the attack recorded familiar streets and an even more familiar skyline. Not only had Baton Rouge been her home during her years as Louisiana's governor, it was also the site of her alma mater, LSU. She'd spent nearly a decade of her life among the easy-going, laid back Louisianans who lived there. They were *her* people. Her friends, neighbors, even family.

And fifty-two *hundred* of them were dead, had choked to death in the throes of raw terror as a vicious nerve agent slowly wreaked havoc through their bodies and shut down their lungs. It was a brutal way to die. A barbaric, unthinkable thing.

And it was *her* fault.

"Let me make this perfectly clear," Maggie said. Her voice had descended into a subdued growl. She spoke through her teeth, facing Aimes now. "I don't care what it takes. I don't care what rules are broken, or what methods you use. I don't care if you burn the Geneva Convention and carve that witness into lunch meat. I *want* Abdel Ibrahim. I want him dead, or alive, or in pieces. I want my people to know that they are safe. That they will never again face terror in their own homes. That this *country* is safe. Do you understand me, Madam Director?"

Maggie's voice rose into a crack. Aimes stayed straight-backed, chin up. She didn't blink. She nodded once.

"Absolutely, Madam President."

Aimes left the meeting after another twenty minutes of scathing interrogation by the president. It was brutal, and worse, it was pointless, but what bothered Aimes the most about Trousdale's inquisition was the unexpected nature of it.

Aimes had worked for the Trousdale administration both directly and indirectly since its inception, and she'd never seen Muddy Maggie this way. Not even close. The president looked like she was dying, with pale skin and sunken eyes. She slumped over a lot. She snapped easily, as though she were experiencing sustained pain.

Something was wrong, and it wasn't just the pressure of American terror and backstabbing Washington politics. There was a deeper issue at play.

Aimes took her briefcase and was halfway to the exit of the West Wing when Vice President Stratton appeared behind her, walking tall and buttoning his suit jacket.

"I'll walk you out," he said with a tense smile.

Aimes ducked her head, and Stratton led the way. The halls of the West Wing were quiet as evening closed over the White House, muted voices talking on phones and hands rattling over keyboards in an assortment of aide and intern offices, but none of the chaotic beehive buzz that accompanied a work day in full swing. It might have been peaceful if Aimes weren't riding the edge of mental redline, so overworked that she felt like snapping herself.

Stratton said nothing as he pushed through the exterior door and stepped into another muggy Washington summer night. Aimes's car waited for her on the drive, but her gut told her that the VP had something to say. He'd never accompanied her out of a meeting this way, and it hadn't been a typical meeting, anyway.

"Way to take the pressure," Stratton said, stopping by the car. "You'll do well as director."

"Thank you, Mr. Vice President. I'm not director yet . . . still the confirmation to clear."

"And how's that going? Honestly?"

Stratton's piercing gaze fixated on Aimes. She stood awkwardly by the car, unsure what to say. She knew he wouldn't accept a dismissal. She also wasn't ready to dive into the nitty gritty.

"Not well," she said at last. "The committee keeps demanding further discovery. Documents, reference statements from my old colleagues, travel logs. A lot of nonsense, frankly. If I were to be blunt, I'd say they were dragging their feet."

"They are," Stratton said. "Matt Roper is a political hack and a grimy parasite. He's been gunning for majority leader since the Democrats took the Senate. Sometimes I think his sights might be set even higher. He was always a pain when I worked on the Hill . . . no reason to think anything has changed. He'll nurse this thing for every ounce of political exposure he can extract."

"I know he voted against President Trousdale's confirmation when she became VP . . ." Aimes let the comment hang. It was something she had wondered about for a while, but hadn't been sure how to ask. She couldn't ask Roper directly. She couldn't ask Trousdale. It made her wonder if a personal vendetta was in play.

"That was because of Brandt," Stratton said. "When Brandt was running for president, he promised Roper a cabinet position in exchange for help in delivering Iowa. Secretary of the Treasury, I believe. Roper delivered, but Brandt reneged on the appointment. I think something came back in the vetting process. I really don't know. Whatever the case, when Brandt nominated Maggie to fill the VP's office, Roper opposed her. Probably out of pure spite. Of course, it didn't matter, Brandt had plenty of votes."

"So Roper is still bitter?" Aimes asked. "He's driving a lot of the pushback."

"It's certainly possible. The man is an elephant, he never forgets anything. But I don't think this has anything to do with Brandt. Roper is smarter than that. He plays chess, not checkers."

"Should I be concerned?" Aimes was already concerned, but she didn't want to admit it. She preferred to put on a strong face. It kept her options open.

"Not yet," Stratton said. "Keep doing what you're doing. I'll make some calls to my old chums in the Senate. We'll grease the wheels and get things moving again. In the meantime, the president is right. Your focus should be on locating Ibrahim."

Aimes swapped her briefcase to the other hand. She fought back the urge to snap, and kept herself calm. "We're really doing everything we can, Mr. Vice President. I can pressure our contacts in the Middle East, but—"

"I don't want you to pressure." Stratton's voice lowered. He took a half step closer. "I want you to focus. I want you to think outside the box. And when you find something, I want you to come to me . . . *first*."

A dull chill ran up Aimes's spine. Stratton didn't so much as blink.

"Do you understand, Madam Director?"

Aimes swallowed. "Of course, Mr. Vice President. Whatever you say."

Stratton flashed a smile. "Excellent. Now get some rest. You've got another hearing tomorrow! We'll see what we can do to whip old Roper into line."

5

Beirut, Lebanon

The Liberian freighter made dock just after midnight, local time. That suited Ibrahim just fine. The darkness made it all the easier for him to depart the hidden cabin inside the modified shipping container, and to reach shore without detection. It had been a prolonged journey from Montréal to the Levant, with a stop in Casablanca to make engine repairs. The ship was old and somewhat unreliable. Ibrahim was restless, knowing that each wasted day brought him closer to the jaws of the pursuing Americans.

But despite the pressure, the moment he set foot back onto the stable sands of his homeland, a weight lifted off his shoulders. He imagined it must be a similar feeling to what astronauts felt when they safely returned to Earth. A sort of peace. A sense of belonging.

But not a permanence, because just like an astronaut, Ibrahim was a man destined for other worlds. Hostile, ugly worlds, where the judgment of fate would rain like hellfire from the skies.

He took a cab into the interior of the sprawling coastal city, bumping along crowded streets between glimmering high-rises. The cab driver was

Jordanian. He wouldn't shut up about football. Ibrahim flatly ignored him, ruminating in his mind about the toxic poison of Western culture.

It had seeped across his homeland and stained the souls of so many of his brethren. Not only the money—so much money, greedily exchanged for the black gold pumped from beneath the sand—but the pop culture. The movies. The music. The *sports*.

Things that so easily bought the hearts and minds of a culture once dedicated to independence at any cost. Many of the true believers, scattered from Damascus to Tehran, blamed their hardships on the military might of the Americans, but that was a short-sighted viewpoint. America's true weapon was her opulence. Her indulgence. Her insidious culture of greed, lust, and glamour, which so quickly turned warriors into fattened slobs, ready for slaughter.

It was the culture Ibrahim had declared war on. The culture that had stolen his brother's soul long before American murderers stole his brother's life. The Cardinals hat Ibrahim wore into battle at St. Louis was a reminder of who the real enemy was—the American spirit. The fabric of a society drunk on wealth and power.

Destroy the spirit, and the body would quickly die. No matter how many guns and rockets America possessed.

The cab driver dropped Ibrahim at a warehouse outside the city. Ibrahim paid but didn't tip. He departed the car without a word, and waited for it to disappear around the next turn before he faced the sprawling building. It was an old agricultural warehouse. A place for storing grain, or maybe animal feed. Whatever the case, the slow erosion of time and weather had broken the place down. There were holes in the walls, and one door slumped against the ground.

It was forgotten. That made it perfect.

Ibrahim dug the flashlight out of his pocket and stepped inside. Dust hung in the air, the concrete floor crunchy with a layer of sand. The building was empty—or nearly empty. Only one item stood beneath the beams of moonlight that blasted through the holes in the roof. It was a truck. A heavy truck, with an enclosed bed. The license plate was white with black letters, "GE" printed beneath a red and white flag on the left side. The national signifier of Georgia.

As Ibrahim regarded the truck, a figure appeared from the shadows. A tall man with a face pitted and scarred by a long, hard life. Bulky shoulders. A cigarette dangling from his lips. He met Ibrahim's gaze without comment, and Ibrahim tilted his chin toward the truck.

The man with the pitted face blew smoke from his nostrils. He nodded once.

And smiled.

6

Nashville, Tennessee

The apartment situated on the fourth floor of the Gulch high-rise was a great deal nicer than Reed's previous address off Nolensville Road. It featured granite countertops, two spacious bedrooms, a balcony, and a view of midtown . . . which was simply a view of more glass-encased high-rises.

Following his assistance in the prevention of the St. Louis chemical weapons attack, Reed had received another deposit from the CIA. It was dwarfed in comparison to his paychecks from the North Korean and Venezuelan operations, but it was still sufficient to upgrade his family's living conditions. Banks liked the Gulch. She liked the easy access to fine dining, cutesy coffee shops and boutiques, and most important of all . . . Music Row.

Banks's dreams of becoming a famed singer/songwriter were finally taking off. Quite literally. Her fame following her near-death experience at the heart of Abdel Ibrahim's first attack had spread her story across social media platforms the world around, resulting in millions of streams of the handful of songs she had uploaded to various music platforms. Every record label in Nashville had fallen over themselves to make her an offer.

The promises were big—seven figures big. Touring contracts. Multiple album deals.

The only hiccup, of course, was Banks herself. Because she couldn't yet sing . . . or walk. Or even stand for long periods unassisted. The bomb blast that had shredded her torso with dozens of tiny ball bearings had done a number on her digestive system. Surgeries stacked up and physical therapy ground on like a torture mechanism, but the cold reality of recovery couldn't be rushed.

Banks needed time, and until she was ready to actually deliver multiple albums, nobody was quite ready to hand her any fat checks. This was still business, after all.

Reed's plane landed at Nashville's BNA airport just after two a.m., and he and Turk split ways with a fist bump, taking separate Ubers to their separate addresses. The city sparkled beneath a black sky, the dozens of new towers that crowded downtown reflecting light onto the dozens more still under construction. Reed sat slumped in the back seat with his backpack in his lap, struggling to keep his eyes open while the driver prattled on about comic books and superheroes. He managed little more than a grunt of thanks when he finally reached his apartment building, and struggled with his key fob to gain access via an electronic lock. The elevator was slow. The hallway smelled like a hotel. His door looked exactly the same as every other door in the building.

Reed fumbled his key before getting the lock open. He tried to move slowly through the kitchen, setting the backpack on the counter and stretching. Baxter the English bulldog snored from his bed next to the refrigerator, his loose lips dripping saliva while all four legs jutted straight into the air. Reed's old pet had slept that way for as long as Reed could remember, but there was a stiffness to his body now that reminded Reed of his age. A brittleness to his greasy coat of brown and white hair.

Life had taken a toll . . . and not just on the bulldog.

Reed fished a beer from the fridge and twisted the cap off with his shirt. Then he kicked his boots off and stepped into the living room.

And stopped.

Banks sat in the glider rocker Reed had bought her for their first house, back when Davy was a baby. She looked out the sliding glass door at the city, her head leaned back, blonde locks falling over her shoulders. She wore a bathrobe tied tightly around her waist, and she held her belly.

An empty whiskey glass sat on the arm of the rocker.

"Isn't it beautiful?" Banks mumbled.

Reed looked through the glass. A hospital glimmered a few blocks away. More apartment complexes. A bank tower.

It wasn't what he would call beautiful. To him it was pretty average, but he wouldn't rain on any parades.

"It's great," he said, sitting with a sigh on the couch across from her. He sipped the beer, and his throat burned.

"Can't sleep?" Reed asked.

Banks shrugged. She rotated the empty whiskey glass, and Reed noted the bottle sitting on the floor next to her. Also almost empty.

"The doctor said—" Reed began.

"I know." Banks's voice tried to snap, but came out a little closer to a slur. Reed sipped his beer and gave it up. It wasn't the first time he'd come home to find Banks drunk, and he didn't have much of a leg to stand on when it came to condemning medication by alcohol.

"How was work?" Banks's voice slurred again, but this time there was an undertone of sarcasm. It cut, and Reed knew why. Banks hadn't known where he was going, exactly, but she knew what he was up to. He'd reneged on his commitment to retire from operator life only months after making it. He knew she felt betrayed.

But that commitment was made before the bombing. Before Banks was hurtled to the ground in a spray of blood. Before their child . . .

"Fine," Reed said, cutting his own train of thought short before it could lead to a place he was too weary to face. Banks nodded slowly. She still hadn't looked at him.

"You think we'll ever actually be normal?" Banks said.

Reed hesitated. He picked at the beer label with one nail, and searched for an answer that would pacify Banks and maybe get her to go to bed. He was too tired for a discussion on the outlook of life. Too jaded by his visit to Cuba.

And the prison camp.

"What is normal?" Reed said at last.

Banks didn't answer. Her eyes glistened, and once more Reed knew why. He felt the same pain in his gut. It redoubled whenever he looked at his wife's swollen stomach, bandaged and scarred, tormenting her with burning agony whenever she moved. Reminding them both of the life that once lived there, and the future lives, maybe, that would now be impossible.

"When I sign this deal, you're going to quit," Banks said. She fixated on the window, and her lip quivered. "We won't need the money anymore. We'll have plenty. You can quit."

She faced him for the first time. A hot tear slipped down her cheek. Reed's stomach descended into knots.

"It's not about the money, Banks," he said.

"Isn't it?"

Reed gritted his teeth. His fingers closed around the bottle. He thought of Ibrahim, in St. Louis. The moment America's greatest enemy slipped away . . . right out of his grasp.

It wasn't just the personal injury. It was the failure. The misery of feeling *responsible* for what had happened. He'd stood there next to the stage in Rutherford County when Ibrahim's men positioned the bomb. If he'd moved a little quicker, drawn and fired from the middle of the crowd . . .

It didn't matter now. Yes, Reed had money problems. Banks had been uninsured when the bomb went off, and the funds generously donated by thousands of her new fans barely served to cover her hospital costs. In fact, the bills were still rolling in. But the promise of a CIA paycheck wasn't what drove Reed out of bed each morning. The only thing that mattered now was the hunt. He would find Abdel Ibrahim, no matter how long it took. He would find Abdel's friends. His partners. His associates and his brotherhood.

He would kill them all.

Reed's eyes blurred, and he blinked the fog away. It was only then that he noticed Banks staring at him. There was something vacant in her eyes. Something very distant. She looked like a shell.

"What's happening to us, Reed? It was never supposed to be this way."

Her lip trembled. The glass fell from the arm of the rocker and crashed on the floor, but Reed didn't so much as flinch. He knew he should hold her. He knew he should kiss her forehead and pull her close and tell her it would all be okay. That all the loss and pain and heartbreak didn't change a thing.

But it had. And it still was. Reed was numb all over. The only thing he could really feel was the rage—that thirst for blood.

"Nothing's changed, Banks. This is what the world's always been."

Banks shook her head. "No . . . I won't believe that."

Reed stood. He drained the beer and threw the bottle across the room at the trash can. It hit the wall instead and shattered. Banks jumped, but Reed just stared.

It wasn't the alcohol. It was the numbness. He started for the door.

"Where are you going?" Banks called.

"Out."

"Reed, please. You should be here. You just got home—"

Reed ignored her. He found the Camaro keys lying on the counter and returned to the hotel hallway where all the doors looked the same. Where nothing smelled like home.

He left Banks in the rocking chair and walked quickly to the garage. The old car fired up with a guttural roar of classic American muscle. Reed had invested a little of his CIA earnings into some basic repairs and maintenance. The vehicle still looked like a rusted junker, but it ran more reliably than it had in decades. He powered out of the garage and hit 12th Avenue. He took I-65 south out of the city, and gave the car its head. The old Z/28 roared and threw him back in the seat, rushing out of Nashville, through Franklin, and deep into Williamson County.

Reed didn't stop until he reached the little block building sitting out in the middle of nowhere, an empty gravel parking lot stretching out in front of it. The sign still read *Jarhead Fitness*, but Reed and Turk had closed their failed gym venture following Ibrahim's attacks. They'd rolled the metal doors shut and locked them. They'd pushed all the gym equipment against the walls. The lockers had been replaced by gun safes. The wrestling mats with tables and computers.

He cut the Camaro off in a storm of gravel dust and unlocked the gym door with an eight-digit code. Fluorescent lights illuminated the space while a giant fan recirculated the hot Tennessee air. Reed stepped past a table dirty with gun oil and another laden with chest rigs and armor plates to reach his laptop in the corner. It was hardwired into the internet—no Wi-Fi. It powered up and unlocked with a thumbprint and a fifteen-digit code. He navigated to a secure web portal and input additional codes. His heart thumped with adrenaline as he reached a message portal and filled out a brief after action report.

Met with prisoner. Extensive conversation, no intel. Opinion: Prisoner knows nothing of value. Should investigate leads overseas, consider terrorist strike funding and weaponry. On standby to deploy inside of six hours.

Reed smacked the send button and folded his arms. The continued thump of his heart signaled that despite the late hour, his body was awake and alive with nervous energy, but none of that energy made it to his mind. None of it made it to his actual consciousness. When he closed his eyes, he only saw two things.

The flash of red as the bomb detonated next to the stage. And the face of Abdel Ibrahim.

7

George Bush Center for Intelligence
Langley, Virginia

Aimes had the whole of former director Bill O'Brien's executive office stripped and steam cleaned. It wasn't that O'Brien was a nasty person. At least, not physically. It was just the aura of the place that bothered her, as though it couldn't really be *hers* without a fresh start.

The place had been outdated, anyway. Fresh carpet, a bright coat of paint, and updated furniture made a world of difference. Aimes also had a large portion of the wall between her desk and the rest of the executive floor replaced with plate glass. She wasn't a dictator sitting atop an ivory tower. She was a leader. People needed to be able to see her, and she needed to be able to see them.

When they were around, anyway. Nobody was around at two a.m. except Aimes herself. She sat behind the desk, poring over reports from intel sources across the Middle East and Eastern Europe. There were hundreds of pages of photographs, transcripts, and detailed tracking logs of various HVTs—high-value targets. Generally, this sort of review work would be reserved for any one of the hundreds of analysts the agency employed.

But Aimes knew she had to pull out the stops. It wasn't enough to crack a whip and push her people harder. She had to get her own hands dirty.

She had to find *answers*.

Her computer chimed when the message came in from the Prosecution Force. It was short and curt—likely written by Montgomery himself—and it contained nothing of value. Montgomery and Turkman had come up empty-handed following their visit to Gitmo, which was just as Aimes suspected. She'd only sent them there as a last resort, and also perhaps to keep them busy. Montgomery and his team of misfit black ops specialists were her most lethal secret weapon. Aimes had gone out of her way to secure their services following her appointment to the directorate of the CIA, and the president knew nothing about them. Nobody knew. That was what made the arrangement so useful.

But restricting knowledge of the Prosecution Force program had its definite downsides, also. It meant that Aimes was left to manage Montgomery herself, and that was already turning out to be a pain in the ass. The man was on fire to find Ibrahim. He messaged her regularly. He wanted answers. He wanted a target.

He wanted to kill.

Aimes couldn't blame him, given what had happened to his wife. She knew about the lost baby, and she could only imagine that for a trained assassin like Montgomery, he would go mad if he wasn't given a mission. But that didn't help her find a target, and she couldn't deal with an additional voice in her head right then, so she chose not to reply to his message. Montgomery could wait.

Aimes pushed the documents aside and went to work on her keyboard, digging through daily research reports from her financial analysis division. She would never tell him, of course, but Montgomery was right about the financial leads. When all else failed, following the money always led to something. It might not be what she wanted, but it was better than beating her head against a block wall.

Pages of spreadsheets and annotated reports from forensic accountants working for the agency filled her dual monitors, and Aimes blinked back a blur in her eyes. Her back hurt. Her head throbbed. She wanted to sleep so bad it was almost the only thing she could think about.

That, and the Senate hearings scheduled for the next day. More jump rope with Chairman Roper and his friends.

Amazing.

The phone chimed on Aimes's desk and she sat bolt upright, realizing she'd drifted off while thinking about not drifting off. Her gaze snapped to the display, where the caller ID read an international number coupled with *CSIS*. The Canadian Security Intelligence Service, a sort of blend between the American FBI and CIA.

The phone rang again, and Aimes rocked her water bottle back. She swished the water to help wake herself up and clear her throat, then she mashed the speaker button.

"This is Aimes."

There were only a handful of officers at the CSIS who held Aimes's direct line. None of them would call without a reason, and none of them would call at two a.m. without a *great* reason.

"Madam Director, it's Jean-Luc. I'm glad I caught you."

The voice crackling through the speaker carried a heavy French-Canadian accent, but still sounded clearer and more alert than Aimes herself. Jean-Luc Morin was the director of the CSIS, and had been for the past decade. Aimes had interacted with him only a few times, but she always liked him. He was direct. Personable, but he didn't waste time. And most importantly, he was good at his job.

"Good evening Jean-Luc . . . or good morning, I guess. How are things in the great white north?"

"Busy, as ever. I am calling to deliver good news . . . sort of."

Aimes sat up. She lifted the phone and cradled it against one ear. "Did you find him?"

"The news isn't *that* good, I'm afraid. We found where he was, anyway. And maybe where he was going. The Nissan Sentra your border security photographed in Detroit was discovered in an impound lot in Montréal. Apparently it was abandoned at a Provigo market and towed after a week. The clerk who recorded the details at the impound lot screwed up the vehicle identification number, which is part of why it took us so long to locate it."

"Did you find anything inside it?" Aimes could barely control the urgency in her voice. Jean-Luc remained calm.

"Nothing thus far. Forensics are just beginning. But we obtained security footage from the Provigo and patched together similar footage from across the city. We tracked your suspect on foot for a mile before we lost him in a camera gap. The interesting thing, however, was the region he was walking through. It was very close to the port. So we pulled port footage, and—"

"He boarded a boat," Aimes said.

"Yes, he did. A Liberian flagged container ship, specifically. She set sail shortly thereafter, running up the St. Lawrence River to Quebec City before entering the Atlantic. She was bound for Beirut. She reached port yesterday. I've already collected a file containing all the photographs, along with the details on the ship. I'm emailing it to you now."

Beirut.

It was a city on the other side of the world. Millions of occupants. A gateway to the Middle East. Probably a portal for Ibrahim to lose himself.

But it was still a lead, and the first solid lead Aimes had uncovered in weeks.

"You're a rockstar, Jean-Luc. Thank you. Keep us posted with the Sentra."

"Will do, and likewise. Have a great morning."

The CSIS director hung up, and Aimes set the handset down. She chewed her lip and pivoted back to the computer, pulling up a world map. Zeroing in on the Mediterranean, and then the Levant.

Lebanon. Beirut. A capital city resting right on the coast.

Her email chimed and she scanned quickly through the documents Jean-Luc had sent her. The file was fat—it would take hours to fully analyze. She might not find anything the Canadians hadn't already uncovered.

But all of that was secondary. The primary concern was putting boots on the ground, ASAP.

Aimes orbited back to her computer and tabbed to the secure messaging service that linked her to Montgomery. She typed out a quick message. She read it back once, and then hit send.

It was time to deploy the Prosecution Force.

8

Williamson County, Tennessee

The chime of Aimes's incoming secure message woke Reed as he slept in his desk chair, passed out next to the computer. He scrubbed his eyes and read the details quickly.

Then the text messages began—three of them, rocketing out across the city to call the troops into action. By sunrise, Turk had arrived, piloting his race-red Jeep Gladiator on mud tires into the slot next to Reed's Camaro, and landing on booted feet with a backpack slung over one shoulder. Then came Kirsten Corbyn, the ex-British SIS officer and Royal Air Force Chinook pilot. She zipped into the lot astride a brand new, jet-black Triumph Rocket 3, an absolute beast of a motorcycle that rumbled twice as loud as Reed's Camaro. The bike was a product of her CIA paychecks, alongside a green card and a ticket back into the action . . . which was what she really cared about.

Wolfgang was last. He arrived in a gray Mercedes S-Class coupe, several years old, badged with New York plates. Reed knew Wolfgang hadn't even visited his home in New York in months. He'd acquired an apartment in Franklin, and while the Wolf would never admit it, Reed thought he preferred the warmer southern climate.

It was likely better on his amputated right leg, replaced now by an advanced prosthetic built of lightweight titanium and carbon fiber. There was a compartment concealed inside the fake calf where Wolfgang was known to keep a Glock 29 chambered in 10mm automatic. Ten rounds in the mag, one in the pipe, ready to go and matched with a medical card dismissing metal detector alerts as caused by his prosthetic leg. He could glide through security with ease, armed to the teeth the entire time.

The Mercedes ground to a stop next to the Jeep, and both doors popped open. Reed squinted into the sunrise as Wolfgang appeared from the driver's side. The passenger's side door closed, but he couldn't see anyone over the hulking mass of the Jeep. Wolfgang appeared behind the car . . . and then he was joined by Lucy Byrne.

Reed shot Turk a sideways look. The bigger man was also fixed on the incoming woman. She was petite to the point of being tiny. Five-foot and change, but not much change. Auburn red hair and a loose cotton shirt. Yoga pants and combat boots. She had a backpack slung over one shoulder. She popped gum as she walked.

Reed straightened from the table as Wolfgang and Lucy entered. Corbyn was already inside, rich brown hair pinned back in a ponytail, aviator sunglasses riding halfway down her nose. Pilot swag.

"Wassup, mates?"'

Reed ignored Corbyn's greeting and stared at Lucy. Lucy blew a bubble with her gum until it popped. "Good morning, Reed."

Reed nodded once. "LB." Then he turned to Wolfgang. He cocked an eyebrow.

"Your invite didn't include a plus-one."

Wolfgang tossed a duffel bag on the floor. "Come off it, Reed. We were hanging out when you texted me."

Reed shot another look at Turk. He received only a sigh in return.

"What are you doing, LB?"

Lucy set her bag on the table. "What does it look like? I'm deploying."

"Right. Except, you don't deploy anymore. Remember?"

Following the blast that sent Banks hurtling to the ground in a spray of blood, Reed had reached out to Lucy Byrne to protect Banks while he hunted Ibrahim. It was a logical move, considering Lucy's background as a trained assassin with enough blade skills to filet a concrete wall. The two killers had known each other for years, at one time working side by side as part of an underground criminal kill ring.

Each of their lives had taken some turns since then. Reed had gone straight, or tried to. Lucy had vanished into Southeast Asia, surfacing months later with severe injuries and a heavy opioid addiction. Reed secured help for her at a rehab facility. It was there that Lucy found God, and put the life of an assassin behind her.

She told Reed as much when he returned from thwarting Ibrahim's attempted strike in St. Louis. She explained her faith. She talked about the Bible.

Reed didn't get it, and didn't want to get it. He respected her decision to embrace a new life, but he hadn't spoken to her since. As far as he was concerned, they were now on two different playing fields.

Lucy didn't answer Reed's challenge. She simply rested her hands on top of the backpack and smiled. Reed dropped his pen and jerked his head to one side. Lucy followed him into a corner.

"What are you doing?" Reed kept his voice low as he repeated the question. Lucy remained relaxed.

"I'm helping," she said, simply. "I was with Wolfgang when the text came through. I've got no place to be. So here I am. I still owe you one, remember?"

"No. No you don't. We settled that when you covered Banks."

"You say we settled it. I have a different view. You saved my life—we won't be square until I return the favor in kind."

Reed inhaled slowly. He didn't want to snap, but he really didn't have time for this, either.

"Look. I really appreciate the gesture, but you already told me you're out. I don't have time to jump through any religious hoops. We're wheels up before lunch."

"I never asked you to jump through any hoops, religious or otherwise. I also never said I was out. I said I was done murdering people, which is a perfectly reasonable thing for anybody to say, faith aside."

"And what do you think I'm headed to do?" Reed's voice dropped. Lucy didn't flinch.

"You're headed to protect your country. You're headed to do a job."

"I'm headed to *kill* somebody, LB. As painfully as possible."

Lucy chewed gum. Her perfectly calm nature was starting to get under Reed's skin.

"Not all killing is murder," she said, simply.

No, Reed thought. *It's not. But I don't need an arbitrator on my plane calling the morality of my shots.*

"Everybody you have is a field operator," Lucy said. "You've never run a team this big before. You need somebody to manage coms and keep everything organized. An eye in the sky. Somebody to mediate between personalities and handle all the BS logistical stuff. Food, for instance. Have you made a plan to keep everybody fed?"

Reed hadn't. He hadn't even considered his own breakfast.

"Also, there's medical. I studied a lot of first aid at rehab. I'm not combat trained, but I know how to stop bleeding and deal with hypothermia and cardiac arrest. Something is better than nothing. Plus, I'm cute and I have a great sense of humor. I'm basically amazing."

Reed closed his mouth. He didn't say anything. He glowered down and weighed his options, evaluating whether it would be easier to ditch Lucy Byrne or to throw her into the meat grinder and test her abilities in the field.

The assassin Reed always knew as *LB* was unthinkably stubborn, which was part of what made her so good. Her faith experience didn't seem to have changed that, and she wasn't wrong that he needed a hub for all the logistical headaches of a fast-moving operation to pivot around.

Maybe it would be easier not to argue.

"If I hear one judgmental word out of you—"

"I'm not here to judge anything," Lucy cut him off. "I'm here because I was told to be."

"By Wolfgang?"

Lucy smiled. She popped gum. "By Somebody higher up the chain."

Right.

Reed ran a hand through his hair and turned back to the table. He snapped his fingers.

"All right! Circle in. I'm only going to say this once."

The team gathered around the middle table. It was spread with computers and an eleven-inch tablet computer. Reed traced his finger across the tablet's screen to expand a map of the globe—Canada to Europe.

"Our target is Abdel Ibrahim. He vanished after escaping St. Louis, and border patrol picked him up on camera at the Detroit/Windsor border crossing. From there Canadian intelligence traced him to the Port of Montréal, where he boarded a Liberian flagged freighter bound for Beirut. That freighter made port twenty-three hours ago, which means we're already way behind the eight ball. Langley wants us in the air and headed east, ASAP."

"We have a tail on him now?" Wolfgang asked.

Turk snorted. "Wouldn't that be nice . . . "

"We don't know where he is," Reed said. "Hopefully, still in Beirut. Langley is working leads with local assets as we speak. If they pin him down, we need to be ready. Which is why we're wheels up as soon as everyone is packed."

"What did they give us?" Corbyn's question was predictable. Reed could detect the gleam in her eye through the moderately shaded sunglasses.

"Gulfstream V, 6,500 nautical mile range. It's just over 5,500 miles to Beirut, so we can fly straight through. Langley has provided a co-pilot. You'll take command. The plane is fueled and waiting at Leiper's Fork."

The gleam in Corbyn's eye spilled into a grin. Reed straightened from the table, meeting each member of the team in the eye. Making sure they were zeroed in.

"Let me make one thing perfectly clear—this isn't a snatch and grab. Langley has requested for Ibrahim to be brought in alive, if possible. I have zero intentions of facilitating that request. They'll get a loaded body bag, and nothing more. If any of you has an ethical problem with that, speak up now."

Reed's gaze stopped on Lucy. She continued to chew gum. She said nothing. Neither did anyone else.

"Okay then. Everybody gear up and meet in the parking lot. We're wheels up within the hour."

The team dispersed rapidly, gear spread across tables and sliding quickly into packs. Turk grabbed guns and ammo. Lucy worked through a heavy black backpack with a white cross stitched to the face—medical. Corbyn studied maps and made flight plans.

Reed met Wolfgang at the side of the room as the one-legged killer packed an APC10 Pro submachine gun into a duffel bag alongside stacks of twenty-four-round Glock-made 10mm magazines.

"Any word from your friend?" Reed's voice lowered so that only Wolfgang could hear. The Wolf continued packing, not looking up as he replied.

"Who's asking?"

"Who do you think?"

It was an obvious point. Reed himself couldn't care less about what had become of Ivan Sidorov, the former Russian intelligence officer who had fed critical intel to the CIA via Wolfgang over the past ten months. Ivan knew a lot of things. Things about Russia. Things about Venezuela. Even things about Ukrainian arms dealers who sold VX to radical Islamic terrorists.

He was a gold mine of intelligence, but he'd vanished shortly after he and Wolfgang slaughtered the aforementioned Ukrainian arms dealer aboard his yacht off the coast of Thessaloniki. Reed didn't mind, because Reed understood. He was a creature of the shadows himself.

But the CIA wanted their gold mine back, and Aimes was regularly hitting Reed up for leads on Ivan.

"I left him in Greece when I flew back to the States," Wolfgang said. "No contact since then. I honestly have no idea where he is." Wolfgang zipped the bag and shouldered it. He faced Reed. "You can tell Director Aimes that she's welcome to phone me. She doesn't have to make you the middleman."

Reed snorted. "What if I told you the CIA is intimidated by you?"

"I'd say they're smarter than they look."

"And you'd be flattering yourself."

A dry smile crept across Wolfgang's face. He slipped his sunglasses on. Reed caught him with a final word as the Wolf turned for the door.

"Hanging out, huh?"

Wolfgang stopped. He looked over one shoulder. Reed cocked an eyebrow and tilted his head an inch toward Lucy.

"Worry about your mission, Prosecutor," Wolfgang said. "We've got a terrorist to kill."

9

Belgrade, Serbia

The poker den resting two stories beneath the rain-soaked streets hung thick with cigar smoke, empty bottles of Russian-made vodka scattered about the countertops of a kitchenette while a single exhaust fan struggled to keep up with the smog. There was a pair of cots in one corner. A toilet standing in the other. The room was no more than five hundred square feet in size, with rickety wooden stairs leading upward to the basement of the house overhead.

Condensation and rain runoff dropped slowly from an overhead rafter. A mouse scuttled from the kitchenette to a hole in the wall, vanishing from sight. The four men circled around the card table in the middle of the room ignored the mess, drinking vodka from plastic cups and smoking thick-rolled Turkish cigars. The cards were as worn and grimy as the rest of the room. The game was five-card draw, and the stakes were high—cheap plastic chips backed by expensive American dollars. Nobody was playing any aces from their sleeves.

There were too many guns in the room.

Former Russian intelligence officer Ivan Sidorov sat with his back to the wall, a cigar jammed between his teeth and a cup of vodka close to hand. It was his fifth drink of the night, but he wasn't even close to intoxicated as he dealt the next hand clockwise around the table. Smoke blew from his crooked nose, obscuring a little of his vision.

But he didn't need to see very far. He only needed to watch the three other men gathered at the table—one Ukrainian, one Belarusian, and one German. All world-class criminals, estranged from their homelands, on the run from Interpol, and ruthless to their very core.

Ivan's kind of people.

The hand was dealt, and everyone pitched a grungy white chip into the pot to pay the ante. Ten American dollars. Ivan checked his hand and found three diamonds, a spade, and a heart. Enough to make a flush, maybe, with a little luck. Not much else.

"I heard a rumor of you, Ivan." It was the Ukrainian who spoke, which was typical. The man's lips were as loose as his morals, and that was saying something.

"You should not believe everything you hear," Ivan said. The Belarusian to his left pitched fifty dollars into the pot. The German folded. The Ukrainian sucked his cigar and called. Ivan matched the bet.

"This rumor was from a reliable source," the Ukrainian said. "One of my old chums from the Kremlin. He said there was an upheaval recently. A little scare at the SVR. Apparently, a ranking intelligence officer went missing. They say he is wanted for treason."

Ivan looked over his cards, cocking an eyebrow. The Ukrainian grinned around his cigar.

"Perhaps if I had ever served in the SVR, I could contribute to your rumor," Ivan said slowly. "It's too bad."

The Ukrainian exchanged a glance with the Belarusian and the German. Then he laughed.

"Too bad indeed."

Cards hit the table. Ivan dealt from the deck, exchanging his spade and his heart in hopes of two more diamonds. No such luck, but he did score a pair of sixes. Enough to keep him in the game.

Enough to keep the poker ring talking.

Another round of betting. Ivan called at sixty more dollars. Cards hit the table. Ivan's hand was easily trounced by a straight from the German.

Chips slid around the table, and Ivan passed the deck to his left. It was the Belarusian's turn to deal.

"I also heard a rumor," Ivan said.

"Oh?" It was the Ukrainian again.

"Da. It was about one of your countrymen, in fact. Dear old Melnyk."

Ivan flicked a lighter, pretending to relight his cigar while he watched the table from his peripheral vision. All three stiffened at the mention of Melnyk, but that didn't necessarily mean anything. The man was an arms dealer from Odesa. A complete savage, and a kingpin of the arms industry.

Or he had been, anyway. Until Wolfgang Pierce and Ivan Sidorov conspired to kidnap him, and Ivan ran a folding knife through his guts.

"Funny you should mention Melnyk," the German said. "I heard he retired. Quite suddenly, in fact. Nobody can get a hold of him, myself included. He owes me a commission on a little connection I arranged. Three crates of RPGs into South Sudan. A lot of future business, too."

"I wouldn't hold my breath for the commission," Ivan said.

"Oh?" The German looked up.

"I heard he was dead," Ivan said.

Nobody spoke. The Belarusian stopped mid-shuffle, and the Ukrainian cocked his head.

Then the German laughed. "You're out of your mind."

Ivan shrugged, sucking on the cigar. Playing it off as though it were just a joke.

But he noticed the Belarusian giving him the side eye. Evaluating him, even as he dealt the next hand.

"Speaking of Melnyk." Ivan lifted his cards and arranged them in his hand. A little more luck this time. Two jacks. He would trade the rest and hope for three of a kind.

"What about him?" The Ukrainian said.

"There may be a chance for another sort of commission," Ivan said, tone still casual.

"How much money?" That was the German. No surprise. Ivan had known the German for nearly a decade and the man was always eager to make a buck, no matter how many people had to die.

"I'm not sure," Ivan said. "Enough, I should think. If a connection can be arranged."

Chips hit the table. Ivan traded in three cards. A seven, a ten, and a jack landed in his hand. *Bingo*.

"A connection between *who?*" the German pressed.

"Between Melnyk," Ivan continued. "And the United States."

He looked up as he spoke. Everybody froze again, and this time nobody smiled. The German set his cigar down. The Ukrainian lowered his cards.

The Belarusian just stared, eyes as cold as ice.

"What would the United States want with a man like Melnyk?" The German spoke slowly, and for once the Ukrainian seemed content to listen.

Ivan tossed more chips on the table, shrugging as though it were nothing. "I do not have specifics. An old friend mentioned it. Apparently, the CIA has an interest in him. They think he might be connected with that . . . what was it?" Ivan trailed off as though he were searching for the right word. Then he snapped his fingers. "The VX! That nerve agent in Louisiana. The terrorist thing. They think Melnyk may have supplied it."

Ivan dragged on the cigar and studied his cards. None of the other three men looked away from him. Nobody blinked.

"Since when are we in the business of trading with the Americans?" The Belarusian spoke for the first time. It was a predictable question, but the tone of his voice was harsher than Ivan would have hoped. He'd arrived in this rathole nearly four hours earlier. He'd spent a lot of time trading war stories and breaking open bottles of vodka from the case he had brought.

He'd worked hard to loosen the mood. To get each of his three acquaintances from Europe's criminal underworld as drunk as guarded men could become, hoping for careless conversation to follow.

Clearly, he'd made his move too soon.

"Relax," Ivan sighed. "I thought you were all in the business of making money? I heard of an opportunity, this is all. I only mention it because you mention Melnyk."

The Ukrainian and the German both shrugged it off, looking back to their cards. The Belarusian didn't break eye contact. He hadn't so much as glanced at his hand. His gaze was fixed on Ivan.

"*You* brought up Melnyk. Not us."

Ivan cocked his head. "Did I?"

The German and the Ukrainian exchanged a glance. The Ukrainian was too drunk to be sure, his eyes misting over after another pour of Russia's finest. The German sighed.

"Oh whatever, who cares? Are you in or out, Pavel?"

The Belarusian looked slowly to his cards. He made a bet. The bet circled to Ivan, and he matched it. Then came the great reveal.

Ivan's trio of jacks seized the pot, and the deal moved to the German.

"You know, on the subject of Melnyk." It was the Belarusian. His voice was flat and cold, the same as it had always been every time Ivan had encountered the man. "I also heard a rumor."

"What's that?" The Ukrainian hiccupped halfway through his question. The Belarusian didn't notice. He was staring at Ivan again.

"I heard that there were men, a few months ago, asking about Melnyk. Whispering in the shadows. Seeking his location. And then, not long after, one of Melnyk's warehouses on the Danube was struck. Bulgarian police overtook it. This was right before Melnyk went missing."

Nobody moved as the tension in the room spiked. Card game forgotten, all eyes were fixed on Pavel, the Belarusian, while he stared dead at Ivan.

"What a story," Ivan said slowly. He sat with both arms on the table, one holding his cards, the other cradling his cup of vodka.

Pavel leaned forward, teeth flashing as his lips curled. Voice dropping.

"And you know what else I heard? I heard the two men looking for Melnyk . . . one was a Russian. Very big. Broken nose. A lot like you, in fact. And the other? *He was American*."

And there it is.

Ivan knew the gambit was up the moment the words left Pavel's lips. The Ukrainian was wasted, and the German was stupid, but neither mental handicap would overpower instincts born of long years spent far beneath the surface of Europe's criminal underworld. Survival was the name of the game—the name of every game—and drunk and stupid or not, they could smell the danger.

Ivan moved first, flicking his wrist left and hurling vodka straight into Pavel's face—the immediate threat. The Belarusian choked and shifted backward, hand dropping to his waistband. Ivan was already on his feet, cup abandoned, a Russian-made Grach handgun appearing from his waistband. The Ukrainian and the German scrambled. A SIG SAUER appeared over the table. Gunshots blasted across the confined space, and the Ukrainian hurtled backward with the top of his head blown off only a moment before the German caught two slugs to his face.

Pavel was out of his chair. His own weapon flashed beneath the table. The muzzle of a Glock 19 orbited toward Ivan.

Ivan didn't try to outrun it. He slung himself left instead, across the top of the bloody table like a running back hurtling over the top of an offensive line. His shoulder collided with Pavel's arm just as the Glock cracked. A bullet raced past Ivan's ribcage, and then he was on top of Pavel. They both hit the ground. Ivan's right hand struck like a snake, slamming the muzzle of the Grach straight into Pavel's left eye. Blood sprayed. Pavel screamed. He fired again, but only shot the wall.

Ivan pinned Pavel's gun arm with one knee. He ripped the Glock away. He pounded Pavel's face until the Belarusian writhed and choked on his own blood.

Then he hauled him up by the collar and shoved him onto the couch that ran along one wall. He didn't even glance at the two dead men growing cold on the floor behind him. He rammed the muzzle of the Grach beneath Pavel's throat, and placed his finger on the trigger.

"Now, old friend," Ivan snarled. "You will tell me what you know about where Oleksiy Melnyk acquired *Russian-made* VX."

10

Langley, Virginia

In her newly remodeled executive office, interim director Dr. Sarah Aimes stood over an eight-seat conference table spread with photographs. Not digital ones—not screens. These were printouts, generated by the massive printers housed in Langley's operations division and carted in under the arm of Silas Rigby, Aimes's newly appointed deputy director of operations.

Rigby's new job was Aimes's old one, and he had a unique approach to it. Barely thirty-two years old and a little too blue-blooded for Aimes's taste, Rigby was Vermont born and Yale educated. Always dressed to the nines and a stickler for details to the point that he sometimes tripped over himself. He was a rookie in the world of leadership, and not much better than a rookie in terms of intelligence work. His appointment to the directorate of operations was one of the many sticking points of Aimes's own confirmation as director. The Senate Select Committee on Intelligence didn't like the idea of somebody so green running the CIA's core functions.

But Aimes was willing to stick to her guns on this one—not only because she believed Rigby had tremendous potential as both a leader and a spook, but because she valued his youth and malleability. She liked the idea of soft clay, not yet baked by decades of habit and prejudice that made him either unwilling or unable to think outside the box. Rigby was *hers*—not the CIA's. He would listen. He would think.

He wouldn't play games and pull strings behind her back the way Aimes herself had been forced to do with Victor O'Brien, her predecessor. Rigby was uncut stone, and Aimes was going to shape him into a deputy she could bet her life on.

"We're still communicating with assets in Beirut," Rigby said. "We've got eyes on the freighter and a search net running through the city. It seems logical that Ibrahim would have fled Lebanon shortly after making port, but if he's still in the vicinity, we'll run him down. I'm confident."

Aimes surveyed the printed photographs of the Liberian flagged freighter, *Cartova,* and the surrounding dock. It had been Rigby's idea to print them instead of using iPads or computer screens. He wanted to blow them up. He wanted to inspect for subdued details that one might miss in a small image. He wanted to challenge his own process.

Aimes liked that.

Most of the images were black-and-white, taken from what sparse security cameras filmed of the bustling port. Rigby had obtained the images from Lebanese officials, who only surrendered them under pressure. The government in Beirut was still salty over the short notice Washington had provided before deploying helicopters loaded with American spec ops soldiers through their airspace as though it were a public highway. Now they were inclined to be obstinate, to stall and play games.

Rigby had pushed—hard. He'd obtained a lot of still images from the cameras at the time the Liberian freighter made port and began to offload her cargo. Very little of it was relevant, maybe none of it. But it was still the most tangible lead the CIA had in locating the world's most wanted terrorist.

"Is the freighter still in port?" Aimes asked.

"She's left port this morning, headed for Guyana. We just missed her."

Of course we did.

Aimes would have liked to have put a field officer aboard with a pocket full of American dollars, ready to bribe any member of the crew who would talk. It was already too late for that.

She dismissed the *Cartova* from her mind and lifted a magnifying glass over one of the images. Aimes felt a little silly doing it—like a Sherlock Holmes wannabe. But she couldn't deny that Rigby's instincts were right on the money when it came to blowing up the images. She was seeing things she might not have. Things like a large blind-corner mirror mounted to the side of a warehouse. In its reflection she found the rear bumper of a Mercedes sedan. Not new—maybe two decades old. Battered. Muddy. There was no taxi sign on the roof, but she made out the outline of a driver's head behind the wheel.

And there was a passenger getting in—a lone man dressed in a jacket with a ball cap pulled low over his ears. Aimes couldn't determine any identifying characteristics in the grainy reflection of the mirror, but something about the man's posture sent a tingle up her spine. The way he ducked his head low, the collar of his jacket turned up.

Even in the baking Beirut heat.

"What's this?" Aimes placed a finger on the image. Rigby circled the table and accepted the magnifying glass. A slow smile crept across his face.

"I believe that's a lead."

Only half of the Mercedes's plate was visible. It was white, with a blue stripe across the top. The digits Aimes could read were all numerals: *58446*.

"Send this to Lebanese authorities," Aimes said. "And have our people scour the port area to see if any other cameras may have caught a better view."

"Will do." Rigby reached for his phone. Aimes returned to her desk and unlocked her computer. She pressed her palm against the biometric scanner to authorize the secure messaging service. She opened the thread and quickly scanned the latest update.

It was good news—Reed and his team were preparing to take off.

"Silas?" Aimes exited the software and looked over the top of her monitor. Rigby lowered his phone.

"Yes, ma'am?"

"Can I trust you?"

The hint of a frown passed across Rigby's face. He slid the phone into his suit jacket. His chin lifted.

"Implicitly, ma'am."

Aimes nodded slowly. Then she motioned to the chair across from her. "Have a seat. There's something you need to know about."

11

The Presidential Residence
The White House

Maggie took her midday meal in the private dining room situated on the second floor of the residence. She could have taken it in the West Wing, or even the Oval Office. But as the morning grind of another executive workday kicked in, the pain returned. It erupted in her stomach and consumed her thoughts.

It was all she could do to sit up straight. All she could do to keep her voice steady as she addressed her chief of staff, or made phone calls to the Senate, campaigning for Aimes's confirmation. The mental grit Maggie had leaned on for the duration of her political career strained and trembled under the pressure of this latest challenge, and for the first time in her adult life, Maggie truly wondered if she was about to break.

Not only mentally, but in every way. If she was about to fold under pressure too strong for anybody to face.

Lunch in the residence might not be a break sufficient to power her through the remainder of the day, but it was a good place to start. Maggie had a Cobb salad delivered to the dining room and sat slouched in her chair, breathing through the pain. Concentrating on the food. Trying not to think of her doctor's prophecies of imminent doom.

And trying not to cry.

I can't fail like this. I won't accept it.

When the door opened, Maggie blinked back the fog in her eyes to find that she'd barely touched her salad. A quick glance at the clock on the wall confirmed that she'd been gone from the West Wing for the better part of an hour. She had a meeting scheduled with FBI director Bill Purcell in twenty minutes to discuss the bureau's progress on the Ibrahim investigation. There were a lot of big questions in the air, like how a terrorist cell nobody had ever heard of sprang out of the rocks with a weapon like VX and a tool like the robocall system they had used to blanket the nation in fear.

All of those things felt vaguely out of touch to Maggie as she raised her face to the door, expecting a White House steward, maybe come to refill her water glass. It wasn't a steward. The man standing in the doorway was tall, broad, and wore an expression of deep concern as he closed the door behind him. He walked quickly to the end of the table and placed a hand on her arm.

"Are you okay?"

James O'Dell's voice was heavy with a Cajun drawl as he squeezed her arm. Maggie blinked the fog back and jabbed with her fork, spearing boiled egg and lettuce. She crunched down and nodded.

"Fine. Didn't sleep well."

O'Dell relaxed his grip, but she could tell through her peripheral vision that he didn't believe her. She could see it in the same deep brown eyes that had so often expressed such genuine pain and concern for her well-being. A love that she somehow didn't feel that she deserved.

O'Dell took a seat next to her, and Maggie focused on her meal. She felt vaguely annoyed to no longer be alone—like she was back on duty, under the watchful eye of the nation. Was romance meant to feel this way? Her relationship with her former bodyguard had blossomed into something more intimate a few months prior, and initially, Maggie had been excited. She'd always liked O'Dell. She'd always felt comfortable around him. She was willing to be open-minded and exploratory about the potential for a deeper connection.

Yet something had felt broken between the two of them for several weeks now, though Maggie routinely pushed it to the back of her mind. She had enough problems on her plate without adding personal ones.

"What did the doctor say?" O'Dell asked.

Another flash of frustration washed through Maggie's chest. It was a reasonable question, especially given their relationship. Somehow, it still felt like an intrusion.

"All good," Maggie said. "More rest, more vitamins."

O'Dell pursed his lips and nodded softly. His arms were crossed. He didn't reply, and eventually Maggie looked up.

"What?"

"I'm just wondering why you're lying to me." O'Dell's voice was calm, but she could detect the frustration in it. That tone did nothing to assuage her own feelings of irritation.

"Excuse me?"

"I know you're not okay. Everyone does. You're pushing too hard, and your health is melting away right before my eyes. I'm allowed to be concerned about that."

"Oh, are you?" Maggie wasn't sure why her voice had become so cutting. O'Dell remained unfazed.

"You have to back off," he said. "You're literally going to kill yourself. I don't understand why you won't confide in me. Why you insist on bearing everything by yourself."

"Because it's *mine* to bear." Maggie's voice cracked like a bullwhip. "Because this is my job."

O'Dell's jaw tightened and his dark eyes flashed with sudden frustration. For the first time in her life, Maggie felt the heat of his anger directed her way.

"What is *my* job?" O'Dell demanded.

It was a simple question, but it felt like a gut punch. Maggie sat with the fork hovering over her untouched plate. Her stomach throbbed, more hot pain ripping into her chest. Her fingers trembled, but she shoved it all back. She wouldn't acknowledge it. She wouldn't give it power.

"What does that mean?" Maggie said.

"You know what it means. It means, who am I? Why am I here? What do you even want from me?"

So there it was.

The tension boiling beneath the surface for so many long, stressful weeks was finally erupting to the surface. The big question: what was this? Did Maggie even know? Did she even have the heart for it?

When she woke up in a Chicago hospital, barely clinging to life, O'Dell was the only one there. He'd waited for her. He'd spent every waking minute by her side. He'd *fought* for her. There was something there . . .

Or hadn't there been? Was it just the raw emotion of survival? Of loneliness? Of one soul clinging to another?

Maggie set the fork down. She ran both hands through her hair. Her head ached. Her body throbbed. Thoughts of her meeting with Purcell, and Aimes's stalling confirmation vote, and a terrorist on the loose while America threatened to crumble before her very eyes shut out any personal concerns. She was overloaded. This was the straw that broke the camel's back.

"I can't deal with this right now." Maggie's voice was colder than she intended, but maybe this was how she really felt.

"What does that mean?" O'Dell said.

"It means what I said. I don't have time for this."

"Time for this? Or time for me?"

And there it was again.

Maggie faced O'Dell. He didn't blink. His arms were crossed. He wasn't backing down . . . not this time.

"You won't answer my calls." O'Dell's voice trembled. "You push me to the side in the West Wing. You've given me a meaningless title and an office in a closet. We never see each other, we never talk. I'm left to watch you fall apart one bloody day at a time . . . and you don't have *time* to talk about it?"

Maggie's stomach quaked. Her hand trembled. The heat in her chest redoubled. She couldn't even tell if it was pain anymore. She couldn't tell anything. The brain fog was taking over. The pressure was breaking her.

She couldn't do this. Not now, maybe not ever. She was about to break. Something had to give.

A hot tear slipped out of her eye, and Maggie dug someplace deep beneath the carnage and found an ounce of courage.

"I don't have time for *you*," she said.

The words struck home like a ballistic missile. O'Dell flinched, his eyes rimming red. Maggie wanted to take the blow back, but she couldn't. She couldn't force herself through another empty conversation. She had nothing left to give.

"You should go," Maggie said. "I'm sorry."

O'Dell's deep eyes blinked slowly. He swallowed.

And then he nodded once. He stood and left the room without another word. The door closed. Maggie trembled.

Then she fell against the table and sobbed.

12

Leiper's Fork, Tennessee

The order for deployment reached Reed three hours after the team assembled. Everybody loaded into their individual vehicles and drove ten miles deeper into the county to a rural little community buried in the Tennessee hills. Leiper's Fork featured only a handful of businesses and no traffic lights. The private airport was pilot-controlled—no tower. The hangars were mostly small, mostly open-faced.

But the largest of the hangars featured twin rolling doors that concealed the 2005 Gulfstream V, a fourteen-passenger business jet owned and operated by a consulting firm based in Arlington, Virginia. Not all that far from Langley.

The pilot waiting for them next to the jet wore a t-shirt and cargo shorts. He was young, and had a definite military look about him. Air Force, likely. Perhaps Navy. He still kept a haircut that Reed associated with an airman—high, tight, and cleaner than a jarhead's chaotic lifestyle would allow. Reed met him at the nose of the jet, and the guy extended a hand.

"Mr. Montgomery?"

"That's right."

"Kyle Strickland. I'll be your pilot in command today. I understand you brought me a co-pilot?"

"I brought you a PIC. You'll be the co-pilot. Strickland, meet Kirsten Corbyn."

Reed jabbed a thumb over his shoulder, ignoring Strickland's flush of indignation. Corbyn appeared in her flight jacket, a tight tank top and tighter jeans matching black combat boots and aviator shades that once again rode halfway down her nose. She extended a closed fist.

"Wassup, mate?"

Reed left the two pilots to squabble about command while he and Turk unloaded the gear. There was a lot of it. Probably a lot more than the Lebanese would allow through customs, but that was Aimes's problem to solve. If the Prosecution Force was going to run Ibrahim down, they would need all the firepower they could get. Reed expected nothing less than a raw gunfight.

The Gulfstream was larger than any of the planes the CIA had allocated in the past. Reed figured that was an indicator of his promotion among the ranks. There was plenty of room to secure the gear in the back next to a table laden with premade Subway sandwiches and an ice chest full of bottled water. Seats were clad in worn leather, the carpet a little threadbare but still holding up. There was a lavatory and even a small berth.

It would do.

Reed returned to the tarmac to find Strickland beet-red and Corbyn as cool as a cucumber. He jerked his head at the plane.

"Somebody move that thing so we can park."

Corbyn swung aboard, and Strickland rushed to follow. Jet engines wound to life five minutes later. The plane taxied slowly out onto the airstrip, and Turk and Wolfgang helped Reed relocate all the vehicles inside the hangar. The doors rumbled shut, and Turk padlocked them. From behind the Gulfstream's windshield Reed could see Corbyn seated in the lefthand chair, looking over her glasses and popping gum while she ran through her pre-flight. Strickland sat next to her, still cherry red, but no longer speaking.

A dull chill ran up Reed's spine, defying the Tennessee heat that boiled down from the late summer sun. It was an electric feeling. A rush of anticipation. A chemical instinct bred by years of moments just like this.

The thunder of jet engines. The promise of incoming action.

Only, this time was different. When Reed closed his eyes and thought about Ibrahim, he also thought about the dream. That vision he had enjoyed in the fuzzy moments between life and death. The field, and the light.

And his daughter.

Reed opened his eyes and lifted his phone. His blood ran hot as he dialed Banks. He didn't expect her to pick up. She had read his text message alerting her to his departure, and she had never responded.

Right on cue, the call routed to voicemail. Reed waited for Banks's cheery message to play while the Gulfstream howled across the airfield. The voicemail beeped, and he found himself standing dumbly, unsure what to say. He could only think about Ibrahim . . . and his daughter.

"I love you," he said at last. "I'll call you when I'm headed back."

Then Reed hung up. He pocketed the phone. He met Turk and accepted half a burnt cigarette as the two of them started toward the plane. The smoke flooded his lungs, and the nicotine collided with the combat anticipation. It wasn't enough to neutralize the raw energy coursing through his body, just enough to control it.

Reed was ready to kill.

13

United States Capitol
Washington, DC

"Dr. Aimes, how do you justify a complete overhaul of the CIA's leadership structure during your tenure as interim director?"

Aimes sat behind a table in the middle of a triangular Senate chamber, a series of seventeen United States senators spread along a curving table that sat a few feet higher than her own. There were witnesses in the room —cameras for C-SPAN, and media photographers snapping pictures. It was warmer than Aimes would have liked. Sweat trickled down her back as she sat upright in front of the chair and endured the hail of questions hurtling toward her like artillery shells.

Not just from one party, but from both parties, and the single independent who joined them. All guns were turned on her like a broadside from a battleship, and three hours in, the shells just kept landing.

The most recent blast came from Carrie Anderson of Utah, a junior senator and member of the Democratic Party. She was the youngest member of the body by far at barely thirty-one, and Aimes didn't miss the irony of her questioning.

She just couldn't acknowledge it.

"Senator, as I'm sure you're aware, U.S. law stipulates that the DDCI is appointed by the president and confirmed by this body, much as my own position. That's not a matter I control."

It was a sidestep of Anderson's challenge, but a legally sound one. Anderson redoubled.

"Dr. Aimes, we're all adults. We all read between the lines. The nomination that President Trousdale submitted to this body for Silas Rigby to assume the position of DDCI may have come on White House letterhead, but it's beyond question that your recommendation birthed it."

Aimes said nothing. Anderson raised both eyebrows.

"I'm not sure I understand the question, Senator," Aimes said coolly.

Anderson leaned close to the mic. "I'm asking whether you endorse handing the second most powerful position in the CIA to a man who's barely out of grad school."

And yet he's older than you.

Aimes could have said it, but it wouldn't have helped. She decided to keep things simple.

"Mr. Rigby is an outstanding member of the intelligence community and a dedicated servant of the nation, Senator. He is both highly intelligent and a talented leader. He enjoys my full support."

Anderson pursed her lips. Aimes could feel the edge in the senator's cold glare, and she couldn't help but wonder *why*.

Of course the nation was terrified. Of course these were uncertain times. Everybody wanted answers. But why all the direct targeting of her as a nominee? It felt vaguely personal . . . and that led her mind back to Roper.

The senator from Iowa sat perched in the middle of the curved table, staring dead at her, his thick black hair coiffed and streaked with gray, a pen clicking slowly opening and closing in his right hand. He'd kept up that annoying habit for nearly an hour, and nobody had challenged him. Nobody dared.

Roper ran this committee like a team of beaten draft horses.

"Let me pivot to other concerns, Dr. Aimes." Anderson resumed her line of questioning. "You may not directly control the nomination of the

DDCI, but you do control many lower-level management and director positions within the agency. During the last three weeks you've made no less than eight replacements along your chain of command. While the nation is in such desperate need of security, how do you explain overhauling the very structure of our intelligence service?"

It was a dumb question, and it clearly reflected a lack of understanding in how the CIA functioned. Aimes hadn't replaced anyone who didn't deserve it, and she'd only replaced them so quickly *because* the nation was so desperate for security. There was no time to fool around.

"Senator, the responsibility I've been entrusted with while serving as the interim director of the CIA necessitates decisive action. In the wake of the August terrorist attacks which left so many of our countrymen dead, the burden on the CIA to provide a location for Abdel Ibrahim is immediate and preeminent. I rely on a stalwart team of intelligence professionals to accomplish that mission. As with any team, sometimes you have to make substitutions and call players off the bench. There's nothing unusual about that."

Anderson's lips parted. Then she looked back to the clock. Her time had expired. Roper leaned toward the mic.

"The chair now recognizes the senator from Iowa . . . that being me."

Here we go.

Aimes braced herself as Roper arranged his notes. Anderson had been persistent, but the questions were easy enough to dodge. Roper would be tougher, just as he'd been in each of the three afternoons she'd spent in this miserable room. Roper would come for blood.

"Dr. Aimes, last week I inquired about classified portions of your service record with the CIA which had not been provided to this committee."

Aimes nodded. "Yes, Senator. As requested, I gave directions to my staff to ensure all such records were furnished immediately to this committee as mandated by law."

"I appreciate that. But this morning I was looking over some of your records from the early part of your career during which time you served as a field officer stationed in the Middle East. I noted that in 2002 you spent time at a known CIA black site near Bagram Air Force Base in

Afghanistan codenamed *Salt Pit.* We now know that during this period many prisoners held at Salt Pit were subjected to so-called 'enhanced interrogation techniques,' which is, of course, a colloquialism for torture. Prisoners recount being chained in uncomfortable positions, left for hours in the darkness, denied food and water or given filthy food and water. Some accounts even described forced nudity, waterboarding, and threats of sexual violence."

Roper looked up from his notes. Aimes stiffened. She could feel the punchline coming.

"Dr. Aimes, did you participate in any of these torturous interrogations?"

Aimes's blood ran cold. She focused on not swallowing or twitching. She could feel every eye in the room fixated on her.

"As I stated previously, Senator, all records of my service to the agency, classified or otherwise, have been willingly submitted to this committee."

Roper removed his glasses. "Right. But I'm asking you a question about what is *not* contained in those records. Did you participate in enhanced interrogation techniques at any point during your career with the CIA?"

Aimes's chest tightened. She kept both arms on the table and took her time. There was no right answer to the question. A blunt denial would be deemed dishonest. An admission would be worse.

"Senator, as detailed in my numerous service evaluations, I have served the agency and this country with honor and a strict moral compass, conducting all of my missions in adherence with U.S. law."

"So . . . that's a yes?" Roper cocked his head. "Or no?"

He raised both eyebrows. The silence was deafening. Aimes's stomach descended into knots. She was hyperaware of every camera in the room broadcasting this interaction across a shell-shocked and desperate nation, and she knew Roper was also. The senator knew exactly what he was doing. He didn't really care about the answer to his question. Anybody who had served in the CIA immediately following 9/11 could be faced with similar questions. This was about putting her on the spot. Setting her up to fail.

"Senator, wars aren't perfect. Least of all a war such as the war against terror. I don't think I have to tell you that."

Roper winced, just slightly. His eyes turned cold, and Aimes glanced to the USMC pin affixed to his lapel. Her point was made.

"How about I ask you a different question?" Roper said. "Does the CIA *now*, under your guidance, practice *any* enhanced interrogation techniques as part of or in relation to your search for Abdel Ibrahim?"

Aimes's face felt hot. She hoped she hadn't flushed. She kicked the ball right back.

"The CIA follows the law, Senator."

"Does the CIA under your leadership practice torture?"

"The CIA interrogates intelligence subjects in adherence with U.S. and international guidelines."

"And does that include torture? Has it ever included torture under your guidance?"

"It includes any legal method available to us, Senator. Just as it always has." Aimes's voice snapped with sudden vitriol. She found herself sitting up and leaning forward before she could stop herself. "We've got nearly six thousand dead Americans in Tennessee and Louisiana, and a terrorist on the loose who has promised to unleash more carnage at the very next opportunity. I'm not paid to grandstand or nitpick, I'm paid to keep this country safe. Whatever happens after that is the jurisdiction of elected officials, *sir*."

A low murmur erupted from the crowd of reporters gathered behind Aimes. Cameras clicked and flashed. Every eye was fixed on her. Aimes fumed.

But Roper remained relaxed. He sat in the center of the curved table, eyes locked on hers. Glasses cradled in one hand.

The hint of a smile playing at the corners of his mouth.

Aimes left the chamber twenty minutes later. Two more senators questioned her, but neither of the conversations made it beyond clipped answers and abrupt verbal swordplay. Roper called a recess for the day. Aimes pushed past the reporters without comment, joined by security as she routed for her executive car back to Langley.

Her blood ran hot. Her head pounded. Her chest felt tight.

She thought of Bagram and the so-called "Salt Pit." She thought of the detainees who called the place *dark prison*.

Oh yes, there were stories to tell. Screams and shouted demands. Pleas and surrendered answers. Targets given. Targets located. American lives saved.

To hell with Roper.

Aimes reached the limo and slid inside. The heavy door slammed. Her security officer climbed behind the steering wheel. She'd barely made it a block from the capitol before the secure phone built into the seat next to her rang. Aimes braced herself, ready for absolutely anyone—including the president—to be calling.

The hearing hadn't gone well. She was ready to suffer the consequences.

"Aimes."

"Director, it's Silas. I've got an update from Beirut."

Aimes sat up. Thoughts of the hearing evaporated as her mind raced back to Lebanon.

"What is it?"

"It's from Mossad," Rigby said. His voice chirped with edgy excitement. "We found nothing on the car, but we did snag another security camera image of the sedan passing out of the port a block away. A passenger is barely visible. No clear face. But the driver . . . he might as well have been posing."

"*And?*" Aimes pressed.

"And Mossad had a match. His name is Bilal Mousa. He's a Lebanese national with known associations with the Islamic State. Mossad has an address and they're already moving on him. We hope to have updates within the hour."

Aimes checked her watch. It had been five hours since she'd deployed Reed. The plane would be well in the air, someplace over the Atlantic. A full tank of fuel and open skies.

The Prosecution Force would be ready the moment Mossad gave them a target.

"Silas, you remember what we talked about?"

Aimes didn't want to say it out loud, and she didn't have to. Rigby had received knowledge of the Prosecution Force without blinking. It didn't bother him. He was a practical guy. He wanted the job done . . . just like Aimes.

"I do," Rigby said.

"Make contact," Aimes said. "Tell them to gear up. We're moving on this the moment we have an address."

14

42,000 feet over the North Atlantic

The field was bright and golden—maybe from the wheat bending gently in a hot summer breeze, maybe from the sun beating down almost directly from overhead. Reed looked in every direction, but he only saw empty horizon. No clouds, no trees, no geographic landmarks of any sort. The ground was perfectly flat, the field endless. He stood in the middle like a speck in a desert—a raft on the ocean. The air was heavy in his lungs, his chest compressing with each gasp. A weight bore down on his shoulders like a Marine rucksack loaded with bricks.

He gasped for breath and peered directly upward into the sun's glare. It burned his eyes, but he couldn't close them. His mouth was as dry as the Iraqi desert, his tongue swollen and stiff.

Reed hit his knees, swallowing hard. He tried to shout, but he couldn't get past the lump in his throat. The heat washing down from above redoubled, but Reed didn't sweat. He was too dehydrated. His head swam as he peered slowly through the wheat, his vision swaying.

He'd been here before. Something about this place felt familiar. Even as he remained rooted to the ground, the field rolled beneath another blast of wind. A hill appeared out of nowhere, a tall oak tree rooted in the top.

Gnarled limbs reached for the ground, emerald leaves fluttering in the breeze. The tree drew nearer, only fifty yards away, and Reed longed for the relieving shade. He struggled to lift one leg, but his knee was sealed to the ground as though it were locked into concrete. He couldn't budge.

Then he heard the laugh. Soft and melodic, the sound was both familiar and foreign all at once. It reminded him a little of Banks, but was too high-pitched. Too innocent.

Reed saw the child the same moment he saw the tire swing. It hung from a limb of the oak tree, spinning out over the sloping side of the hill and rotating under the wash of the sun. The child sat with her legs running through the tire's core, both hands wrapped around the rope that suspended it, bright blonde hair flowing in the breeze as she rocked her head back and laughed.

And laughed.

Molten pain cut through Reed's chest like a storm of bullets. His mouth dropped open and he reached for the tree. He recognized the face, now. He recognized the smile. The bright blue eyes the child had stolen from her mother.

He'd met this girl before—together in a dream as VX nerve agent fought to claim his life. It was *his* child. His daughter.

"April!"

The name croaked from his throat as a rasp. The girl didn't hear him, and Reed gritted his teeth. He dug one hand into the ground, fingers rooting among wheat and rich soil, and he clawed his way forward.

One knee broke free. Then the other. He fought to his feet. The sun was fading behind a sudden bank of storm clouds, but still the child clung to the swing, all alone on the hill.

"April!" This time Reed screamed the name, and this time the child saw him. Her beautiful rosy face rotated toward him as the swing began to slow, hair still caught in the wind. The sunshine had vanished, leaving an eerie blue light washing over her face. The smile began to fade.

"April . . . it's me. It's Daddy."

The words were raw. Reed barely recognized his own voice. He took a faltering step forward, and the child smiled again. She reached a pudgy hand toward him.

Then her face washed with sudden terror, and a heavy hand descended over Reed's shoulder. His body was yanked back by the strength of a giant, shoulders crashing into the ground.

A face leered overhead, eyes bloodshot, teeth stained crimson. Olive skin was scalded by chemical burns, lips busted and breath ragged. It was a face Reed would have recognized anywhere in the world—the face of the world's most wanted man.

"You go no further, Montgomery," Ibrahim's voice growled like a demon of the underworld. His fingers crunched down around Reed's shoulders, digging into unprotected flesh. Reed screamed and thrashed, one hand dropping to his hip in search of a sidearm. But he was unarmed. He couldn't even find his knife.

Ibrahim leaned closer, blood dripping from his teeth. He grinned.

"The child is mine now. I'm taking her to Hell."

Reed sat up with a lurch in the back of the Gulfstream, eyes snapping open as he gasped for air. The hot pain in his shoulder vanished with the vision, but the pressure remained, fingers clamping down. Reed's hand dropped to his thigh-mounted drop holster and closed around the grip of the SIG P226 strapped there. Finger on the trigger, barrel clearing the Kydex. Up and right, moving toward the threat.

"Reed!"

Turk's voice broke through the brain fog as the hand on Reed's shoulder shook. He blinked, and suddenly he saw the interior of the Gulfstream. Wolfgang and Lucy were watching Reed with intense, concerned eyes from a few seats away as Turk leaned down directly alongside him. Reed's gaze snapped up toward the face of his old friend, and he gasped again. His arm shook. Turk put a gentle hand on the SIG and pressed it slowly down.

"You're good, man . . . you're good. Let it go."

Reed blinked and looked down. He noted his index finger curled around the SIG's trigger, and a new wash of panic coursed through his chest. He rammed the gun back into the holster. Sweat ran from his forehead and he scrubbed it away with one hand.

Turk squatted next to him. "You okay?"

Reed avoided his gaze, sitting up quickly in the leather-backed chair and reaching for the glass of Old Forester he'd left on the side table. It was almost empty, and the bottle resting in the seat next to him was nearly half empty. He knocked back what remained in the glass, throat burning.

He blinked hard, but the images in his head wouldn't go away. He still saw the field. The hill. The tree and the swing. The face of the girl . . . *his* girl.

And then Ibrahim.

Reed's chest tightened and he reached for the bottle. Turk squeezed his arm.

"Maybe you should drink some water."

"Piss off," Reed snarled. "Haven't you ever had a bad dream?"

He shoved Turk with his shoulder, and the big man stood. Reed poured himself another glass and shot a lethal glare down the length of the plane. Wolfgang and Lucy looked slowly away, Wolfgang returning to a movie on an iPad, Lucy returning to an open Bible. Turk patted Reed once on his shoulder and gave him space.

Reed drank the bourbon in a gulp and wiped his mouth with the back of one hand. He still saw Ibrahim and his demon face, but with effort he was able to rewind his mind. Back to the moments before, in the field, under the bright sun. He saw the child . . . and he heard his own voice.

April.

He hadn't thought to call the child that. It had simply popped out, as naturally as addressing an old friend. It just fell off his lips, confusing him for a moment. And then making perfect sense.

April was Banks's middle name, just like David was Reed's. They'd named their son in honor of that lineage . . . would they have named their daughter in the same way?

Renewed heat raced through Reed's gut, and he thought he caught Turk looking at him from across the aisle. Reed took another gulp and pushed the vision from his mind, forcing himself to return to the present. He glanced at his watch as jet engines howled outside the cabin, and a sudden memory lurched to the front of his mind like a freight train.

It was Wednesday. He'd almost missed it.

Sweeping up his own iPad, Reed connected to the satellite internet feed provided by the CIA and navigated immediately to a favorited website. It was a local Nashville area media that featured a popular radio show. Banks was scheduled to join hosts *Bobbie and Billie*—both women—for a rush hour chat. Reed had almost forgotten all about it, and another gut punch landed like a fist as he recalled the previous evening. How he'd stormed out.

He hadn't even thought of the early morning show, then. Banks must have been excited, or maybe nervous. He should have talked with her about it. He should have shared the moment.

As it was, he was left to listen to the replay via noise-canceling headphones while the jet rocketed eastward. Both his wife and his son left far behind.

"Now, Banks. You've become a little famous for being something of an enigma in the celebrity world. Not much is known about your personal life. You'd don't post very often on social media. Is that intentional?"

It was Bobbie who spoke, or maybe Billie. They had introduced themselves at the start of the show, but they sounded the same to Reed.

Banks laughed a little. It was a melodic sound, but Reed detected the strain in it. Carefully hidden, like bruises beneath makeup.

"You know, I guess I've never been on social media much. It's just not really my thing."

"Well, you've never been a celebrity before!"

"Is that what I am?" Banks laughed again.

"Closer to a sensation, I think. I remember the moment I first heard about you. It was right after the attack . . . I was still in shock. I mean, we all were. It was such an ugly moment. So much fear. But then, we hear this story. A young singer blown down by the bomb in Rutherford County. Clinging to life by a thread. And then we heard your music . . . *Banks*. You have a gift. Do you know that?"

A pause. Banks's voice softened. "It's very kind of you to say so. I feel like the most special thing about my life has to be the gift of still living it. The bomb . . . I mean . . . "

Banks's voice choked. The sound sent knives through Reed's chest. His wife wasn't faking it. That wasn't her style. She was as raw and authentic on the radio as she was in her own living room. It was one of the things that made her so special.

"We know it's been hard," one of the women said. "We can only imagine how hard. And we have to tell you, you're not the only one blessed by your survival. Over thirty *million* streams of your music since the blast . . . you're a national story!"

"I guess . . . I mean, it's hard to wrap my mind around. I always wanted to be a singer. When I lived in Atlanta, I used to play bars and nightclubs. And that was always enough. I didn't need it to be big. I just wanted it to be real."

"Oh, it's real, Banks. It's special. But people want to know about *you!* They want to know the girl behind the mic. You're such a mystery."

Another nervous laugh. "Well . . . that's not intentional. It just kinda happened that way."

"So what can you tell us? Who *is* Banks Montgomery? Are you single? I know a lot of guys are hopeful."

A cheeky chuckle from the host. Reed flushed.

"No, not single. I'm married, actually."

"Oh?"

"Yes. His name is Reed. We met in Atlanta."

"Another singer? A hot guitarist, maybe?"

Reed sat up. The whiskey cradled in one hand, his attention fixed on the screen. Banks paused.

"He's . . . I mean. I don't really know how to say it. Reed was a Marine. Now he works for the government. He keeps us safe."

"*More mystery!* I love it."

Laughs all around. Reed grimaced. He would have preferred Banks not to mention his occupation at all. Call him a mechanic, or an accountant. Say he was a bum who played video games all day and rarely showered. Whatever.

After the voicemail—after the *threat*—Reed didn't relish anybody knowing anything about him. It brought too much attention on Banks, not from radio show hosts with cutesy names, but from America's worst enemies.

He would have to say something later. For now, he was grateful that

Banks had skirted the question. The interview proceeded to Banks's musical influences and future plans, with more conversation about Davy and Baxter than the mysterious former Marine who kept Americans safe in bed.

Reed was fine with that. He found it hard to focus on the verbal wit and flippant jokes of the radio hosts. His mind kept fading back to the dream . . . or the nightmare. The child's laugh. *April's* laugh.

And Ibrahim.

A notification appeared at the top of Reed's iPad screen, jarring his mind back to the present. A new message waited from Langley—a tight group of three lines, high-level details, with more promised.

Reed's heart rate spiked and he sat up. He read the message over again, assimilating quickly. Already spinning ahead to next steps.

CtrlCmnd: Be advised: Mossad located possible location for target. Warehouse on outskirts of Beirut, details pending. Land and prepare for immediate action.

Reed shot a message back.

PF: Advised, will notify on landing.

He flicked the iPad into sleep mode and tore his headphones off.

"Corbyn! What's our ETA?"

The Brit appeared through the open door to the cockpit, bending around her captain's chair. Wolfgang and Turk both sat up with her. Lucy twisted from the seat next to Reed, anticipation hanging in the air like a storm cloud.

"Seven hours, forty-five," Corbyn said. "What's up?"

"Make it seven flat. We've got a target."

15

Belgrade, Serbia

Pavel the Belarusian knew things, and he shared them. Not easily. Not without blood and a lot of artful manipulations of Ivan's folding knife. A lot of desperate shrieks suppressed by a wadded-up t-shirt.

Ivan took his time. Not because he enjoyed it, but because he was patient. Screams no longer resonated with his blackened soul. Pleading rang hollow in the caverns of his empty chest. He only knew the objective, and the path to achieving it.

Unfortunately for Pavel, he was the path. Ivan brutalized him for two hours before he got everything he wanted, all recorded on a voice memo on Ivan's smartphone for future replay and analysis.

Much as Ivan knew before he set foot in the grungy Serbian basement, Pavel was more than a sly card player. He was a trader, a sort of wholesaler of the black markets of eastern Europe and the third world. But unlike Oleksiy Melnyk, Pavel wasn't a direct trader of hard goods. No, the machinations of his particular industry were more nuanced, and much less tangible. But also more valuable, by far.

Pavel's merchandise consisted entirely of information. Of connections and opportunities. He was a man who knew men. A master of criminal networking, like a human Rolodex, but also a smoke screen. If you needed something in the criminal underworld and didn't know where to find it, Pavel could make a call. He could source a product, or a service.

He could do it without revealing the identities of either party, which was part of what made him so useful. He was discreet—masterfully so.

That made him difficult to break, but Ivan was an artisan of breaking people. He had nowhere else to be. Nothing better to do. He removed hope from the equation. He tore Pavel's mind down like an old skyscraper, chipping steadily away at the foundations until eventually . . .

Everything collapsed.

Pavel knew Melnyk. He knew him well. He also knew where Melnyk had acquired three fifty-five gallon drums of lethal nerve agent—the VX used by Abdel Ibrahim in his American attacks. The Belarusian knew, because the Belarusian had sourced them himself, from a forgotten Soviet-era weapons stash hidden deep in rural Georgia.

Not the state—the country. Not far from the capital city of Tbilisi. It was a small stash, but diverse in nature. Pavel had made a pretty penny by connecting the discoverer of the stash with various purchasers of such rare merchandise. Melnyk bought some. Warlords in Africa and rural Asia bought some. Some might still remain.

Pavel swore he knew nothing about the attacks. He swore there was no more VX to be had, and nothing more lethal. He pleaded for mercy. He choked on his own blood.

He died with agony plastered over his face.

Ivan washed his knife in the sink and cleaned his hands. He collected his personal items and used a cast iron frying pan to bust a copper gas line running along the underside of the rafters overhead. It was natural gas, piped in to operate heaters during the coldest months. It flooded the basement in mere seconds as Ivan climbed back to the surface. He lit a Russian cigarette in the alley outside. He smoked half of it while he ruminated on what Pavel had said.

Then he laid the cigarette on the doorstep and set off in a brisk walk. He had just made it to the end of the alley when the gas caught. It detonated with a thunderclap, blowing out windows and hurtling metal trash cans against the adjacent building. Flames consumed the doorway, hot and ravenous.

Long before the local fire department arrived, the basement would be lost. The building would cave in on top of it. If the bodies were ever found, it would take days, maybe weeks.

Ivan would be long gone by then. He already knew his next destination. He would fly to Tbilisi. Find transport to the rural weapons stash Pavel had described. Do a little of his own investigation.

Because Ivan Sidorov had been around a long time. He remembered the Soviet days. He remembered the weapons stashes, spread all across the Union. He remembered when they were abandoned, cleaned out, and sold off.

Plenty of small arms had found their way to Africa and the Middle East. Southeast Asia and South America. AK-47s alongside millions of rounds of ammunition. Sniper rifles and RPGs. Tanks, even.

But VX? Weapons of mass destruction?

Russia had reclaimed those. Every one, very carefully. Because the risk was too great. It was certainly possible that some had slipped through the cracks. Certainly possible that a weapons stash had been forgotten.

But Ivan didn't buy it. His gut told him there was more to the story, and the folding knife in his pocket was sharp and ready to test that theory.

16

Beirut, Lebanon

The Gulfstream touched down at just after midnight, local time. Nobody had slept much on the flight. Reed spent most of his time using the iPad to survey details of the location reported by Mossad—a warehouse four kilometers from the heart of downtown, triangulated between the heart of the city and the city's port. Based on the aerial view, it was dilapidated, but it wasn't out of use. There were vehicles visible in the adjacent parking lots, and tire marks running in and out of the dusty entrance of the facility. A high fence surrounded an open lot next door, and the gravel there also looked disturbed by recent vehicle movement.

Mossad reported that the facility had once been used in agriculture, but they weren't certain of its present purpose. It seemed to be between tenants. On short notice, it was difficult to obtain further details. The CIA was leaning on local assets, of course, but in the middle of the night with a strike team already touching down, everybody was running short on time.

The smart play would have been to stall, mine additional intelligence, and establish a more calculated plan of action. Reed wasn't in the mood to wait for the smart play, and much to his satisfaction, neither was Langley. Aimes arranged for the Mossad agent on the ground to meet them at the airport. Lebanese customs were being difficult about the entrance of American operatives into their capital city, so the CIA had sidestepped them altogether by logging the flight as corporate executive transport related to the oil industry, something Lebanese officials wouldn't bat an eye at.

Reed and his team wouldn't be able to take any of their hardware off the plane, but Mossad was sympathetic to the cause of eliminating a radical Islamic terrorist hellbent on jihad against the Free World. They were willing to outfit Reed's team from their own stash, hidden inside Beirut.

That would suffice.

Corbyn parked the jet on the tarmac near a refueling station and powered it down. Then she left the cockpit with a quick smack across Strickland's shoulder.

"Top 'er off, will ya? And get those buggers off the windscreen."

Strickland glowered but said nothing as the Prosecution Force departed the plane. Reed figured that Strickland had been under-informed about the exact nature of the mission at hand, and the pilot probably liked it that way. It was simpler. He would refuel the plane and remain on standby.

Corbyn would accompany them. Probably not directly into the gunfight to come, but close by. Reed had learned through repeated experience that the ex-RAF pilot was quick on her feet and relentlessly useful in a pinch.

Customs cleared the line of mismatched Americans and one Brit without complaint. The airport was a small one, not used for much commercial travel so much as private. Reed figured that the weary Lebanese officials running the desk were used to late-night flights packed with foreigners who weren't eager to answer intrusive questions.

These were oil executives, after all. Shabby clothes or otherwise. This was normal. Reed, Turk, Wolfgang, and Corbyn all had fake passports at the ready. Lucy was forced to use her real passport, but it also glided past inspection and received a stamp without hiccup.

Outside the airport a gunmetal grey Toyota Prado waited in an express pickup parking lot, windows heavily tinted, engine running but headlights off. As Reed cleared the automatic doors of the airport, a haze of pollution flooded his lungs. The lights of sprawling downtown Beirut stretched across the horizon, obscured by the same cloud of smog, car horns, and distant sirens rising between tightly packed apartment buildings and mid-rise business towers. The air tasted of salt and oil. The ground was baking hot beneath his boots even long after sunset. The wind was cool and blew in from the coast.

It was different from any place Reed had ever set foot . . . and at the same time, it was exactly the same. Another city in another country with a target hiding someplace amid millions of innocent and guilty souls alike. He wasn't here for the landscape or the local cuisine.

He was here to kill somebody.

"That's it," Reed said, comparing the license plate on the front bumper of the Toyota with the number in his mind. It made him nervous to approach an unknown vehicle, unarmed in an unfamiliar environment. Instincts deep in Reed's gut warned him that a more careful approach would be well advised.

But Abdel Ibrahim had landed in Lebanon almost eighteen hours prior. The Prosecution Force was out of time to be careful.

Reed approached the passenger side. Turk flanked to his left, while everyone else fell in step a few yards behind. Of the five of them, Wolfgang was the only one still armed. His backup Glock had remained encased in his fake leg as he breezed through the customs metal detector with a sheepish shrug and a flash of his medical card.

Reed shot him a sideways look, and Wolfgang nodded once. Then Reed approached the passenger glass as it buzzed downward. A cloud of vapor drifted out, joined by a rush of air-conditioned breeze.

"Good evening. Do you know where I could find a movie rental store?" The voice was smooth. Not local, but definitely regional. Israeli, Reed thought. English was comfortable for the speaker, but not native.

Reed stopped next to the door, peering inside. The vehicle was empty save for a single occupant—a man behind the wheel, sucking on a vape stick. Dark-skinned, dark-eyed, dark-haired. Very handsome. Lithe and muscular, with a strong five o'clock shadow speckled with gray. Reed could tell in an instant that he was looking at a fellow killer. Everything about the man's aura radiated calm confidence and awareness, not just mental, but physical.

"They all went out of business," Reed said. "But I could sell you DVDs."

"Do you have any of the Rambo movies?"

"Only the first two."

The man nodded softly and hit a switch on his door. The locks clicked. Reed glanced over his shoulder and nodded once. Wolfgang's hand twitched, and his right pant leg dropped a few inches over the fake leg. Reed opened the front passenger's door and piled inside.

"Reed Montgomery, I presume."

"That's right." Reed shut the door and wound up the window. The Toyota smelled like candy—sour, fruity candy. He guessed it was the vape stick. "And you?"

"Amir Mizrahi," the man said.

The Toyota rocked as Turk clambered in behind Reed. Wolfgang took the seat behind Amir, which suited Reed just fine. That Glock 10mm would punch right through the driver's seat if anything should go sideways. Corbyn and Lucy huddled into the back, Lucy shooting sharp eyes through the tinted windows and around the parking lot, Corbyn popping gum and still wearing her aviator sunglasses . . . even in the dark.

Amir looked into the rearview mirror, his gaze switching from one face to the next. He sucked on his vape stick and held the cloud, then breathed sideways against his own glass. The tangy sweet odor of candy redoubled.

"You have been briefed by your agency on our intel?"

Reed grunted. "Warehouse on the outskirts. Probable location."

Amir shook his head. "That is optimistic to say. We obtained footage of a cab driver picking up a passenger near the docks after the Liberian freighter made port. Whether this man was Ibrahim, we cannot be sure. I paid a visit to the cab driver to inquire."

"And?" Reed asked.

Amir shrugged. "He was easy to buy. He dropped the man at the warehouse. He didn't recall much about his appearance, only that he was Middle Eastern, but . . . this is the Middle East."

Reed considered. It was a less promising report than he'd hoped for, and less certain than Langley had led him to believe, but he didn't care. Abdel Ibrahim had been aboard that freighter. This was as strong a lead as they had yet to find.

"It's enough," Reed said.

Amir sucked on his vape stick and shifted into drive. The Toyota powered out of the parking lot.

"Do you like hip-hop?" Amir asked.

Reed shrugged. "Sure."

Amir cranked up the radio. It was American music—Reed recognized neither the song nor the artist, but the cadence of urban rap was impossible to misidentify. Amir breathed vapor through his nose. Already the cabin of the Toyota was clouded with it. He turned for the highway with a flick of his turn signal and mashed the gas. The big engine roared.

"I understand you could use some hardware," Amir said.

"Whatever you can spare," Reed replied.

A dry smile crept across the Israeli's face, breaking his icy composure for the first time. "Dream big, my friend. Dream big."

17

Amir was as good as his word. The Toyota purred across the city, rushing through traffic and zipping off the freeway with downtown lost in a smoggy haze to their left. He finally pulled down a grungy street lined by ten- and fifteen-story apartment towers, sunbaked and sand-blasted. Balconies were lined by colorful clothing flapping from makeshift clotheslines, and windows were foggy with dust and dim light.

Amir turned the Toyota into the entrance of an underground parking garage and navigated to the back. Reed tensed with instinctual unease, and the Israeli detected it. He lifted a calming hand, then pressed a button on his sun visor. A metal door groaned, then lifted slowly in flat sections to reveal a two-car garage on the far side.

One half was empty, with an oil spot in the middle. The other was stacked with plastic containers, like a storage unit. Amir pulled over the oil spot and mashed the button again. He cut the engine, but waited for the metal door to close before he exited the car. Reed stepped onto smooth concrete, and Amir flicked a light on. A fluorescent glow spilled over the plastic containers as the remainder of the Prosecution Force exited the Toyota.

Amir approached the containers, still sucking on his vape stick. He bent and flipped a container lid off with a casual flick of one hand. It hit the floor, and the overhead lights flushed the interior with light.

Rifles lay inside—half a dozen of them. Reed recognized the black outlines as Galil ACEs chambered in 7.62x39mm, judging by the curved steel magazines stacked alongside them. Holographic sights rode the Picatinny rails above the receivers, and polymer weapons lights were mounted near the muzzles.

Amir gestured with his vape stick, breathing vapor between his teeth. "Jericho 941s to your left. Body armor, combat clothes, and communications to your right. Help yourself, friend."

The Israeli gear was different from the American stuff Reed was accustomed to, but ten minutes after sifting through the containers, his entire team was outfitted heavily enough to storm a bunker. Turk, Reed, and Wolfgang all accepted Galil rifles with spare magazines, chest and back plate body armor, black pants and shirts that were too short and snug for Reed and Turk but fit Wolfgang well, and Jericho 941 handguns chambered in 9mm. Turk found breaching charges in the bottom of an ammo container, but much to his disappointment he didn't find grenades.

Corbyn and Lucy each took handguns before Lucy dug into the communications gear, unpacking five headsets and corresponding belt units and powering them on to ensure functionality before she distributed them.

"I'll serve as the communications hub," she volunteered. "I can also run overwatch."

Reed nodded. "That'll work. Corbyn, you stick next to her. I like the idea of having you on standby if we need a getaway pilot."

That earned a smug grin from Corbyn, but Amir held up a hand.

"We don't need any theatrics here. Especially with Israeli small arms. Mossad's preference would be for you to pull your man without any gunfire."

"Mossad's and my own," Reed said. "But this guy has already killed over five thousand Americans. He won't go down without a fight."

Amir thought about that between puffs of vapor. He glanced to the Toyota.

"Put your communications with me. They can operate from the back seat. When you have your man, I'll pull you out. With God's providence we can have you back to the plane before sunrise, no one the wiser."

"With God's providence?" Lucy cocked an eyebrow, a smile playing at her lips. Amir returned the smile.

"He is faithful."

Reed inspected the Toyota and thought about angles. From the ground, Lucy and Corbyn's aid as overwatch would be minimal. But there was a definite positive to having Amir behind the wheel. If things went sideways, somebody who knew the city would be a benefit. It shouldn't have surprised Reed that Amir wasn't going to hand them a full loadout of weaponry and simply cut them loose.

"That'll work," Reed said. "But just so we're clear, my orders are to eliminate the threat. I'm not here to play politics. If this jerk so much as twitches, he's getting two in the face and a mag dump in the chest. Can you deal with that?"

Amir sucked the vape. Held it. Breathed out in a cloud. Then he reached for his keys.

"*Yalla.* Let's go."

18

Dim city lights lit the way as the Toyota powered back into the city. Reed rode in the back this time, keeping his Galil beneath the window line while Corbyn sat shotgun and scanned the passing buildings with her sunglasses slid halfway down her nose. Everybody was quiet. Turk press-checked his Jericho twice, and fidgeted with the red dot affixed to the top of his rifle before removing it altogether using the quick-detach lever.

Reed couldn't blame him. Untested, the optic was more of a risk than factory irons. He'd likely remove his, also.

"The building sits between a textile plant and an empty lot surrounded by a high fence," Amir said. "I've monitored it for most of the past ten hours. There is certainly somebody inside . . . there are small noises, and once a car left and returned. I did not see any faces."

"Multiple occupants?" Reed asked.

"I think so."

Reed would have assumed multiple occupants, regardless. Saying it out loud still tightened his chest a little. It was always a risk kicking a door down. Much more of a risk doing so with zero knowledge of the layout of the building's interior, to say nothing of how many armed occupants might wait within.

Missions like this should take time to plan. Days, maybe, and a lot of careful surveillance. At least an attempt to obtain the structure's layout via blueprints or images. But Langley didn't have time for that, and neither did Reed. This was the nature of working on a nonexistent strike team. They wouldn't be able to do this the spec ops way, with extensive prior planning and the best technology the military could offer. This would be done the black ops way. Quick, dirty, and highly dangerous.

Reed withdrew the iPad from his pack and checked communication from Langley. There was a standing request for a sitrep. He punched out a quick update.

PF: Arrived on site. Preparing to breach. Will advise.

"Do you want a pass or do you prefer to go in blind?" Amir asked.

It was a good question. There were risks either way. Reed chose to take the chance of being spotted in favor of at least the pretense of reconnaissance.

"One pass," he said. "Don't slow."

Amir hit his blinker and turned right down a city block. It was an industrial part of town, with a lot of warehouses and small factories. There were vehicles in plenty, but nobody walking the sidewalks or loitering on street corners. Beirut was as fast asleep as any big city ever was. It was just past two a.m., but Reed didn't trust the calm.

Amir slowed at a stop sign, then hung a quick left. He accelerated, bumping along like any other late-night traveler headed toward downtown. A lot appeared on the right, surrounded by a high chain-link fence that was obscured by privacy slats. Fresh tire marks ran through loose gravel near the chained gate.

Then came the warehouse. Single story, built of sand-blasted block coated in beige paint. A metal roof. Fifty yards wide, and twice as many long. Running right up to the sidewalk with a rolling metal door large enough to admit a semitruck, and a human-sized door standing next to it. Both closed.

Amir breezed right past a textile plant before hanging another left at the next block. Trash blew across the street and dim streetlights gleamed over the Toyota's dirty windshield. Amir shot Reed a sideways glance.

"Well?"

Reed's mind was already spinning. His brief glimpse of the target structure had told him a lot. There were no side entrances, but the satellite view on his iPad already told him there was a back entrance leading into a narrow alley. He would need to split his team in two—have somebody watch the back door while he breached through the front. It would be risky, no matter how fast he moved. They were going in completely blind. For all he knew, there could be a shaped charge and a trip wire attached to the front door. He could kick his way in only to be blown in half.

But that didn't change anything. Not really. There was still a better-than-random chance that Abdel Ibrahim was sheltered inside that building. That his daughter's killer waited, only a block away. There wasn't anything on earth that would stop Reed from smashing through that door.

"Wolf, I want you on the back. Anything that exits that way gets two in the chest and one in the face. Turk, you're with me. Lucy, run coms."

A chorus of grunts rose from the back seat. Amir stopped the Toyota two blocks from the warehouse and pulled against the curb. Reed double-checked his Galil and flipped the safety off. He went ahead and disposed of the red dot, also, but he kept the weapon light. He, Turk, and Wolfgang dismounted the vehicle with ease.

And then so did Amir. The Israeli tossed Corbyn the Toyota's keys and withdrew an Uzi with a collapsible stock from beneath his seat. A Jericho 9mm slid into a holster on his hip.

"What are you doing?" Reed challenged.

"Protecting the Promised Land," Amir said. "You don't own a monopoly on killing terrorists, friend."

Reed's mind worked quickly. He almost refused. Then he figured four guns were better than three. With so many variables piling in like storm surge, he might as well add an unproven fighter to the mix. If Mossad's reputation was worth its salt, Amir would be handy to have around.

"Go with Wolf. Two in the chest, one in the head."

Earpieces slid into place. Lucy double-checked coms. Corbyn started the Toyota with a rumble and pulled away from the curb.

Then the two teams split. Reed went right, ready to circle in from the west. Amir led Wolf south, the two men fading like shadows into the night.

Half-cocked and accelerated beyond reason, the mission was a go.

19

Reed reached the block opposing the face of the warehouse five minutes later. His heart rate was up, but that was mostly due to adrenaline and anticipation. Even after a brisk jog, his breathing remained easy. He crouched in the shadows across the street from Turk and surveyed the face of the warehouse.

Details that Reed had missed during the rapid drive-by now caught his eye. He noted the cigarette butts gathered on the sidewalk near the smaller of the two doors. The black trail of a tire's scuff mark running against the curb—relatively fresh. Dust cleared away from the single window, allowing an occupant to obtain a clear view of the street. A fresh deadbolt affixed to the metal door, gleaming in bright contrast to the otherwise faded and corroded metal.

There was most definitely somebody inside, and they were on guard. That was strangely reassuring.

"Prosecutor to Wolf, sitrep."

"In position," Wolfgang replied almost immediately. "Clear view of the back door and street. Be advised, two vehicles are present. One Land Rover, one pickup truck. Both appear operational and are parked near the back door."

Reed considered. Then he thumbed the mic. "Wolf, can you approach without breaking cover?"

The reply was immediate. "Affirmative."

"Slash the tires and check back in."

Reed relaxed against the wall, counting the moments and studying the warehouse. Searching for any break in pattern. Any shift in detail. A blink of a security light, a flash of a shadow passing behind the window. Anything that would indicate occupants housed within.

It was the adjacent lot that bothered him. He wasn't sure why. The high chain-link fence fit with privacy slats seemed strangely out of place relative to the rest of the district. Not that there was anything particularly unusual about a chain-link fence near a warehouse. But the fence seemed . . . too high. Twelve feet, with no razor wire. And the slats looked fresh, as yet undamaged by the brutal Levant sun.

"Done," Wolfgang radioed. "Both vehicles out of commission."

Reed hit his mic again. "Can either of you see inside that fenced lot?"

"Negative," Wolfgang said. "We're on the ground."

"Amir?"

"I climbed to the top of a nearby building early yesterday," Amir said. "The lot was empty then. Just an abandoned forklift and an old truck."

Reed sucked his teeth and glanced sideways across the street to Turk. He raised both eyebrows. Turk remained fixated on the high chain-link fence, chewing gum silently. Then he looked to Reed and nodded once. The go-ahead.

Reed hit the mic. "Prosecutor to all channels. We're moving in. Stand by."

The radio chirped four times as Wolfgang and Lucy confirmed the transmission, then Reed left the shadows first, dashing across the street and avoiding the dim streetlights with ease while Turk covered him from the shadows. The moment his back was pressed against the warehouse wall, adjacent to the window, Reed pivoted the Galil down the length of the wall toward the door and waved two fingers at Turk.

The big Tennessean broke from cover and loped with ease to the far side of the door. His boots didn't make a sound as he reached the sidewalk. The Galil swung in low ready, Turk's finger just above the trigger guard. He inched his way past the rolling metal door while Reed pressed his ear close to the edge of the window and listened.

The Lebanese night was strangely still. Distant traffic noises rang from downtown Beirut, and a couple blocks away a horn beeped. Background noises that Reed filtered out with ease as he fixated on whatever lay inside the warehouse.

He heard something. A soft clink, like metal on metal. It brought his old Camaro to mind, a box of greasy wrenches resting next to him while he dug beneath the hood. The clink repeated, and he was sure of it now. They were tool noises.

Somebody was indeed inside, and they were awake. Working on something.

Reed beckoned with his free hand. Turk inched forward. The big man remained in a crouch as he reached for the doorknob. Reed covered him with his Galil. The knob twisted with ease, but the door didn't open.

The deadbolt was fixed.

"*Breach*," Reed mouthed.

Turk rested his rifle against the warehouse wall, then reached into his cargo pockets. The Israeli-made breaching charge was compact, built into a disposable plastic box with magnets on one side, a detachable detonator and an arming switch mounted to the other. A very handy little piece of hardware, not much bigger than a deck of playing cards.

But a lot louder, Reed knew. They would need to move quickly once the door was open.

Turk fixed the charge to the door and inserted the detonator. He double-checked the position and pulled a little to ensure the magnets were firmly clamped to the metal door. Then he shot a thumbs-up and retrieved his rifle. Reed inched back a couple of yards. Turk flipped the switch and scuttled away. Reed thumbed his mic switch once, sending a chirp through the coms. The signal that the party had started.

The breaching charge detonated with an earsplitting blast. There was no flame, but a lot of smoke. The deadbolt blew out of the door amid tangled fingers of jagged metal.

Then Reed and Turk were on it—Reed swinging automatically into the point position while Turk covered from the rear. Fingers on triggers, now, every sense hyperfocused. Reed's ears still rang from the blast as he reached the door and pivoted left. Turk grabbed the knob and yanked. The door swung open and Reed's weapon light flashed on.

Then the gunshots began. They snarled from someplace inside the warehouse—a desperate cough of bullets that sprayed at random toward Reed's position. It was an Uzi. Reed recognized the unique growl of 9mm slugs spat at a rate of six hundred rounds per minute even as he rolled to the floor.

Turk opened fire from behind as bullets skipped off the concrete, sending dust exploding into the air. The warehouse was dark save for a bright pool of light right in the center, where a pile of wooden crates marked with black paint stood in a circle around workshop lights that blazed down on the sheltered core of the circle. Like a child's fort, except this fort was occupied by armed men.

Reed saw the muzzle flashes even as he landed in a crouch behind the only cover he could find—an abandoned water heater. It was one of the skinny residential models. Not really a safe place to hide, but Reed didn't plan to stay for long. He swung the Galil's iron sights in line with the crates and clamped down on the trigger. Heavy 7.62mm slugs ripped through the air and splintered the crates, silencing one Uzi even as two more opened up. Turk was inside now, scrambling left and maintaining fire. The pair of Galils barked in unison, weapon lights flashing on and off as Reed and Turk used them selectively to illuminate targets. Reed counted at least four men from beneath the glare of the work lights. One of them was already dead, his head split open by a slug from Reed's Galil. He lay over the top of a crate with a bloody Uzi resting next to him. The other three moved as shadows, ducking and scrambling. Vanishing into the dark.

"Close in! Close in!" Reed called.

He left the cover of the water heater and sprinted for the next line of cover. It was one of the crates, the nearest to his position. Four feet tall and twice as broad, it was built of battered spruce wood with the same stenciled black markings printed on the outside. Reed's weapon light flashed across them for a split second, just long enough to read the text.

Except he couldn't read the text. It was all written in Cyrillic, with only one symbol recognizable amid the mix. The emblem of the Soviet Union—a hammer and sickle sprayed in red instead of black.

Reed saw it, then his attention was ratcheted back to the present by a fresh blast of Uzi gunfire. Nine-millimeter slugs danced across the top of the crate, sending a shower of spruce shards raining over his head and spraying into his face. Reed rolled left and returned fire, blasting straight through the corner of the crate with the much heavier 7.62mm ammunition. Somebody screamed and a weapon clattered across the floor. Lights exploded overhead as crazed gunfire blew them out. The warehouse went dark, and Turk shouted from Reed's left.

It was a pained cry, followed by a crash and clatter. Reed hit the weapon light and swung the Galil left. A bright beam cut across Turk as he slammed against another crate, a heavily muscled man bent over him with a long combat knife cocked. Turk's Galil was trapped against his chest, and blood ran from his neck.

Reed rotated his rifle up and flicked his trigger finger in one smooth motion. Turk's assailant collapsed in a spray of blood and brain matter, the knife clattering to the ground. But even before the body reached the floor, another sound burst through the warehouse from the direction of the enclosed lot. A chopping, thundering sound. The beat of rotor blades against hot Middle Eastern wind.

A helicopter.

20

"Chopper in the lot!"

Wolfgang's voice burst through the coms, but Reed didn't need it. He'd already heard the aircraft, the rising thunder of jet engines and rotor blades pounding like a hurricane blast against the block walls of the warehouse. He pivoted in the direction of the noise, switching the weapon light to full blast and leaving it on this time. Reed pivoted around the crate and leapt over a fallen body. Shattered glass crunched beneath his boots from the obliterated overhead lamps, and Reed passed two heavy workbenches laden with tools. More empty crates and wood shavings littered his path to a pair of large double doors that stood open at the end of the building.

Reed couldn't see the chopper outside. It sat to one side of the doors, obscured from view, but his weapon light illuminated twin tire marks leaving dark black streaks along the concrete, all the way to the door. A heavy payload had been transported away from the crates, away from the bodies.

Toward the chopper.

"Keep it down, keep it down!" Reed shouted into the mic as Turk scrambled to follow. Outside the warehouse, the howl of jet engines had reached a fever pitch. Years of combat and dozens of helicopter missions communicated the inevitable to Reed without him needing to actually *see* the aircraft. The chopper was lifting off. The rotors were at full pitch, a tornado's force of wind defying both nature and gravity as a multi-ton chunk of metal was yanked off the ground like a leaf in the wind.

Reed reached the door even as Wolfgang opened fire from across the street. The bark of an Israeli Galil was lost amid the thunder of the rotors as Reed pivoted right and exploded into the open lot, his own rifle rising into his shoulder.

The air was awash with a cloud of dust so thick even Reed's weapon light barely broke through, but the chopper wasn't difficult to find. It rose fifty feet off the ground, shooting straight up and orbiting at the same time, the tail rotor sucking the nose of the bird around even as the pilot brought the aircraft into a bank. In the dark and dust Reed couldn't recognize the make or model, let alone any identifying markings. None of that mattered. He already knew who was on board, and he wasn't about to let him escape unscathed.

Reed selected center mass, just beneath the core of the rotor, and clamped down on the trigger. The Galil thundered, joined quickly by Turk's rifle while Wolfgang squeezed off more precise shots from the alley behind the warehouse. Brass rained across the gravel, and full-metal jacket rounds whistled into the sky like reverse hail. The chopper twitched, and sparks erupted against the blackness as copper skipped over steel. Reed thought he heard glass shatter.

But the chopper kept rising. It banked hard left, taking the bulk of the ground fire across its belly in the split second it took to adjust the rotors and gain forward momentum. Then the bird raced into the darkness like a ghost. The engine noises continued, but the navigation lights remained black. The chopper outran the beams of Reed and Turk's weapon lights within two seconds.

And then it was simply gone.

Reed lowered the Galil after the bolt locked open over an empty magazine. His chest heaved, his head a cloud of surging adrenaline and maddened frustration. He bit back a curse and wanted to hurl the rifle. He wanted to drive his fist through the first wall he saw.

Instead he simply stood, hands trembling against the rifle. He spat saliva and dirt through his teeth and keyed the radio.

"Prosecutor to all channels. Anybody got eyes on that bird?"

He already knew the answer, but he had to ask. One by one the other members of his team radioed back in the negative as the distant voice of the helicopter faded over the city. It had vanished so quickly that Reed couldn't be exactly sure which direction it had taken. South, maybe.

But it easily could have turned. Assuming the aircraft had escaped without any significant damage, it could be a hundred miles away in mere minutes. The passengers—Abdel Ibrahim, and whoever was with him—could depart and flee from there on foot.

They might as well be on Mars.

"Sirens incoming." Amir's voice was calm over the radio, but crisp enough to jar Reed out of his irate fixation on the sky. He heard the sirens also, and wasn't particularly concerned about them.

But there was still the matter of the warehouse—the crates, and what they contained.

"Corbyn, prepare for extraction." Reed's voice was equally calm. "Everybody else, rendezvous at the warehouse for inventory. Let's move!"

Corbyn chirped her radio in affirmation while Reed circled back with Turk. A fresh magazine rocked into the Galil's receiver, and Reed left the weapon light on while Turk produced a cell phone and went to work snapping pictures.

There were tools, greasy rags abandoned on the floor, and a lot of wood shavings spilling out of the open crates. Reed held the light to illuminate Turk's photographs as Amir and Wolfgang burst in through the back door. The sirens rang louder, but Reed took his time. He directed Corbyn to pilot the Toyota to the back door as Amir produced his own camera and joined Turk's documentation.

"Get the crates," Reed said, poking a finger toward the spray-painted markings illuminated by LED light. Cyrillic text, and an emblazoned Soviet symbol. Turk snapped pictures, and Corbyn's voice burst over the radio.

"In position! Be advised, coppers on the main drag. No more than thirty seconds out."

Reed jerked his head, and he and Turk turned for the door, leading with the rifles. They made it halfway before Wolfgang's voice cut through the warehouse.

"Reed! You need to see this."

Reed glanced over one shoulder even as the first gleam of bright emergency lights flashed through the warehouse's front windows. Wolfgang stood over a smaller crate, removed from the rest. Painted with the same markings, and riddled by bullet holes. He shone a light inside, rifle dangling across his chest as he fixated on the contents.

Reed signaled Turk with one hand to cover the front entrance while he sprinted for the crate. He reached it just as the first Beirut patrol car squealed to a stop in front of the building. Wolfgang's light illuminated the contents, and Reed's blood ran cold.

"Cops inbound!" Turk shouted.

Reed exchanged a glance with Wolfgang—a split second of confirmation. *You see what I see.* Amir appeared at the edge of the crate and snapped a picture. Then all four of them broke for the back door, sprinting through even as an Arabic shout boomed through a loudspeaker. They reached the Toyota and hurtled inside. Corbyn mashed the gas before the doors were even shut. Turk slumped in the back seat, holding his neck with one hand. Blood streamed from it, and Lucy went to work with a medical kit before anyone could ask.

Reed slumped into the front passenger seat with the rifle held between his legs. He stripped off his gloves and extended a hand over one shoulder. Amir passed him the camera without objection, and Reed scanned back through the last three images.

Checking, then double-checking. Just to be sure.

His first inspection had been an accurate one. He'd seen exactly what he thought he saw.

The Toyota reached the end of the alley and Corbyn hauled the Toyota onto a two-lane, gunning the motor. Turk was the first to speak.

"NBC suits," he said. It wasn't a question.

Reed simply nodded. "A lot of them."

21

Langley, Virginia

Rigby arrived ten minutes after the Prosecution Force reported "no joy" on their Beirut incursion—mission failed. The negative report hit Aimes in the chest like a battering ram, but the rational part of her knew the chances of capturing Ibrahim on such short notice and with such little planning had been slim from the start.

Maybe they should have waited. Planned a little longer. Scoped out the warehouse and confirmed the occupants before risking a breach. Maybe this thing had gone off half-cocked, and that was her fault.

There was no use second-guessing now. Rigby shut the door of Aimes's executive office and placed an iPad on her desk. There were photographs snapped from on the scene. Rigby spoke quickly as Aimes flicked through them.

"Three combatants killed on site—none of them Ibrahim. A helicopter was parked in the adjacent lot behind a fence. Whoever else was inside the warehouse escaped via the chopper before the PF could ground it."

They didn't freaking check the empty lot?

Aimes gritted her teeth, not bothering to ask if any of the Prosecution Force were killed or injured in action. Reed's team was Reed's problem.

"Did they identify Ibrahim?" she demanded.

Rigby shook his head. "No. Nobody saw him. They think at least two people fled in the chopper, plus some cargo. If you look here, you can see tire marks on the pavement leading to the empty lot. Something heavy."

Aimes squinted at the parallel trails running across the dusty concrete floor. They were a little irregular, wider in some places than others, and splitting into four tracks through the course of a shallow turn. It was some kind of four-wheeled cart, she figured. A heavy item on casters.

A *very* heavy item. She noted crushed bits of rock near the door where loose gravel had fallen beneath the caster's wheels, and chipped concrete at the edge of the warehouse floor. Whatever item had ridden atop that cart, it had left a mark.

"We have no idea what this was?"

"Well. We have some idea." Rigby's voice dropped a notch, and Aimes glanced up. She didn't like the chilling undertone that hung beneath his words. Rigby motioned, and Aimes flicked to the next series of pictures.

Then she stopped. Three images completed the lineup, all taken at a downward angle into an open-topped crate. Yellow plastic filled that crate, with a face mask visible. The message printed on a rubber sleeve was written in a foreign language—possibly Russian, it looked to be Cyrillic—but Aimes didn't need to know what the text said to know what she was looking at.

They were NBC suits—nuclear, biological, and chemical protective gear used by militaries and weapons labs to shield soldiers and scientists from the scourge of their own weapons of mass destruction. Weapons like the one Abdel Ibrahim had already deployed to great effect in Baton Rouge.

Aimes's gaze snapped up. "Did they search the other crates? Were any unopened?"

"No time," Rigby said. "The Lebanese police arrived just as they were exfiltrating."

"And the chopper?"

"No idea. It was pitch black . . . could be anywhere. One of the PF did manage to capture a partial tail number, though. Our people are working that lead now."

Aimes's heart thumped. She looked once back to the iPad, racing thoughts and raw adrenaline rushing into her mind and forcing out any concern about Matt Roper and his witch-hunting committee. Now she felt only absolute focus.

And just the hint of fear. Ibrahim had already proven himself to be a resourceful enemy with access to wicked tools. He'd been wearing an NBC suit in St. Louis when Reed almost captured him—protection against the VX.

Had Ibrahim somehow located *more* nerve agent? Or perhaps . . . something nastier.

"Order the PF to go to ground and remain on standby," Aimes said. "Put all your resources behind locating that chopper. Advise Mossad. I'll deal with the Lebanese."

Rigby retrieved the iPad. He was out of the office just as Aimes reached for her phone. Her assistant picked up.

"Get me the White House," Aimes said.

22

Eastern Hemisphere
Undisclosed Location

The chopper touched down in a clacking storm of rotor wash, and Abdel Ibrahim stepped off. Blood ran from his left cheekbone where a near miss from a thundering Israeli Galil had come within an inch of switching his lights off. A pounding headache was joined by an even worse pounding heart. His fingers felt numb.

His mind was awash with raw, desperate energy. They'd *almost* had him. Exploding out of the darkness like wraiths, the Americans had descended upon the warehouse with the pure vengeance known only to the recently and demonstrably injured. Ibrahim would know—he'd launched his attack against America out of the same pain, but that didn't mean he was blind to the possibility of it backfiring on him.

The jaws of death had snapped against his heels tonight, and Ibrahim felt the terror. He'd grown bold in Beirut. He'd thought he was safe, at least for a few more days. The Americans had moved quickly. Now he questioned everything.

If the weapon hadn't already been loaded on the chopper, he would have lost it.

The helicopter spun down in the darkness as the pilot removed his helmet. Salt wind blasted Ibrahim's face, and he turned for the entrance of the nearest structure. The door burst open before he could reach it, and the *man* appeared. Ibrahim's shadowy ally, the scar-faced man who had proved so useful in Ibrahim's quest for blood over the last few months, but had now transformed into something larger.

Something a lot more controlling.

"What happened?" The voice was eastern European, demanding and harsh. Not the least bit expressive of sympathy.

"Americans," Ibrahim snarled. "They stormed the warehouse. Four, maybe five. I barely got out alive."

The man barreling across the helipad barely seemed to hear. He ran straight to the chopper, yanking the door back as panic crossed his face.

The panic melted quickly when he saw the crate. Massive, shrouded by a black tarpaulin, and carefully strapped down. Undamaged by gunfire despite the storm of it that had risen from the Americans.

A bit of luck.

"Is it complete?" the man barked.

Ibrahim scrubbed blood from his face. He nodded. "Yes."

The man considered. Then he slammed the chopper's heavy door shut. "Then all is well. Clean yourself up. We proceed."

Ibrahim stood in semi-confusion, the salt wind now increased to a steady blast that ripped at his sunbaked face. He wasn't certain he had heard correctly.

"You can't be serious. They're right on our heels. We must go to ground —conceal the weapon. Bide our time—"

The man put a heavy hand on Ibrahim's shoulder. He squeezed with thick fingers, and Ibrahim winced despite himself.

"Have you lost your nerve?" the man growled.

Ibrahim hadn't. He'd dreamt of this moment for years. Longed for it. *Thirsted* for it.

But he'd survived Detroit by the skin of his teeth, and Beirut by an even thinner margin. No. This was a long game. A play that couldn't afford to fail.

"We need *time*," Ibrahim said. "Another few weeks. Fly me inland. I have friends in Syria—"

"The Americans know of your friends," the man said. "Apparently, they know all about you. There is no safe place anymore. Your only chance now is to move quickly . . . and trust your allies."

Allies.

Ibrahim could have trusted them more easily if he knew their names. They were the shadowy benefactors who'd financed his assault on Tennessee and Louisiana, and supplied the weapon now resting inside the chopper.

For a man motivated by religious zeal, Ibrahim's faith was in short supply.

"Find your balls," the ally growled. "We're not stopping anything."

23

The White House
Washington, DC

The Cabinet Room was packed, every chair around the expansive table occupied by officials and secretaries, but from Maggie's seat midway down on the outside, she felt like she was viewing the meeting through the walls of a fish tank. Her ears rang. A vague brain fog pursued the edges of her tired mind, hampering clear thought as FBI Director Bill Purcell completed his report on the bureau's efforts to trace the terrorist Abdel Ibrahim.

But Maggie didn't need to be clear-headed to understand the implications of failure. The FBI had been tasked with backtracking the automated calls that had blanketed America with panic following the Tennessee bombing and directly preceding the VX attacks. It seemed like a simple task to Maggie, especially considering her creative leveraging of the Communications Act, which had provided the FBI with an open door into every cell service provider in the country, privacy concerns be damned.

Yet still, Purcell and his crew had hit nothing save block walls. The automated calls were international, that was obvious. They thought perhaps that they had originated someplace in the Middle East, but there were a lot of proxy servers and forwarding services in play—technical things that Maggie struggled to wrap her clouded mind around.

Excuses.

"Do you have nothing, then?" Maggie cut Purcell off in the middle of a sentence. The director hesitated over his notes, and the room hung in awkward silence. Fresh pain lanced up Maggie's core, and she masked it with an angry glower down the length of the table.

"Does *anybody* have anything?"

More silence, broken at length by Purcell.

"We're optimistic about our Middle East leads. Another day or two, and—"

"We haven't *got* another day or two. Did you see the agency's report or not?"

Maggie hadn't concealed Aimes's report of a near capture of Abdel Ibrahim in Beirut, or the NBC suits that were found on the scene. The prospect of yet another weapon of mass destruction in the hands of a man like Ibrahim was unthinkable. Unbelievable, really.

And yet, the implications were too dreadful to ignore.

"I don't have *time* for your excuses, Director. If your people aren't uncovering leads, perhaps they aren't properly motivated."

Purcell bristled just a little. His chubby face rose, sweat glistening from a bald head. "Madam President, you can rest assured that is not the case."

Maggie wanted to push her point, but the pain in her gut had faded rapidly into a wash of overwhelming exhaustion. She blinked, and the table wavered. It was difficult to make out Purcell's face. The silence lingered into an awkward phase, and Maggie stalled by fixating on her water glass. To her elbow, Jill Easterling, White House chief of staff, took the cue and slid in to rescue the conversation.

"We may be running short on time, Director. Congress is rapidly closing on a final draft of a bill to override the president's emergency use of the Communications Act. There's support in the Senate. We're looking at a veto-proof majority. Once that bill is passed, you'll be barred from access to the telecommunications sector. You'll be back to begging for warrants and subpoenas."

"I have a suggestion on that." It was Stratton who spoke. The VP sat two chairs down from Maggie, rotating a Montblanc pen on the cover of a leather portfolio. Maggie's eyes burned as she glanced his way. Stratton's profile wavered a little in her line of sight. She blinked hard.

"I've made some calls," Stratton said. "Old friends in the Senate who owe me favors. We may be able to stall the passage of the bill . . . a week, perhaps two."

"At what price?" Easterling voiced the question everyone was thinking.

Stratton sucked his teeth. He seemed hesitant. "There is a . . . growing perception on the Hill that the White House has no regard for the legislative branch."

"What does that mean?" Maggie barked.

Stratton faced her. "It means we've pissed them off. They don't feel suitably valued. They feel steamrolled, and they're inclined to return the favor."

"By ramming a veto-proof bill down my throat?"

"By putting you on a *leash*," Stratton said. "This isn't just about overriding your veto. It's about constraining your powers. It's a national rebuke. We're approaching the election cycle, and there are statements to be made. A lot of power players want to send a signal to the American people that Congress is the boss. Whatever magic we leveraged by winning as independents is rapidly fading. We have no friends now. No side of the aisle to claim as our own. We're a breath away from the entire Washington machine turning against us."

Someplace deep in her psyche, the political instincts Maggie had long denied told her Stratton was right. She knew she had neglected Congress during her tumultuous early years as president. In the face of imminent war, global catastrophe, and terrorist attacks, petty things like the legislative agenda paled in comparison. She thought she had pacified the Hill by giving them their head on the most recent spending bill. She'd signed what they sent her without complaint or pushback.

Maybe that had only served to undermine her authority as president. Maybe the problem wasn't a lack of friendship, but a lack of control.

Then again, if Congress stripped her of the emergency powers she had exercised via the Communications Act, she'd have less of both.

"What do they want?" Maggie demanded.

"A softer touch," Stratton said. "A more attentive ear. They want to be courted. We can't stop this bill—national support is too universal. But we can slow it long enough to locate Ibrahim, and that will leave us with political capital even when it passes. Ideally, you wouldn't even veto it. You could say we did what we had to do to protect America, and now you're submitting to the will of the people. It's a win-win . . . pacify Congress while preserving the trust of the electorate."

Even through the brain fog and aching pain, Maggie couldn't deny the political wisdom in Stratton's words. She could feel the wall pressing against her shoulders even as the rock of Congress and a panicked public careened straight for her face.

She knew she had to play this smart. She knew she had to *be* the politician. Embrace the game.

But when she closed her eyes, all she could see were the photos. The piles of bodies in Louisiana. The thousands left dead by Ibrahim's bombs and poison. The stench of death rising across the nation in a boiling wave of fear.

Ibrahim had won. Even if he never took another life, he had *won*. He had backed the most powerful person in the Free World into a corner, handcuffed by her own democracy.

Maggie hadn't been elected to be handcuffed. She'd sworn an oath to protect her people, and she'd already failed. She wouldn't allow failures to stack.

"You have an ear in the Senate?" Maggie asked.

Stratton nodded. "I can arrange a meeting this afternoon, or manage it myself, if you like. We should meet with both party leaders. Make this bipartisan. Senator Gallin should be compliant. Whitaker might make a fuss—"

"No," Maggie said.

Stratton stopped. "I'm sorry?"

"No," Maggie repeated, speaking through gritted teeth now. "I won't be meeting with Congress. You get on the phone with Harvey Whitaker and tell that spineless ball of Maryland crab crap to find his nerve or get the hell out of my way."

Maggie's voice rose and cracked as she spoke. She placed both hands on the edge of the table and half rose out of her chair. Nobody spoke. Stratton flushed. Maggie kept going.

"I wasn't elected president to quake in the face of bureaucrats. We have a *job* to do, Mr. Vice President, and come hell or high water, it's gonna get done. Mr. Director, you have my authorization to leverage my emergency powers in whatever way you see fit. You can take over every data center in North America, if you need to. To hell with Congress, to hell with legislation. *Get me Ibrahim*."

24

Beirut, Lebanon

Langley's next order arrived shortly after Reed transmitted the photographs of the bright yellow NBC suits found in the warehouse. The CIA wanted further details, of course. They wanted additional photos, and they had lots of questions about any unopened crates.

But what Reed knew he'd already told them, and it wasn't an option to go back in. Lebanese authorities had descended on the sight of the gun battle and locked it down tighter than Fort Knox. Soldiers were deployed. A full investigation was underway. Langley could request access, of course. But given the fact that the CIA had never actually obtained permission to deploy a team into Beirut in the first place, and in the context of the Lebanese's existing frustration with American intrusion, that was going to be tricky. Reed might have to shoot his way in, and the diplomatic headaches of that were more present a threat than the need for further information.

So the order was given for the Prosecution Force to stand down and stand by.

Back aboard the Gulfstream V, Reed stripped his chest plate off and threw it to the floor with a curse. Amir had driven them back, and now invited himself aboard without comment. Nobody had stopped their car along the way, and as yet their presence at the scene of Ibrahim's operation appeared undetected. That might change. Reed didn't care. He was a lot less concerned about Lebanese authorities than he was with the pressing question of *where* Ibrahim had fled.

"Who's got that tail number?" Reed demanded.

The Prosecution Force had gathered in the midsection of the plane, Strickland standing in the door of the cockpit, and Lucy quietly closing the door to isolate Reed's shouts. Corbyn sipped some kind of fruity energy drink from a bottle, sunglasses folded neatly inside her free hand. She looked as cool and collected as ever, and that made Reed want to put his hand through the wall.

"Right here," Corbyn said. "Or at least a part of it."

She held up a notepad with a number scrawled on it. That number had already been transmitted to Langley, but Reed wasn't interested in waiting for the CIA to get back to him.

"Run a search," he said. "See what you can find. Somebody hand me an iPad."

The device appeared on the lone table situated between rotating captain's chairs. Reed called up a map of the city and circled Ibrahim's warehouse using a stylus. Then he zoomed out.

"How far?" he asked, glancing sideways at Corbyn. The pilot shrugged as she tapped on her own device, running searches on the partial tail number through whatever aviation applications pilots used. Reed didn't know and didn't care.

"Impossible to say," Corbyn said. "I don't know what kind of bird it was. I don't know how much fuel it held. Could be three hundred, maybe four hundred klicks. By now it could be out of the country."

Reed already knew the facts before he asked. He still hoped for something. Even though he'd never actually *seen* Ibrahim in the warehouse, he somehow knew the terrorist had been there. Just like he knew that Banks's unborn child had been a girl, and her name was April. Yanked away before her time, slaughtered by a monster. It was instinctual and consuming, like fire racing through his veins and turning his blood to steam. He could barely focus on the iPad screen. A tremor ran down his arm, and his eyes stung.

He *almost* had him. He was *so* close.

"The aircraft was a Leonardo AW139." Amir spoke so softly Reed barely registered the words at first. He looked up to see the Israeli standing with his arms crossed, a little sweaty but looking as steady as a statue in contrast to Reed's thumping heart.

"What the hell is that?" Reed said.

"Italian helicopter," Amir said. "Fifteen seats, pretty high payload capacity. Very popular around the Middle East, especially in the Gulf. We see them a lot."

"Military?" Turk asked.

Amir nodded. "Sometimes. The Lebanese Air Force uses them, but those are usually painted gray or green. This one was black with yellow trim."

Reed licked his lips. His mind spun. He thought about the surrounding region, and all the places a helicopter of that size could reach in the two hours that had passed since it took flight. All the places it could have originated from.

A corporate headquarters? A private airfield? A hospital?

"He's right," Corbyn said. "I can't find the specific bird, but the first part of this tail number is pulling up a lot of offshore aircraft owned by a charter flight company here in Beirut."

"Offshore?" Reed looked up.

"Oil platforms," Amir said. "Transportation for the oil rig workers."

Bingo. Reed knew it as soon as the words were spoken. Something in his gut simply clicked—it felt right.

"Are there any platforms in the region?" he demanded.

Amir laughed for the first time. "Are you serious?"

Nobody spoke, and Amir approached the table. Brushing Reed's hand aside, he zoomed the map out and traced a massive circle with the stylus, highlighting the coastline running south from Syria all the way to Haifa in northern Israel.

"This is called the Levant Basin. There has been a lot of contention between Beirut and Tel Aviv in recent years over territorial drilling rights in the region. Mostly, the interest is in natural gas. However, there are a few dozen oil platforms as well, all within easy reach of that chopper. It would actually make a lot of sense to hide on a platform. You're in the middle of nowhere, with little or no direct government oversight. Also, it would be easy to slip away on any number of passing ships."

"So it's still a needle in a haystack," Wolfgang muttered.

Amir bit his lip. He straightened over the table and rolled the stylus between his fingers. He cocked his head.

Reed let him think. He could feel an idea coming, birthed out of a clever and cunning mind. The mind of a man who made his living thinking like his enemies.

"Many of the platforms are occupied by hundreds of workers. A lot of people to hide from, none of which can be assumed to be Ibrahim's friends. He could buy them off, of course, but it's not like he could come and go at his pleasure. Not without explanations to be made."

"And there's the payload," Turk said.

Reed nodded. "We have to assume he carted something away on that chopper. Most of those crates were empty. A lot was missing."

"So he'll need something more remote, then," Amir said. "Something with less people, but still a place to land the chopper . . . "

He trailed off. Then he leaned over the iPad and zoomed. The satellite image loaded slowly. It clarified. At last Reed saw a dot on the open blue water. The dot grew into the mass of a steel superstructure suspended on four giant legs.

An oil platform, filthy with exposure to corrosive wind. Just a few klicks off the Lebanese coast.

"Intrepid Oil Anchor," Amir said. "It was built ten or twelve years ago by a joint British-Lebanese venture. A lot of corporate dollars were invested into tapping the Block 4 oil field. I don't know the details, but the venture fell through. Financing problems, I think. The platform was left semi-completed for years, with purchasing agreements never quite closing. Mossad's financial division actually investigated it. We thought it might be a front for terrorist money laundering. In the end it was simply a case of gross corporate mismanagement. I think they finally sold it last year to some Russian energy conglomerate. Lenksy . . . Liken . . . "

"Lenkov International," Reed said.

Amir looked up. "That's the one. You know them?"

Reed's mind stalled for a moment as he rewound. Back behind Ibrahim, behind the attacks in Baton Rouge and Tennessee, all the way to his previous mission. Before he retired.

Following the attempted assassination of President Trousdale, Reed and his team had deployed to Caracas, Venezuela, where a fleeing Russian oligarch was linked to the president's would-be assassin. That oligarch's name was Stepan Belsky, and he was the owner of Lenkov International.

A coincidence? Reed looked to Turk, and the big man shook his head once.

No chance.

"That's the one," Reed said. "We'll go tonight. Can you arrange a boat?"

The question was directed at Amir. He didn't even hesitate.

"I'll have something ready by midnight. We can drive to the coast. I'll refit your arsenal and acquire some night vision. We'll make it clean."

Amir was already reaching for his phone as Lucy crowded in, a hand riding Reed's arm.

"Hold up a second. We've been put on standby. What about the CIA?"

Reed drew breath, but he never got the chance to answer. Corbyn cut him off with a silly grin.

"Let me guess . . . they can make passionate love to themselves."

It wasn't funny—not really. But Reed smiled anyway, because he was already envisioning Ibrahim's head pinned against the wet steel of an oil platform's deck. His own fingers wrapped around the terrorist's throat.

"All night long," Reed said. "Let's roll."

25

36 kilometers west of Tbilisi
Georgia

The weapons depot had lain abandoned since the late nineties, not long after the collapse of the Soviet Union and the resulting intrusion of Western powers. Georgia was little better than a third world country back then. Ravished by the economic decay of an empire determined to weaponize itself into invincibility, and sabotaged in the end by the Achilles' heel of empire breakers.

Failure from within. A lack of belief. A slow erosion of faith in the very system everybody was fighting so hard to protect. Ivan Sidorov had been a young man, then. A soldier not long retired from the Red Army to join the "Committee for State Security"—known to the motherland's enemies as the KGB. He watched Moscow lose control of Reagan's evil empire like a house flying apart under the winds of a cyclone. It was slow, at first. Tremors and shudders, a lost shingle here and a rebellious Baltic state there.

Then it all just disintegrated. Georgia was one of the first to leave, declaring independence from the USSR not long before that union's total collapse. Ivan had hated the Georgians then for being one of the first dominos to fall, but that anger had long ago faded into a more realistic understanding of the world, and a more self-aware appreciation for the mistakes of the Soviets.

The union had deserved to collapse. It had failed in its most basic promises to its people. The workers' paradise was no paradise at all, with more bullets than bread.

Bullets packed in warehouses across two continents . . . enough to bring America into its grave. Enough to make the world stop spinning. Tens of millions of Kalashnikov rifles, shoulder-fired rockets, anti-tank missiles, tanks themselves, aircraft- and heat-seeking missiles designed to blow aircraft from the skies.

And heavier, nastier things. Weapons that humanity was never meant to discover. Biological plagues that would horrify a witch. Radiological masterpieces that Oppenheimer himself could have never imagined. And chemical cocktails that could inflict mass death in the most agonizing and absolute form known to man. Things like gases, and nerve agents.

Things like VX.

Ivan dismounted the Land Rover he had rented in Tbilisi and stood for a moment in the blast of an early autumn breeze drifting down out of the mountains. It was already chilly in Georgia, and he pulled his coat a little tighter around his barrel chest as he surveyed the road leading between twin rock ridges and around a bend into a sheltered valley. There were guardhouses and gates, partially torn down by local villagers who had repurposed their materials into agricultural fencing instead of military. The curled barbed wire was all gone, the signs marking the entrance of the depot stripped away, leaving only rusting chains to rattle in the wind.

But if you looked closely, all the hallmarks of yesteryear were still present. The faded messages painted on one wall of the guardhouse were written not only in Georgian Mkhedruli but also in Russian Cyrillic. The even more faded gold of a hammer-and-sickle symbol.

Ivan pocketed his hands and left the Land Rover, one fist closing around a flashlight, the other around the grip of his Grach handgun. He ignored the messages and their accompanying graffiti as he worked his way up the roadbed, thighs burning and lungs crisp with the mountain air. He passed barracks on his right and an administrative structure on his left, both stripped of their roofing tin and their windows. Vacant holes gazed out at him, and more Cyrillic, here covered over in a spray-paint depiction of a Georgian valley, dotted not by tanks but by sheep. A mural of peace.

This hadn't been merely a weapons depot, but a Red Army outpost. Ivan had never visited before, but he was familiar with it. As an anchor of the Caucasus and the oil fields they contained, Georgia was an invaluable tactical holding for Moscow. It must be protected at all costs.

Too bad the Russians hadn't seen the enemy within.

Heavy steel doors guarded the semitruck-sized entrances of the depot warehouses, all carved directly out of the side of the mountain. The doors also were covered over by graffiti, but much of it was faded beyond recognition. Now that the Georgian government had stripped away the military assets, and the villagers had stripped away any usable agricultural material, there was no reason for anyone to drive this far into the mountains. No reason to venture through the torn-away door standing next to the warehouse entrances, and wander into the dark.

It could be dangerous. There could be vagrants, or wolves. Bears, even. But Ivan knew that these mountain pits used to hold far worse things, and he didn't hesitate as he clicked the flashlight on.

He saw the tire marks almost immediately. The door he ventured through was barely four feet wide, not really suitable for transporting any significant cargo, but the larger doors were operable only by heavy hydraulic mechanisms, and the engines that ran those mechanisms had long ago been salvaged.

The tire marks were just a little narrower than the door, grinding over dirty concrete under the weight of a heavy load. In turns the marks broke apart, indicative, Ivan thought, of some kind of four-wheel cart.

And the marks were fresh.

Ivan drew the Grach and rested his finger on the trigger as he shone the light across the open warehouse space. The beam was powerful—nearly a thousand lumens—but it fell far short of reaching the wall. The space was massive, more easily measured in square kilometers than square meters. Relics of pallet racks and rotten ammunition crates littered the ground in places, along with indicators of inhabitation by vagrants. Scraped tents and messy bedrolls. Human feces near one of the massive steel doors. All of it old and forgotten.

But mostly, the place was empty. Hauntingly so, as though even the ghosts of yesteryear had abandoned this place.

A chill ran down Ivan's spine, but he didn't hesitate to follow the tire marks. They faded in places, and he was forced to use his light in concentric circles to relocate them. But always, they ventured toward the furthest corner of the warehouse. Behind the racks where rifle crates were kept. Beyond the gnarled concrete where tank tracks had rumbled. All the way to the far rock wall, now laden with condensation . . .

And then nothing. The tracks simply vanished. Ivan stopped and swept his light around, then resumed his circular search pattern. The floor was filthy with abandoned trash and dust, but the dirt should only have made it easier to trace the tire marks.

He found nothing. Only the spot where black rubber left a trail, and that trail abruptly ended. He stopped over the point where the tracks vanished and focused the light, allowing himself time to think. Ivan knew that tires didn't usually leave tracks on concrete, not unless they skidded or burned.

But what if that cart had been heavily overloaded? Could that be the answer to the riddle? Had the weight been removed, relaxing enough pressure on the tires to cease the scuff marks they had previously left? Or, more likely, this was the place where weight had initially been loaded onto the cart. Something very, very heavy.

But . . . from where? There was nothing here. No pallet racks. No brackets in the walls anchored there to hold shelves or scrapes on the floors where artillery may have been parked. Only empty concrete and . . .

Ivan's light fell over a rough patch in the floor, ten meters away. It was so laden with dirt he barely noticed the change in texture at first, but when he approached he noted the clear outline of a square perimeter, swept clean enough to identify a narrow crack that separated concrete from something else. Something speckled with regular little lumps, like mushroom caps.

Ivan knelt and swept his hand across the crack, and then he knew. The change in material was a switch from concrete to steel, the rough texture the result of lead-based paint bubbling up from the surface. The mushroom caps were rivet heads, and the object was a door. A very large door.

It took nearly ten minutes for Ivan to identify the latch and disarm it, but the door itself lifted with only gentle pressure. It was heavily counterweighted, and the hole beneath was fit with smooth concrete steps leading down into the dark.

Ivan didn't hesitate. The door hung open under the pressure of the counterweights, and he started quickly down the steps. His flashlight cast a thick beam ahead. The stairs turned just as his head descended beneath the floor above. The wall was scraped and scratched where some heavy objects had been dragged by—recently. There were more rubber scuff marks on the floor. Abandoned nylon strapping, too new to date back to the Cold War.

And then he found it. A channel carved out of the rock, framed and roofed by concrete, ten meters wide and four times as long. Tight lines of electrical wiring hung from the ceiling, feeding rows of fluorescent lights untouched by the scavengers. The walls to Ivan's left were occupied by barrel racks—half a dozen of them, each marked with a Soviet-era chemical hazard symbol. Ivan's heart rate spiked, and he swept the light farther down the channel.

The barrel racks were empty on both sides, and tall crates labeled in stenciled Cyrillic as tactical artillery shells stood just as empty next to them. Ivan accelerated, following fresh tire tracks down the length of the channel, beyond tool racks both dusty and forgotten, spiderwebs clinging to the rusting surfaces of hammers and wrenches. Beyond an alarm system bolted to the wall, also irredeemably corroded.

All the way to the end, where a final metal rack stood. Also empty. Painted bright orange, with a single sign spray-painted by stencil on the rock wall behind it.

Ivan's flashlight focused on the spot, and his blood ran cold.

26

The West Wing
The White House

Vice President Jordan Stratton never imagined when he accepted Muddy Maggie Trousdale's invitation to join her rebel administration that he would age this quickly. It wasn't just the streaks of gray so rapidly joining his normally thick black hair, or the lines on his face and the black bags under his eyes. Stratton felt the strain in his very bones. His joints ached when he rose before sunrise, and his mind failed to shut down when he finally went to bed long after sunset.

He hadn't shared more than a passing word with his wife in nearly a month. He hadn't spent more than a passing moment with either of his twin daughters in much longer. Too much caffeine served to spike his energy level, while an overindulgence in illegal Cuban cigars helped to take the edge off the stress. Stratton ran like a machine, not because it was sustainable or even very effective, but because it was the only option. Despite a lineage populated by blue-blooded criminals and conniving political superstars, Stratton counted himself a true statesman. One of the last of a dying breed.

He meant every word of his vice presidential oath. The glory and the power were his fuel, but the purpose was something greater. He signed on with Muddy Maggie because he bought what she was selling. He liked her outlaw spirit and willingness to overturn political tables. He knew that America liked it, also. He knew it was special.

He wanted to be a part of it. He never imagined it would fly off the rails this quickly.

By the time the West Wing wound down and Stratton stepped out of his vice presidential office, it was nearly eight p.m. The sun had set over the East Coast, and the buzz amid the corridors of American power had subsided, but Stratton himself was hours away from calling it a day. Most of the afternoon had been consumed by his telephone—exhausting hours spent connecting with old friends and allies from the United States Senate. People Stratton had served alongside during his years as an Illinois senator, many of whom still owed him favors.

Despite Maggie's impassioned order for him to lift a middle finger to Congress, Stratton wanted to make a last-ditch effort to court his old friends. To cash in those favors. The president needed the Referendum on Executive Control Act stalled. Shut down would be ideal, but Stratton was a realist. There was far too much national support for RECA to ever bite the dust. It would pass, he assured them. He only needed a few more weeks of unfettered FBI intrusion into the communications sector to locate Ibrahim first. Then, he promised, Maggie would sign the bill willingly. There would be no need for a veto-proof majority. Whether or not he could actually talk Maggie into making good on that promise remained to be seen. For the moment, he simply had to stall RECA.

A Republican by heritage, Stratton was ready for the conservative backlash to Maggie's aggressive leverage of the Communications Act. His old chums called it "an invasion of American privacy," while their liberal colleagues from across the aisle were much harsher, terming Maggie's actions a "fascist application of emergency power." It was all very consistent with party line, but what Stratton did *not* expect was how quickly the enemies of his friends had turned his friends into enemies. Bipartisanship was flourishing in Congress on an unprecedented scale, and it was all hell-bent against Muddy Maggie Trousdale.

Stratton's Senate buddies were stalling him, and the message was clear.

Old favors were no longer being honored. If Stratton wanted help, he was going to have to pay for it, and it wouldn't come cheap.

A new day. More problems.

Stratton pulled his suit jacket on and ran a hand through his hair on the way to the Oval. He had requested the meeting with Maggie two hours prior, and half expected her to decline. A larger portion of executive responsibility was falling on Stratton's shoulders every week, but he still resisted the urge to take the bull by the horns and cut Maggie out. She was still president.

For now.

Stratton knocked once and eased the door open. Maggie sat behind the Resolute Desk, hair pinned back in a ponytail while she overlooked a field of documents with a pen in hand. A desk lamp burned next to her. A glass of water was nearly empty. Stratton retrieved a pitcher to refill it before taking a seat across from Maggie.

"Vote counts?" he asked.

Maggie removed a pair of reading glasses and rubbed her eyes. She hadn't worn glasses when Stratton first met her. The strain was getting to the president even more quickly than it was tearing down the VP. Graying hair, sagging cheeks, and haunted eyes. But it was worse than that, also. Maggie looked yellowish under the pale light. Her skin seemed oddly loose, her body frail.

She looked like she was dying.

"They have the votes," Maggie said, simply. "I made calls all afternoon. There's no stopping it. I'm even losing Louisiana."

Stratton already knew. He hadn't even bothered to estimate the vote count in the House of Representatives. RECA would pass with flying colors. It might even be unanimous.

He couldn't help but wonder if the political pandering Maggie had finally agreed to attempt had worsened the problem. Maggie didn't have a pandering bone in her body. She'd likely resorted to threats.

"Where do we stand with the Senate?" Maggie slurped water and slouched into her chair. Her face twisted as her head met the headrest, and Stratton caught a profile he hadn't seen before. It was difficult to look at. Maggie's eyes were sunken, her cheeks hollow.

He looked away quickly and poured a glass of his own. "I'm working old contacts. Some promising leads. Give me another day and we may have a solution."

It was a BS answer and Stratton knew it. He expected Maggie to call him on it, but instead she simply nodded. Her gaze was fixed on the oil painting of George Washington that hung over the mantle. Stratton wondered if she was thinking about greatness, and how evasive it could be.

Certainly, he was.

Stratton set his glass down and leaned toward the desk. "There's something else. Maybe something more pressing."

Maggie pivoted toward him. She lifted both eyebrows.

"Roper," Stratton said. He didn't have to explain further. Maggie's lip lifted in a default snarl.

"What now?"

"I finally got him on the phone. He wouldn't even discuss RECA. He only wanted to discuss Aimes. He's blocking her confirmation. He all but said it. She'll never get the votes."

"That's not up to him. It's a seventeen-seat committee."

"Sure. But he owns the votes of eight of those seats, himself included. And he's doing a good job poaching support from the Republicans. I think this is personal."

"Personal how? I barely know the man. Did you piss him off?"

"Not me. Brandt."

Maggie breathed a curse. "You can't be serious. The man is *dead*."

"But the grudge lives on. Brandt promised Roper a cabinet position. Then he reneged. Roper has had it out for him ever since."

"I'm not *him*."

"Apparently that doesn't matter. You've become the surrogate target for Roper's vendetta, and that's a problem. I don't think we can fight two battles at once. RECA may already be a lost cause, but we *cannot* allow Aimes to be shut down in confirmations. We need her now more than ever. Somehow, we've got to win him over."

Maggie said nothing, lips pinched together as she pondered, slowly. Stratton knew what she was about to say before she said it, and he also knew he wouldn't be able to talk her out of it. No matter how bad an idea it might be.

"I want to meet with him," Maggie said.

"With respect, Madam President, that's not a good idea."

"Why not?" Her voice snapped a little.

Because you look like death and have the political tact of a bull in a china shop.

Stratton wanted to say it, but he knew it wouldn't help. Just like his friends in the Senate, Maggie needed to be won over.

"I think Roper can be bought," he said. "That may be all he's fishing for."

"Bought?"

"Brandt promised him a cabinet position. You can make good on that promise."

"You can't be serious . . . "

Stratton held up a hand. "Just hear me out. You can give him something less than secretary of Treasury. That seat is occupied anyway, but we could make him an under secretary of state, with a promise of promotion when an opportunity—"

"Jordan. I'm not *paying* the man off." Maggie's cheeks flushed. She sat up and set her water glass down with a thump of glass on wood.

Stratton inhaled slowly. He adjusted his coat. "We're running out of options. Roper is a powerful man. I can sweet-talk him all day long, but without something tangible to offer, it won't matter. An under secretary position could be enough to get Aimes through confirmation and stall RECA—"

"While making me appear crooked as hell," Maggie said. "He's been fighting us all month. Suddenly he becomes our best friend, then two weeks later he joins my cabinet? Do you know how that looks?"

"It looks like you're *in control*," Stratton said. "It will send a message to Congress. They can't stonewall you. You're willing to be creative. You—"

"No." Maggie's hand smacked the desktop with a soft crack sudden enough to make Stratton flinch. Her eyes blazed. She spoke through her teeth. "You get Roper on the phone and you get his ass into this office. I want to see him—tomorrow. We're going to meet person to person. If you can't handle him, I will."

Stratton remained calm. He could feel the blood rising into his face, but he didn't indulge it. Maggie was coming undone. He needed to tread carefully now. He couldn't afford to fight fire with fire.

"As your vice president and your friend, I'm obligated to tell you, that's a mistake."

"So noted. Now make the freaking call."

Stratton ran his tongue over his teeth. Then he stood and buttoned his jacket.

"I'll call him first thing in the morning."

He turned for the door, but made it only halfway before Maggie's tired voice called after him.

"Jordan . . . "

"Yes, ma'am?"

"I'm . . . sorry. For snapping."

He looked back. Maggie sat slumped in the chair, her gaze drifting aimlessly across the carpet. Chin down. Eyes hollow.

Seeing her that way tore into his chest, despite himself. It wasn't the president he knew.

"Are you okay, ma'am?"

Maggie opened her mouth to answer, then stopped. She faced him. Laughed a little.

"Are any of us?"

He stepped slowly back to the desk. This time he didn't sit. "The rest of us aren't president. You're the one who matters."

She grunted softly, one hand picking at the edge of the desk. Her next comment took him by surprise.

"I sent O'Dell home."

Stratton squinted. He hadn't seen the president's "special advisor" in a couple of days, but that didn't necessarily mean anything. He'd been busy.

"Why?"

Maggie shrugged. "Can't deal with the distraction. I have to focus."

Stratton didn't say it, but he understood. His mind flashed to Louise and

Lindy, his beautiful twin daughters who would celebrate their eleventh birthday in a week or so.

No. They *had* celebrated their eleventh birthday a week prior, and he was just now remembering it.

Stratton winced. The West Wing demanded a brutal price for admission.

Maggie looked up. “This office is mine, Jordan. For better or for worse, come what may. I have to be the captain. I have to steer the ship. And you have to trust me.”

“I do,” he said. “And I have your back.”

Maggie forced a smile. “Call Roper in the morning. I’ll use a light touch. We’ll see if the Muddy Maggie brand has any magic left in it.”

27

Beirut, Lebanon

Amir was as good as his word. The clock had just reached midnight over the Levant when Reed took a call from an unknown domestic number. Amir answered in two clipped sentences, providing the confirmation of a vessel and a rendezvous point in a small town on the Lebanese coast, just a few klicks from Intrepid Oil Anchor.

Reed hung up and spun his finger in the air to signal the passed-out team sprawled around the cabin of the Gulfstream like the scene after a frat party. Turk snored and Wolfgang gave him a kick with his fake leg. Corbyn left the cockpit and Strickland followed. Only Lucy remained seated, focused on the iPad that Reed had designated for communication with Langley.

"We've got a boat," Reed said. "Wolf, Turk, Corbyn—you're with me. LB, stay on coms in case Langley comes through with something. Strickland . . . keep the seats warm."

Reed started toward the door when Lucy called out from the table: "Wait one! We may already have something."

Reed turned back, and Lucy spun the iPad. A message waited from Langley, joined this time by a photograph. The image was shot in lime green through a night vision lens, and depicted a sprawling section of black tarmac with a helipad sitting front and center.

A chopper filled the view, jet black with yellow trim, and the first five digits of the tail number matched what Corbyn had seen on Ibrahim's fleeing bird.

Reed's heart thumped, and his gaze flicked to Aimes's message.

CntrlCmmd: Helicopter matching partial tail number provided found at Queen Alia International Airport, Amman Jordan. Deploy immediately to intercept, advise when in air.

Lucy looked up, excitement playing across green eyes, and Corbyn cut loose with a confident grunt. "Ace!"

But Reed didn't move. His gaze remained frozen on the screen, fixating on the image. Something didn't feel right. He read the tail number back twice, and knew it matched. The chopper looked identical to the one that fled Beirut earlier that night. He even thought he saw a few bullet holes marring a fuselage panel, barely visible in the grainy photo.

But what did that prove?

"Ignore it," Reed said. "Let's move."

Lucy blinked. Corbyn let out a little laugh.

"Are you serious? That's the chopper!"

"That's *a* chopper," Reed corrected. "With only a partially confirmed tail number. You heard Amir. Those things are common down here. That could be anybody."

"But the bullet holes," Lucy said.

"So there's bullet holes," Reed retorted. "It's not like those are difficult to replicate. Even if that *is* the correct bird, why should we assume Ibrahim is still with it? He's either lost in Amman or he was dropped off someplace along the way. Use your heads. We stick to the plan."

Reed moved to the door and twisted the latch. Steps swung down under hydraulic control. Everybody else lingered near the iPad. Then Turk grunted.

"You heard the man. Move out!"

Bags rustled and Reed returned to the sticky Lebanon airfield. They were already cleared through customs, but they had to pass through security to exit the airport. The Toyota waited ten yards away, on loan from

Amir. The Galils and assorted other weapons were with their new Mossad friend. Reed felt a little naked as he set his phone's GPS for the rendezvous point and powered into the city. He didn't really expect Ibrahim to be waiting for an ambush—the terrorist was long gone by now, wherever he had fled.

He could be in Amman, lost in the Levant's largest city where he would never be found. Flying to Queen Alia now wouldn't change that. Reed put himself in the shoes of the bad guys, switching his brain into hunting mode, and he knew the oil platform still made sense. Not only because there had been plenty of time for the chopper to drop Ibrahim and its cargo off before reaching Jordan, but because of who owned the platform. Because of Lenkov.

It was a coincidence he simply couldn't accept.

Nobody spoke as the cramped streets of Beirut passed in a tangle, streetlights illuminating the potholes and dashed lines while the buildings on either side descended into full darkness. The city was asleep, and Reed could only assume that the oil rig would be also. The ocean would be black. They could strike from the shadows before anybody knew they were coming.

The rendezvous point lay north of the downtown, just east of the Port of Beirut. Reed rumbled past a pair of Lebanese patrol cops without interference, then guided the Toyota through an open chain-link gate onto a concrete pier that jutted out over inky dark Mediterranean water. He spotted Amir waiting alongside a Nissan pickup, tugging on his vape stick and pretending to work beneath the vehicle's hood. Reed shifted into park and looked out to sea.

It was more than darkness—there was fog, also, and heavy cloud cover. No moon, no stars. A perfect night for a strike.

"You sure about this?" Wolfgang was the first to break the silence.

Reed wasn't sure. There was no such thing as certainty in his line of work. But he had a feeling.

"We go," he said, simply. Then everybody dismounted the Toyota and met Amir at the hood of the Nissan just as the Israeli dropped it closed. The guy looked seriously pissed, teeth clamped around the vape stick and lips curled into a snarl.

"What's up?" Reed said.

Amir muttered something in Hebrew, then jerked his head toward the waterline. Reed and his team followed him to the edge of the pier, where a simple metal ladder led down to the lapping edge of the sea. A fifteen-foot rigid-hulled inflatable boat rested there, a Suzuki 80-horse outboard motor hanging off the back, with a center console and a bench seat. The vessel was dark gray, and forward of the console an oversized duffel bag lay heavy with gear. A digital screen on the dash displayed GPS navigation.

Amir blew vapor through his nose. "She's fully fueled. You've got about a fifteen-mile range. The rig is already programmed into the GPS, four miles out. Don't stray off course—the currents are strong tonight."

Reed detected the frustrated undertone beneath Amir's instructions, and connected the dots.

"You got sidelined." It wasn't a question.

Amir pocketed the vape stick. "Headquarters. They don't want any Israeli fingerprints if this goes sideways."

CYA, Reed thought. It was an international principle.

"If things go sideways, fingerprints are the least of our concerns." Reed said it even though he knew it wouldn't make Amir feel any better. The Israeli simply extended a hand.

"God be with you. Show them an early grave."

Reed shook once. Amir turned for the Nissan. Corbyn was already shinnying down the ladder, making her way by default to the controls. By the time the three men found their way into the boat's bow, the Suzuki motor had rumbled to life. Wolfgang loosed the line, and the boat pulled away from the pier. Turk dug into the duffel bag and located fresh Galil rifles, fully equipped with multiple magazines, night vision headsets, tactical gloves, and communications gear.

Reed faced out to sea as the pier faded rapidly behind them. He couldn't see the platform. He could barely see a hundred yards under the fading light of Beirut.

He tilted his head anyway, and Corbyn dropped the hammer. The front of the boat rose skyward, and they were off.

28

Eastern Hemisphere
Undisclosed Location

The room was large—fifteen meters wide and twice as long, with workbenches and plenty of tools. The weapon fit easily into the middle of the space, rolling in on a heavy cart with rubber tires that squished under the weight. Ibrahim scuttled around like a mother hen looking after her chicks as the team of five true believers transferred the precious cargo safely inside. Then the helicopter thundered away, banking south toward Jordan.

A decoy.

Other helicopters landed. Ibrahim's ally arrived even as the weapon was removed by chain hoist and placed inside a heavy crate. The walls were nailed shut. The crate was taken by another chain hoist and long metal rails through a cargo door and onto its next method of conveyance.

Its final method of conveyance.

Ibrahim watched from a rain-streaked window as the weapon disappeared. Something hot burned deep in his gut, more than the bloodthirst or hunger for revenge he had endured for so many months. This was frustration. A sudden flash of irritation as he turned back to the true believers laboring on the second weapon—welding and modifying. Customizing for a use altogether unlike this weapon's original purpose.

Making it more lethal, and yet still only a fraction of the threat of that precious crate that had just vanished into the dark.

Ibrahim's ally had lied to him. He'd been lying all along, promising a freedom he now yanked back like a rug from beneath Ibrahim's feet. Choking him on a leash Ibrahim never intended to wear.

"This wasn't what we agreed to," Ibrahim spoke through his teeth as his ally stepped next to him, grinding his thumb across a lighter to ignite a tarry Russian cigarette. The air clouded with smoke. Ibrahim glared.

"The plans changed," the ally said. "You still have a role to play."

"I'm not here to play roles. I'm not an actor. You promised me that I would go with it. You promised me—"

"And *you* promised *us* three devastated cities," his ally snarled, sudden fire lacing his voice. "Your benefactor is not Santa Claus. You do not place your orders without payment. You failed in America, so now you will do what *we* tell you."

The ally sucked slowly on the cigarette, inhaling deeply. Not blinking, his big red eyes fixated on Ibrahim. Defying him to argue further.

"Unless you would rather *not?*"

The implication was clear. Ibrahim gritted his teeth, knowing that it was his own fault that his back was against the wall. He'd made a deal with the devil to obtain the VX that wrecked Baton Rouge and brought so many Americans into an early grave, to say nothing of the complex mechanisms that had further plagued America with tens of thousands of automated phone calls. It was a bargain none of the brotherhood would have struck, but Ibrahim was a pragmatist. He understood the value of making friends out of his enemy's enemies.

This was the cost.

"You had better make them *bleed*," Ibrahim growled.

The ally sucked on the cigarette. He grinned, exposing brown teeth. He exhaled smoke as he spoke.

"Of that you can be assured."

29

The Mediterranean Sea

Corbyn ran the boat like she ran an airplane. The moment the bow was pointed in the direction of the GPS arrow and they were safely removed from the pier, she ramped the throttle up as though she were preparing for takeoff, and the Suzuki howled. Reed huddled low in the nose of the boat, his mind flashing back to the last time he'd crashed over open water in a similar vessel. It hadn't been that long ago, but back then he'd been fleeing the western coast of North Korea.

He hadn't been racing into combat. Somehow, this felt better. It felt more like control.

The Galils were clean and fresh, and this time Reed kept his red dot. Amir had proven himself enough for Reed to trust the gear he provided, and the optic would be invaluable in the dark. Turk and Wolfgang similarly geared up, pulling chest plates over their shoulders and strapping them in place. Weapon lights were affixed to the rifles as before, but this time they were joined by IR lasers to correspond to the night vision goggles buried in the bottom of the bag. There was also additional communications gear similar to what they had used in Beirut.

Reed tested everything, slipping the goggles on and sweeping the laser across the open water before unleashing two rounds from the Galil.

Function check complete.

"Wind it down as we close in!" he shouted over the wind. "I don't want them hearing us."

Corbyn nodded from behind the controls, her long brown hair swept back as she wore the now trademark sunglasses as protection against the wind. How she could see anything in the dark was an enigma to Reed, but he left that to her.

He'd learned the hard way that it was easier to trust his team to do things their own way. They hadn't failed him yet.

The seas were relatively calm as the bow rose from the water and the bottom of the boat skated across gentle swells, but two miles offshore the rain began. Not a thunderstorm so much as a steady shower, beating down on Reed's head and quickly soaking all of them. Despite the warm Mediterranean air, the rain was cold. A chill ran up Reed's spine, and he double-checked the trio of spare mags affixed to his chest rig.

He could feel it in his bones. This wasn't a wild goose chase. They were headed for pay dirt, and with it, plenty of gunfire.

Corbyn eased the throttle back ten minutes later. Reed could already see the rig on the horizon, still three miles distant but marked by a handful of security lights. It was massive, rising from the ocean like a floating city. Under the aid of the night vision goggles, Reed made out two levels, standing something like the decks of a parking garage, with a hollow core. Two cranes were mounted to opposing corners of the top deck, while a drilling mechanism overhung the open core. There were a pair of buildings on the top deck, each about the size of three semitruck trailers parked alongside each other, and a mess of machinery on the lower deck. The entire structure was upheld by four giant legs, splayed out and disappearing into the dark water.

It was an imposing sight, but what drew Reed's eye was the helipad overhanging the left side of the rig, two hundred feet off the water and highlighted by marker lights. He made out the outlines of two separate aircraft resting on the oversized pad, their rotors restrained against the wind as the rain beat down. From nearly two miles away it was impossible to determine make or model, but the implication was clear.

The rig wasn't abandoned. Somebody was on board . . . and that somebody just might be Abdel Ibrahim.

"Lock and load," Reed called.

Wolfgang and Turk were already locked and loaded, but they double-checked everything in silent routine. Corbyn slowed the boat again, bringing it gently off plane. The throb of the motor was lost among the wind, but Reed thought she was right not to risk it.

"Ladder on the front left leg," Wolfgang called. He peered through a pair of binoculars, water streaming from his wind-matted brown hair. Corbyn adjusted their heading and the boat swung wide.

Reed kept his eyes on the rig, sweeping from the helipad to the barnlike metal buildings resting on the upper level. They faded out of view as the boat approached, and he swept the machinery on the second level instead. The drill itself was not lowered into the water—according to Amir, it never had been. The rig's only connections with the ocean were the four legs that plummeted to the sea floor, but one of them included a welded metal ladder leading eighty feet off the surface to the lower level.

Reed turned from the bow of the boat. "Turk, Wolfgang, you're with me. I'll take point. Corbyn, stay with the boat and keep your com open. We get in and we get out. If anything goes sideways, we bail and Corbyn picks us up."

"Are you kidding me?" Corbyn protested. "What, you don't want a girl watching your back?"

Reed rolled his eyes. "Relax, Brit. It's better than getting shot at."

Corbyn descended into a string of British cursing Reed only half understood. He blocked it out as the boat rose and fell slowly over the swells. It was so dark with the sky blackened by clouds that he wasn't worried about being spotted. If the engine was quiet enough not to be heard over the wind, they would remain within perfect concealment until they reached the lower level of the rig.

At least . . . that was the plan.

The front left leg loomed out of the darkness like a tower of its own. The ladder was rain-soaked and narrow, leading out of the swells and into the pitch blackness above. Reed slung his rifle into low ready and braced himself against the inflated gunwales of the boat. Corbyn lowered the throttle another notch and drove the boat sideways toward the leg. The ladder loomed close.

Reed jumped. He caught a rung with two gloved hands and hauled himself upward even as the boat swung away again. Then he was climbing, one foot over the other, thighs burning and rain puddling on the lenses of his NV goggles. Green glow illuminated the underside of the lower platform as water streamed from the metal grates it consisted of. It was a long way. Reed glanced between his knees to see Turk monkeying up behind him like a gorilla climbing a tree. Wolfgang lagged a few feet farther behind, struggling a little with the prosthetic leg.

Reed had thought about asking him if he could manage the ladder. He'd decided against it. Much like Corbyn and her sunglasses, Wolfgang's situation was Wolfgang's situation.

The top of the ladder was closed off by a metal trapdoor. Reed slowed as he approached, inspecting for a padlock or nearby personnel. He saw neither, and used his right arm to ease the door up. The rain had doubled in intensity during the climb, and was now pouring in a steady deluge that ran behind the goggles and into his eyes. The door was heavy, and he pressed down with his boots to add leg power. It swung up with a groan and landed open with a clang. Reed raced the rest of the way onto the deck, swinging the Galil into his shoulder and flicking the IR laser on. It appeared in his night vision as a white beam cutting through the dark and racing from object to object as he swept his surroundings.

He was alone. The lower level of the platform was crowded with tangles of thick iron pipes and hefty valves, electrical wires housed within steel conduits with corresponding warning labels painted in three different languages. The floor was an open grate with a clear view of the ocean far below. Reed saw Corbyn drifting a little ways from the rig, peering up at him in those fool sunglasses.

"Prosecutor to Hotshot. We're on the lower level. Keep the engine warm."

"Up yours, Prosecutor."

Reed indulged in a dry grin as Turk hauled himself off the ladder and fell into position to his right. Wolfgang took a while longer, but he didn't complain as he reached the lower level with a heave and wrestled his rifle out of a tangled sling.

"All good?" Reed said.

"Roger," Turk drawled. Wolfgang shot a thumbs-up.

Reed rose out of the crouch and turned left down the first corridor he could find. It led amid the pipes and machinery toward the core of the rig. The metal grates squeaked a little under his boots, but Reed still wasn't worried about being heard. The beat of the rain was now louder than the wind, pounding against steel and pinging off iron. He reached the end of the corridor and swept his muzzle to the right as Turk swung automatically to cover the left.

Nothing. More corridors, more machinery. More pounding rain.

Reed thought quickly and put himself in Ibrahim's shoes. He thought about the helicopter, and what it might contain. The two barnlike buildings on the second level.

If Ibrahim was here—if he was using this place as an operations center—there would be no need to descend to the lower level. All the resources he would need would rest on the top.

They needed to find stairs.

Reed led the way with the Galil riding at eye level, the darting beam of the laser still jumping from one point of fire to the next, his finger held just above the trigger guard. Wolfgang's steps dragged a little from behind, but when Reed glanced back he was gratified to see the third member of his little strike team covering their rear like a pro.

They cleared two more paths amid the pipes and crossed near the core of the rig. Reed leaned out and peered upward toward the drilling mechanism hanging high above. It was difficult to see anything through the deluge, but he caught sight of the second-floor railing. He also caught sight of a shadow moving against the wind.

And then a flash of orange, like a little flame. A cigarette lighter.

Reed put two fingers to his eyes, then pointed upward. Turk nodded once, then Reed swung right. There were stairs ahead. Three flights of them, leading to the second level. The steps were wet but not slick—treads were stamped into them, offering robust traction as Reed ascended. By the time he reached the first landing, he was well over a hundred feet off the rolling swells below, and his stomach rolled with them.

Don't look down.

The top of the last flight connected with the outside of the second level. The nearest barnlike building stood only fifty yards to Reed's right. There was a crane to his left, mounted on the outside of the rig and swaying a little in the wind. The helipad lay on the far side of the platform beyond the drilling mechanism, near the second barn building. Reed saw the twin aircraft as mere shadows, but it was now possible to determine airframe types. The first was large, like the bird Ibrahim fled Beirut in. The second was much smaller, and looked to be a Bell model. Maybe a JetRanger.

So there were a lot of people on board, then. Probably sheltering in the barn buildings. But Reed had seen somebody standing guard near the core . . .

He swept the rifle left while crouching at the top of the stairs, not covered but concealed by the darkness. He saw the shadow again, standing just beneath the edge of a pavilion. The flash of orange blazed brighter for a moment, and now he knew it had to be a cigarette. He couldn't smell it, but he recognized the visual signature of a bent arm rising toward a mouth.

And a cell phone. Maybe a sat phone, with a thick antenna rising above the man's head. A rifle leaned against the railing behind him.

Reed signaled Turk, and Turk covered the guy while Reed swept right. Even with the aid of the night vision, the rain made it difficult to see. He mapped out a second crane and a fuel depot—heavy drums marked as diesel and jet fuel, likely for the choppers. Not much else.

"I've got nobody," Reed hissed.

"Same," Turk replied. "Take him by hand?"

Reed nodded once. Turk left the darkness without further instruction, starting across the platform. Reed covered him with the Galil while Wolfgang filled the position next to him. Turk approached from behind, lowering his rifle as he moved. Readying his right arm to throttle the man from behind.

It was an assumption that the guy wasn't a legitimate oil rig worker. But then again, what oil rig worker comes armed with an AK-47?

Turk made it halfway, and Reed held his breath. He dropped a finger over the trigger, just in case.

And then everything hit the fan. A shout burst from someplace to Reed's left. Wolfgang yanked his Galil that way as Turk hesitated. The shout repeated from the corner of the platform, lost in the shadows out of Reed's view. Then a pistol cracked.

Wolfgang answered with three quick rounds from the Galil. The man with the cigarette turned and reached for his gun. Turk abandoned his throttling approach and snatched the Galil up. A burst cut the guy through the stomach, and he toppled.

"Contact! Contact!" Turk called. "Going hot!"

30

If Reed had any doubts about the nature of the men gathered on the oil rig, those doubts evaporated within the next five seconds. By the time Turk obtained cover and Reed swept his rifle back toward the helipad, a storm of gunfire had erupted from the second barn building. Through open windows and a door, hot yellow light streamed while muzzle flash blazed. Bullets pinged off pipes and the metal grating beneath their feet as Reed split right and Wolfgang went left, each finding more robust cover behind machinery.

The first of the two barn buildings lay directly ahead of Reed, and even as he approached the front door blew open and a tall Middle Eastern guy appeared with an AK. He took two in the chest and one in the head before he even knew what was happening, and Reed stitched a line of heavy thirty-caliber rounds through the walls of the building for good measure. A scream rent the air as Reed slid to his knees behind a two-foot iron pipe to change mags. Turk dumped fire from his position on the far side of the drilling mechanism, and Reed swept his gaze across the platform.

There were no less than six shooters dug into the second barn building. The rifles sounded like more AKs, bullets zipping through the rain like angry hornets. It was pray and spray type fire, but it was reasonably effective. Already Reed was pinned down, unable to easily move. He couldn't approach the second barn building without clearing the first, and he couldn't retreat toward the stairs without exposing his left side.

Reed rotated the Galil across the top of the pipe and squeezed two careful shots through a window sixty yards away. Blood sprayed across the glass and a body fell as Turk's voice burst through the coms.

"Two tangos left of the building! I think they're moving toward the choppers."

"Can you circle in from that side?" Reed called.

"Affirmative. I've got cover."

"Do it! Wolf, cover me. I'm clearing the first building."

Wolfgang's Galil switched to full auto in a snarl of death as Reed sprang from behind the pipe and sprinted for the nearest barn building. He didn't look to his left to watch for muzzle flash from the second building. It didn't matter. If they were going to shoot him, they'd hit him before he saw it coming. His best bet was to dash.

Reed cleared the body of the man he shot and leapt through the open door just as a hail of gunfire ripped across the mesh flooring behind him. Dull lights shone from overhead, dimming the power of his night vision as he hit his knees and instinctively yanked the Galil right. A handgun cracked, and a round zipped over his head.

There was a man on the floor, laid up against the wall with one arm clutched around his stomach. Blood pooled around him, and his mouth hung open. A rifle lay on the floor next to him, but he fired a Glock handgun instead, his arm swaying wildly as he fought to obtain an accurate shot.

Reed was quicker. The laser cut across the room and found the guy's chest. Three thunderclaps split the confined space, and Reed's ears rang. He fought his way to his feet and swept the rifle in the opposite direction.

The building was a dormitory. Bunk beds stood on all sides, with a door leading to a kitchen. Reed kicked through it, passing dirty dishes and a table laden with bottles of water. There was a dining room, then a theater room. They were all empty. He swept one after the other as gunfire continued from outside, and Turk called in updates on the chopper.

"They're loading something on the bigger bird!"

"Can you see it?"

"Negative. I . . . I can't . . . "

Turk's voice crackled in and out amid another storm of fire.

"I'm pinned down!" Turk shouted.

"I'm coming!" Reed replied. "Wolf, move if you can. Give him some cover fire!"

"Copy," Wolfgang chirped.

Reed exploded through a large shower room into an even larger storage room. Stacks of dry goods and food were heaped against the wall, followed by another metal door. One strike of his boot sent it crashing open, then Reed was on the far side of the platform. He circled left, toward the last barn building. It was still eighty yards away, but from this angle no windows overlooked his position. Reed held the Galil in low ready and sprinted, breath whistling through his teeth and heart thundering. On the far side of the drilling mechanism, Turk and Wolfgang unloaded on the building from twenty yards apart, twin starlights of muzzle flash unleashing rounds in full auto.

"I'm almost to the building!" Reed called. "Don't freaking shoot me!"

He reached the end of the barn and yanked on the door. It opened without resistance just as a guy appeared in the doorway. He was tall and bearded, blood streaming from one shoulder. He wielded an AK, frantically snatching it up just as Reed's Galil descended over his torso. The Israeli rifle cracked, and he went down. Reed stumbled over the body and into the building, feet thundering on rough plywood.

It wasn't another dormitory. This building consisted of one giant room, with rows of workbenches and tool racks running along either side. There were heavy metal carts built of angle steel with thick rubber tires. Grease on the floor, and tangles of wires lying on a workbench. Tools scattered about and chain hoists running on I-beams overhead. The air was thick with an acrid ammonium smell, and blood ran in rivers and gathered in small lakes nearly everywhere. There were four bodies on the floor, rifles fallen at their sides. Holes riddled the wall and glass lay like fallen stars, gleaming in Reed's night vision.

But there were no combatants. Not anymore. Whatever survivors had fled the building had departed through a large rolling metal door that consumed the far wall. It was open, and rain poured down in torrents outside. Reed noted thick black tread marks running from the workbenches toward the door and disappearing outside.

It didn't take a genius to know what had happened here. It didn't take a genius to know what the next sound was, either. A whirring, whining shriek. A thumping shudder.

One of the helicopters was spinning up.

"They're aboard the bigger chopper!" Turk shouted. "I've got a shot."

"No!" Reed called. "Hold your fire! Hold your fire! They may have a bomb."

He sprinted again, thundering across the bloody plywood toward the open rolling door. By the time he reached it the air was alive with the howl of the aircraft. Reed saw the helicopter another eighty yards away, perched on the helipad alongside its smaller twin. He yanked the rifle into his shoulder and played the laser across the chopper's windshield, but from his current angle he couldn't draw a bead on the pilot. The windshield was slick with rain and obscured his view.

Reed swung right instead, looking for the open side door. The NV goggles penetrated the darkness and he detected the silhouette of a man crouched within, huddled next to a giant wooden crate. The man's face turned, and Reed's heart stopped.

It was Ibrahim—he was sure of it. The snarling demon face from his nightmares was highlighted in a rain-obscured profile as he crouched near the crate. Reed's finger dropped to the trigger and the laser raced sideways toward his target. His heartbeat resumed with a drumroll thud that pounded in his ears. The chopper lifted off the helipad and rose slowly. Reed contemplated the box behind Ibrahim and what it might contain—a deadly pathogen that would explode into the air, suffocating them all. A biological plague, maybe. A slow death.

He could face death. It was worth it. He began to squeeze the trigger.

No, Daddy.

The girl's voice rang softly in his ears, as clear as if she were standing right beside him. Reed's mind deadlocked, and his finger froze. The chopper lurched upward, and the shot was gone. In an instant, a storm of automatic fire erupted from the still-open side door, showering his position. Reed stumbled back, sliding into cover as heavy slugs whistled overhead. His hands shook, his mind semi-blurred. He couldn't process a clear thought.

"They're getting away!" Turk shouted.

He's getting away.

That was enough to liberate Reed's mired brain. He blinked once, then screamed into his own mic.

"Corbyn, get up here! Move it!"

"Already on my way!" Corbyn called back. Reed swung out from his concealment just inside the open door and lifted the rifle. The gunfire had ceased, but the chopper was now two hundred feet up and banking hard. He scrambled back to his feet and snatched the Galil into his shoulder.

Nothing. No shot at all. Ibrahim was yet again slipping through his fingers.

"Turk, Wolf! Secure the second chopper," Reed ordered. "I'm headed your way."

Reed wheeled on the interior of the building, his brain now buzzing with surges of adrenaline that muted the child's voice in his memory. Instincts took over, and he remembered his objective. He started moving without really knowing what he was doing.

Out came his cell phone. He snapped a series of quick pictures of the makeshift workshop. They were hurried and incomplete, but better than nothing. He was just sweeping back to the right, half his field of view capturing the fuel depot outside the open rolling door, when something gleamed brighter than it should have from the darkness outside. Reed moved quickly, flipping his goggles back down and pivoting around the edge of the doorframe toward the looming jet fuel tanks.

He knew what it was before he even stopped, but the sight of it still sent his stomach plummeting into his boots.

A small digital screen lay pinned beneath the fuel tanks alongside a pair of nondescript fifty-five-gallon drums. Wires ran from the screen to the tops of the drums. The screen was a clock.

The clock ready forty seconds, and counted down.

"Bomb! Bomb!" Reed shouted. He turned for the helipad and broke into a mad dash even as Corbyn appeared from the top of the stairs on the far side of the rig. Turk had already wrenched the JetRanger's door open and sat inside, soaked to the bone and still covering Reed's approach with his Galil. Wolfgang had strapped himself into the co-pilot's seat. In Reed's mind he saw the clock, still ticking down. Thirty-five seconds, now? Was it thirty?

"*Move*, Corbyn!"

Reed hurled himself into the JetRanger and scrambled across the floor. Corbyn's long legs carried her with an awkward hitching motion, pain igniting across her face with each fall of her left leg. Reed remembered her Royal Air Force injury but didn't have time to sympathize. He screamed a curse into the darkness and beckoned.

Corbyn reached the JetRanger just as the clock in Reed's head reached twenty seconds. She slid into the cockpit like a fighter pilot, hands running across the controls with practiced ease, lips recounting a silent flight procedure. Her saturated hair dripped rainwater while the aviator sunglasses remained perched halfway down her nose.

The JetRanger coughed. The engines howled. Corbyn flicked something on the dash and grabbed the cyclic.

Then the rotor turned. Slowly at first, but rapidly gaining speed. The clock in Reed's mind reached ten seconds. Then nine. The rotors thundered louder. He looked back to the fuel drums and wondered if he should have attempted to disarm the device.

He wouldn't have had time to determine how.

The JetRanger hopped once on the helipad, and Corbyn managed the collective.

"Stay in the boat, Corbyn," she said. "No girls welcome here, Corbyn!"

"Will you shut up and fly?" Wolfgang screamed.

"How about I shut up and make you a sandwich?"

"*Move!*" Reed shouted.

The JetRanger lunged off the helipad with a sudden dump of power, and Corbyn banked hard to the left. Reed slid across the floor and caught himself with one boot pressed against the door frame. The Galil dragged against his neck, still dangling by the strap. Turk grabbed his arm and pinned him back. The chopper soared two hundred yards from the platform.

I love you, Daddy.

The child's voice echoed through his mind only a split second before the bomb detonated. A thunderclap of hot orange fire and deafening noise flooded the night, and then the rig simply disappeared.

31

The Oval Office
The White House

Maggie rose early for her meeting with the chairman of the Senate Select Committee on Intelligence, Senator Matthew R. Roper. She showered. She took her time with her makeup, and selected a flattering deep blue dress with half-length sleeves. She put her hair up in a tight bun. She doubled her regular pain medication and swallowed it with two cups of black coffee.

She was *determined* to look awake and alive, ready for battle. By the time she reached the Oval the pain was muted in her gut, and her head floated a little despite the charge of caffeine. She took her place behind the Resolute desk and resolved to only stand once when Roper entered. Shake his hand, and then quickly move to the couch.

There couldn't be any risk of appearing injured or feeble today. The tabloids' favorite nickname for her, "Lame Duck Maggie," was gaining enough traction as it was. The previous day, a congresswoman from Kentucky had even used the title on the House floor while campaigning for RECA.

The last thing Maggie needed was to give Roper a front-stage pass to tabloid validation.

The Senator arrived eight minutes late, which irritated Maggie, and she couldn't help thinking that it was intentional. He strolled into the Oval with a broad smile and an unbuttoned suit jacket. Tall and muscular with a definite "corn-fed" appearance, Roper was the poster boy for his home state of Iowa. Maggie knew from her tour of his Wikipedia page the night before that he'd played middle linebacker for the University of Iowa's Hawkeyes, generating a stat line that featured an impressive number of tackles, forced fumbles, and sacks. One of those sacks left the rival Cornhusker quarterback with a broken collarbone and two fractured ribs, effectively terminating a promising Heisman run.

Moving down the page to Roper's political career, Maggie wasn't surprised to find much of the same behavior along the linebacker's progression into politics. Roper had progressed directly from sacking quarterbacks to sacking political rivals, rising up the ladder more quickly than any young law student had business rising. He skipped the House of Representatives altogether, jumping directly from the Iowa State Legislature to the United States Senate.

Another impressive stat line, but Maggie wasn't intimidated. She'd sacked more than her share of political opponents in her own short career, rising far higher and far more quickly than Roper dreamed. He should have shown up on time—with a buttoned suit jacket.

"Good morning, Madam President! It's such a pleasure to finally meet you."

Maggie extended a hand with a warm smile she certainly didn't feel. Roper squeezed harder than he should have, but Maggie didn't wince. She shook his hand with the confidence of a swamp girl raised to wrestle bigger gators than those found on Capitol Hill.

"Senator, thank you for joining me. Can I get you something to drink?"

"Coffee? Black would be amazing."

Maggie gestured for him to sit while she poured two cups of rich black Colombian blend. Already she felt a little unsteady on her feet. The fogginess in her brain had only intensified over the past hour, making her second-guess her decision to double up on the pain meds. Maybe she would have been better off with the fire in her gut.

Maggie handed off a china cup on a china plate, then took a seat across from Roper. The senator sat with one leg crossed over the other, kicked back like he was relaxing in his own living room. It pissed Maggie off. It made her want to open the conversation with a warning shot.

"I read that you played for Iowa. Middle linebacker?"

Roper beamed. "That's right. Four years. Had a little interest from the league, but pro ball was never my aim. I always wanted to be in public service."

Maggie doubted very seriously whether pro scouts had ever sincerely considered Roper, but she didn't mind indulging the flex. It would only make the fall that much more satisfying.

"You played LSU once, didn't you?"

Her smile didn't waver. Roper's faded, just for a moment.

"Ah, yes. The Death Valley game. I was there. Tough loss . . . the Tigers always bring the heat!"

Like you would know, watching from the sidelines.

Maggie knew that Roper had been ejected in the first quarter of that game for unsportsmanlike conduct. He'd yanked the helmet off the head of an LSU Tiger's offensive lineman and shot him the bird. Rumor had it, he'd even indulged in a racial slur.

Of course, Roper denied those claims. Maggie didn't need to make the point. Mentioning the game was sufficient to put him on notice.

"I won't waste any of your valuable time, Senator. I'm sure you know why you're here."

Roper nodded, slurping coffee. The cup made a little *clink* as it resumed its position on the plate. "RECA, yes. Jordan called me yesterday about it. Wanted a feeler on the Senate's position. Of course, it's still early, but if the House should pass it—"

"Actually, I wanted to talk to you about Sarah Aimes." Maggie skated right past Roper's casual reference to the Vice President of the United States by his first name, and went straight for the throat. Roper lowered the saucer and cocked his head, playing dumb.

"The confirmation hearings?"

"Right."

"Ah." The saucer found his knee. Roper leaned back, inhaling deeply and grimacing, as though it were a tough subject.

"I'm not sure there's much I can tell you about that, Madam President. The committee is still reviewing evidence. Of course, we like to keep all that close to the chest until we're ready to announce our findings. I'm sure there will be further interviews, possibly additional testimony . . . "

Roper droned on, never using three words when six could be extrapolated. Maggie's eyes glazed over as she sipped coffee, waiting for him to reach an inevitable conclusion, which could easily have been distilled into a simple: *Screw off, Madam President.*

"Matt," Maggie set her cup down. "May I call you Matt?"

A twinkle shone behind Roper's gaze. A sort of vague amusement. He ducked his head. "Of course, ma'am."

"Allow me to shoot straight with you, Matt. One homegrown American to another."

Roper cocked his head again. Maggie felt the vague urge to punch him in the throat. She pressed on.

"I need you to cut the drama and confirm Dr. Aimes. She should have been confirmed two weeks ago, but the hearings and discovery proceedings continue. I respect the fact that you and I may hold differing views on the issue of national security, but surely you must appreciate the urgency of devoting the full attention of this administration and the CIA to locating the actors responsible for the Tennessee and Baton Rouge attacks. We don't have time for bureaucratic logjams. We need this done."

Roper raised both eyebrows. He did the slow breathing thing again, this time only through his nose. Then he relaxed into the couch.

"Well. They told me you were blunt."

"I'm a woman with a long to-do list, Senator."

Roper nodded a few times, and something changed behind his eyes. They grew colder . . . and more calculative.

"Well, then. Since you set the precedent, allow me to be just as blunt."

Maggie gestured for him to proceed. Roper didn't hold back.

"I don't like your nominee, ma'am. I don't like her background, I don't like her pedigree, and I don't like her approach to intelligence. She's heavy-handed and evasive over the most basic questions. Much of her resume is shrouded by classified records I'm only just beginning to investigate. She's a loose cannon in a time when America can't afford any mistakes. She—"

"Who would you nominate, Senator?" Maggie cut Roper off. Roper's mouth hung half-open as he hesitated. Then he frowned.

"I'm not sure how that's relevant."

"Oh, I think it's quite relevant. You clearly have some well-developed ideological complaints about the nature of my nominee. You've served on the Select Committee for Intelligence for nearly five years. You must be familiar with the intelligence community. Surely there's somebody you like."

Roper pinched his eyebrows together, as though he were contemplating the question. Maggie knew he wasn't, just like she knew he didn't really have a problem with Aimes. There was nothing to have a problem with. Anybody with sufficient intelligence experience to qualify for the director's job would have a resume "shrouded by classified records." It was a given.

Roper was playing games, and she knew it. He was showboating. But why?

"Honestly, ma'am, I would need to get back with you on that. I've invested all my current time into reviewing your nominee. If you're seriously interested in replacing her—"

"I'm not."

He squinted. "So why ask?"

"Because I need to make a point. You're a practical man. If you really objected to Dr. Aimes on an ideological level, you should have some idea of who you would prefer. At least a name that came to mind. But you don't. So . . ."

Roper remained impassive. Not blinking. Daring her to say it.

Maggie decided to go for the throat.

"Is this about Brandt?"

A flash of fire flicked across Roper's gaze. There and gone in the blink of an eye, carefully smothered out. But Maggie saw it.

"Why would you say that?" Roper asked.

"I know about the cabinet position. Secretary of the Treasury, wasn't it? An enviable post. You rallied a lot of support for Brandt on the campaign trail. You even managed to secure Iowa . . . no easy task, I admit. I've done it. That put six electoral votes in Brandt's pocket. And then he pulled the rug out from under you."

The fire returned, and this time it remained. Roper took a long pull of coffee. Maggie threw her cards on the table.

"What do you want, Mr. Roper? We're both practical people. Let's make a deal."

Maggie's offer was as sincere as Roper's complaints about Aimes, but she couldn't squash the man without first identifying a vulnerability. The moment he admitted to a desire, she would have a target.

Roper swallowed coffee, taking his time. He adjusted the suit jacket, then the corn-fed smile returned.

"I appreciate your candor, Madam President, but this really isn't a matter of negotiation. I'm simply trying to serve the best interests of the American people."

"The interests of the American people would be best served by confirming Dr. Aimes so that she can focus on her work."

"A matter of opinion."

"A matter of *fact*." Maggie turned the heat on in her voice. She leaned forward, squinting a little. Roper remained unfazed, as polished and austere as the portrait of George Washington overlooking them. Not the least bit interested in engaging.

Why?

"What are you up to, Mr. Roper?"

No answer. Maggie's mind worked quickly. The brain fog was still there. The pain. The foggy vision. But the instincts that had brought Muddy Maggie Trousdale from the swamps to the Oval Office weren't completely smothered. She could still think.

And she thought she saw it.

"You want the attention, don't you?" Maggie said.

Roper feigned innocence. "I'm sorry?"

"You're sucking the limelight. Using these confirmation hearings to develop your national brand. You're . . . thinking of running, aren't you?"

The smile didn't so much as flicker. Roper's plate clicked as he returned it to the coffee table.

"You know, Madam President. Life is such a funny thing. It's a little like football. Sometimes you make a mistake and draw a penalty flag. Sometimes, you get benched when you were promised a starting slot. You have to watch from the sidelines while everybody else hogs up the moment. But then, sometimes . . . the team loses. Badly. Then they're embarrassed, and they remember who they left riding the bench. Meanwhile, you've been pumping iron. You've been making use of the time. You've been waiting. Because the thing about football . . . "

Roper leaned forward. The smile became a grin. "There's *always* another game."

Maggie didn't budge. Roper stood, finally buttoning his jacket. Shoulders square, broad chin held high.

"See you on the gridiron, Madam President. I'm really looking forward to it. Who knows . . . maybe you'll pick a jersey by then! Would be a shame to see you get sacked by both teams."

Maggie's blood boiled, but she didn't stand. She didn't comment. She didn't so much as flinch as Roper turned for the door and disappeared without being excused.

32

Langley, Virginia

Aimes was ready to break necks. She arrived at Langley early, but the reports from Lebanon were already streaming in. Somehow, the Lebanese had connected the CIA to the strike at the warehouse in Beirut. They didn't have any actual evidence, but the State Department was fielding a storm of inquiries from the Lebanese embassy, and that meant that Aimes was fielding a storm of inquiries from the State Department.

Secretary of State Lisa Gorman wanted answers. She wanted details. Aimes couldn't offer them, but she might have been able to stall both Gorman and the Lebanese had it not been for the next report to strike her desk like a sidewinder missile: a detonated oil platform only five miles from the Lebanese coast. Witness statements of heavy small-arms fire from a commercial freighter passing nearby. And a Prosecution Force who was most definitely *not* in Amman, Jordan.

"Where are they?" Aimes barked the question the moment that Rigby stepped through the door. He put up a hand, urging calm even as he closed the door. Aimes wasn't interested in calm any more than she was interested in the iced latte he set on her desk.

She wanted Reed Montgomery. She wanted him in the chair seated across from her. She wanted to break her keyboard over his face.

"They're back in Beirut," Rigby said. "They managed to escape the platform just as it went up. I'm still gathering details."

"What were they even *doing* there?"

Aimes barely recognized her own voice. The cool and calm had melted. Hot fire boiled in her stomach, and she knew it was a direct result of the stress. She didn't have *time* for this. She couldn't afford for Montgomery and his crew of miscreants to run off script and start blowing things up.

She needed to be focused, right now. She still had Roper and another one of his hearings to attend to in barely three hours. She needed to prep her testimony. She needed for Roper to *not* be questioning her about Lebanese accusations of illegal American covert action.

"We've had only limited contact since last night," Rigby said. "We're still working on it. It seems that Montgomery obtained a lead of his own about the oil platform. He chose to investigate. He claims they made contact with Ibrahim."

Aimes's head snapped up. "What? They have him?"

"No. He made the slip, again. But Montgomery claims they found evidence of a weapons lab on the platform. Apparently, it was currently out of use. Between owners, or just recently sold. Like I said, we're still working on it. He sent photos."

Out came another iPad. Aimes scrolled quickly through a number of cell phone snapshots. Many were blurry and out of focus, taken on the fly. More than a few featured bodies on the floor, chests and faces riddled with bullet holes. Brass lay everywhere.

The "weapons lab" sat on the upper deck of the platform inside an enclosed structure. Some kind of mechanical room, stripped of its usual components and stocked instead with workbenches and tools.

And explosive paraphernalia. It was all there. Aimes wasn't any sort of bomb expert, but she'd viewed enough photographs of terrorist bomb labs to recognize some of the equipment. It was all conventional, not nuclear. Nothing that would justify radiation suits.

Aimes tossed the iPad down and gritted her teeth. A part of her wondered how Reed had even *reached* the platform, but she didn't have to wonder long. It was a simple enough riddle.

Mossad, definitely. Loose cannons with axes to grind and enough weaponry to keep Israel alive while surrounded by tens of millions who wanted her exterminated. She should have put Montgomery on a shorter leash.

"Get in contact," Aimes snapped. "I want everything he has, a full mission brief. Then get them *the hell* out of Lebanon. I don't need any more diplomatic drama."

"Where do you want them?"

"I don't care. Just park them someplace out of the way and keep them there. Get every detail you can on the platform and how Ibrahim escaped. Is there anything left to investigate?"

Rigby grimaced. "Not really. The platform was pretty well destroyed by the blast. Apparently it was rigged to blow. Montgomery thinks Ibrahim triggered it on his way out."

Of course.

Aimes lifted the latte despite herself and slurped from the lid. It was cold and shockingly sweet. She grimaced and set it down.

"Get our local people as close to the platform as they can to find whatever they can, and get me Montgomery's full report, ASAP. We'll go from there."

Rigby turned for the door. Aimes turned for her computer.

"Silas?"

"Yeah?"

"No sugar next time."

Rigby shot her a casual salute, as calm and collected as ever. "You got it."

He departed the room, and Aimes opened her email. There was a slew of internal reports and requests from various departments for authorization on various operations. A mess of things she could barely keep up with, but one email stood out. It wasn't internal, it was external. From the office of Senator Matthew R. Roper.

. . .

Dear Madam,

Please be advised that today's hearing of the Senate Select Committee on Intelligence concerning your confirmation of candidacy for the position of Director of the Central Intelligence Agency has been postponed while the committee reviews new evidence regarding your eligibility. We will advise further as appropriate.

Sincerely,

Senator M. R. Roper

Aimes had barely finished reading the email before her phone rang. Her mind spun, and she almost bumped the call. Then her gaze flickered across the caller ID.

This wasn't a call she could bump.

Aimes mashed the speaker button even while she was rereading the email.

"Good morning, Madam Pre—"

"Sarah, what the hell? What am I looking at?"

"Ma'am?" Aimes played dumb, unwilling to show her hand until she knew whether Maggie was calling about Beirut or the email.

"Roper's *email*. What is he talking about? What evidence?"

Aimes leaned back in her desk chair. Her body felt suddenly cold. Her stomach leaden.

She decided to tell the truth. It was really her only option.

"I have no idea, Madam President."

33

Yalta, Crimea

Situated in a little cleft between the fingers of the Crimean Mountains, the resort city sparkled with a relaxed vibrancy that defied the recent violence spilling across the region. Traditionally recognized as a part of Ukraine, but now under Russian control, the Crimean Peninsula was as beautiful as it was ecologically diverse. Rolling green forests, towering mountain peaks, and beautiful white sand beaches.

Ivan had visited Crimea a number of times during his long career as a KGB and then SVR agent, and had even passed time in Yalta on occasion, but he hadn't set foot in Russian-controlled territory since fleeing Moscow several months prior. The SVR, he knew, was actively looking for him. They had a finger on most of his false identities and pseudonyms, having issued many of his fake passports themselves. He was ninety-nine percent sure they didn't know about *all* of his false identities and pseudonyms. He'd crafted a few on his own time, reserved for an emergency need just such as this. He'd hidden his tracks well, paid in cash, and only dealt with very reputable underground dealers of such things as manufactured passports and falsified government ID numbers. He'd done a good job.

Yet he was still only ninety-nine percent sure, because you could never truly be certain where the SVR was concerned. In Russia there was no such thing as a secret, and that made venturing into Crimea extremely dangerous, even under the guise of the Polish passport which recorded his name as Jakub Nowak, an agricultural pesticides merchant from Kraków. If the Russian authorities detected him at the airport in Sevastopol or snagged him somewhere along the short mountain drive to Yalta, he would be a dead man. He couldn't bring his Grach handgun on the flight from Tbilisi. He was too deep inside Russian territory to hope for escape.

And yet Ivan boarded the plane willingly, and didn't stress about the risks. There was no point. He had to go—he had to see the man in Yalta. He needed answers, and anyway, the SVR wouldn't expect to find him right under their noses.

At least, that was what he told himself as he pulled the rented Renault off the highway on the outskirts of the beach town and took the mountain road onto a ridge overlooking the Black Sea. Two kilometers along the ridge Ivan turned off the paved two-lane onto a gravel track marked only by a mailbox leaning on a rotting wooden post. Trees bowed low over the path, trailing limbs scratching the roof of the Renault like nails on a chalkboard. Ivan kept his foot on the gas and his eyes moving, conscious of the fact that he was driving himself into a corner with little opportunity for escape if things went sideways, but he drove along anyway.

Not because he liked the odds.

Because he didn't have a choice.

The house at the end of the drive sat by itself, isolated from the two-lane by thick groves of overgrown brush and scraggly trees, perched only a few strides away from a fifty-meter cliff that dropped straight into the Black Sea. It was a small house, but well built. There were no windows facing the drive, only a tall door built of steel with a lot of fancy trim and a fresh coat of paint.

It was a reasonably aesthetic look, but Ivan knew the door was specially designed to repel bullets. The occupant of this house was a very careful man, and he had doubtless detected Ivan's approach. The Renault had already passed no fewer than five security cameras hidden among the trees, not to mention carefully disguised motion detectors and pressure plates hidden beneath the gravel, some of them likely equipped with remote-controlled explosive charges.

The house had its back against the cliff because the occupant only wanted to watch one side. He didn't care about being rammed into a corner, because he wasn't the kind of man to run from a fight. He just wanted to be sure that if anybody came after him, they would regret it.

Ivan parked the Renault ten meters from the house and left his hands on top of the steering wheel, making direct eye contact with the security camera shrouded behind a wreath at the top of the door. It was only semi-hidden, and maintained a clear view of the entire front yard. After thirty seconds, Ivan stepped out of the car and peeled his jacket off. It was cool at the top of the cliff, but he wanted to demonstrate that he was unarmed. That would be considered polite.

At last he approached the door, pressing the bell button mounted on the frame and again gazing into the security camera lens. A little light blinked. He waited. Then the electric rumble of automated bolts growled through the door. The windowless face of the house stood like a wall as the door swung open with a rush of salt air, and a skinny man with long gray hair and a neatly trimmed beard stepped out.

"Ivan! You old dog. How are you?"

The skinny man wrapped Ivan in a heartfelt embrace, and Ivan returned the hug with a gentle pat. He couldn't help but notice the bulge of a handgun protruding from the small of the man's back, but he chose not to comment on it.

"Serge, my friend. It is so good to see you."

Serge pushed Ivan back, sweeping him up and down for a moment and squeezing both biceps. The old man smiled, but shook his head.

"Ivan . . . you look like hell! The years have not been kind to you."

"You know what they say. It is not the years, but the mileage."

That brought another laugh. Serge beckoned inward.

"Come, my friend. I just made a pot of strong tea. The view is excellent in the morning. Not too hot."

The door closed automatically behind them as Ivan followed Serge down a bare hallway lined by security control panels and a coat rack. The living room was better decorated, with a large television and leather-clad furniture. There was a mini bar and a dining room with picture windows that overlooked the cliff and the water beyond. A veranda with cushioned patio furniture and a table, also overlooking the sea.

Serge proceeded into the kitchen where he set a teapot on a tray already laden with cups—two of them—and danishes. Everything smelled amazing, and Ivan's stomach growled. He hadn't eaten in nearly a day. He hadn't found the time.

A sliding glass door led to the veranda. Ivan followed Serge into a blast of sea breeze, breathing deeply and enjoying the flavor. The view was stunning—south facing, so there would never be a proper sunrise or sunset, but with this much ocean spread out in place of a backyard . . . who would complain?

"Milk and sugar?" Serge asked.

"Just tea."

Ivan took a seat across the table from Serge, settling into the cushioned chair. It was indeed comfortable, and a welcome relief after the undersized Renault. Ivan sipped good Russian tea and took a man-sized bite out of a danish. It was as fresh and delicious as anything he'd ever tasted.

"You like?" Serge asked.

"It's magnificent."

"I baked it myself."

"No!"

Serge grinned. "Every week. I figure, if I'm going to be retired . . . I may as well spoil myself."

"And here I thought you could only bake enemies of the Motherland."

That brought a deeper laugh from the old man, even though the memory of interrogating Soviet traitors was a gory one. Serge had run a gulag interrogation center at one stage of his lengthy career. He was among the KGB's most ruthless agents, and it was that same ruthlessness he had instilled in Ivan when he first took the young man under his wing.

"How long has it been, Ivan?"

Ivan licked his fingers and eyed a second danish. Serge motioned invitingly, and Ivan went to work.

"Six years," he spoke through a mouthful. "Back in Vladivostok. That thing with the Koreans."

Serge snapped his fingers. "Was that six years ago? Time flies when you're having fun."

Ivan polished off the danish and sipped black tea. It soothed his throat and slowly brought energy back to his weary body. He hadn't realized how exhausted he was.

"I hear you've not been having so much fun, lately . . . " Serge spoke carefully, and Ivan eyeballed him without blinking or commenting.

It didn't surprise Ivan that Serge had heard of his ousting from Moscow. It was no great secret that the two were old friends, or that Serge had schooled Ivan during his early years in the KGB. That they trusted one another. The SVR probably sent agents directly to Yalta to inquire of the old man as to whether he had heard from Ivan.

Serge wouldn't have told them anything even if he had. Sure, he was a long-time servant of the motherland, riding the waves of the Cold War before eventually riding the collapse of the Union. He was a patriot, some might say. A dedicated comrade.

But he was also a ruthless pragmatist, and a man who had been burned himself. When Ivan made contact via the secure online chat he and his old mentor had once used to communicate while ratting American spies out of the SVR, Serge hadn't hesitated. He'd given him an address. He'd promised a warm pot of tea.

And here Ivan was, with a cup of the promised beverage, and a lot of questions.

"I need your help, my friend," Ivan said.

Serge cocked an eyebrow and waited.

"I have been working a case," Ivan continued. "An inquiry. It began while I was still in Moscow. You have read the news of the tumult in America?"

Serge grunted.

"There are links, Serge. The assassin was a Russian, and he was hired by Stepan Belsky."

"The oligarch?" Serge's tone carried no hint of surprise. Both men had dealings with the oligarchs. Both men understood how treacherous they could be.

"*Da*. But there is more. It appears Belsky had support. He fled to

Venezuela to establish a partnership with the Moreno regime. An attempt to resurrect the Venezuelan oil trade."

"I heard there were hiccups . . . " Serge swirled his tea gently. Ivan nodded.

"You could say so. The Americans, of course. Moreno was killed and they installed Rivas as president. They captured the oil trade."

"A neat little piece of business."

"And it might have stayed that way, but there is still the link, Serge. The link between Belsky . . . and whoever was supporting him."

Ivan trailed off, and Serge hesitated over his tea. He cocked his head. He squinted. His own voice dropped a notch.

"What are you suggesting, my friend?"

"It is him, Serge. I confirmed his communications with Belsky just prior to being ousted from Moscow, and now I have further determined that the nerve agent used in the recent terrorist attacks was of Soviet origin. It was sourced from a forgotten weapons stash in Georgia. Sold through a Ukrainian arms dealer named Oleksiy Melnyk to the terrorist Abdel Ibrahim. Or so we are meant to believe."

Serge didn't blink. His lips tightened, and he set his tea down very slowly. He waited, but Ivan didn't continue. The implication was already there, sitting like an elephant on the table, waiting for Serge to acknowledge it.

But Serge acknowledged nothing. He feigned ignorance.

"What are you suggesting, Ivan?" he repeated.

"I'm not suggesting anything. I'm only following the evidence, and the evidence says what we have long suspected. He is making a play, Serge. Nikitin is attempting a global coup. He is going after the Americans."

Serge finally blinked. His nostrils flared, and his jaw set. He stood and walked to the veranda's glass railing, placing both hands atop it and looking out over the Black Sea. Ivan crossed his arms.

"We always knew this would happen, Serge. From the day he took power. It was never enough in Crimea, never enough in Ukraine. Never enough until the glories of the old Union are restored. Nikitin isn't like his predecessors. He knows he cannot directly confront the West, so he will sabotage them slowly. Erode their government, their economy, the fabric of their very society. Wear them down by proxy attacks, as long as it takes. The smarter they become, the harder he will strike. He will not stop until the world burns."

Serge still faced away. His shoulders bunched, and his knuckles turned white atop the railing. He breathed slowly.

At last, he said, "I never thought I would see the day, my friend, when a good Russian would trade in American propaganda."

Ivan blinked. A cold chill ran up his spine, and he sat up. He placed both arms on the table.

"Excuse me?"

Serge turned. His face was hard now. Very cold. "You cannot *honestly* expect me to believe this nonsense?"

"Serge. I interrogated Melnyk myself. I spoke to old contacts in Belgrade. The rumor is that the weapons were obtained in Georgia, but I viewed the weapons locker. There was a vault buried beneath the main room. Storage for WMDs. But we never kept them that way, Serge. We never stored weapons in such lockers, and even if we had, we would have recovered them. This was part of your job, was it not? After the fall?"

Serge said nothing, arms crossed, standing with his back to the cliff. Ivan leaned closer.

"Somebody is *supplying* the terrorists, Serge. Handing them lethal weapons, then setting up this weapons stash as a cover. As a smoke screen, so we do not know who is really responsible. Can't you see? It is him, Serge. It is Nikitin. He is plotting—"

"Listen to yourself!" Serge's voice cracked. His face twisted in disbelief. "What has happened to you, Ivan? These are not the investigatory skills I taught you. This is tin hat madness concocted on the internet!"

"No. No, it is not. I heard Nikitin speak with Belsky with my own ears. I know it was his plan to infiltrate Caracas—"

"And this proves *what?* That Nikitin has interests in oil overseas?"

"It proves that he had connections with the man who hired Trousdale's would-be killer. Does that not tell you everything?"

Serge sighed. He returned slowly to his seat and sat with a restrained grunt. He looked suddenly very old, and very tired. He rested his arms in his lap.

"It tells me, Ivan, what it should tell you. That the nature of our homeland will always be a complicated thing. Much business is conducted beneath the table. There are mysteries we will never understand. This is Russia."

Ivan shook his head. "No. This is not Russia. This is *him*. This is the government we have given sweat and blood to build. Now it will kill us all, if we do not stop it. It will be the *death* of Russia—the real Russia. The farmer in the field. The mechanic in the shop. The school mother making lunch buckets. They will all suffer because of this insanity."

Serge sucked his teeth. Ivan leaned across the table. He placed both heavy hands on either side of the teacup. His voice lowered.

"There was an empty weapons rack at the end of the locker. It wasn't for a barrel, it was for something much larger—much heavier. Serge . . . it was labeled *radioactive*."

The cold wind raking up off the Black Sea seemed to drop a few degrees as the words left Ivan's lips. Serge flinched, but he didn't budge. His arms remained crossed. Ivan spoke through his teeth.

"He is *arming* them, Serge. Whatever will come next is a blow the world cannot sustain. You must help me. We must forestall this madness."

Serge's chest rose in gentle breaths. He stared without blinking. Then he spoke in barely above a whisper.

"I urge you, Ivan. As your friend. *Drop this*."

"What?"

"There is nothing but pain for you on this path. A true patriot would walk away."

"A true patriot would protect his people!"

"So protect them. Finish your tea. Walk away now."

Ivan squinted. A sudden chill ran up his spine. His lips parted.

"Did they get to you, old man?"

Then he heard the tires. Rolling heavy and fast up the gravel road, crashing toward the house on the cliff. He heard the click beneath the table, where Serge's hands lay out of sight. The distinctive snap of a Makarov pistol's safety disengaging. It was a sound Ivan had heard a few thousand times and would have recognized anywhere.

Serge's face turned very sad. "I am sorry, old friend."

34

Beirut, Lebanon

The Prosecution Force was effectively barricaded inside their Gulfstream.

Corbyn had barely set the helicopter down on the tarmac near the airport before the authorities arrived. They made it back to the CIA's jet with just enough time to shut the door on a group of irate Lebanese officials, proceeding to completely ignore them while Strickland and Lucy, who had been waiting on the airplane, were quickly brought up to speed. Reed, meanwhile, was communicating with Langley.

He sent the pictures. He sent a full report along with the name of the rig: Intrepid Oil Anchor. Then the storm came. Not the rain that still beat down outside, but the verbal storm from the computer. Reed had zero doubt that Aimes herself was operating the keyboard. Many of the orders were in all caps, and the message itself was clear.

Stay on the plane. Do *not* move. Do *not* run any further unauthorized ops.

Reed was far less concerned about Aimes's directions than he was about the greater question of where the chopper had gone. There hadn't been a chance of finding it after the oil platform went up. The blast itself sent the

JetRanger into a tailspin, forcing Corbyn to wrestle with the controls and nearly dumping them all back into the raging sea.

By the time the chopper finally leveled off, not even the light from the blazing oil rig could help them locate the missing second bird. It had faded into the darkness like a ghost, and there was no equipment inside the dated JetRanger suitable to track it.

The only thing to do was to return to base, evaded twice in a span of hours. Reed made his reports and shut the iPad off when Aimes became nasty, then he stormed to the back of the plane and sat by himself, facing a wall. The rain beating down on the aircraft's fuselage sounded like dry beans cascading across a metal pan, as loud as the twin jet engines when the aircraft was in flight. Thunder joined the mix, and Reed's head pounded. He fished the bottle of Old Forrester from his go bag and drank directly from it, swigging good Kentucky bourbon to drown out the voices in his head.

He still heard her—the child. Not the way he heard her on the oil platform, as a voice both crisp and clear in his ear. Now he heard the girl as a memory, those two crisp lines spoken at the strangest of moments.

Daddy!

I love you.

Reed's hand trembled as he lowered the bottle, and he blinked away a growing fogginess in his eyes. The liquor was hitting him hard, landing in an empty stomach and going straight to work on his exhausted brain. He felt as though he hadn't slept in days, but he couldn't even close his eyes.

He thought of Ibrahim. The moment the laser settled over his chest, Reed's finger on the trigger.

Why hadn't he taken the shot? There was a good chance he would have missed. It was a long shot, and a rushed one. The laser was an imperfect aiming device at such a distance.

But he should have *tried*. Ibrahim was right there. Right under his nose. Why had his daughter's ghost revisited him at that worst possible moment? Was it a trick of his frayed mind? Was he losing it?

In the front of the plane, Corbyn and Strickland were already working an iPad equipped with some kind of aviation app to predict the possible destinations of the fleeing chopper. Discussions of range, fuel capacity, and burn efficiency under payload were all tossed around like they actually mattered.

Reed already knew the truth. In this part of the world, that aircraft could be bound for six or eight different nations, many of them favorable places for scum like Ibrahim to hide. They wouldn't catch him by guessing a second time. Ibrahim wouldn't repeat a simple shell game like he had with the helicopter in Jordan. This time he would go to ground, well and truly.

They needed a bigger break.

Reed chugged bourbon and embraced the pain of it burning in his empty stomach. He deserved the pain. He deserved more of it. He had one job to do, and he froze up. He didn't shoot.

What's wrong with me?

"You okay, Reed?"

Lucy appeared from the front of the airplane, resting a gentle hand on Reed's shoulder. He flinched and looked up, eyes stinging. Even standing while he was sitting, Lucy's head only rose a few inches over his own. She offered a smile, and momentary mental deadlock returned to Reed's brain. He froze up, unable to reply. Unable to remember what it was he wanted to say. For a split second, he even forgot who he was looking at.

She was just . . . a person.

"Reed?"

This time it was Turk who spoke. Reed realized the airplane had gone quiet, even Corbyn and Strickland falling silent. He blinked, and a sudden flash of anger twisted his stomach. Not anger at them—anger at himself.

"I'm fine," he snapped, turning quickly away. A long moment passed, then the buzz of voices resumed behind him.

But Lucy didn't leave. She settled into the seat across from him instead, resting her arms in her lap with a subtle smile. She wore loose cotton pants, much as she always had since . . .

Well. Southeast Asia. The burns. The rape. It was an abrupt departure from the skin-tight leather pants Lucy used to prefer, but something about the subdued appearance suited her. She looked . . . calmer, somehow. More collected.

"You'll get him, Reed," Lucy said. "You always do."

Reed avoided her gaze, fixating on the bottle. Picking the label with one thumbnail, and again returning to the shot.

Was it even Ibrahim? Had he imagined the face?

We should have let him have it, Reed thought. He should have given the order for Turk and Wolfgang to unload on the chopper, WMD or no WMD. They should have driven Ibrahim and whoever else was inside that bird straight into the Mediterranean, riddled with bullets and gasping for breath—

"You wanna talk about it?" Lucy's next question terminated Reed's line of thought. He looked up suddenly, realizing he'd already forgotten that she was there. His mind had fixated on the oil rig and the blast. On Ibrahim, missed opportunities, and voices in his head.

On a blonde-haired child with her mother's eyes.

"You're not alone, Reed," Lucy said gently. "And I don't mean the team. There's Somebody else."

Reed blinked. His vision cleared. The child and her happy smile faded. He shut her voice from his mind.

He only saw the face of her killer—his next target.

Reed stood abruptly and swigged bourbon. He wiped his lips, then reached for the door to the aft cabin. He left Lucy and the team without another word, and descended into darkness.

35

Langley, Virginia

"We've got him!"

With her latest confirmation hearings postponed, Aimes had remained at Langley for the day to drive the Ibrahim investigation. She was standing in a computer lab overlooking financial data captured from the late Oleksiy Melnyk's Swiss bank accounts when Rigby burst in. Waving an iPad and grinning like a schoolchild, Rigby didn't look like the second most powerful person in the agency. He looked like a nerdy enthusiast with a new toy, and that was exactly the kind of energy Aimes needed.

She swept her glasses off as she straightened up from the computer. Rigby met her behind the desk as the gathering of soda-slurping, unbathed analysts around the room all peered at them with unabashed fascination.

Rigby passed the iPad off. Aimes flicked quickly through the photographs. They were black-and-white, stripped from a security camera with text printed in one corner to mark the date, time, and location. At least, she assumed that's what the text represented. She couldn't actually read any of it. The letters weren't even Latin.

"Is that . . . ?"

"Greek," Rigby said with a grin.

"He landed in Greece?"

Rigby shook his head. "Cyprus. This is from an airport just outside Larnaca. The footage is six hours old."

Aimes zoomed the grainy photos. They depicted a helicopter, quite similar to the one they had traced to Jordan, but with a different tail number. Four men departed, all dressed in simple Western clothes, two with bags slung over their shoulders. Two of their faces were tilted toward the camera, but both were so distorted as to make them unrecognizable.

"How do we know this is Ibrahim?" Aimes looked up.

Rigby's grin widened. "That's the fun part. See, we have this AI program now that can correlate a clear picture of somebody's face with a distorted one, looking for unique angles and correlating identifiers that might—"

Aimes held up a hand. "Let me rephrase. I don't care how. *Do* we know that one of these men is Ibrahim?"

"We do. Keep scrolling."

The next several photos were zoomed in. They focused on the man on the right. The original image had been cropped and zoomed to focus on his face, leaving the overall picture even more grainy and distorted than before. But as Aimes proceeded to the end of the photo chain, that photo clarified. The AI went to work, filling in the gaps and making its own educated guesses about what the man could look like.

And revealing a face that was absolutely Abdel Ibrahim.

Aimes's gaze snapped back up again. "Where is he?"

"I've already reached out to the Cypriot authorities. They searched the helicopter and found it empty. Security footage of the area is limited, but shortly after the chopper landed a private flight departed on a one-way flight plan . . . for London."

Aimes's chest tightened. She shoved the iPad back, already estimating travel distance and time elapsed. If Ibrahim had departed Cyprus six hours ago, he would already be in London, likely slipping into the country under a fake passport. They were once more behind the eight ball. He was about to strike again.

"Get in touch with the PF. I want them back in the air immediately. Do everything you can to trace that plane to a destination airport. Tell Montgomery to dump the fuel on. I need them on the ground, *pronto*."

Aimes started for the door.

"And the British?" Rigby called after her.

"I'll call the British," Aimes said. "You just make sure they have backup."

36

The Roosevelt Room
The White House

"Roper is running for president," Maggie said. "He all but said so. He'll seek the Democratic nomination."

White House Chief of Staff Jill Easterling let out a groan, while Stratton simply shook his head. There was no surprise in his face. The three of them sat around one end of the polished conference table, flags of the United States and every branch of the armed forces standing in the background. The room was smaller than the Cabinet Room, sandwiched between the Oval Office and Stratton's vice presidential office. There were no windows, and all the doors were shut. Maggie had the lights turned down dim.

It helped her headache. It aided her strained eyes. Something about the Roosevelt Room felt vaguely like a cavern in contrast to the window-lined Oval Office. It felt safer.

"It's inevitable," Stratton said after a moment of contemplation. "We knew we'd face onslaughts from both parties in the next election. We beat them before, and we can do it again."

"We didn't expect onslaughts this *soon*," Easterling said. Maggie's squeaky chief of staff sat with little plastic glasses perched on her nose, platinum blonde hair swept back into a clip. An iPad joined to a keyboard sat in front of her alongside a coffee mug that was half as large as she was.

Maybe it was Maggie's own sense of pain and decay reflected onto another individual, but she couldn't help thinking that Easterling looked a little more tired than usual. More worn.

More out of answers.

"We'll deal with Roper when the time is right," Stratton said, still projecting confidence. "Honestly, this could be a good thing. The man has skeletons. I may know where to find them, and now I have plenty of time to do so. This isn't a fight he should have picked."

"I'm not worried about the election," Maggie said. "I'm worried about the Senate. RECA aside, he's blockading Aimes's confirmation, and now he claims to have an additional witness. I have zero idea who. This is becoming a media circus. We don't have *time* for this."

Maggie's tone rose in intensity as she spoke, turning hoarse near the end. She noted Stratton and Easterling exchanging a glance, and she sucked down coffee to collect herself.

The pain in her gut had developed to an almost blinding level. It was difficult to process clear thoughts. She'd taken her painkillers, and they simply weren't working. Her brain felt fogged. Her entire body was hot. It was like she was burning from the inside out.

And through it all, Maggie felt cornered. Not just by Congress, by Ibrahim, or by the hometown bodies she saw every time she closed her eyes. She felt the pressure of a panicked nation crushing her against the wall. She'd read all the headlines—Americans were rapidly losing faith. They hadn't even seen their president in nearly a month. She couldn't make television appearances, and any sort of voice-only broadcast would be too obvious in the digital age.

She wasn't presentable. She was falling apart. She needed . . .

Maggie's mind faded. Her vision blurred. She blinked hard.

"Are you okay?" Stratton spoke first. Maggie looked across the table and barely saw him. He was a blob, wavering in his chair. She blinked again, forcing back the confusion, and focused.

She *had* to focus.

"I'm good," she said. "I want us back on the offensive. We're losing on every front. We need a win—*now*."

"I agree," Easterling said. "But I think our agenda has been mandated, at this point. I don't see how we launch any initiative without dealing with RECA or the confirmation block. We've remained silent on both for too long."

"It was your idea to remain silent on the continued hearings," Maggie said. "You said it would make them look petty. Beneath us."

"You're right. And that was a bad call. I never expected them to gain this much steam."

"Well they have, Jill. And now they're about to steamroll us all."

Maggie's voice cracked and broke. Stratton held up a hand.

"We can only move forward. I recommend we select a priority and lean into that. Hopefully diminish the other fight. We know we want to stall RECA, and we know public support is against us. So I say we focus on the confirmation hearings. Make a strong statement—condemn the Senate for endangering American lives by distracting the CIA. Roper will go on the defensive. If we get lucky, he might slip up."

Easterling chewed her lip. Maggie's head spun. From the door behind her, a soft knock sounded. Stratton called an admittance, and a steward entered. Fresh coffee and donuts. Maggie fought to focus on Stratton's recommendations for a statement. They would release something through the White House press secretary, Farah Rahman. Make it a strong, almost bombastic condemnation. Then Stratton would strategically expose himself to the press pool, offering an opportunity for them to question him on the subject. That would allow the administration to generate a few direct sound bites without it *looking* like Stratton was filling in for Maggie.

It wasn't ideal. Not even close. But Easterling thought it was a better idea than Maggie appearing on camera in her present condition. As bad as the words stung, Maggie thought she might be right.

"This came for you, ma'am." The steward placed an envelope on the tabletop next to Maggie. It was addressed simply to "Madam President." Typed, not handwritten. There was no letterhead or return address.

Maggie lifted the envelope and flipped it over as Stratton and Easterling continued to strategize. She pulled at the closure, ripping paper. A simple card fell out, thick and heavy, made of cream paper with a symbol emblazoned on one side.

It was the crest of the Central Intelligence Agency. Maggie flipped the card over to find a single word printed in blue ink. Bold handwriting, written with passion. Dotted with a period.

Karma.

Sudden dread descended over her like a black cloud. Maggie flipped the card again and looked back inside the envelope. There was nothing. She was just pivoting to Stratton when Easterling breathed a curse from the end of the table. Maggie ratcheted that way instead. Easterling was fixated on her iPad.

"What is it?" Maggie snapped.

Easterling didn't answer. Instead, she simply rotated the iPad. The screen displayed an article from CNN. The timestamp was only two minutes old. The photograph was of a bald man with glasses and owl eyes, a face Maggie knew well.

The headline read: FORMER CIA DIRECTOR TO TESTIFY BEFORE SENATE INTELLIGENCE COMMITTEE, CLAIMS: "PRESIDENT GUILTY OF CRIMINAL PRACTICES."

Maggie's heart lurched. The pain in her stomach redoubled, so sharp and sudden she couldn't help but wince. Stratton stood and scooped up the iPad. Maggie placed both hands on the edge of the table and moved to stand. Her knees went rigid halfway up, and the pain raced from her gut straight up her spine and into her head.

It detonated there like a hand grenade. Maggie stumbled halfway out of the chair. Stratton's gaze snapped up, and panic crossed his face. The iPad fell. He shouted something, but Maggie didn't hear a word.

She only heard her own heartbeat, thundering like a drum. She felt the table slide away from her hands as she pitched sideways, gliding past the chair. The ceiling spun overhead in slow motion as she plummeted toward the floor.

And then everything went black.

37

London, England

Abdel Ibrahim landed at a private airfield ten klicks outside the city and departed the plane immediately. There was a rental car waiting, hired under the shield of a British shell company set up by Ibrahim's shadowy ally.

The man calling all the shots. The man who had provided—and then *taken*—the weapon.

Ibrahim was joined by two soldiers from Afghanistan. They had been Taliban, at one point. Now they thirsted for something more aggressive. It was Ibrahim's ally who'd connected the three men. One of them was a helicopter pilot, trained by the Americans, no less, before defecting to the side of true believers. The other was little better than a bullet sponge, but he was big and strong and could help move large and heavy things.

That sort of brutish skillset would be useful in the near future. For now, Ibrahim only needed to know that he was safe from the pursuing dogs biting at his heels—the American dogs. He really had no idea how they had found him on the oil platform. He'd thought the trick with the helicopter parked in Amman would buy him some time. Clearly, he was dealing with quick thinkers. A smart enemy.

And a lethal enemy.

In east London, Ibrahim ditched the rental car in favor of a battered Volkswagen left in a parking garage. Another gift from the ally. It was less flashy than the rental, and even less linked to Ibrahim. He rode in the back seat, conscious of the thousands of security cameras that blanketed the British capital like a net. One clear shot of his face, and the next stage of this plan could be terminated before it even got started.

At least London was in no way short of Middle Eastern men. There was nothing unusual about three brown guys riding in an anonymous silver car through winding streets crowded by buildings two and three hundred years old.

When they reached the warehouse on London's industrial side, not far from the River Thames, Ibrahim instructed the ex–helicopter pilot to pull straight inside. The door rolled shut behind them. The space was empty save for a single shipping crate pushed up against one wall. Chinese letters adorned the box, sloppily stenciled in black spray paint. The English translation printed beneath it marked the shipment as a load of children's car seats.

Ibrahim knew there were no car seats housed within. At least, not beneath the uppermost layer. Instead he would find the equipment necessary to complete the next phase of his mission. Tools, dry food, water, and weapons.

More gifts from his generous and controlling ally.

Ibrahim stepped out of the car and walked into the shadows furthest from the crate while his men went to work opening it. He drew a sat phone. He dialed a long international number.

The ally didn't keep him waiting.

"You have arrived?"

"Yes," Ibrahim said.

"Everything is in order?"

"Yes."

"Any signs of a tail?"

"No."

Ibrahim's voice was clipped and direct, not only because he disliked communicating with a person he still didn't have a name for, but because he was still suppressing his own irritation.

In a place like London, the weapon's destructive power could be . . . incredible. Magnificent. An unprecedented throat punch to the West, never before seen in jihad. He could have transported it here. Even now, he could be ready to detonate it.

But his ally had other plans, and Ibrahim was short on leverage. There would still be blood spilt in London—a lot of it. The one-two punch the ally had arranged would unleash terror true believers could thrive on for years.

Although . . . maybe not Ibrahim.

"Your shipment is on schedule," the ally said.

"You got it out of Cyprus?" Ibrahim made no effort to hide his surprise. With the Americans so close on his heels, it might have been reasonable to assume this phase of the plan would have already failed.

"We're good at what we do," the ally said. "The shipment will arrive as planned. Remain under cover and stand by for delivery updates."

Ibrahim hung up without comment and pocketed the phone. He watched his men unpacking fresh MP5 submachine guns from the crate, pre-loaded with thirty-round magazines of 9mm hollow points. More magazines lay in the box.

Enough firepower to lay down a few dozen people . . .

Or keep Ibrahim and his men alive long enough to slaughter many more.

38

Beirut, Lebanon

"London, London! Let's go. Wheels up!"

Reed hadn't slept well in the tail of the Gulfstream. The buzz of the bourbon clouded his mind, and as soon as he closed his eyes he saw his child again—April. Not as a clear vision of fields of gold with the oak tree and tire swing, but as vague and blurry images that came and went but never really disappeared.

Her face was always there. Her voice in the background, happy laughter irregularly broken by horrific, panicked screams. Total desperation, absolute fear.

And then Ibrahim—then it was always the demon face of her killer, blood dripping from his lips, leering down at Reed.

It was Lucy who woke him with a tap on the cabin door. Reed sat up with a lurch, his t-shirt soaked with sweat and sticking to his chest. A quick inspection of his watch confirmed that three full hours had passed. The rain still beat down from outside as he called Lucy in. She extended the iPad. Reed read the messages from Langley.

And then he was on his feet. The nightmares were relegated to the back of his mind and he was lurching into the main cabin, calling to his team. Directing Corbyn and Strickland back into the cockpit.

CntrlCmmd: Wheels up. We have a new target.

The CIA had traced Ibrahim straight into England's capital city, and based solely on the evidence collected by the Prosecution Force in Beirut and on the deck of the oil platform, they had to assume he was carrying a WMD. It was a five-hour direct flight from Beirut to London, and Aimes wanted the Prosecution Force in the air immediately.

She didn't have to ask twice. Even as the Gulfstream taxied to the runway, Reed knew his team was yet again behind. He could feel the crushing pressure in his chest as he strapped into a captain's chair and the jet engines howled in his ears. Corbyn drove the plane like a sports car, dumping power and lifting off with enough aggression to qualify her for naval air service.

Strickland sat alongside her, but he'd given up arguing or attempting to regain any control. Corbyn was in charge, aviator sunglasses slid halfway down her nose as she chewed gum and banked hard northwest.

Toward England.

"The agency thinks he took a private plane out of Cyprus," Lucy reported. "They have people on the ground in Larnaca inspecting an abandoned helicopter and searching for leads. They'll keep us updated if anything is discovered, but the assumption is that he's already in London."

"He is," Reed said. "He wouldn't have sat still twice. We're already behind."

He leaned out from the seat and shouted toward the cockpit. "Hey, Brit! You got contacts in the SIS?"

Before Corbyn could answer, Lucy jumped back in.

"I'm already arranging for the agency to connect with SIS headquarters and facilitate our arrival. They'll meet us at the airstrip and provide transportation."

Reed shot Lucy an approving nod. She flashed a smile. "I told you I would be good for something."

Reed couldn't deny it was nice to have somebody ironing out the logistics, but he was a great deal less thrilled by Lucy's next statement.

"Langley is placing us under the temporary authority of the British so long as we're in London. We won't be armed. We're there in an advisory and support role only. The agency wanted me to emphasize that. No heroics."

Yeah. Okay.

Reed pivoted in the seat to address Turk and Wolfgang. Both men sat across the aisle from him on either side of the narrow table. Wolfgang was busy cleaning his concealed Glock 29, scrubbing away any chance of contamination from rainwater that may have leaked inside his prosthetic during the oil platform gunfight. Turk was eating—per usual.

"You can get that thing past sophisticated security?" Reed asked.

Wolfgang snorted. "What do you think?"

"Good. Turk, see if you can slip anything into your pack. At least a couple handguns. I don't want to be left relying on the Brits if things go sideways."

"I heard that!" Corbyn shouted.

Reed ignored her. "As soon as we get to London, we go to work with whatever we have. This guy does *not* slip away again. Period. I don't care what we have to burn down."

Even as Reed spoke, his mind traveled back to the oil platform. He'd seen it in his dreams, also. He'd envisioned the shot he didn't take, but already his mind was playing tricks on him. Had there even *been* a shot? Had he imagined it?

Turk wiped his mouth with the back of one hand, then exchanged a glance with Wolfgang. Neither man spoke.

"What?" Reed snapped.

Turk lowered his sandwich and pivoted in the seat. "You square, dude?"

"What do you mean, am I square?"

"I mean, are you sure you're up for this? You're starting to sound a little frazzled. That crap on the oil platform—"

"What about it?" Reed's body went rigid, sudden uncertainty clouding his mind. Had Turk *seen* him hesitate? Did he already know?

"It was gonna happen," Turk drawled. "You made the right call letting him go. We don't know what he had on that chopper. We lost a round. That's okay. We stay cool."

They were reassuring words and Reed knew that Turk meant them, but they did nothing to calm the acidic burn in his stomach. Even when he divorced his mind from the oil platform, he instantly thought back to Tennessee. To the bomb blast. To the hot kiss of fire on his face. To Banks pitching over the stage, torn through by shrapnel.

To the life that would never be, obliterated in a second.

"When this guy goes after *your* family, then you talk about staying cool," Reed snarled. "Until then, you keep your opinions to yourself, or get the hell off the plane."

Turk's eyebrows rose. He held Reed's gaze. Then he simply resumed his meal, not saying a word. The rest of the plane had gone quiet also, but Reed didn't care. It needed to be said.

He leaned back in his seat and closed his eyes, breathing slowly. He saw fire. He saw blood.

He saw his unborn daughter fading into the black.

"God save us . . . "

It was Lucy who spoke. Reed's eyes snapped open to find her fixated on her iPad, her jaw hanging slack. He sat up.

"What?"

Lucy didn't answer. She simply passed him the iPad, and Reed scanned the screen. It was MSNBC—a news article. He only needed to read the headline to get the message.

PRESIDENT TROUSDALE COLLAPSES AT WHITE HOUSE, RUSHED TO HOSPITAL. DOCTORS SUSPECT LIVER FAILURE.

39

Walter Reed National Military Medical Center
Bethesda, Maryland

Stratton remained in the conference room attached to the presidential medical center while Maggie was under observation. She'd passed out in the Roosevelt Room. She hadn't resumed consciousness even when the medical staff arrived. The airlift to Bethesda had been immediate.

Somewhere along the way word had leaked. Already reports of the president's condition were spreading like wildfire across the media. Stratton gave a cursory glance to the headlines before sending a quick email to Farah Rahman instructing her on an address from the press room. It would be short, sweet, and light on details. Just enough to pacify the media while Stratton figured out what the hell to do next.

The stress that descended on his shoulders the moment Maggie collapsed was instant, but he couldn't pretend to be surprised. He'd been monitoring his boss's condition for weeks, and it was obvious that her health was in decline. He'd tried to broach the subject with her multiple times. Maggie had shut him down across the board.

He always knew this was a possibility. It was the very nature of the vice presidency, to remain on standby for an emergency, and this wasn't even the first time. It still felt like a punch to the gut. With Ibrahim on the loose, Congress on the offensive, and America on a rollercoaster of fear, this couldn't have come at a worse time.

Stratton's phone rang and he answered without checking. He already knew who it was. Jill Easterling's high-pitched voice was undercut by strain, but she remained calm. A true professional.

"Any update, sir?"

"I'm waiting for the doctor now. She's been under examination for nearly two hours. It can't be good."

A brief pause.

"What do you need from me, Mr. Acting President?"

Good woman.

Stratton didn't need to hear the title to know it was his, but he appreciated Easterling saying it. Another sign of a true professional, Maggie's chief of staff understood the importance of keeping the machine running. Just because the lead actress had collapsed on center stage didn't mean the show could stop.

"Are you familiar with the philosophies of Rahm Emanuel?" Stratton asked.

"Never let a crisis go to waste," Easterling said.

"Exactly. The president's condition is out of our control, but we can strike while our enemies think we are down. I've already instructed Rahman on a press release. Work with her to weave in a statement about the Senate hamstringing the White House. I want Roper to feel the pressure."

"I think he's already feeling it. He postponed his hearing with former director O'Brien."

Stratton grunted. "That's an unexpected win."

A long moment of silence. Easterling's voice quieted. "Do you . . . have any idea what O'Brien may know?"

Stratton had been considering that question since the moment he read the CNN headline. *Criminal practices* was both a bold accusation and also a vague one. Any number of things could fall under that general umbrella.

Technically speaking, jaywalking constituted a criminal practice. It was against the law.

Somehow, Stratton didn't think Maggie had been caught jaywalking. He'd only known O'Brien for a couple of short years, but his interactions with the man had taught him that the former director of the CIA wasn't the type to make idle threats. The very nature of his previous employment was indicative of a man who knew things.

Stratton would need to find a way to shut him down—hard—without appearing to be on the defensive. It was another problem atop a growing heap.

"No idea," Stratton said at last. "But it can't be good. Work with your people and see what you can find out. Whoever leaked the subject of O'Brien's testimony to CNN could be a lead. It's safe to say Roper's cabinet knows something. Let's make some phone calls."

"Will do, sir. Please call if you think of anything else."

The door swung open at the end of the room, and Stratton ended the call. The woman who stepped in wore white scrubs and glasses, her hair restrained behind a surgical cap. She offered a tight nod and extended her hand as Stratton stood.

"Mr. Vice President. Thank you for being here."

"Absolutely, Doctor. Please have a seat."

Doctor Fletcher joined him at the table. Stratton closed his laptop and folded his hands. He didn't ask. He didn't have to.

"The president has experienced traumatic liver failure," Fletcher said. "I'm not exactly sure what triggered it, but I would presume that it was extreme stress. It's been a concern for a while. The regeneration of her injured liver from the assassination attempt has stalled to the point of total failure. Toxins in her blood built to the level of triggering unconsciousness. That's what made her pass out."

"We couldn't see this coming?" Stratton knew his question sounded like an accusation, but he couldn't help it.

"We could, sir. But that doesn't mean we could stop it. I advised the president to step away from public service, but of course I couldn't make her. Once her liver failed, the toxins developed quickly. She would have died if we got her here a half hour later."

Stratton ran his tongue beneath his upper lip and sorted quickly through the data. It was a lot to be hit with, but really only one thing mattered.

"What's her prognosis?"

"We have her sedated currently. An induced coma. Likely, she'll need to remain in that state until we can find a transplant."

"A transplant?"

"There's no saving her liver at this stage. We can use hemodialysis to filter her blood in the short term, but eventually she'll die without the transplant."

"How long do we have?" Stratton's tone remained direct and emotionless. There was no point in panicking now.

"Impossible to say. Days. Maybe weeks. A month, at the most. I've already given directions for her to be placed on the donor list, but I should warn you that several critical cases stand ahead of her. It's a complete roll of the dice. We might have four suitable livers available tomorrow, or we might not have one for weeks. I really can't say."

Stratton chewed his lip, trying to imagine what in the world he was supposed to do next. He'd mentally prepared himself for this possibility months ago, but that didn't make it easy.

Especially with half a dozen house fires raging through the White House.

"Thank you for your help, Doctor. Please keep me updated, and let me know if there's any way my office can assist."

Fletcher shook his hand, then departed the room. Stratton ran one hand through his graying black hair and breathed slowly. He wanted a drink, and somehow that felt very disrespectful in light of Maggie's current predicament. Maybe too many drinks and too much stress had been the problem.

Pick a target, Jordan. Make a punch list. One fight at a time.

Stratton's phone buzzed, and he lifted it to find a message from Easterling. Short and straight to the point.

Roper rescheduled O'Brien's testimony for Monday. He's not backing down.

Stratton's gaze flicked to the top of his cell phone screen, where the day was displayed. It was Wednesday. Roper was turning up the heat.

Stratton put his thumbs on the screen and shot back a quick reply.

Get in touch with O'Brien. I want to meet with him—in person.

40

Galați, Romania

Ivan's ribcage still burned like fire as he handed the driver a colorful roll of euros and stepped out of the cab. Technically speaking, Romania didn't use the euro as an official currency, favoring their own *leu* instead, but Ivan had overpaid and the driver didn't complain. As the car rushed away Ivan stepped onto the sidewalk, one arm hoisting a small duffel bag while the other remained clamped to his side, adding pressure to the wound.

He'd bled a lot as Serge's gunshot ripped through flesh and scraped a rib, coming only a few inches from shattering his heart. If he hadn't grabbed the table and shoved it into the old man's chest, Serge wouldn't have missed. He was a good shot. He always had been.

But Serge was also old, and he had missed. He moved more slowly than he used to, and Ivan didn't hesitate. He rammed the table even as the pain erupted in his side. Serge toppled out of his chair and fumbled the Makarov. Ivan exploded out of his own chair and rammed a foot over Serge's hand. He found the gun.

He shot his mentor in the forehead even as Serge stared up at him with heartbroken, apologetic eyes. Ivan himself could barely see those devastated eyes. His own had blurred over, hot tears bubbling up for the first time in decades.

Then came the soldiers. They leapt from their vehicle and ran straight to the door, attempting at first to breach it by force instead of using explosives. It was a stupid mistake that cost them valuable time, and then their lives. Ivan found his way into the house and located Serge's weapons stash with ease. He knew how the old man thought, and knew there would be heavy weaponry near the core of the house where a person was most likely to shelter in the event of an invasion. As the soldiers were busy setting the charge, Ivan found the locker hidden beneath the coffee table. He ripped the door open. He located a row of small arms, including two AK-12s, an American-built Remington sniper rifle, a Croatian-made 12-gauge shotgun, and a French-built FAMAS rifle chambered in 5.56 NATO.

Ivan went for the FAMAS. Not because he liked or even respected the NATO cartridge, but because the FAMAS dumped those cartridges at a rate of over a thousand rounds per minute.

The first round slammed into the rifle's chamber as the breaching charge slammed against the outside door. He could hear the soldiers shouting, repeating familiar commands in Russian. They would back up next, taking temporary cover. Pressing their backs against the wall on either side of the door while the charge detonated. Then would come flash bangs before the entry.

More wasted time.

Ivan returned to the veranda and leapt over the glass rail onto the narrow ledge of rock running alongside the back of the house. With the cliff to his left, he walked quickly around the corner. He passed the trash cans and a small garden. It was neat and orderly, lush with green produce.

Ivan's eyes stung again.

He reached the face of the house just as the breaching charge erupted. Smoke blasted from the face of the house, and one of the soldiers shouted.

Ivan never stopped walking. He pulled the FAMAS into his shoulder and clamped down on the trigger, unleashing short bursts of death nearly back to back, moving quickly from one target to the next. The first guy went down before he knew what hit him. The second turned and caught 5.56

NATO rounds to the face. The third was fumbling with his gun when his lights went out.

The fourth actually got off a shot, but it was wild and way off target. By the time Ivan reached the front door, the FAMAS was empty, and the reverberating gunshots evaporated over the cliffside. He inspected each man to ensure death before stripping away Udav pistols and AM-17 rifles. The dead men wore the black uniforms of Russian FSB agents—the policing grandchild of the KGB. Ivan couldn't help but think that if the four bodies in front of him had *actually* been KGB, they would have put up a better fight.

He torched the house before he left, piling the bodies in the living room and flooding the home with propane using the gas stovetop. A match was all it took for the home to erupt into flames, quickly building into a beacon atop the cliff. The fire wouldn't truly hide anything, but it would at least slow down his pursuers.

Ivan took the Mercedes SUV used by the FSB agents and fled Crimea. He used the causeway, so frequently blasted by Ukrainian missiles during the war, to access Russian-controlled Ukraine. There was a pair of checkpoints, but none of the frontline soldiers working them knew to be on the lookout for a fleeing SVR agent who knew too much.

Hours later, he'd switched vehicles twice. He ditched all the weapons save a Udav handgun before attempting a border crossing into Romania. He used his fake Polish passport. He reached Galați.

And now he was here, still on the run. Still fighting a nagging wound in his side that had been hastily and improperly sealed using one of the FSB agents' med kits. His head pounded. His chest was drum-tight.

But he kept going, because yet again he knew something that could put the fate of the world in jeopardy. He reached a hostel and checked in with cash—more euros. The clerk didn't complain. He found an isolated corner of the second-floor room with nobody around and dug out his cell phone.

There was only one American number in his contact list, but one would be enough.

41

RAF Station Northolt
Hillingdon, London

The Gulfstream touched down in the United Kingdom under Strickland's control with a gentle kiss of tires on pavement. Through the windows Reed noted a row of hangars, some of which were open to expose the noses of Dassault Falcon 900LX jets awaiting use. The airfield buzzed, but it didn't appear overly military. There were civilian aircraft visible, also, and multiple helicopters.

"Multi-use airfield," Corbyn said, catching him looking. "Executive military transport, mostly. Some protection wing stuff. Flown out of here loads of times."

The Gulfstream stopped, and the engines wound down. Reed looked to Turk as the big man shouldered his backpack. Turk nodded once. Wolfgang had already replaced the Glock 29 inside the hidden compartment in his prosthetic and walked easily to the door.

"Can I stretch my legs this time?" Strickland didn't bother to hide the irritation in his voice.

Corbyn grinned and ruffled the top of his head. "Sure thing, mate. Get yourself some fish and chips! You've earned it."

Strickland glowered, but he kept quiet. The stairway struck the tarmac, and Reed was the first to depart.

It was cold in England, much more so than he expected. Gray clouds covered the horizon, and a steady breeze tore at the Union Jack hoisted atop a nearby flagpole. Even before the remainder of his team had departed the jet, a pair of black Mercedes SUVs were racing toward them from across the airfield. At a distance, Reed detected black suits and dark sunglasses from behind the glass, and noticed Corbyn tense.

"Oh, goodie . . ." she said.

Reed didn't bother to ask. He figured the truth would be revealed in short order, and he wasn't wrong. The two SUVs ground to a halt at the nose of the Gulfstream, and the black suits stepped out. From the rear seat of the nearer SUV a tall man with thick gray hair and a rosy face appeared, buttoning his jacket as he approached. He didn't even look at Reed.

He looked at Corbyn.

"Well, old girl. You just can't stay away, can you?"

Corbyn offered a sheepish smile. "Deputy Director."

The tall man didn't extend his hand. He looked instead to Reed, taking a moment to size him up. Pursing his lips, and thinking. Reed didn't so much as blink.

"I take it you're *The Prosecutor*?"

"That's right."

"Aimes warned me you were cold."

"Not a lot to smile about at the moment."

"No . . . I suppose there isn't." The deputy director swept his gaze across the small crowd, moving quickly across Wolfgang before he stopped on Turk. He snorted.

"Looks like somebody ate their porridge."

Turk didn't miss a beat. "Got any more?"

That brought the hint of a smile. The deputy director turned back for the SUV.

"Come along then, Yanks. We've made room for you."

Reed and Wolfgang slid into the back seat of the Mercedes that the deputy director took shotgun in. Turk, left with only the middle seat in the back, opted for the second vehicle. Corbyn seemed only too happy to join him. Lucy would remain with Strickland to monitor communication from Langley, as before.

The moment the doors closed, the driver shifted into gear and the tires spun. The airfield faded quickly around them, and Reed noted the digital compass built into the dash reading SE—they were headed deeper into the city.

"I'm Deputy Director John Arnold," the man in the left seat said, leaning back with his fingers interlaced and his thumbs twiddling steadily. "Your boss—Sarah Aimes—and I go way back. She wouldn't say much about who or what you are. I suppose I can guess. I'll be a little more upfront about who I am. I'm a man with an agency directorate to run, and precious little time for bollocks. I've even less time for reckless heroics. Am I clear?"

Reed nodded.

"Excellent. So tell me what you know."

Reed began at Tennessee and ran quickly through the highlights. He figured Arnold already knew most of the details. Aimes would have sent him a full report, along with a dossier on Ibrahim. He recounted the highlights anyway, because he couldn't be sure what detail might be important. Arnold listened in rapt silence as the Mercedes blazed through the outskirts of London.

"And you have no idea what this weapon could be?" Arnold asked once Reed had concluded.

"The NBC suits we located in Beirut are indicative of a WMD. He's favored chemical weapons and small bombs before. That seems the most logical possibility."

Arnold simply grunted, his lips pursed tightly together. Reed thought he detected increased agitation in the sound—maybe more stress. Reed felt it in his own chest. It somehow hurt to breathe.

"We must presume the worst," Arnold said at last. "I've already contacted the military and the local bobbies. We've swept the airport, of course. The aircraft your agency marked landed six hours ago. A hired car departed, but it seems the occupants traded vehicles shortly after. We found the hire abandoned."

Wolfgang's phone rang as the deputy director spoke, and he dug it out with a squint at the screen. Reed barely noticed, the knots in his gut twisting as he pictured Ibrahim departing the jet, taking the rental car, and driving into the city.

He's here.

The demon face returned to his mind, along with a flashing memory of his child's scream. The mental sound temporarily disoriented him, and he blinked hard. His heart rate had quickened. His hands felt clammy.

I'm going to kill him. I'm going to kill him.

Reed's repeated train of thought was derailed by a single word from Wolfgang.

"*What?*"

He turned to see the Wolf sitting bolt upright with his cell phone clamped against one ear, eyes wide. "You're *sure?* When? *Georgia?*"

Reed pivoted in his seat, and Arnold looked into the rearview mirror. The strain on the Wolf's face was both instant and absolute, a far cry from the practiced calm he had exhibited only minutes prior. It looked almost like panic.

"What else do you have?" A pause. "Send me everything, immediately."

Wolfgang hung up the phone. He turned to Reed.

"That was Ivan."

Reed squinted. "He's resurfaced?"

"Apparently. And he's been busy. He backtracked Melnyk's sourcing of the VX. It led him to an abandoned Soviet weapons depot in Georgia. He found evidence of missing VX . . . and something else."

Arnold spun around the seat. He didn't bother to ask who Ivan was. It was a moot point.

"What else?" Arnold and Reed said it together.

"Those NBC suits weren't being used for the C," Wolfgang said. "They were being used for the N. Ibrahim got his hands on a nuke."

42

Langley, Virginia

Aimes received the call from SIS headquarters in London only minutes after the Prosecution Force landed. It was John Arnold on the line, and in stark contrast to his usual jovial manner, the deputy director sounded alive with tension.

And frustration.

She listened in perfect silence for twenty seconds, her own blood running cold. Then she pressed the speaker button so that Rigby could hear. Her own deputy sat across the desk from her, notepad at the ready.

"Are my people there?" Aimes said.

"Right here," Arnold said. "You're on speaker."

"You spoke directly to the contact, Wolfgang?"

"Yes."

"Who was it?"

No answer. Aimes gritted her teeth. She might have smacked Wolfgang if he were sitting across from her, but it really didn't matter. She already knew the contact was Ivan Sidorov, the Russian semi-defector who seemed always to be playing on the sidelines of the Prosecution Force. Wolfgang had protected him over his Belsky intelligence. He'd protected him again over the Melnyk VX intelligence. When Wolfgang had flown to the U.S. to deliver the news of a possible chemical weapons attack, Ivan had remained behind. Apparently the Russian didn't trust America, even if he was willing to go out of his way to help protect her.

None of that really mattered. Ivan was two for two on the accuracy of his intelligence. She could only assume he was correct again.

"Is the weapon mobile?" Another question Aimes already assumed the answer to, but she might as well ask.

"My contact indicated that it could be," Wolfgang said. "Possibly a low-yield or tactical device. Something easy enough to shift around on a helicopter or a small airplane."

Aimes breathed a curse. She bit her lip. There wasn't a lot she could say to Arnold other than "so sorry about this." Not that it was her fault, but if Ibrahim had never escaped America, this wouldn't be happening.

"You have the full use of my people, John. We'll work the lead from our end. Whatever you need, let me know. I'll be in my office."

"Thank you, Sarah." Arnold's voice was clipped but calm. A true professional. The line terminated, and Aimes immediately dialed her assistant.

"Yes, ma'am?"

"Get me the White House. I need to speak to the acting president."

"Yes, ma'am."

Aimes lifted the receiver and held it against her face while it rang. She pivoted to Rigby.

"Welcome to the big leagues, Silas. This is where the circus gets real."

43

Washington, DC

James O'Dell left his mother's sagging Louisiana double-wide the moment he saw the news about the president. He'd only recently arrived, in fact, taking a detour through New Orleans after Maggie kicked him out of the White House. He wasn't much of a drinker—not usually—but the hot knives of unexpected pain that lanced through his gut the moment she told him to leave were as bad as the moment he'd walked in on Vickie, his ex-wife, tangled in the sheets of his own bed with a fellow Louisiana State Police officer. As bad as the day a Louisiana judge had ruled in favor of Vickie taking full custody of their nine-year-old daughter Holly.

As bad as the day that both Vickie and Holly departed Louisiana altogether, fully abandoning him. It was crushing, it was absolute, it was overwhelming. O'Dell wasn't an emotional man, and he never knew how to process pain. So while he may not have been much of a drinker during good times, he knew exactly where to turn in bad times—Bourbon Street. One bar after another, knocking back anything the bartender would pour until the days blended together and he could no longer stumble back to his hotel. Then he would catch a cab out into the parish, and show up on his widowed mother's rotting front porch to sleep it off.

He was only seven hours into that recovery phase when his mother's Cajun shout roused him from the bedroom. She was watching TV and chain-smoking, much as she always did. The dated television set displayed a newscast about how Muddy Maggie Trousdale had collapsed in the White House and was thought to be undergoing liver failure.

O'Dell left immediately, throwing a few basic essentials into a backpack before he called another cab back to Louis Armstrong Airport, ignoring the profanity-laden shouts of his mother and purchasing a one-way ticket to DC on the way. The flight was direct. The hours dragged by in slow motion. O'Dell sat folded into a window seat overlooking the 737's lefthand engine and returning to a practice he only ever indulged in when even the alcohol failed him—prayer.

As a born and raised Catholic, O'Dell considered himself a religious man only so much as it concerned census papers. But he knew how to pray, and he'd prayed for Maggie more than he'd prayed for anyone except Holly. He'd prayed for her when she was cut down by a would-be assassin's bullet. He'd prayed for her while she clung to life in Chicago, while she recovered slowly, while they fell into each other's arms during those many passionate nights in the White House residence.

He'd even prayed for her over his beer on Bourbon Street. Not only for her to want him back, but more importantly for her to recover. To be strong, to lead the country into greatness. He couldn't explain his commitment to America's swamp girl any more than he could define his own obsessive-compulsive tendencies to throw his body over any and every grenade that threatened her. It looked like love, and maybe it was, but despite their intimate relationship O'Dell struggled to view Maggie in a romantic light.

It was closer to obsession. Blind and total loyalty. A compulsive desire to be near her and see her protected. Maybe it was all the failures that had stacked up over his long life of mediocrity and defeat, but he *believed* in Maggie. He'd attached his own fortunes and identity to her in a way that now felt impossible to reverse.

If she was lying on a hospital bed, clinging to life and in need of a liver, he was ready to donate his own. They would probably need to let it detox first. Let the vodka clear out. But then they could have it. He'd eat a bullet if necessary.

Why not? Maggie was all he had left to live for.

But when he reached Walter Reed Medical Center, he never got the chance to offer his liver, or even see the president. They barred him from entry. Even his White House ID wasn't enough to gain access. They wouldn't update him on her condition, and they wouldn't even let him past the first round of secure-access doors.

They denied him everything, so O'Dell turned to the next logical point of attack—Maggie's temporary replacement. He took a cab to the White House, still dressed in stained jeans and a smelly t-shirt, and used his ID to get in. He found Stratton in the West Wing, marching from his vice presidential office toward the Oval, a crowd of aides rushing at his side.

Stratton's gaze widened when he saw O'Dell, first surprised, then a little put off. Probably by the smell. Finally the trace of compassion crossed the VP's strained face.

But only for a moment. The man was on a warpath. O'Dell didn't know and didn't care what the latest and greatest national emergency was. He only cared about Maggie.

"I need to see her," O'Dell said.

Stratton paused in the hallway, hesitating, then quickly dismissing the aides. They scuttled off. He turned back to O'Dell.

"I thought you left," he said, simply.

"I did. I need to see her."

The repeated request was met by no indicator of agreement from Stratton. He simply sighed.

"Is she dying?" O'Dell asked. His voice wavered.

"We don't know," Stratton said. "Possibly. Her liver is failing. She may—"

"She can have mine."

The words spilled out before O'Dell could stop them. Stratton took a half step forward and put a hand on O'Dell's shoulder.

"They're doing everything they can, James. You have to trust that."

"Can I see her?" he pressed. Once more his voice almost broke. Stratton squeezed his shoulder.

"Go get yourself cleaned up. The residence is empty. Shower off and rest . . . we'll talk soon."

O'Dell was already shaking his head. "No. I want—"

He never got the chance to finish. The aides returned, somebody calling out after Stratton. The voice was alarmed. Apparently Interim Director Aimes was on the phone. The message was urgent.

"I have to go," Stratton said. "Clean yourself up."

The acting president turned away before O'Dell could stop him. In an instant he was gone, stepping into the Cabinet Room. The door shut with a thud, leaving O'Dell suddenly alone in the hallway. His eyes fogged over and his throat went dry. He tried to swallow and couldn't.

He could only think of Maggie.

44

Eastern Hemisphere
Undisclosed Location

The hotel room's windows were covered in blackout curtains, the door double-latched, and towels laid against the bottom to muffle whatever subdued noises might leak out. The room was on the eleventh floor—not a cheap hotel, but not an expensive one, either. Right in the middle, it was a working-class type of place with a great view that the man inside couldn't care less about.

He kept the lights off and headphones clamped over his ears for stealthy communication. He sat at the little desk with a pair of laptops propped open, neither of them linked to the hotel's complimentary internet connection. He used satellite connectivity instead, which was a risk, because it could give away his position. Then again, it was so heavily encrypted that the risk of discovery was minimal, and nobody was looking for him anyway.

Not yet.

The righthand computer screen ran thick with a multitude of windows, ranging from deep corners of the dark web—and dark corners of the deep web—to encrypted email servers and even American news websites. Those news websites were alive with reports of President Trousdale's recent admittance into a hospital for liver failure. Apparently, she had collapsed.

That was both unexpected and interesting. Perhaps Fedor Volkov's impossible shot hadn't been a complete waste of effort after all.

Pivoting away from CNN, the man focused instead on a chat box. It was one of those dark corners of the deep web, a place not indexed by search engines or guarded by a simple firewall. It was a place you had to be looking for to find, like an obscure village in the middle of Siberia. The chat window itself was double encrypted, providing additional layers of security. The person on the other end was codenamed *Cyclops.* He was a deep cover asset it had taken years to develop. The man in the hotel room hadn't done that work himself, of course. He was a manager and a technical genius, not so much a handler. His bosses had done the development. Now that development was paying off. Cyclops was coming through with a new message, a critical piece of data.

Americans have arrived in London and rendezvoused with SIS deputy director at RAF Station Northolt. Now at Vauxhall.

The man in the hotel read the message, but didn't reply. There was no need to. Cyclops wouldn't be monitoring the chat box anyway, and there was nothing more the man in the hotel needed to know. This was sufficient.

It told him the plot had succeeded.

He switched to another deep web window, this one used for voice communication, and input a password. He selected a digital contact. His headphone chimed with a digital ringtone. The voice that answered on the other end was distorted, sounding a little like a robot in an American science fiction film. The man in the hotel room knew who it was, of course, but that didn't matter either. It was only a middleman.

"The distraction is working," he said. "Notify Centaur that the Americans have followed Ibrahim to London. They'll track him there."

"What about the little one?" the robot voice asked.

"We found a small cargo plane in Cyprus. The little one arrived on schedule in London. Ibrahim has picked it up. It's ready to go."

"And the big one?"

The man in the hotel looked away from the deep web screens, pivoting instead to the second laptop. It displayed a single window—a satellite feed with a view of the North Atlantic. A lone beacon blipped, now well clear of the Mediterranean and closing on the Americas. Still chugging steadily westward.

The man in the hotel smiled. "It's right on schedule."

45

Vauxhall Cross
London, England

Reed had once heard that the United Kingdom boasted one surveillance camera for every fourteen people, and moments after stepping into the operations center at SIS headquarters, he believed it. The bank of screens running along the far wall was alive with active video feeds from not only London but the entire southeastern corner of the country. While advanced computer software zipped through thousands of still and moving images, scanning faces and comparing them to photos of Abdel Ibrahim, dozens of analysts examined every possible match by hand, marking anything of further interest for escalated review.

The system was breathtaking—both massive and finely tuned, running with an efficiency that would put an automobile factory to shame. The room was loud with ringing phones and profanity-laden shouts, but order remained paramount. Nobody panicked.

Everyone was hell-bent on locating the United Kingdom's new number-one enemy.

"We have security footage posted at intersections, public areas, ports, parking garages . . . pretty much everywhere." Deputy Director John Arnold stood on an elevated walkway alongside Reed, gesturing openly to the operations center. "We use an advanced form of facial recognition software supercharged by AI. It targets not only facial features but also behavioral characteristics. Things like the way he walks, or how he might move his hands while speaking."

Arnold turned to Reed, his face very grim but confident. "Do you know the difference between Brits and Americans, Yank?"

"One of us knows that chips come in a bag?"

The joke bounced off Arnold as though it had struck a block wall. "Americans think a hundred years is a long time. Brits think a hundred miles is a long ways. This is a small island, relatively speaking. A little less total dirt than your state of Colorado. We've been able to blanket almost the entire thing with security surveillance. If this bugger made it onto our shores . . . we'll find him."

The outlaw in Reed wanted to object to such an absolute application of electronic oversight. He'd seen enough third world nations consumed by the rise of violent dictators to know that any protection measure was only one bad election away from being weaponized by a police state.

But for the time being, he couldn't deny the usefulness. He nodded once, and Arnold gestured for the Prosecution Force to follow him into an annexed conference room with a windowed view of the operations center. Whatever plate glass was used to construct the windows must have been thick, because the buzz of activity was almost completely shut out. Bottled water waited on the table. Arnold motioned for everyone to take a seat while he remained standing.

Reed didn't sit. He crossed his arms.

"What now?"

During the forty-five-minute drive from RAF Station Northolt, Reed had effectively briefed Arnold on everything he knew. Much of it Aimes had probably already communicated, but Reed seized the opportunity to reinforce the potential evil Ibrahim could be ready to unleash.

He wanted Arnold scared. He wanted to be handed a gun and an open door. He should have known better. The British had spent most of the last century staring down the muzzle of fascist, communist, and religious extremist threats much closer to their shores than they were to America's. They weren't easily rattled.

"Now you wait," Arnold said, his tone offering no invitation for discussion. "And we do our job."

Reed tensed. Arnold held up a hand.

"This is not your Wild West, Mr. Prosecutor. This is our show. We'll let you know if we have need of you. You stay in this room."

The last comment was directed at Corbyn. She flushed a little, and focused on her fingernails. Arnold left the room and Reed pivoted to overlook the operations center. Focusing on the screens, joining the AI overwatch.

Longing for a glimpse. Praying for Ibrahim to slip up.

When he did, the entirety of His Majesty's Armed Forces couldn't keep Reed in that room.

46

The Oval Office
The White House

It was early afternoon before Stratton could find time to slip away from the turmoil enveloping the West Wing and meet with the former director of the CIA, Victor O'Brien. News of a possible nuclear weapon in the hands of America's most wanted terrorist had chilled Stratton to the bone, but after a brief conversation with Aimes and his SecDef, Stratton knew there really wasn't much he could do about it for the time being. His people were in motion, and he remained on standby to make difficult choices. He wouldn't leave the White House.

But he still had work to do, and that work waited for him in the Oval Office. It was a deliberate choice on Stratton's part to host the meeting there. News out of Walter Reed Medical Center was sparse and bleak, but Stratton wanted O'Brien to know that whether or not Muddy Maggie Trousdale survived, somebody sat behind the Resolute desk. The administration was intact.

And they were a dangerous animal to corner.

O'Brien arrived in a suit coat and slacks, but no tie. In stark contrast to the stiff and proper man Stratton remembered from the numerous Situation Room meetings the two had shared over the past eighteen months, O'Brien now looked vaguely aloof. A little disinterested.

As though he were thoroughly disenfranchised from the very concept of American presidential power, and no longer interested in impressing it.

Stratton greeted him with a warm handshake and a broad smile anyway, choosing to put on a relaxed posture, as though nothing in the world were wrong, as he offered O'Brien a drink from the minibar. Bottles of rare and very expensive bourbon were on display. Stratton knew that O'Brien was a bourbon man, much as himself, and had asked the White House steward to bring in some of his personal stash on a conspicuous cart.

A little strong drink never hurt a difficult conversation.

"I'm good, thank you." O'Brien's tone was cold and detached. Stratton remained relaxed.

"You sure? I've got a bottle of Pappy twenty-year. A friend in the industry hooked me up. A little rich for my blood, but when it's free . . ."

Stratton shot O'Brien a mischievous smirk. O'Brien remained stone-faced.

"You know, Mr. Vice President, a gift that valuable could constitute bribery. I hope you disclosed it to the ethics committee."

Stratton stopped with the bottle half rocked over his tumbler. He faced O'Brien. His smile never flickered.

He poured the drink without blinking, then corked the bottle.

"Well, I'm having one."

He circled one of the Oval Office couches and motioned for O'Brien to have a seat across from him. The round glasses perched on O'Brien's face were likely responsible for the owlish look Maggie always accused him of, Stratton thought. Or maybe it was the hook nose. The expressionless stare.

He wasn't pleasant to look at, but something in Stratton's gut told him that the disgraced intelligence director would be a great deal less pleasant to look at on C-SPAN, testifying before Matt Roper and his cohorts. Stratton remained loose as he crossed one leg over the other and indulged in a deep sip.

The Pappy was exquisite, obviously. Stratton had never tasted Pappy that wasn't. A twenty-year bottle could be reasonably classified as *opulent* at five to seven grand a bottle. Of course, Stratton hadn't paid for it. It had been a gift. And yes, maybe that gift had been preceded by a phone call to a regulatory commission which had cleared away a little red tape for a friend in the industry. Maybe that constituted bribery.

But let them prove it.

"You know, Victor. You're missing out."

Stratton sloshed the bourbon gently, ice clinking against the tumbler's walls. O'Brien didn't so much as blink.

"I came here as a professional courtesy, Mr. Vice President."

The tone was curt. Stratton's smile faded. He didn't really care about titles—not unless they were useful. The title of *acting president* was a great deal less useful than the powers it entailed, but maybe it was time to fire a warning shot. O'Brien was clearly uninterested in playing nice.

"Mr. Acting President," Stratton corrected. "But it's okay, Victor. Titles can be funny things. They come and go, sometimes. And then come back around."

He cocked his head. The implication was clear. For the first time, O'Brien's blank face shifted. He smirked.

"What?" Stratton said.

"You don't seriously think you can bribe me with the offer of a new job, do you?"

"Bribe you?" Stratton feigned confusion. "Why would I want to bribe you?"

"Oh, please, Mr. *Acting President.* We're both important men. I think we can dispense with the foreplay. You only invited me here because you believe I have damaging evidence against Trousdale. You might even know what it is. Or maybe not. Regardless, you'll fish for information first. You'll ask me what I know, and what I'm going to tell Roper. Then you'll offer me a deal to do otherwise."

Stratton didn't break eye contact. He sat perfectly still, bourbon evaporating on his lips. Then he smiled. A little chuckle rolled out of his throat. He lowered the glass and dropped one leg off the other. He sat forward.

"You know, Victor. I'm not like Maggie. I missed out on that Southern charm. I'm from Chicago, where we call it like we see it. And what I see right now is a complete idiot if you actually think anything you just said is true."

O'Brien flushed crimson. His nostrils flared a little as he inhaled and sat up. Stratton charged on.

"I didn't call you here to bribe you, let alone to tamper with whatever testimony you plan to offer the Senate. You may recall that I used to serve in that chamber myself. Matthew Roper is a friend, as are many of the members on that committee. If I wanted your testimony shut down, all I would need to do is make a phone call. But then . . . that would be breaking the law. And despite your sultry viewpoints about the origins of my bourbon, I'm not in the habit of breaking the law."

O'Brien's lips flexed, his back rigid as an iron rod. Stratton could feel the wounded pride in him burning like a bonfire. It was dangerous—it was probably the origin of his decision to testify in the first place. O'Brien couldn't have enjoyed being canned by Maggie, especially after he was sidelined during the Ibrahim crisis in favor of his deputy director of operations, Dr. Sarah Aimes.

But that pride could also be useful, if Stratton was careful. It was all about playing his cards right.

"I called you here because you're a professional," Stratton said. "You've served in the intelligence community for a very long time. You understand the landscape, and how critical it is for the country to have both eyes open with a terrorist on the loose. We've got people hunting Ibrahim now, and we're very close. But with so much fear in the air, there's a lot at stake. It would be helpful if you could consider slowing your roll on whatever campaign you're on until Ibrahim is caught."

O'Brien's eyes cooled to someplace below freezing. Stratton remained loose.

"That sounds like witness tampering to me, Mr. Acting President."

"Not at all. Just a request for temporary postponement . . . in the interest of national security."

This time O'Brien did laugh. The sound was slow, and dry, and very soft. It was the first time Stratton had ever heard the man utter anything but a monotone sentence.

Something about it sounded vaguely unhinged.

"If you wanted this postponed, it seems like you could have called one of your friends . . . you know. On the *intelligence committee*."

Stratton's smile faded. He sipped bourbon, considering the remaining cards in his hand and measuring them against the hatred in O'Brien's eyes. Whatever the man's motivation for testifying against Maggie, it was burning deep within him. It was the real deal. He was consumed by it.

A simple favor wouldn't be enough to shut him down. And yet . . . O'Brien was here.

"Okay," Stratton said, his own voice flat now. "Cut to the chase, then. You didn't travel all the way into town simply to laugh in my face. What do you want?"

O'Brien shrugged innocently. "You invited me . . . "

Yes, Stratton thought. *And we both know I can't say why.*

"What are you doing, Victor?" Stratton put a little edge in his tone. Maybe enough to cut through the BS.

"Me?" O'Brien feigned innocence.

Stratton set the glass down. He lowered his voice to barely above a whisper.

"If you testify about classified matters on C-SPAN, I'll have the attorney general down your throat so fast you'll choke."

"Ah, and now we have witness intimidation. You're assembling quite a rap sheet, Mr. Acting President."

"If I wanted to intimidate you I would have made a threat, Victor. That was a promise, and you can tell anybody you want that I made it. This administration enforces the law."

"And breaks it," O'Brien said. "Repeatedly. Tell me . . . does the name *Reed Montgomery* mean anything to you?"

Sudden ice flashed through Stratton's veins, stiffening his posture before he could stop it. O'Brien must have noticed, because the dry, lifeless laugh returned.

"Oh yes. I know all about Mr. Montgomery and his band of merry men. The president's 'secret weapon.'"

"You were there, Victor." Stratton spoke through clenched teeth. "If you testify—"

"I would be incriminating myself," O'Brien cut him off. "I know. But what about things that happened *before* Trousdale became president? You know, back in *Louisiana*? I'm sure the public would be very curious about any intelligence the agency was able to gather concerning that. It's quite a colorful story, Jordan. A lot of unanswered questions about just how, exactly, Muddy Maggie and Reed Montgomery became such good friends."

Now the grin was wolfish, exposing a mouth full of gleaming teeth. O'Brien's owl eyes sparkled like a kid's. He looked crazed.

Stratton spoke in another monotone. "Okay, Victor. Now I'm warning you."

O'Brien leaned forward, cocking his head. Still smiling. "You're what now? Say it, Jordan. Go ahead and say it."

"You want me to say it?"

Teeth flashed. Stratton stood.

"Okay, Victor. I'll say it. In plain English, simple enough for your mud brain to comprehend. If you testify against this administration—if you threaten or damage or attempt to blackmail us in any way—I will *bury* you. Your body will be rotting in a shallow grave before the police even know you're missing, and when they find you fifty years from now, they won't be able to identify your teeth, because they won't be there. Just like your fingers. And your toes."

O'Brien's smile faded. The color drained out of his face. His head rocked back to follow Stratton as the VP stepped around the end of the table.

"You think you can intimidate me with other people's power, you little rat? I was *born* with more cunning for this game than you'll learn in a dozen lifetimes. I've got friends in every office of every department of every branch of government from here to Chicago, and they *all* owe me favors. I could erase you like the wrong answer to a math problem without ever getting my suit dirty, and I *will*."

Stratton leaned down, his face only inches from O'Brien's. A little trickle of sweat crept down O'Brien's face. Stratton spoke through his teeth.

"You wanna go tell the Senate intelligence committee that the White House tried to intimidate you? *Be my guest*."

O'Brien blinked. Stratton didn't. The stare remained unbroken. Then O'Brien got up abruptly and walked to the end of the couch, facing away. His breath was loud enough for Stratton to hear as the VP recovered his drink and took a long sip of bourbon.

"Man," Stratton chuckled, smacking his lips. "That's good."

He drained the glass and walked to the desk. He sat in Maggie's chair. O'Brien faced him from ten feet away, looking flushed again.

But still sweating.

"You'll make the right decision, Victor," Stratton said, cheerily. "I have faith in you."

O'Brien's teeth clenched. His face turned a darker shade of scarlet. Then he left the room in a rush, a White House visitor pass flapping against his chest.

The moment he was gone, the smile evaporated from Stratton's lips. His chest tightened, and he leaned back against the chair. He sucked his teeth and replayed the conversation in his mind, nausea growing in his stomach. Not only because he had no idea what O'Brien knew . . . he also had very little ability to make good on his threats. What friends Stratton had from the Senate were evaporating quickly as the winds of politics changed course.

O'Brien could never prove that the VP tried to intimidate him, and he likely wouldn't try. But the Trousdale-Stratton administration was weak. Vulnerable. Maggie was unconscious. Stratton couldn't ask her what O'Brien might know, or how to prepare to counter it. His hands were already full with Ibrahim.

If O'Brien elected to testify, they could well be finished.

The phone on the desk chimed once, and Stratton scooped up the handset, eager for a distraction.

"Yes?"

"Mr. Acting President, we need you in the Situation Room. There's been an update in London. They think they've found him."

47

Vauxhall Cross
London, England

"We may have something!"

Reed saw the flutter of activity around a particular analyst's desk and let himself out of the conference room. Nearly eight hours had passed since they'd arrived at SIS headquarters. It was full dark in London, and a new shift had arrived to relieve the exhausted day workers. Arnold had food sent to the Prosecution Force—chicken tikka masala, which Corbyn was proud to declare was actually a British invention, not an Indian one.

Reed didn't care. He didn't have an appetite—at least not for food. When the first indicator of a lead presented itself, he pounced like a waiting jungle cat. Arnold himself appeared next to the bank of screens spread across the front of the analyst's desk, peering at a particular black-and-white image of a vehicle moving down a highway. It was a glimpse, and then it was gone. How the analyst or the AI-powered software had caught a still image of the driver at all was beyond Reed. The picture was grainy, and there was a great deal of debate about who sat behind the wheel.

At least for the British. Not for Reed.

"That's him," Reed snapped. "Where is he?"

Arnold looked up from the desk with an irate curse. "Get back in the—"

"*Where is he?*" Reed snarled.

"He's on the M20," the analyst said. "Southbound, just outside of Ashford . . . "

The man trailed off, and Reed squinted at the map he called up. Ashford sat southeast of London, with the M20 highway running out of the British capital and across the southeastern cross-section of the nation, all the way to the coast.

"*Away* from the city?" Arnold said.

It gave Reed pause also. He thought of Wolfgang's warning of a small weapon, possibly a portable or a tactical nuclear bomb. Reed wasn't an expert on nuclear weapons any more than he was an expert on British geography, but the basics of blast yield and death toll were simple enough equations. A tactical nuke was a battlefield weapon, designed to assault military targets with concentrated bursts of radioactive energy. Compared to a modern strategic nuclear weapon, or even the atomic bomb that leveled Hiroshima in World War II, a tactical nuke was small.

Which meant if you were a terrorist, you would want to cart that thing into the very heart of a concentrated populace. Find a *lot* of people close together. London would be ideal.

But Ashford?

"We just got him again," another analyst chimed from a nearby desk. "The vehicle is a Ford Transit, commercial plates. He didn't stop in Ashford. He's still headed south."

"What's south?" Reed popped off the question before Arnold could intrude. The analyst panned the map along the arcing path of the M20 highway, beyond the town of Ashford into the heart of the county of Kent.

"Nothing really. A few villages, some farmland. The highway ends at Folkestone on the coast."

"Folkestone?" Reed questioned.

Arnold stood upright, a sudden flush passing across his face. "The Chunnel!" he snapped. "Bloody hell. He's headed to France!"

Arnold wheeled away, and Reed followed. The deputy director was on the phone in the blink of an eye, calling rapt orders to half a dozen different departments. He wanted the military on standby. Coastal assets of the Royal Navy, and a special advisory to authorities in Paris. The tempo of the operations center spiked again, and the rest of the Prosecution Force exploded from the conference room. Reed caught Arnold by the arm and wheeled him around.

"*What is the Chunnel?*"

Arnold hung up the phone. The relaxed undertone that had hallmarked his personality since Reed met him was long gone. The man looked stretched, like a rubber band. Like everything was boiling to the surface.

"The bloody transit tunnel, through the Channel. The Eurostar line runs from Folkestone to Calais. Freight and automobile transport. There's a train leaving in twenty minutes."

Again Arnold turned away. Wolfgang, Turk, and Corbyn had arrived. Reed caught the director by the elbow again and sank his fingers in, wrenching him back around.

"*Talk to me*," Reed barked. "How deep is that tunnel?"

Arnold yanked his arm away, teeth gritted. He shouted an order across the room at an analyst standing with a phone pressed against his ear. The buzz had intensified to beehive status. Reed blocked it all out.

"Mr. Prosecutor, if you don't return to that conference room—"

Reed closed the distance between them and spoke through gritted teeth, just loud enough for Arnold to hear. "*Listen to me.* That prick has already unleashed one WMD. It's reasonable to assume he's got his hands on another. Whatever his rationale for entering the tunnel, it could be an opportunity. You need to think about isolating the threat. About *containment*."

Momentary hesitation flashed behind Arnold's eyes. Reed knew that he'd finally broken through. The deputy director was getting the picture.

"How deep is the tunnel?" Reed repeated.

"About seventy meters," Arnold said. "It's tunneled through the seabed. Through chalk marl. Why?"

Reed thought quickly. He pictured the blast. The eruption of radiation and a mushroom cloud, accompanied by an unthinkable blast of energy. Enough to obliterate any sort of tunnel, but seventy meters beneath the surface, barricaded by chalk and ocean water, the devastation could be minimized.

"Can you shut down the train?" Reed asked.

"How do you mean?"

"Can you cut off the power halfway through the tunnel? Leave it stranded?"

"I suppose so."

"Then tell your people to back off," Reed said. "Let him onto the train and send it into the tunnel. Stop it halfway."

"Mr. Prosecutor, there are *people* on that train!"

"And there's a hell of a lot more people off it. If this jerk has another WMD, you *want* it at the bottom of that tunnel."

"But then we have a hostage situation."

"No," Reed shook his head. "Not when I get there. I'll go in after him myself."

"You must be out of your mind," Corbyn broke in for the first time. Reed ignored her.

"I've hunted this guy before, Mr. Arnold. I know how he thinks. And I don't care if I don't walk out alive. This is what I do—let me do it."

Arnold hesitated. Reed could see the wheels turning in his mind. The uncertainty. And then the inevitable conclusion. Reed's math was solid. If there was any risk of a WMD, the needs of the majority spread out across the English and French coastlines trumped the needs of the few locked inside that train. Isolating the weapon at the bottom of the Chunnel could save lives.

And if a rogue operator was going to throw his life away trying to stop the attack . . . better a random American than one of Arnold's own.

"We could phone the station," Arnold said. "Try to get as many people off as we can."

"You'll spook him if you do," Turk said.

"And then he's likely to trigger the attack in Folkestone," Wolfgang added.

"Let me do my job," Reed hissed. "Get me to the coast. Give me a gun. And stand the hell back."

Another moment of consideration. Then Arnold was bought in.

"We've got an executive transport helicopter on the roof," he said.

"I'll fly!" Corbyn was already headed for the door. Arnold kept speaking.

"I can give you something from our weapons locker and arrange for transport into the tunnel. That's . . . really all I have."

"That's enough," Reed said. "I'll take it from there."

48

Folkestone, England

The ride out of London was smoother than Ibrahim expected. The Ford panel van ran well even with a fifteen-hundred-pound load packed into the cargo area, strapped to the floor and wired to a car battery for detonation. A safety switch was in play, of course. A pair of them, actually, along with a timer.

It wouldn't be a lot of time. It might be enough. If not . . . Ibrahim was prepared for that, also.

He sat behind the wheel, no longer bothering to hide his face from the cameras lined alongside the M20 highway. He didn't relax off the accelerator as they blazed through Ashford and followed signs toward the coast.

LeShuttle was the automotive and freight service that ran through the Channel Tunnel, colloquially known as the "Chunnel." That specific service was called *Eurotunnel*, and included trains as long as eight hundred meters long, consisting of carriages designed to transport vehicles at up to 140 kilometers per hour.

The journey would take exactly thirty-five minutes, and run through one of a pair of 7.6-meter-wide tunnels built 30 meters apart with a 4.8-meter service tunnel running directly between. Passageways built every

375 meters connected the three tunnels, offering access to the service tunnel.

That service tunnel would be Ibrahim's path out, if there was a path at all. He pictured the blueprints in his mind as he approached the digital kiosk built alongside the first of a trio of gates, and punched a button for his ticket. A trickle of sweat ran across his scalp, and he glanced down at his phone to see a message from his ally. The man who had disappeared shortly after Ibrahim had departed the oil platform, but had not ceased to remain in contact.

Because somehow, despite Ibrahim's fierce independence and dedication . . . the ally had become the boss.

Message me when you enter the tunnel, the message said.

Ibrahim shot back a quick reply. Entering now.

Then he looked over his shoulder to the only other passenger of the van. The dumb Afghan—the man Ibrahim barely knew and couldn't really trust. A far cry from the true believers who had accompanied Ibrahim into America for his first wave of attacks, but this mission didn't require intelligence. Only relentless dedication, and at least the Afghan offered plenty of that. The hellfire in his eyes was almost as bad as what Ibrahim saw in the mirror. Maybe British troops had killed his family during the lengthy occupation of his homeland. Maybe he was thirsty for vengeance.

Or maybe he actually believed that somehow, some way, this was bigger than humanity. That Allah actually cared.

"Allahu akbar," Ibrahim said.

The Afghan nodded once and repeated the phrase in a dull monotone as Ibrahim turned back to the road ahead. He followed the signs. He obeyed the guidance of a conductor who directed him onto a flat car before he turned through an open rolling metal door into the automobile carriage. Even in mid-evening, the carriage was full, packed with a diverse assortment of vans, trucks, and cars. Average, everyday people on their way to France.

The doors rolled shut, and soft lights glowed from the ceiling. Ibrahim relaxed into his seat with the van switched off, and closed his eyes.

He thought about home. He thought about his brother, gunned down by the Americans. He thought about the family he'd lost, all the uncles and cousins and friends. He thought about his shattered home and the long years of torment.

He thought about the weapon, somewhere far away in the midst of the ocean. Churning steadily westward. The device sitting behind him would yield a fraction of the devastation, but Ibrahim had now resigned himself to the plan. It was better than he could do on his own.

It would bring the West to its knees.

49

The Situation Room
The West Wing

"Are we certain that's our man?"

Stratton stood halfway down the conference table, bent over the polished wood surface just in front of the chair Maggie had so often occupied during one unfolding crisis after another. Somehow, it felt wrong to sit there.

"SIS is ninety percent, sir. He's driving southeast of London and toward the trans-channel tunnel."

Stratton fixated on the picture displayed at the end of the room. It was black-and-white, some kind of security footage. The man sitting behind the wheel of a white panel van had his face turned a little to the left. The profile was clear, but not properly illuminated.

It looked like Abdel Ibrahim.

"You have people on the ground?" Stratton said.

Interim Director Aimes spoke from the speakerphone. "That's correct, sir."

"Put them at the full disposal of the British. Have your people update us every ten minutes."

"Will do, sir."

Aimes hung up. Stratton pivoted his attention down the bustling row of aides and cabinet personnel to Easterling. Maggie's chief of staff ran the meeting room with now practiced efficiency, keeping everybody occupied to prevent them from adding to the chaos.

She was good at her job. But then, she ought to be.

"Are we in touch with London?" Stratton said.

"I've got Prime Minister Wright on the line now."

Stratton scooped up the handset, still not allowing himself to sit.

"Prime Minister, what do you need?"

Stratton cut to the chase—not only because he could feel the crushing weight of evaporating time bearing down on him like a hundred feet of water, but because he knew that Victoria Wright appreciated directness. She'd only served as the British PM for a little over two years, but during that time he'd encountered her on a few occasions.

Wright was a lot like Maggie. She was all business. She was a good leader.

But for all that, she took a moment to be polite.

"Acting President Stratton. I was so sorry to hear about Maggie. We're keeping her in our prayers."

"I appreciate that, ma'am. She'll pull through. How can we help?"

Wright seamlessly switched gears into battle mode. "I'll be blunt, Jordan. I need to know that your people aren't going to get trigger-happy on us. My naval advisors indicated that you've put your Sixth Fleet on full alert. I don't need planes ripping through the Channel. Cooler heads must prevail."

"That was only a precaution," Stratton said. "But I do want to be clear—you *are* aware that we have obtained intelligence indicating that Abdel Ibrahim may be in possession of a WMD? Possibly a nuclear one."

The Situation Room went quiet at that statement. Wright remained composed.

"I'm aware. We running radiological detectors at all of our ports. There are no indicators that any such weapon was smuggled in. It seems that Ibrahim is heading for the Channel Tunnel. We're going to put him in it, and shut down the line. If he does have a weapon, that should help contain it."

A hint of uncertainty crept into Wright's voice. Stratton couldn't blame her. This was an unprecedented situation, and she was right. It would be easy to become hot-blooded. To move too quickly, and make a catastrophic mistake.

Cooler heads must prevail.

"We've got your back, Prime Minister. I'll remain by the phone."

"Thank you, Mr. Acting President."

The phone clicked off. The buzz of activity resumed. Stratton placed both palms on the table and looked back to the picture of the moving van.

It wasn't a large vehicle. Any weapon it contained couldn't be very large, either. But what if Ibrahim had already planted a weapon in London? What if he was fleeing the city before setting it off remotely?

Even in that case, the tunnel was a good idea. It might isolate whatever triggering method he planned to use. In any event, the next sixty minutes could be the worst sixty minutes in British history.

"Sir, a word?"

General Yellin appeared at Stratton's elbow, his bulldog shoulders tensed beneath an Army uniform heavy with medals. Stratton followed him to the corner of the room where the general lowered his voice to barely above a whisper.

"I'd like to recommend we advance to DEFCON 2—*Fast Pace*. If there's even a chance there's a nuke ready to blast in Europe, we need to be ready to respond at a moment's notice. We'd want to lock down our borders and put our air forces on full alert. At DEFCON 2, I'm only six hours away from full military action."

Stratton hesitated. He knew the Pentagon was already operating at DEFCON 3, code-named *Round House*. They had been since Ibrahim's chemical weapons attacks earlier that summer, keeping the entire bulk of the U.S. armed forces at increased readiness for . . . whatever came next. It only made sense.

But DEFCON 2 was something else. It was a much bigger jump. Stratton had witnessed it before during the North Korean crisis earlier in Maggie's tenure as president. He remembered the shockwaves it sent ripping through every corner of Washington and the military complex. With so many nerves already running ragged, he couldn't see how the additional tension would help.

"We're not at risk of being attacked, General."

"Not presently," Yellin said. "But the risk of a nuclear attack even in Europe could easily trigger a chain reaction. We need to put our allies on alert, specifically France. They've got nukes of their own, and if a bomb goes off on their side of the Channel, even a small one, we need to be in position to manage an international crisis. It's not just about launching weapons ourselves. It's about keeping everybody else from freaking out and launching them."

France. The UK. Pakistan. India. Russia. North Korea. Israel . . . unofficially, of course. China.

Stratton ran through the growing list of nuclear-armed nations and knew Yellin was right. He'd been thinking too narrowly. This wasn't just about America's ability to prevent or respond to an attack on her own shores. This was about managing a nuclear world.

"Do it," Stratton said. "Move us to DEFCON 2."

50

London, England

The helicopter Corbyn led them to was indeed an executive transport. It sat on a helipad sheltered by the upper walls of the SIS building, some kind of Eurocopter with polished black body panels and a glimmering windshield.

By the time Reed, Wolfgang, and Turk reached the helipad, Corbyn had loosed the tie-downs binding the aircraft against the wind and rolled back the side door. The interior was leather-clad and carpeted. Turk slung his backpack in ahead of him while Wolfgang removed his G29 from his prosthetic leg and tucked it into his belt. Corbyn slipped into the cockpit and talked her way through a pre-flight, muttering profanities into the microphone at whatever local air traffic control was refusing her flight request.

"Listen, tosser. I'm not bloody asking. Tango two-seven-seven fox is taking air from Vauxhall. Clear the skies!"

A steel door exploded open behind them, and Arnold himself appeared on the roof. He walked at a fast trot with a duffel bag riding from one hand. He still looked uncertain.

But he didn't look like he was going to argue.

The helicopter's jet engines fired and Arnold put his arm up to block the blast. He slowed near Reed and gave him a once-over. "You know how to ride a motorbike, son?"

Reed nodded.

"One of my analysts lives in Folkestone. He rides some kind of crotch rocket, and he'll make sure the service tunnel is open for you. The train just left the station—we've given word for it to run at three-quarter speed. Any slower and we might tip him off."

Arnold extended the bag. Reed took the handle and the top fell open.

Two Heckler and Koch MP5 submachine guns lay inside, fully equipped with red dot optics, weapons lights, and spare magazines. A complete loadout.

Reed looked up.

"Aimes tells me you're one of her best," Arnold said. "From where I'm standing, you're one of her craziest."

"He murdered my child," Reed said simply.

Arnold winced, a flash of empathetic pain crossing his face. Reed shouldered the bag and turned for the plane. Arnold put a strong hand on his shoulder.

"Mr. Montgomery."

Reed tensed. He'd never given Arnold his name. It must have been Aimes. He looked back.

"We'll stop the train at mid-tunnel," Arnold said. "After that . . . he's all yours. You should know, there's at least three hundred people on board."

A trace of pain shot through Arnold's gaze.

"Notify your navy," Reed said. "If this thing goes sideways, be ready to rescue survivors."

Arnold stepped back. "Godspeed, Prosecutor."

Reed leapt through the open door, tossing the bag ahead of him. Turk caught it and expertly flipped the first submachine gun out, locking in a magazine and running the bolt even as Corbyn applied power to the rotors. The Eurocopter rose from the helipad, and Arnold turned back for the door. Then Corbyn banked left, still shouting profanities into her headset as London raced far below.

Reed accepted an MP5 from Turk and rammed two extra magazines into his pocket. His knees bent over the edge of the helicopter's floor, the open side door howling with a thunder of wind. He checked his watch and saw that it was just past nine p.m., but the sky was gray with a reflection of ten million city lights. The roads and buildings faded below as Corbyn nosed down. If Reed closed his eyes, he didn't think of London at all.

He thought of Iraq. Baghdad. South America. The Yellow Sea.

The specific geographic location had ceased to matter a long time ago. The only thing that remained was the target, and the long road to placing that target under the muzzle of a weapon.

"Eight minutes!" Corbyn shouted.

Reed unfolded the MP5's sling and wrapped it around his shoulder. Then he thought of the motorcycle waiting for him in Folkestone, and he tightened the strap until the submachine gun was locked tight against his chest.

Just in case.

The entrance of the service tunnel was marked by a wide concrete frame, a two-lane road dropping out of sight beneath the English coastline just a little ways inland of the Channel. Hot yellow security lights blazed across an open parking lot long cleared of cars, people appearing as dots rushing back and forth near the mouth of the tunnel as Corbyn spun the Eurocopter in midair and prepared for descent.

"I'm gonna set her down in the car park!" Corbyn shouted. "Hang on!"

The chopper went down in a smooth swoop, Reed's ears almost numb by the blast of jet engines. As they approached, a man in a yellow reflective vest appeared to guide them in, motioning with two arms like a ground controller at an airport.

Corbyn ignored him, selecting her own spot fifty yards from the tunnel entrance and dropping straight down. She applied cyclic at the last moment, easing the descent and resting all three wheels of the helicopter at once with a gentle thump

Reed was already out, followed closely by Wolfgang and Turk. He bent beneath the slowing blast of the rotors and turned for the mouth of the tunnel.

The guy in the reflective vest stopped him, shouting over the noise. "Are you Montgomery?"

So now everybody knows my name.

"Where's the bike?" Reed barked.

"This way!"

The guy ran. Reed kept pace, locking the MP5 into his belt as they neared the tunnel. The motorcycle in question was parked just outside, a beast of a thing resting on two meaty tires with glossy red body panels reflecting the overhead security lights. Reed recognized it in an instant, not because he knew a lot about bikes, but because he'd seen an identical bike barely a day prior, all the way back in Leiper's Fork, Tennessee.

It was a Triumph Rocket 3, the same muscle cruiser Corbyn rode. It looked even more gnarly just outside the entrance of the tunnel, with a modified exhaust painted matte black and the massive pair of headlights covered over in dark tint.

"The tank is full," the guy said, a little hesitantly. "The deputy director said you needed it . . . "

"Keys," Reed snapped. The guy passed him a little black key fob, and Reed threw his leg over the saddle. The ignition was keyless. The moment Reed located the engine stop switch on the right handgrip and flipped it to *engine run*, the digital dash illuminated with a Triumph logo and a lot of little readout lights. The guy approached and extended one arm, offering a helmet. It looked about two sizes too small. Reed brushed him off.

"Where's mine?"

Reed had anticipated the anger in Turk's voice when he learned that he would be left behind, which was why Reed hadn't told him.

"You two remain on standby with Corbyn. Be ready to haul ass if this goes sideways."

"Reed!" Before Turk could object, Corbyn raced in with a cell phone extended. Reed took it and flicked it to speaker mode.

"Prosecutor?"

It was Arnold.

"I'm about to enter the service tunnel."

"Very good. The train is almost halfway to France. It'll hit the deep point in six minutes . . . we're stopping it there. Look for service passageway 78R. Good luck, son."

Reed handed the phone back. He clamped on the clutch and hit the starter switch. The bike erupted to life like a bomb blast of its own, all thundering muscle and throaty wrath. Reed had ridden bikes before, plenty of times. He'd ridden some big ones—heavy cruisers and lightning-fast sport bikes. This was both, heavy between his knees but equipped with earth-shaking amounts of power. He twisted the throttle to earn a rip of modified exhaust as loud as the Eurocopter behind him. The tachometer spiked, and Reed dropped his foot over the gear shift. A click signaled first gear.

"Reed!"

He looked up to see Turk leaning close. The big man put a hand on Reed's shoulder. He squeezed. His eyes flashed.

But he didn't argue.

"Waste 'em," Turk said.

Reed relaxed on the clutch and rolled on the throttle. The back tire chirped, and he launched forward as though he'd been released from a slingshot. In an instant the mouth of the service tunnel closed around him. The ground dropped off. Wind tore at his hair and the front suspension decompressed as the bike lifted from the pavement. Concrete walls reflected the blast of exhaust like a thunderstorm, and Reed ratcheted his foot into second gear.

Then the tunnel swallowed him.

51

The Channel Tunnel
Midway between England and France

Ibrahim and his associate disabled the carriage's security cameras with a quick slash of their feed wires, and then proceeded to kill everyone inside the moment the Eurotunnel train vanished beneath the English Channel. There were seven cars aboard the carriage in total, lined up with tall rolling metal doors blocking them in on either end. Four trucks, another van, and two sedans. Their windows disintegrated under the suppressed fire of Glock 9mm handguns aimed at close range. The last car was packed full of French college girls headed back to school. They saw the oncoming death and attempted to escape.

They caught bullets in the backs of their heads even as they scrambled for the emergency alarm mounted to the interior wall of the carriage. Ibrahim stepped over the bodies with the Glock hanging at his side, allowing his companion to deliver additional headshots just for good measure.

He couldn't blame the man. French, English, or American. They were all Westerners. They were all the enemy.

Once the last college girl lay lifeless on the floor, Ibrahim and his companion were free to move about the interior of the carriage without disturbance. They returned to the van under the glow of LED lights mounted high into the roof above them, the wheels below clacking rhythmically with every joint in the underwater track. Ibrahim's ears flooded with the rush of noise outside the carriage, but his mind focused. He opened the rear doors of the Ford. He accessed the device within. He went to work with his companion, communicating quietly in Arabic—the only language both men understood.

The wiring had been completed aboard the oil platform, but now the ignition sequence had to be prepped. The timer on Ibrahim's wristwatch counted down the minutes of the Channel transit, allowing him to estimate the moment when they had reached the escape passageway seventy percent through the journey. It was just on the other side of the deepest point of the ride, and would provide access to the service tunnel.

If everything went off without a hitch, he and his Afghan companion would reach France before the bomb detonated, but if Ibrahim was honest he didn't really expect to survive this attack. Neither did the man sitting next to him, silently handing him tools upon request. This wasn't like America. It wasn't like the battles Ibrahim had fought in the Middle East. This attack would be a great deal less lethal than the nerve agent strike in Baton Rouge.

But it would serve a more sinister purpose. It would spread the fear from America to the European continent. And besides . . . it was the price Ibrahim had agreed to pay in exchange for his shadowy ally's help.

Ibrahim would keep his end of the bargain. He would see this through to the end.

The wristwatch chimed, and Ibrahim cocked his head toward the wall of the carriage. "Prepare to pull the stop."

There were emergency stop levers mounted on the inside of the wall alongside the same emergency alert levers the university girls had been fleeing toward. The levers didn't actually stop the train, but they sent an emergency signal to the controller, and the controller would stop the train, after which Ibrahim would start the bomb timer and attempt his escape.

The Afghan stood and dropped out of the back of the van. He started toward the emergency lever, swaying a little on his feet while Ibrahim toiled over the bomb. He made it halfway there.

Then the train lurched. Brakes squealed. Metal shrieked, and speed bled away rapidly. Ibrahim looked up, squinting at his watch.

It was too soon. His companion hadn't even reached the wall, let alone pulled the lever.

"Abdel?" His companion asked.

The train lurched again, and Ibrahim caught himself against the device. His companion fell. The train scraped and ground, then completed a stop. Not at the seventy percent mark, where Ibrahim had planned. This was much sooner, just past halfway between England and France. The deep point.

Ibrahim looked back up the carriage, past the bodies and toward the doors. He didn't have to wonder what had happened. It was blatantly obvious, and it would force his hand.

The British had found him.

52

The Channel Tunnel
Service Tunnel

By the time Reed reached fifth gear on the Triumph he was already blazing down the service tunnel at nearly two hundred kilometers per hour. The digital display marked a tachometer that spiked toward a redline marker of seven thousand RPM while a three-digit speedometer cranked rapidly upward. He leaned low over the fuel tank, making himself as much one with the bike as possible while the thunder of the exhaust pounded in his ears.

It was unlike anything he'd ever experienced in his life. Not like a helicopter, but just as loud. Not like skydiving, but just as visceral.

Not really like a firefight, but it unleashed the same chemicals of desperation and brutality that whizzing bullets and blazing pain triggered. It was like being trapped inside a tornado, dirt and darkness and flashing bits of light swirling around at a thousand miles per hour. He didn't even feel the gentle loss of elevation as the tunnel dropped beneath the ocean floor. He couldn't read the flashing signs that blinked past him while the Triumph hurtled forward like . . .

Well. A *rocket*.

Reed's toe flicked the bike into sixth gear and the tachometer dropped, but the speedo kept climbing. The shudder of unleashed power howling between his knees sent tremors up his spine and heat waves penetrating his jeans. His knees were bent, his arms locked to reach the handlebars. Each passing kilometer was marked by a blip on the trip odometer, grinding upward like a new high score on a video game.

And Reed saw Ibrahim. He saw the demon face. Even through the rushing howl of the exhaust pounding in his ears, he heard his daughter's voice. Screaming in terror.

I'm gonna kill him.

When the trip odometer read twenty klicks, Reed eased the Rocket 3 down to 150 kmph, allowing him just enough time to read the flashing signs as he clipped past one connecting passageway every 375 meters. Sweat ran down his legs and his heart thundered, but his face and chest were both dry and covered in goosebumps. The air beating against him was cold—chilled by the depth and the crush of cold water surging overhead. If Reed thought about it, his head began to spin. His vision closed in a little.

He focused on the path ahead instead, his gaze catching on a sign that marked a passageway racing by. It read: *76C.*

He was looking for 78R.

The bike thundered again, and the exhaust clapped across the walls. A divot in the pavement sent a tremor through the front wheel, and his arms stiffened. The MP5 was pinned against his chest by the blast. Another series of signs blinked by.

He almost missed 78R. The connecting passageway to the pair of sub-channel tunnels opened on either side, the sign semi-invisible under the shadow of a blown light bulb. He clamped on the clutch and laid on both brakes, the thick back tire of the Triumph sliding left with a squeal. The air ignited with the stench of burning rubber, and the front wheel wobbled. Reed instinctively relaxed on the front brake, but he'd already passed the connecting passageway by a hundred yards. The Triumph finally stopped, and Reed flicked the side stand before swinging off.

A wave of dizziness swept through his mind. The bike was still running, but he barely noticed as he turned back for the passageway and loosed the

MP5's strap. The weapon fell into his hands, and he swept one hand over the Triumph's kill switch.

The big motor choked off, and sudden stillness swept through the service tunnel. Reed's ears rang as though he'd just survived a flash bang, but as the dizziness faded and he jogged toward the connecting passageway, he thought he heard something other than the rushing clack of a train hurtling by.

These were voices. Humans packed tightly together, their words jumbled into a single universal sound recognizable on any continent, in any language.

A desperate cry of fear, mixed with gunshots.

53

The Channel Tunnel

Ibrahim hadn't planned to leave the train car until he was ready to arm the bomb, but the French operators running LeShuttle had other plans. Whatever had triggered the emergency stop brought only momentary calm to the carriage full of parked vehicles and dead bodies—then a voice spoke over an intercom, rattling off a short announcement in French before the same was repeated in English.

"Please remain calm. We have made a temporary stop. Remain in your vehicles."

It might have only been because Ibrahim didn't believe in coincidences, but he knew from the moment the emergency alert had sounded that trouble was headed his way. He snapped an order to his companion to arm himself with one of the pair of MP5 submachine guns housed in the back of the van alongside the device. Ibrahim maintained focus on the job at hand, completing the last of the wiring before activating the detonator and programming the countdown.

It was a simple device, neatly constructed and elegant in its design. Fakir would have been proud. Ibrahim thought of his brother as he input the desired countdown time, now resigned to the fact that he would have to arm the device right where he sat. Fakir had liked countdown timers, likely because of his obsession with American spy films. Equal to his love of St. Louis baseball, Fakir watched espionage and action films en masse, taking a lot of his styling cues from the weapons he saw designed within.

Ibrahim was much less impressed with Hollywood interpretations of the ugly realities of war, but he could appreciate the countdown clock for another reason. It was an homage to his slain brother—the loss that had propelled him into this jihad in the first place.

"Abdel!"

Ibrahim's companion hissed a warning only a moment before a metallic clicking sound rang from the end of the carriage. He froze, looking through the driver's side window of the van to find his companion crouched beneath the sideview mirror, pointing an MP5 toward the sound of oncoming footsteps.

Ibrahim moved instinctually for the second MP5, lifting it silently and flicking the switch to three-round burst. There was already a 9mm cartridge in the chamber. He was ready, and he knew he needed to be, because they hadn't hidden the bodies. Why bother? There was no way to scrub away the blood.

The footsteps pounded closer, at least two pairs of them. A voice spoke in French.

Then the steps halted. Somebody breathed a French exclamation. A flashlight played across the floor. Ibrahim saw the top of a man's head over the roof of the pickup truck parked ahead of them. The guy was lifting his light, shining it through a busted side window at the dead driver lying between. His face washed pale. He pivoted the light to his right, instinctively marking the path ahead. Down the line of cars. Toward the van.

The beam flashed through the windshield across Ibrahim's face. It reached Ibrahim's companion.

And then the Afghan opened fire.

54

Folkestone, England

It wasn't difficult math. From the moment Reed disappeared into the service tunnel, Turk knew there was a better than average chance that he would never resurface. A better than average chance that whatever weapon Abdel Ibrahim had carted onto LeShuttle would detonate in a water-lifting blast heard the world around, terminating hundreds of lives in mere seconds.

Again.

Turk should be down there, he knew. He should have forced Reed's hand. But all that was done now, and he wasn't about to sit silently by the water while the clock wound down. He took command by default—not because anybody had ever accepted him as the Prosecution Force's number two, but because he wasn't interested in democracy.

"Corbyn, spin up the chopper. We're going out over the Channel. Wolfgang, radio SIS and have them signal British naval assets. We'll participate in the search."

Corbyn was already jogging back to the Eurocopter, brown ponytail snapping in the breeze. Wolfgang moved a little slower, a wince ripping across his face as he applied weight to his prosthetic. He must have pulled a muscle on the oil platform.

"Search for *what?*"

It should have been an obvious question. Turk answered it anyway.

"The survivors."

55

The Channel Tunnel

Reed took the passageway with the MP5 held at eye level. The weapon was equipped with an Aimpoint ACRO P-2 red dot sight. Technically designed to be a handgun optic, the sight was low profile and melded close to the receiver. Reed left it on even though he hadn't tested it, because even if it was improperly calibrated, the narrow viewing window would provide a close approximation of his correct point of aim.

And these wouldn't be precision shots. This would be close and dirty work.

The connecting passageway between the service tunnel and the train tunnel was illuminated by dim fluorescent bulbs, glowing yellow over grimy concrete. The walls were built of tightly packed brick, curving a little as they rose over Reed's head. There were fire alarms and fire extinguishers mounted at waist height, along with an emergency locker for medical supplies.

Reed rushed right by it all, because the voice of the gunshots had resumed. The screams he'd detected earlier redoubled, and he could see the tall silver sides of LeShuttle now. It sat on the tracks at a dead standstill, surrounded by the twenty-five-meter tunnel buried in chalk marl seventy meters beneath the churning Channel surface.

The gunfire was automatic, but the bursts were short. Controlled fire from a practiced shooter, ripping from someplace to Reed's right. He narrowed in on that side of the passageway and slid to a stop as he neared the turn. A pinging sound followed by a zipping whine marked a ricochet ripping overhead. Reed dropped instinctively to one knee and looked to the left first, just to be sure. He saw a body lying on the concrete next to the rails—a train conductor with a French flag patch on one arm, a bottle of pepper spray spattered with blood on the ground next to him.

Useless.

The gunfire went silent, and Reed risked a swing around the corner, leading with the MP5. The Aimpoint's reticle played across the metal walls of LeShuttle, tracing quickly to a carriage sixty yards away with an open access door. Lights and shadows played across the darkened tunnel floor from the inside of the carriage, and somebody snapped an order in what sounded like Arabic.

Reed rose back to his feet, finger held above the trigger guard as he skipped the steps and dropped straight into the train tunnel. Boots crunched over dirt and light gravel, and he broke into a sprint. His back was fully exposed—anybody in a carriage farther down could cut him down like a wounded duck.

But he knew Ibrahim hadn't brought an army. There might be only one or two other men in the carriage, armed with weapons that sounded a lot like his own MP5. Reed was ready to roll the dice.

He was ready for blood.

The crunching footfalls may have given him away, or perhaps whatever soldiers joined Ibrahim in the carriage had simply risked a look. Whatever the case, Reed made it only halfway to the open door before the flash of shadow passed across it. He ducked instinctively to the left, closer to the train and lower down. A black barrel appeared and muzzle flash lit the tunnel. A thunderclap of a three-round burst, followed quickly by a second. Bullets zipped past Reed's position and he returned fire, skipping rounds along the side of the carriage and sending at least one through the door. His opponent withdrew, a muted shout ringing through the tunnel.

Reed sprinted. He covered the last thirty yards in a mad dash, swinging deliberately away from the train to obtain a shot through the door, and clamping down on the trigger. The MP5 unleashed a string of ten rounds into the car, pinging off metal and shattering vehicle glass at random. Whoever was inside dove for cover, and Reed slid to a stop next to the door. He dropped the half-empty mag and ratcheted in a fresh one, breathing evenly.

There was no fear. No hesitation. He only knew that somewhere inside that carriage lay a man with blood on his hands.

April's blood.

Reed shouted into the dark.

"*Ibrahim!*"

56

The Channel Tunnel

Ibrahim heard the rattle of automatic gunfire and knew that somebody other than the unarmed French security officers aboard the train had arrived on scene. The Afghan had already rushed toward the noise and unleashed a little gunfire of his own. He called hoarse updates back to Ibrahim in Arabic, the words not quite loud enough to hear through the walls of the van.

Ibrahim blocked it all, focusing on the bomb, finally ready to input the arming code. The clock was already set to count down from ten minutes. It seemed like the right number—enough to offer him the shadow of a hope for escape, while not so long that somebody would have time to disarm it. He would lock the van upon departure. The device was hidden in the back. Somebody would have to know to be looking for it to even find it.

And by then, it would be too late. The blast would rupture the van, rupture the LeShuttle carriage, and tear through the top of the tunnel ceiling. It would blast through meters of chalk marl.

It would reach the Channel with ease, allowing millions of gallons of icy cold water to surge in like a tidal wave. Lights out.

Ibrahim's fingers reached the control panel built on the side of the device. All the keys were printed in Cyrillic, but he'd marked an index card with an Arabic translation for quick reference. The work was a little slower this way, but the potency of the Soviet weapon resting in front of him more than compensated for the inconvenience.

Sweat trickled down his face despite the chill of the subterranean tunnel, and Ibrahim input the code. He had made a mistake on the translation, and a red light flashed. He tried again, slower this time.

Then he froze, blood turning to ice. A voice echoed off the tunnel walls outside, loud and harsh. Angry, and American. A single word.

"*Ibrahim!*"

57

The Channel Tunnel

Nobody answered Reed's call through the tunnel. He swung out from the wall of the carriage and fired twice inside. The metal walls were too thick to shoot through, and his view inside was limited. Whatever tangos waited for his entry no doubt had their weapons zeroed on the door. It was a bad situation in desperate need of a hand grenade.

Reed swept his gaze down the length of the carriage for another entrance, but only the larger, car-sized doors remained, and they were all closed. The sides of the carriage looked like the sides of a metal barn, ribbed and galvanized, rising high over his head. Impenetrable.

But there had to be another way.

Reed backed quickly away from the door and reached the end of the carriage, where a flexible rubber gasket connected it to the next in line. There was no gap or opportunity to force his way through, but at the very end of the occupied carriage a pair of pocket doors stood pressed closed with two glass windows staring out at him. Those windows were speckled with crimson, dirty with tunnel grime.

Reed edged his way closer and pressed his off hand into the gap between the pocket doors. He pried, and the doors slid an inch apart under steady pressure.

There was still no noise from behind. Reed glanced over his shoulder to check, and thought he heard footsteps. The gunman was approaching the previous door again. Time was running out. He threw his shoulder into the door and rammed it apart another eighteen inches just as the gunfire resumed from behind. Bullets zinged overhead and Reed threw himself through the door. He landed on his side and rolled automatically in the direction of the gunfire. A slug tore past his exposed legs, shredding combat pants and drawing blood. Reed thrashed and swung his MP5 up, staring down the interior of the carriage. There were vehicles on his left—a long line of them, many pockmarked by bullet holes and littered with broken glass. Two bodies on the floor, and several more slumped over in driver's seats.

And the shooter, fifty yards down, leaning out of the open door. Reed fixed the Aimpoint's reticle on his center mass and opened fire. The target went down with a scream, arms and legs thrashing. Bullets stitched their way up his chest and across his face, blowing him back across the floor. Blood ran over lifeless eyes, and Reed was back on his feet. He dashed down the aisle between the carriage wall and the row of vehicles, unleashing short bursts of gunfire at random to discourage any potshots from whoever remained.

His ears rang with the thunderclap of enclosed gunfire. The carriage smelled of burnt gunpowder and blood, shattered glass glistening in little cubes on the floor. He saw the Ford Transit that Ibrahim had been spotted in sitting halfway down the row of cars, barricaded in by a parked pickup truck and a small sedan. Bodies lay slumped over steering wheels in both, but the windshield of the van remained untouched. Both front seats were empty.

Reed stepped over the body of his fallen foe and ducked quickly in front of the pickup truck as a snarl of MP5 fire opened up behind the van. Orange muzzle flash grew brighter as 9mm slugs blew out the overhead lights. A loud electric pop signaled the snap of a breaker box responding to a short in bullet-riddled wiring, and everything went pitch black.

Reed's thumb slid forward along the foregrip of the MP5, resting over the thumb switch of the attached weapon light. But he didn't turn it on. He knelt instead, keeping the front left tire of the pickup between himself and his enemy's line of fire as he stole a glance beneath the row of vehicles, thumbing the weapon light for no longer than a second.

He saw no feet. No legs. No target. But the van sat squatted on its suspension just as it had appeared in the security tape, loaded down with some heavy cargo.

A potential nuclear weapon?

Reed's heart hammered as he returned to his feet and listened. His ears still rang, and from farther up the tunnel he thought he detected panicked voices, still stirred to terror by the gunfire.

Those voices had no idea just how panicked they should be.

"You're not getting out of here alive, you swine," Reed snarled. The statement was more tactical than emotional. Reed would express his anger in physical ways, not vocal. But if Ibrahim answered, it might give away his position.

No return shout rang through the near perfect darkness. Reed wanted to thumb the light again, but he'd already rolled the dice by speaking at all. He elected to creep left instead, crab-walking along the front bumper of the pickup to the passenger's side. A similar aisle ran down that side of the carriage, although Reed couldn't see anything in the pitch black. He measured the space with a quick and silent sweep of his arm, then raised the MP5 again.

Abdel Ibrahim beat him to the punch. The snarl of automatic fire ripped beneath the line of vehicles, blowing out the tires of the pickup with a hiss and pinging off the undercarriage of the sedan beyond. Reed placed both hands on the hood of the pickup and instinctively leapt upward, hot lead slicing past his shin a split second before his boots landed on the front bumper. The MP5 slapped against his chest, and Reed let it hang, clawing his way over the truck's hood and onto the windshield. Ibrahim kept firing, dumping three-round bursts at random anywhere a person might stand. He didn't have a weapon light, apparently, and much of the gunfire was aimed by the irregular blast of muzzle flash alone.

Reed's skull thundered with the noise. He kept climbing, reaching the top of the pickup and laying himself over the windshield and roof. He clawed the MP5 back to his shoulder and trained the Aimpoint on the windshield of the Ford Transit sitting only three yards beyond.

Then he thumbed the weapon light.

A beam of hot white light sliced through the darkness and penetrated the Ford's windshield, illuminating two empty seats and an open space between that opened into the van's cargo area. A large metal device framed by angle steel sat in the bed, bright red and yellow wires running out of the top. An LED display flashed red numerals next to it. Tools lay scattered across the floor.

None of that mattered. Reed saw it all in an instant, but he zeroed instead on the shadowy form of a body lying chest-down in the back of the van. Both rear doors were open, and the figure leaned out to fire beneath the vehicle, his left hip and a portion of each leg barely visible around the side of the passenger seat.

Reed chose the hip. He flicked the selector switch to three-round burst and fired. Bullets blew out the windshield and raced into the cargo area as a trio, striking the figure first in the back of his knee before ripping into his upper thigh and then his hip. A shrill scream ripped through the darkness, and the second MP5 went silent. Reed slid sideways, throwing himself off the top of the truck and landing on his feet like a cat. He rushed to the side of the van, the weapon light now blazing down the length of the carriage, Aimpoint reticle sweeping from one possible vulnerability to the next. Searching for another target. Another hidden combatant, waiting to spring out and cut him down.

All he saw were bodies. A bunch of college-aged women riddled with bullets in the sedan behind. An older man slumped behind the wheel of his van.

Reed reached the rear of the Ford and spun left, finger riding the trigger, light blazing. He'd barely cleared the rear cargo door before a blast of automatic fire blazed from only feet away, sending hot lead ripping past his right arm. The shots were hurried and poorly aimed, unleashed in pure desperation. Reed's weapon light illuminated a Middle Eastern man lying on his stomach, his face alive with pain as he struggled with his weapon. The MP5 clenched in his hands ran dry and the bolt clicked. Reed's finger curled around his own trigger and started to constrict.

Then he stopped.

The man in the back of the van was Abdel Ibrahim. There wasn't a doubt in Reed's mind. He lay in a rapidly growing pool of his own blood, deep crimson streaming from his leg as his face washed white. He was already too weak to stand. Too weak to attempt to reload the MP5.

Ibrahim tried anyway, fumbling with the release switch. Reed lowered his submachine gun and stepped quickly over a field of fallen brass, boots crunching. He grabbed Ibrahim's weapon and tore it free of his trembling fingers while his own weapon light continued to blaze at the floor, offering partial illumination.

The terrorist scrambled backward, teeth gritted as he slipped on his own blood. Reed grabbed him by the collar and yanked him forward, halfway out of the van. With a heave, he lifted him upward and slammed him against the vehicle's doorjamb, ribs crushing against hard metal. Ibrahim choked, and Reed cocked his right arm.

The first blow landed like a battering ram, driving Ibrahim's head against the metal and obliterating his nose. Hot pain raced up Reed's arm, but he struck again. A third time. Nasal cartilage collapsed beyond recognition and teeth crunched. Ibrahim choked and struggled to fight back, but he could barely lift his arms now. Streams of blood ran out of the back of the van and splashed over Reed's boots.

And in the background, the weapon beeped.

Reed resumed his two-handed grip on Ibrahim's collar and shook, growling through clenched teeth.

"How do you turn it off?"

Ibrahim rasped. His eyes were bloody and his face torn. Reed allowed him to slump back against the van, the terrorist now too weak to even hold his head up. Raising the dangling MP5, Reed aimed the weapon light across the interior of the van, beyond the superstructure of angled steel to the weapon housed within.

It wasn't makeshift, and it certainly wasn't the handiwork of an amateur in a garage outside of Damascus. There had been professional modifications. A makeshift detonator powered by the car battery, and controlled by a small command screen complete with a keypad.

But the bomb itself was military. All the hallmarks were there. And more than military, it was *aerial,* clearly a rigged version of a heavy ordnance designed to be carried and deployed by an aircraft. Now it hung inside the welded structure of angle steel, removed of its guidance fins and reduced to a simple explosive.

Simple, but not small.

The weapon light flicked across Cyrillic writing inscribed along the outside of the bomb's housing and landed on the control screen. A numeral counted down. That numeral read 4:42 . . . then 4:41.

Reed wheeled back to Ibrahim and rammed the muzzle of the MP5 beneath the terrorist's chin, forcing his face up. Ibrahim offered no resistance, his features now chalk white as shadows crept over his eyes. Reed didn't have to guess why. One of his gunshots had cut Ibrahim's femoral artery. The man was bleeding out now. Rapidly. His life clock counted down from a number much smaller than that displayed by the bomb.

"How do you disable it?" Reed barked.

Ibrahim smiled. He didn't answer.

Reed dropped into a crouch and ran his hand around Ibrahim's leg, searching for the bullet wound that was dumping the most blood. He found it and rammed his fingers in. Ibrahim let out a little cry.

Reed spoke through his teeth. "*How do you disarm it?*"

"Why . . . would I tell you that?" Ibrahim's voice was barely above a whisper. Reed drove the MP5 deeper into his gut.

"Is it a nuke? *Where is the nuke?*"

This time Ibrahim laughed. It was a dry and lifeless sound. Mentally amused, but not emotionally.

"You really do not know, do you?"

Reed dug his fingers deeper into Ibrahim's wounded thigh. Blood still seeped out. There was no stopping it now. A trained surgeon with a mobile hospital couldn't have saved Ibrahim.

"Where is it?" Reed barked.

Ibrahim's lips curled into a smile. He blinked back enough blood to make eye contact.

"I have no idea."

A cold chill ran through Reed's trembling body. He wanted to hit Ibrahim again. He wanted to sink his fingers so deep into the terrorist's leg that he could rip the bones out. He wanted to hear him scream. He wanted to make him *suffer*.

"They are coming for you," Ibrahim hissed.

"Who?" Reed growled.

Ibrahim grinned. "My allies."

A shadow fell across Ibrahim's face. He looked suddenly very gray in the reflected glow of the weapon light bouncing off the carriage wall. His body went limp.

Reed leaned in gripping hard enough to draw a final flinch.

"You killed my *daughter*," he snarled.

Ibrahim's eyes moved slowly to face Reed. The death mist was creeping in so fast Reed thought he could see it, like storm clouds rolling in.

"And your country . . . killed my country," Ibrahim whispered.

Then America's most wanted terrorist flopped over, stone dead. Reed released him and stood quickly, his eyes burning as he stumbled back. A cry boiled up from his stomach, ripping through his throat before he could stop it. He screamed, tears misting over his eyes. His arms shook. His stomach tightened. He slammed his foot down over the body, crushing it into the carriage's floor. Smashing until the skull fractured and the jawbone shattered. He screamed and kicked and thrashed backward, nearly falling.

The doorframe of the van caught him. He slumped and looked sideways.

The bomb remained. The display counted down to two minutes flat.

58

The English Channel

Turk knew the moment the bomb went off. No mushroom cloud erupted from the ocean—no column of water five thousand feet high, swallowing up the Eurocopter in a split second. No earth-shaking release of unthinkable power erasing lives in the blink of an eye.

Instead it was a simple shudder. A section of water about the size of a football field lifted a foot from the rest of the swells, then sprinkled down again in a gentle shower. Shockwaves shot out on all sides, looking little larger than ripples from three thousand feet in the air. Turk thought he may have heard a soft *thud*, but the chopper was too loud to be sure.

Then . . . everything went still. The Channel resumed its perpetual tossing of irritable white caps, many of them washing against a trio of Royal Navy destroyers that were closing on the spot at full speed, ready to assist the survivors.

Except, there wouldn't be any survivors. Turk already knew that.

"That wasn't nuclear." Wolfgang's voice was subdued in the intercom. Turk blinked back a sudden sting in his eyes and nodded once. He gripped the railing next to the open side door and peered out across the open water, desperately hoping . . .

But there was nothing. No debris. No sign of flailing bodies. Just empty gray water.

"Take us down!" Turk called, smacking Corbyn on the arm.

Corbyn shot Wolfgang a hesitant look. Turk faced the door.

"We're going to look," he said. "We have to look."

59

The Situation Room
The White House

The English Channel was under live satellite feed when the bomb detonated. At first, Stratton wasn't sure he had seen anything. General Yellin grew very quiet and squinted at the screen while assistants and technicians rewound and replayed the data.

There was definitely something there. Something that defied the natural rhythms of the oceans as water lifted in a sort of cough . . . but it wasn't nuclear. It wasn't nearly large enough.

"Get London on the line," Stratton ordered.

An aide was already working a phone, ringing through to the halls of the British government. It took another ten minutes to receive the first word. It came from Prime Minister Wright herself.

"What happened, Prime Minister?" Stratton said.

"I don't know. We're communicating with our naval assets now. It seems there was a blast. We're not sure what kind, but it wasn't nuclear. We've lost communication with the train."

Stratton closed his eyes and lowered his head. He took a deep breath, not for himself so much as for the hundreds who no longer could. Even thinking about it brought his blood to a near boil, but there wasn't time to be angry. There wasn't even time for sympathy.

"I'm keeping our forces on full alert," Stratton said. "The full assistance of the United States is at your disposal."

"Thank you, Mr. Acting President. We'll keep you posted."

Wright hung up. Stratton stared at the satellite feed. He saw warships now, three British destroyers circling over the spot that had erupted only minutes prior. He couldn't see people or searchlights from the grainy satellite feed, but the wake patterns of the warships quickly formed into spirals as the vessels fell into a search and rescue formation.

Stratton spoke to Easterling without looking away from the screen. "Notify Langley. We need to know what happened."

60

Calais, France

After twenty minutes of fruitless searching, the pressure bearing down on Turk's chest was near absolute. Corbyn warned him that the Eurocopter was running low on fuel, but he wouldn't let her leave. He kept demanding concentric circles around the site of the blast, leaning out of the window and surveying the water while Corbyn communicated with the warships below.

Debris had begun to surface. Bits of insulation and plastic. A car tire here, still inflated, and a floating vehicle panel there. Most of it was unidentifiable from the air, but after another ten minutes of circling only two bodies had surfaced.

Both were slender and lifeless. Neither was Reed.

"Turk, I gotta put her down," Corbyn said. "We've barely got enough to make it back to shore."

Turk scrubbed a hand across his face, turning away so that nobody would see the wetness building in his eyes. He cleared his throat and spoke gruffly into the mic.

"Take us to France."

"Huh?"

"Take us to Calais. Maybe . . . somebody got out that way."

Corbyn banked the chopper and swept southward, calling into her mic along the way to request an emergency landing. Whoever answered on the other end didn't sound interested in obliging. Corbyn advised him that the chopper was coming down, ready or not, which triggered a string of French shouting.

Turk just watched the water, the aircraft thundering along as the warships faded from behind. Wolfgang squatted beside him and put a gentle hand on his shoulder, squeezing once. Turk assumed it was meant to be comforting, but he couldn't register any sort of emotion at the moment. His chest felt hollow, as though he'd been stripped of every vital organ and was somehow existing as a shell.

I should have gone in. I should have found a vehicle.

The French coastline appeared as a dark shadow marked by bright orange lights. Corbyn chattered on with the French air traffic controller, swapping insults as she zeroed in on the tunnel terminal. Turk thought again about the Triumph Rocket 3, and wondered how fast it was.

Fast enough?

The Eurocopter nosed down, and the terminal raced into view. Emergency vehicles and military trucks sat everywhere, French soldiers racing between buildings and rushing spotlights to the mouth of the service tunnel.

It was awash with seawater, flooding the mouth and completely blocking out any hint of the roadway beneath the Channel. Corbyn breathed a soft curse as she banked and circled the spot, then stopped over an empty parking lot. It wasn't a helipad, and a French soldier rushed out to wave her off. Corbyn set the aircraft down anyway, and the three wheels touched down with a gentle groan before the engine wound down.

Turk was already stepping through the open door, Wolfgang on his heels as they advanced toward the service tunnel. The soldier rushed toward them, extending a palm and shouting in French.

"Were there any survivors?" Turk said.

The Frenchman shouted on, apparently uninterested or unable to speak English.

"Survivors?" Turk repeated, voice rising.

The Frenchman flushed, hand jabbing toward the helicopter.

Turk's MP5 flashed from his belt like a striking snake, ramming against the guy's head as he screamed over the dying jet engines.

"*Survivors?*"

The Frenchman paled, his own hand falling toward a sidearm. He was much too slow, already stumbling back under the pressure of the muzzle. Wolfgang put a hand on Turk's arm and squeezed.

"Turk."

"Where are they?" Turk demanded, shoving the guy off balance. "Who survived?"

His voice choked, vision blurring as the hot tears overcame him. He could barely see. He didn't feel like himself.

"Turk!" Wolfgang shouted, yanking him back. Turk whirled, the pistol pivoting with him, ready to ram it down Wolfgang's throat. He stopped when Wolfgang released him, simply pointing inland.

Turk blinked the tears away and followed the gesture down the service road, away from the tunnel, straight to a curve about half a mile inland. Black tire marks scarred the pavement, there, leading straight into the turn.

And at that turn, lying on its side with the front wheel twisted and buried into the soft French soil, lay a gleaming red Triumph Rocket 3.

Hope ignited in Turk's chest. He holstered the Glock and shoved past the Frenchman, rushing for the road. Additional soldiers met him at the curb, brandishing FAMAS rifles and shouting for him to drop his weapon. Turk flatly ignored them, looking up the road for any sign of Reed.

The two-lane lay empty. Just the tire marks, and one very wrecked motorcycle.

"Montgomery!" Turk roared. "*Montgomery!*"

A French officer put a hand on his arm. Turk yanked free, throwing the guy aside. The soldiers crowded in, FAMAS muzzles rising toward his chest. Turk turned.

And then he saw him. Reed sat on a curb fifty yards away, staring blankly at the mouth of the service tunnel. Dirty seawater lapped at his feet, and a French medic squatted next to him, cleaning an ugly patch of road rash with a soft cloth.

Reed looked dazed. Shell-shocked. Like he didn't know where he was.

Turk rammed through the FAMAS barrels and sprinted across the street, grinding to a stop next to the curb. Reed turned bloodshot eyes on him, tears of his own drying slowly on his cheeks. His gaze was blank and lifeless. He didn't so much as flinch as the medic poured rubbing alcohol onto his raw arm.

"Reed," Turk said. "Are you okay?"

Reed made no answer, he just stared. Turk put a hand on his shoulder and squeezed.

"You're alive, dude. You're gonna make it."

Reed swallowed. His chest constricted, and dry breath rushed between his lips. Then he spoke in a perfect monotone.

"It's not over."

61

Vauxhall, London
England

The Prosecution Force made it back to England after Corbyn finally managed to sweet-talk the French authorities into providing a few gallons of jet fuel for the Eurocopter. Reed suspected that they were only too happy to have the aircraft—and its foreign occupants—out of their hair. Calais was a mess of storming military activity and panic near the tunnel.

The train had not surfaced. Neither had any of its occupants. Thus far, Reed was the only known survivor, and now that the passageways had allowed seawater to flood all three segments of the Chunnel, there was no way to access the deep point where three hundred and twelve people were trapped inside.

Many of them likely already dead.

As Corbyn banked the Eurocopter over the gulf, Reed looked down to see a tangle of British and French warships cutting back and forth across torn Channel seas, spotlights cutting across the water while military helicopters circled overhead, relying on infrared technology to reveal any survivors in the water.

It was an impressive showing, but Reed knew it was pointless. Nobody would escape that tunnel. What survivors somehow managed to barricade themselves into watertight compartments of the train would quickly run out of oxygen while they remained impossible to reach. It certainly hadn't been the attack the West was expecting, but something about its simplicity was deeply sinister. Reed had fought enough radicals to understand that it wasn't the promise of total annihilation that spread the most terror. It was the prospect of random, unexpected carnage.

A bombed school here. A torched office building there. The sorts of things that could, at any given point, kill anybody. It was the ultimate in psychological warfare, and yet Reed's gut told him that Ibrahim's final chess move had been even bigger than psych warfare. It had been a distraction. They had willingly followed him into London and zeroed in on the train, ignoring any and all else.

What had they missed?

Reed stared blankly out the open door of the Eurocopter as London flashed by and Vauxhall appeared on the horizon. Corbyn chattered with the air traffic control and Wolfgang and Turk sat silently behind, watching him, but not commenting. Reed hadn't explained Ibrahim's threat after Turk found him. What was the point? He would say it once, back at SIS headquarters, where something could be done. Until then it was just a waste of words, and Reed was far too spent for that.

He felt . . . nothing. A cavern opened in his chest, hollowing out any sensation of victory he should have enjoyed. He'd found his enemy. He'd watched him die. He'd made him suffer on the way out.

But it didn't feel like victory at all. It felt like . . . nothing. Just nothing.

The chopper touched down and Reed slid out without comment. He led the way to the steel door and down the stairwell into SIS headquarters. The others hurried to catch up, and moments later they were back at Arnold's operations center. The deputy director was still there, working a telephone and fielding a storm of shouts from the analysts and spooks spread across the room while satellite imagery of the English Channel played across the screen. Reed tracked in mud from the bottoms of his blood-stained boots, crimson tracing his arms and dirt sticking to his face. He caught his reflection in a pane of glass and barely recognized himself.

He didn't care.

Arnold caught his eye, and Reed tilted his head toward the conference room. He stepped in without comment and descended into a chair. Turk handed him a bottle of water, and Reed sucked it down. Arnold appeared two minutes later, his suit jacket removed, suspenders supporting his slacks. He shut the door.

"What the bloody hell happened?"

Arnold's voice was a mixture of alarm, frustration, and heartbreak. Reed simply gestured to the telephone resting on the table.

"Get the agency on the line."

"What?"

"The CIA. I'm only going to say this once."

Arnold drew breath to object, but Turk put a hand on his arm and shot him a look. The British deputy director gritted his teeth and mashed a button on the phone. An operator came on. He requested to be conferenced in with Interim Director Aimes in Langley. The line buzzed for only a moment before Dr. Sarah Aimes picked up, her voice taut and direct.

"John? What have you got?"

"I've got your team," Arnold said, the edge of frustration creasing his face.

"Reed?" Aimes said.

Reed capped the water bottle and flicked it into the waste basket. He swallowed. Everyone stood in breathless silence, waiting.

"The weapon was conventional," Reed said, not raising his voice. "Some kind of air-to-ground ordnance modified into a time bomb. Maybe a bunker buster. There was Cyrillic and a Soviet emblem stamped on it. I didn't have time for a closer look."

"No signs of a nuke?" Aimes asked, a hint of relief creeping into her tone.

"Not in the van," Reed said. "But he said there was one."

Arnold leaned across the table, both eyebrows raised. "*Who* said?"

"Ibrahim."

"And is he . . . " Aimes trailed off.

"Dead," Reed said, voice flat.

Another frozen silence descended over the room. Arnold closed his eyes and breathed slowly. Then Aimes cut back to business, because everything else could wait.

"We need everything you have. Anything he said, any clues he gave. Did he indicate where the weapon was?"

"He didn't know," Reed said. "He claimed to have allies—people who were pulling his strings and calling the shots."

"Other terrorists?" Arnold asked.

Reed shot him a look. "Obviously."

"Don't get coy with me, boy. I'm not asking what they're up to, I'm asking who they *are*. More radicals? State sponsorship?"

Reed thought back to his brief interaction with Ibrahim as America's most wanted man bled out on the floor. The bomb counting down. Reed's own body raw with adrenaline and enough surging hate to shatter bones.

It had only been a couple of minutes. It now felt like a fog.

"I don't know," Reed said. "He only referred to them as *they*. As in: *They are coming for you*."

Arnold breathed another curse. "And you're sure he didn't know anything?"

Reed remembered the agony ripping across Ibrahim's face as he pressed down on the bullet wounds. The blood draining from his cheeks. The death creeping into his eyes.

The terrorist may well have known something about the people he claimed to be working with, but he hadn't known the location of the bigger weapon. Reed was certain of that.

"He didn't know," Reed said.

Momentary silence, then Arnold addressed the phone.

"Sarah, I'll call you from my secure line."

"Copy."

The phone call terminated. Arnold turned for the door.

"If you leave this room, I'll have you shot," Arnold said.

He disappeared through the door, leaving the Prosecution Force alone around the table. Reed thought the threat was probably sincere, but it didn't need to be.

There was no place for him to go.

62

The Situation Room
The White House

Stratton hadn't departed the West Wing since the crisis began. Intel was flying thick from the English Channel, and most of his cabinet had now assembled around the lengthy conference table. General John David Yellin, chairman of the Joint Chiefs. The SecDef, Steven Kline. The Secretary of State, Lisa Gorman. Jill Easterling.

Sarah Aimes conferenced in from Langley, where her operations buzzed at full alert in a desperate attempt to scrape together any hint of a clue. Word from England had filtered through the CIA and reached the Situation Room via speakerphone.

There was no fear in Aimes's voice, yet she sounded more focused and strained than Stratton had ever heard her. There wasn't a doubt in his mind that she believed the intelligence flowing out of London, and that brought the temperature in the room down like a blast of blizzard wind.

"Ibrahim is dead, but there is still a weapon in play. We had an American operative on the ground. He was the last to speak to Ibrahim. He reports that Ibrahim claimed to be under the control of bigger actors—somebody pulling his strings. They have the weapon."

"And the weapon is nuclear?" Stratton asked.

"We can't say for sure, but it's possible. Ibrahim indicated an imminent attack. We're leaning on all our Middle East resources now and reviewing what intel we recovered from Beirut and Intrepid Oil Anchor. I'll keep you posted, Mr. Acting President."

Stratton mashed the *end call* button and stared at the phone. From screens around the room, reports were flowing in from the various branches and installations of the American armed forces. Updates of readiness as mandated by DEFCON 2. Lisa Gorman had been on the phone all night, partnering with representatives from the Pentagon to put America's allies—especially her nuclear allies—on alert.

There wasn't a blueprint for this. Not since the Cuban Missile Crisis. Stratton was looking at a map of the globe with a lost weapon capable of changing the fate of that globe, and no idea where to start.

"Mr. Acting President . . . " It was General Yellin. Stratton already knew what he wanted—DEFCON 1. Complete readiness. The ability to respond at a moment's notice.

Stratton fixated on the map and shook his head. "Not yet, General. Not yet."

63

Langley, Virginia

Aimes couldn't have felt more pressure if somebody were standing next to her with a gun to her head. With every flick of the second hand on the wall-mounted clock in her office, the crushing weight of the inevitable descended a little harder on her shoulders.

She'd been in touch with SIS. She'd been in touch with Mossad. She had the Pentagon on an open line. NSA and the FBI had pooled their resources to pursue intelligence leads and assess potential threats.

But nobody really knew anything. The only solid lead they had came from Wolfgang Pierce and his shadowy informant, presumably Ivan Sidorov. She spoke to Pierce in person and asked him to reach back out to his contact. Wolfgang called back ten minutes later with an update that brought her no closer to identifying Ibrahim's plan of attack, but at least gave her a better idea what she was working with.

If the weapon was indeed nuclear, and it had been sourced by Ibrahim from the same place he had sourced the VX used in the Baton Rouge attack, then there were certain assumptions that could be made. First, the bomb was likely Soviet in origin, making it somewhat outdated, but still a serious concern. Additionally, it couldn't be very large, because large nuclear weapons are very heavy, and this one was apparently both portable and light enough to be moved by helicopter.

That narrowed their search parameters considerably. Aimes reached out to the Pentagon, who in turn tasked a collection of military analysts and Cold War weapons experts to review the problem. They generated a possible list of likely options within the hour.

None of them were good. The smallest was the Soviet "suitcase bomb," code-named RA-115 and RA-115-01. The Pentagon still wasn't certain as to whether either of these prototypes had ever entered mass production. They were thought to be fifty or sixty pounds in weight, able to be put in a backpack and delivered on foot. Like the world's worst suicide vest. Output was estimated at less than two kilotons, or about two thousand tons of TNT. A massive explosion, to say nothing of the radiation, but only about an eighth of the size of the bomb used in Hiroshima.

From there the options became dramatically worse. During the early part of the Cold War, when the nuclear arms race was first heating up, the Soviet Union had developed *thousands* of prototypes and designs, most of which never entered mass production, or at least were never confirmed to have entered mass production. After the Strategic Arms Reduction Treaties were signed, many of these weapons were ostensibly disposed of, and United Nations inspections confirmed as much.

But the very concept that a weapon could have been lost assumed that such inspections had overlooked it, which meant any number of bombs built as early as the 1950s could be a risk. The top of the list included the Soviet RDS-4, an air-dropped device code-named "Tatyana," with an estimated yield of thirty kilotons. Almost twice the size of the Hiroshima bomb.

And then there was the risk of a hydrogen bomb. Many of those were too heavy to fit Aimes's assumed parameters, but any such weapon scaled to a size able to be carried by helicopter could still unleash unthinkable results. Not kilotons—*megatons*. Enough destructive force to flatten midsize American cities into unrecognizable ash.

"We're going to have to make some speculative leaps, Madam Director."

The officer on the phone was Colonel James Andrews of the United States Air Force, a Pentagon specialist with a doctorate in military history specializing in Cold War and Soviet weapons. Yes, the Pentagon had one of those. He'd just completed an assessment of the possible options, boiled down with military efficiency and delivered with clinical detachment. Aimes's mind spun ahead through the details of weight, delivery, and yield, focusing on an underlying thread that had been slowly developing over the course of the last few hours.

None of these weapons were ballistic. They were all either air-dropped ordnance, or in some other way delivered via the ground. That made sense, anyway, because if Ibrahim or his partners had the ability to launch an ICBM at the U.S., they already would have done so.

No, this attack would be delivered via transport of some kind, similar to the VX. That turned her mind to aircraft and ships.

"Thank you, Colonel."

Aimes hung up and called across the room to Rigby. Both doors of her office stood open, and a chain of CIA officers, directors, analysts, and subject matter experts were churning in and out, amplifying the space to the decibel level of a trading floor. It was loud, but it wasn't chaos. Aimes had established clear operational protocols, and Rigby was good at enforcing them.

Her youthful deputy director approached the desk, one iPad clasped in his left hand, two more pinned beneath his right arm. Following the recent retirement of notepads and printed documents, Aimes had begun to think there were more tablet computers at Langley than secrets.

"We need to start thinking about delivery," Aimes said. "Forget *what* is coming, let's fast forward to *how* it's coming. That may give us an edge."

"I've already been working on that," Rigby said. "It's got to be a ship or an airplane, right? I've advised the Pentagon and the FAA to be concerned about incoming airliners and cargo planes. They'll tighten security measures and redirect flights as necessary, but there's a lot of security at an airport, even in the Middle East. It would be difficult to smuggle a weapon that way, especially considering that a flight coming from so far away would need to land and refuel. More hoops to jump through."

"You're thinking it's more likely to be a ship?"

"At least equally so. Ibrahim already used transport ships to smuggle the VX into Savannah, so he's familiar with them. A ship could also explain why the attack hasn't already happened. It takes time to steam across the ocean, right? And once you're in port, you're already in position to detonate the bomb. You're close enough to a big city to wreak havoc . . . you don't even have to unload."

And there's hundreds of ships making port every day, Aimes thought.

She bit her lip, her tired mind overloaded on caffeine and running close to redline. She thought about a small weapon, similar to the sizes Colonel Andrews had described, smuggled aboard a shipping container. From the top deck of a cargo ship, the blast radius would be devastating. Any port on the East Coast could be a prime target.

But how could she possibly filter through the hundreds of freighters that might be closing in on the U.S. coastline? They could all be stopped, of course. Searched offshore, one at a time. The economic impacts of that decision could also be devastating, and worse than that, it could be a waste of time. The ship could have already slipped through.

Think, Aimes. Unwind the problem.

She closed her eyes. She put herself in Ibrahim's shoes. She gave him the benefit of mass resources provided by whatever generous ally had provided the bomb. She thought about logistics.

And then her eyes snapped open.

"The oil rig."

"Huh?" Rigby cocked his head.

"We thought he was using the rig as a workshop. Someplace to build the bomb. But Montgomery already reported that the weapon in the Chunnel was a modified aerial bomb, with a welded angle steel frame. That by itself could explain the workshop in his pictures."

"So . . . "

"So, what if the oil rig had a dual purpose? What if it was also a waypoint for a ship to onboard the second weapon—a weapon that couldn't afford to be caught at a port with security measures in place. What if they flew the nuke out to the Intrepid Oil Anchor, then used the onboard cranes to load it onto a ship?"

Rigby snapped his fingers. "We might have satellite imagery!"

"Get on it."

Rigby rushed back to his desk, and Aimes reached for the phone. Conjecture or otherwise, she wanted to update the Pentagon.

64

The Situation Room
The White House

The next call from Langley rang in just past ten p.m. Stratton and his tiring cabinet were still crowded into the Situation Room, the air hanging thick with the greasy smell of pizza and breadsticks. The acting president had long ago stripped away his jacket and tie, and an empty paper plate and half-empty bottle of Diet Coke were resting next to him when Easterling announced the call.

"Put her on speaker," Stratton directed, snapping his fingers for the room to fall quiet. Aimes's voice was taut to the point of cracking as it burst from the digital phone resting on the conference table.

"Mr. Acting President? We have a lead."

"You're on with the cabinet," Stratton said. "What have you got?"

"The Liberian flagged freighter *Cartova*. She's the same vessel that delivered Ibrahim to Beirut from Canada, a four-hundred-foot container ship. *Cartova* departed Beirut six days ago and we caught her on surveillance satellite at the Intrepid Oil Anchor—that's the oil platform where my team found Ibrahim."

The Situation Room fell deathly quiet. Stratton leaned forward.

"And?"

"There was cloud cover that day, sir. The image was unclear, but it seems she stopped alongside the platform and something was loaded on board. A single container. Then she steamed westward."

"Where to?" It was the obvious question. Stratton's fingernails ground into the tabletop as he awaited the answer, each microsecond passing like a millennium.

"We don't know, sir. We picked her up again at the Straits of Gibraltar, passing into the Atlantic. Then the cloud cover got us. The recordings are unreadable."

Stratton bit back a curse. "Did you contact her ownership? Was there not a destination on file?"

"We're trying, sir. It's unclear who owns her. I was able to acquire a manifest from port authorities in Beirut. She states only three crewmen on board—a captain, one deckhand, and a cook."

Stratton squinted. "*Three?* On a four-hundred-foot freighter?"

"I thought the same, sir. Subject matter experts tell me there should be twenty or more."

"Madam Director, General Yellin here." The chairman of the joint chiefs joined the conversation without asking. Stratton gave him room.

"Yes, General?"

"Has your agency developed a list of plausible coastal targets given assumed cruising speed and time elapsed?"

The next logical question. Aimes was ready for it.

"We have, General. I'm transmitting that to my liaison now."

The liaison Aimes referred to was a senior CIA officer in the operations directorate—somebody Aimes trusted and recommended to Stratton as a Situation Room sit-in while she maintained her focus at Langley. It was a forward-thinking approach, and Stratton appreciated it.

The liaison operated a computer connected to the Situation Room's bank of display screens. He flicked his finger across the trackpad and opened a map on the largest screen. It displayed the North Atlantic with dashed white lines leading broad arcs from the Straits of Gibraltar to various key locations along the American seaboard.

Miami. Jacksonville. Savannah. Charleston. Norfolk. Washington and Baltimore. New York City and Boston.

The little dashed lines exceeded every target south of Baltimore, indicating that the Liberian freighter could have already reached those cities. It was still a few hours out from NYC and Boston, but not far.

Stratton turned back to the phone. "Aimes, shoot straight with me. What are the odds there is a nuclear device aboard that vessel?"

Brief pause. "It's possible, sir. I couldn't put a number on it."

Stratton looked back to the map. He paused for a beat to imagine the consequences. Then his mind clicked to the next step—because there had to be one.

"Keep us posted, Aimes."

He mashed the *hang up* button and pivoted directly to Yellin.

"General, scramble some jets. I want the eastern and Gulf seaboards blanketed, Mexico to Canada. Have them armed and ready to fire. I want that ship *found*, ASAP."

Yellin nodded once, but one eyebrow rose in a slight question. The inevitable question.

The next logical step.

Stratton simply nodded, then pivoted his attention to Steven Kline. The SecDef sat with a slice of cold pizza resting between his arms, a mess of tablet computers and printouts scattered around him, his own shirt unbuttoned and sweat-stained. The same question hanging on his face.

"Notify our allies, Mr. Secretary. We're moving to DEFCON 1."

Kline didn't argue. He scooped up the phone resting next to him with a direct line to the Pentagon, and gave the order.

"Immediately advance to DEFCON 1 and place all military departments on maximum alert. Repeat, advance from *Fast Pace* to *Cocked Pistol*. Nuclear threat perceived imminent. This is a White Alert."

Kline's voice droned on as he mechanically worked down a checklist of orders to give and phone calls to make. Yellin was ahead of him, already engaging standing military protocols for all four traditional military branches along with the United States Coast Guard. Ships would be deployed. Nuclear silos around the nation and boomer submarines in all seven seas placed on standby for possible launch orders. Military bases around the globe called to full alert and locked down. Aircraft along the entire eastern seaboard—already fueled, armed, and resting on standby as a result of DEFCON 2—now given the order to launch.

The largest, most deadly military the world had ever seen was gearing up for a war that might never come—or might destroy the globe within the next hour.

As the phones rang and Stratton stared at the map, contemplating any one of dozens of targets now within reach of a potential attack, a throat cleared over his left shoulder.

"Mr. Acting President . . . we'd like to move you to the bunker now."

Stratton looked over one shoulder. It was Special Agent Jim Dorsey, the head of his detail. Stratton simply nodded, reaching for his coat. The rest of the cabinet was already on their feet, prepared to accompany him. On his way to the door Stratton's mind buzzed into high gear, not thinking ahead to what might happen in the next sixty minutes, but rewinding to what had already happened in the last two years. To the conflicts and unexpected catastrophes. To the war that almost erupted, right at the start of Maggie's presidency . . . and the player on the other side of the world who she had faced off with.

Another nuclear power with a war-mongering leader standing behind the trigger.

Stratton found Lisa Gorman walking next to him, punching out an email on her smartphone. He brushed her arm, and she looked up.

"Get me an open line to Moscow, Madam Secretary. I want to speak to President Nikitin directly."

65

Eastern Hemisphere
Undisclosed Location

In the darkened hotel room, Ibrahim's erstwhile ally remained behind the twin screens, zeroed in this time on the blipping green dot creeping westward across open water. Running at full speed, with only a token amount of cargo and a skeleton crew, the Liberian freighter had made excellent time. She was only about ninety minutes from being within reach of her target, although two hours would place her right at the heart of it. That would certainly be more ideal—it would unleash much worse and much more permanent devastation. With each slow tick of the digital clock on the computer screen, the ally's heart thumped a little harder.

He felt a little more hopeful, but also a little more concerned. It had been hours since the bomb went off in the Chunnel. Intelligence from inside the SIS was sketchy at best, but it did seem that the British—or perhaps the Americans—had anticipated that attack ahead of time. They hadn't been able to stop it, but just the fact that they were so close on Ibrahim's heels was a bad sign.

It could mean they were close on the heels of the bigger plan—the plan the Chunnel attack was designed to disguise. If that were the case . . .

No. He wouldn't allow himself to go down that mental path. There wasn't a lot that could be done to stop the Americans at this stage, even if they were zeroing in on the Liberian freighter. It was a simple matter of passing time. Another ninety minutes, maybe a hundred, and all else would be history.

There wasn't any point in worrying now. He should focus, and maybe prepare to celebrate. There was a monster of a promotion coming his way after the successful implementation of this complex scheme. Managing Ibrahim had been hard work, and doing so without any traces leading back to the mastermind standing behind the curtains was even harder. He himself was the plausible deniability, the smoke screen.

But once this was over, he wouldn't need to be. He could be something much bigger. Something more powerful in the world order to come.

The ally sipped raw vodka from a hotel-branded tumbler and suppressed a belch. He focused on the screen. He tried not to stress.

Something in the back of his mind . . . an instinct, or maybe a fear. Something was there . . .

The digital calling software built into his second computer chimed through his headphones. The contact was labeled in code, but there was really only one person the ally expected to be calling, anyway. He hit the answer button.

"Yes?"

"We have an update." The voice was computer-distorted, but the robotic growl sounded a little like the actual, gravelly growl of the real speaker. Even with a few thousand miles separating them, the ally felt his blood pressure spike. Talking to the man on the other end made him nervous. It likely always would.

"Yes?" he said.

"The Americans suspect an attack. They've moved to full alert and are deploying aircraft to search their eastern seaboard. We're running out of time."

The uneasiness in the pit of the ally's stomach blossomed into full-blown nausea. He bumped the volume up.

"What now?"

"Contact the ship. Advise them to ready the weapon. We may need to detonate early."

"We're still ninety minutes out . . . there's nothing within range."

"Contact the ship. We'll worry about the rest."

The call ended. The ally wiped swept from his forehead. He gulped more vodka.

Then he dialed another number.

66

The Kremlin
Moscow, Russia

President Makar Nikitin took the American phone call in his executive office. Not the practical, daily office he used for the business of actual work, but the decorative one lined with opulent gold trim and painted a deep shade of maroon. Plenty of fancy chairs and an ornate desk with a high-backed leather chair. This was the diplomatic office, where he might receive visiting heads of state, or entertain wealthy oligarchs whose support —and money—he required.

It was the showroom. The Russian equivalent of the Oval Office. For some reason, it felt apropos this morning. As the sun rose slowly from Siberia and spilled toward the Russian capital, Nikitin took his Russian tea black, and his call on speaker.

"Mr. Acting President. So good to hear from you. Let me express my sincerest condolences on the condition of President Trousdale. The thoughts and prayers of the Russian people are with her."

"Thank you, Mr. President."

Nikitin had never spoken to Jordan Stratton before, but he recognized the crisp and direct Chicago accent from the number of Stratton's political speeches and press conferences he had viewed. There was an all-business undertone to Stratton's style of address that appealed to Nikitin. He felt power in his pose and confidence in his word choice, qualities he respected in a fellow world leader.

Even a rival one.

"I'll get straight to the point, Mr. President. You've been notified that we're moving our alert status to DEFCON 1?"

"I have." Nikitin sampled his tea. It was bitter—even more than usual. Typically he preferred it that way, but this morning felt special. He reached for the honey.

"You're aware of what this means?" Stratton asked.

"I understand you're concerned about a terrorist threat?"

"Not concerned, Mr. President. We expect an imminent attack. I'm calling to notify you of our intentions as we place our military at full readiness. International U.S. military bases are moving to full alert and locking down. We're deploying aircraft and naval assets around our shores and—"

"And your boomers are traveling to launch depth," Nikitin said.

The line went silent. Nikitin allowed himself a smile, but didn't allow the smile to seep into his tone.

"You are new at this, of course. I have some experience monitoring the activities of your military. We are aware of your . . . preparations."

It wasn't a threat. It was a statement of fact. Nikitin knew the American military had swung into battle mode from one side of the globe to the other, not only because his military intelligence services kept an unblinking eye on them, but because he'd expected them to.

"I want to be sure we don't have any misunderstandings," Stratton said. "This is the sort of situation that could easily boil over."

"You need not fear, Mr. Acting President. Cooler heads there have never been than heads in my cabinet. The Russian military stands ready to assist you should any attack be attempted. We are already deploying assets into the North Sea to remain on standby to assist Britain, should she choose to accept."

"That's part of why I'm calling. I'm told you've moved three missile cruisers and two attack submarines through the Skagerrak. You can understand my concern for such heavily armed vessels—"

"A rescue flotilla!" Nikitin said, feigning indignation. "We want to be sure our friends in the West have every assistance they require to work through this unthinkable tragedy."

Another pause. Nikitin sipped his tea. It was delicious—the honey had really brought out the flavor. He might pour himself a second cup.

"Mr. President," Stratton said. "I would advise you very strongly to take great care in your military activities over the next few hours. As I said before . . . we don't want any misunderstandings."

Nikitin smiled—and this time, he didn't care if his tone betrayed it.

"Your recommendation is taken under advisement, Mr. Acting President. I will keep a line open. Don't hesitate to call."

He mashed a button. The call terminated. He took another slow sip of tea, then faced the man sitting across from him, stiff-backed in an expensive horsehair chair. Dark eyes and a face not even a mother could love. Completely expressionless.

"We're sixty-five minutes out." The man spoke in a gravelly growl, his eyes unblinking.

Nikitin nodded. He rocked the cup and finished the tea. He relaxed in his chair.

"Give the order, Golubev. The time has come."

67

Western Hemisphere
Undisclosed Location

The order arrived via secure transmission over an encrypted email service. It was brief and direct. Just two lines.

Watch for aircraft and warships, Americans on high alert. Arm the weapon.

The captain of the *Cartova* received the message in perfect calm, immediately placing a call to the two men working just beneath the deck inside that one particular container. Nominally a cook and a deckhand, in truth only one of them was trained as a mariner, and neither of them could cook. At least not anything edible. Their real purpose was to assist in the management and preparation of "the package," as they had come to call it.

It sat inside one of the containers hidden below deck, most of the rest stocked with dry rice or nothing at all. The *Cartova* ran high in the water, making excellent speed from its massive fuel-oil-burning engines that had chugged along at full throttle for most of the last twenty-four hours. From the bridge, the captain could monitor both the black sky ahead and the navigation screen that marked his path to the target.

It was now only thirty-two kilometers and about fifty-five minutes away.

Pretty soon it would be time to join his compatriots inside the lifeboat mounted to the *Cartova*'s stern. The emergency vessel had been modified to feature a more powerful engine and enlarged fuel tanks. The improvements gave the lifeboat enough power and stamina to quickly sail out of the water surrounding the target and reach the shores of a friendly safe haven, not far away. A place where the three of them could survive, and cash their generous paychecks.

The *Cartova*, meanwhile, would churn ahead on autopilot. The package in the container just below deck would slowly count down, the time remaining matched to the distance left to travel.

The vessel would reach her mark . . . and then the world would change forever.

But the captain wasn't really worried about any of that. He was already planning how to spend his impending financial windfall—booze, women, and an early retirement.

68

Vauxhall, London
England

When America went to DEFCON 1, the SIS went into overdrive. Reed felt the moment like a light switch powering on stadium lights. The entire tone of the operations center escalated to a fever pitch. All the nervous chitchat and inflammatory cursing evaporated. Nobody spoke unless necessary. Orders were shouted in the fewest possible words.

And Arnold returned to the glass-encased office.

"On your feet, all of you." He snapped his fingers and jerked his head. Reed and his team fell in line, following the fast-walking director down a stairwell to a bank of computer desks standing beneath the projector screens that lined the far wall.

"Sit," Arnold snapped.

Reed hesitated over the computer. Corbyn dropped right into place, sliding a headset over her ears and inputting the passcode displayed on a sticky note.

"*Sit*," Arnold repeated.

Reed sat, a little disillusioned by the unfamiliar buzz around him. All the hallmarks of a combat zone were there—the tension, the operational protocols, the strained faces. He only missed the bullets, or anybody to shoot at.

Reed didn't know what to do without somebody to shoot at.

"All right, you blokes," Arnold said. "Here's the situation. Your government has escalated to a White Alert and is about to blow the planet into smithereens. Apparently this tosser you killed in the Chunnel had a nuke on hand, and Langley believes that nuke to be aboard a Liberian flagged freighter, headed for America."

Reed's blood turned to ice. Arnold remained perfectly calm.

"So here's what you're going to do. Half my analysts are still stuck on trains headed to work. You're going to fill in. The software you're looking at is active global—"

"Active global satellite feed," Corbyn cut him off. "I know. I'll show them. What are we looking for?"

"We're looking for this." Arnold smacked a key on Reed's computer. An image popped up, a little grainy and distorted by distance. It depicted a row of ships in harbor, all commercial-type container vessels and oil tankers. One ship was circled in the middle. Only half of it was visible, but the name *Cartova* was clearly printed on the stern above a city name: *Beirut, Lebanon.*

"That's the best picture you have?" Corbyn said.

Arnold muttered a curse. "We're pulling miracles out of our backside here, Corbyn. Find the ship!"

Then he was gone, leaving Corbyn to tighten her ponytail and exhale an exhausted sigh.

"Okay. Wolfgang, you'll take Newfoundland to New York. Turk, you'll go NYC to Washington, and I'll go from there to Miami. Reed, you've got the Gulf."

"How do you use it?" Turk leaned close and squinted at the screen, one massive hand blanketing the mouse.

"What do mean, how do you use it? Haven't you ever used Google Earth? Pan and zoom. The ship will kick up a white wake. You'll need to get close before you can spot it."

"And how do we know it's the right ship?"

Wolfgang asked the question. Arnold shouted an answer from thirty feet away. "You don't! Circle them and send an IM with coordinates to critical review. We'll determine."

Wolfgang cocked an eyebrow. "Critical—"

"Right here," Corbyn sighed and smacked a key, opening a dialog window. "It's just a messenger. Bloody hell, do they teach you Yanks anything?"

Reed's gaze settled on the screen and immediately blurred. Despite the noise and intensity engulfing him, his heart rate remained perfectly calm. His mind was still, like a vacant room, his fingers a little numb. He rolled his hand over and stared at his palms.

His fingertips were still stained with Ibrahim's blood, creased by callouses and old scars. As he stared, his hands began to tremble, but he couldn't feel them.

He couldn't feel anything—not the room, not the seat beneath him, not the pressure of a probable nuclear weapon churning toward his homeland with the lives of tens, maybe hundreds of thousands held in the balance. He just kept thinking of Ibrahim and the moment the death glaze passed over the terrorist's eyes.

How many kills did this make? There was a time when Reed logged each one in a little black book kept beneath his bed, and each entry carved out a small piece of his soul. But now he'd given up tracking. Given up caring. There might be dozens, there might be two hundred.

And he realized, he hadn't felt a thing when Ibrahim died. None of the rushing satisfaction or hot vengeance he longed for. No flooding relief to fill the void left by his slain unborn child.

Nothing at all.

"Reed! Let's go!" Corbyn shouted from the end of the line, and Reed blinked hard. He caught Turk staring sidelong at him, and he focused on the screen.

A wide open ocean. A clock with an unknown value counting slowly down to brutal, unthinkable carnage. And a room full of desperate analysts searching for a lost ship like World War One biplane pilots searching for enemy artillery.

I've got to move.

The numbness faded as a surge of forced urgency rippled through

Reed's mind. He began at Miami and moved rapidly up Florida's Gulf Coast, panning fifty and a hundred miles out to sea and logging what sparse shipping he could find. On occasion he found clusters of stalled tankers and container vessels, and he assumed the White House had ordered for all incoming vessels to be halted at sea. What ships still churned along fast enough to kick up a wake were much easier to spot. He screenshotted them all alongside pop-up coordinates and dropped them into the instant messenger.

And he ground on. North to the Big Bend. West to white sand beaches and Mobile Bay. Onward to the Louisiana coastline, crowded by oil platforms that stalled his progress.

The Prosecution Force circled and sent ships via the instant messenger, but Reed could tell by the conversation across the open operations center that none of them were the *Cartova*. A few were flagged for investigation by the U.S. Navy or Coast Guard. Most were already quarantined well off the coast.

Reed made it to Houston, and he stopped. His mind still buzzed with brain fog, thoughts moving slowly like a Marine fighting his way through a swamp. He knew something was there . . . something vague, and just out of reach. A thought, caught in the mire but developing slowly.

The *Cartova* shouldn't be in the Gulf, he realized. Not with so many crowded shipping lanes and swarms of aircraft. Churning around the tip of Florida didn't make sense, anyway. Barring Houston, there was no coastal city accessible by the Gulf that was larger than Miami. Why keep sailing? Why not blow the bomb there?

It's not about people.

The thought finally broke free of the mental muck and gleamed under clear sunlight. Reed sat up and blinked hard, his heart rate finally rising to match the tempo of the strained room. He pictured himself in Ibrahim's shoes, and considered the destructive potential of a nuclear weapon hidden aboard a ship, like the world's largest hand grenade.

It hadn't detonated yet, which meant it had sailed right past the most obvious targets. Ibrahim would want to cripple the United States in the worst way possible. And if it wasn't a crowded city . . .

Reed panned left. He zoomed out and raced across the Gulf. His mouse slid and his eyes blurred. He blinked back to focus and squinted at a stretch of coastline thousands of miles removed from America's borders—yet still planted right at the heart of her national interests.

The satellite imagery loaded slowly. Reed zoomed and panned, fingers racing now. Searching. Watching. The trembling returned to his hand as a speck caught his eye, barely visible on the dark oceans but marked by the British satellite's infrared technology.

Only a few miles from the coast. Churning up a tumultuous wake, and driving straight ahead. Reed zoomed. The image loaded.

And then his back went rigid.

69

The Situation Room
The White House

"They found her! The Brits found her!"

The shout rang from the far end of the crowded conference table as an aide slammed his phone down and returned to a computer. Stratton rose from his chair, gaze snapping to the screen at the end of the room. It was a satellite image, and the picture was in motion. Racing far south of the U.S. eastern seaboard, and even south of Florida. Skating across the Gulf in an instant and rocketing toward . . . Central America?

He squinted, momentary confusion playing across his mind. Then the satellite feed stopped over a circle in the western extreme of the Caribbean Sea, only a handful of miles removed from the city of Colón, Panama.

"Is he . . . " Easterling spoke, then broke off. General Yellin filled the gap.

"He's gonna take out the canal!"

Stratton's breath froze over as the feed focused on a ship. He wasn't any sort of an expert when it came to maritime vessels, but the general outline of the container ship as marked by the CIA's advanced spy satellite technology matched that of the rudimentary images he'd seen of *Cartova*. The vessel was moving, rapidly. Wake rushed up across the dark water behind it, the bow pointed straight for the Panamanian coast.

The canal.

It was the last target Stratton would have suspected, but while the prospect of mass American death vacated his mind, very little relief rushed in to take its place. He didn't need to be a maritime expert to understand the strategy. Stretching across the narrowest section of Central America, the canal constituted the only direct shipping route between the Atlantic and the Pacific without spending weeks of wasted time and fuel churning south around Cape Horn. No nation on earth depended so greatly on the regular passage of container ships through that narrow slot of water as the United States.

This wasn't a death blow, it was an *economic* blow.

"Sink it, General," Stratton snapped. "Whatever you've got. Hit it now!"

70

USS *Boxer*
342 nautical miles east of the Panama Canal
The Caribbean Sea

Lieutenant Laura Hutchins was already waiting in the pilot's ward room aboard the 843-foot amphibious assault craft when the order to man her Joint Strike Fighter tore through the speakers like a punch to the gut. She snatched her flight helmet from the table and rose out of her seat, but didn't head for the door as the air boss exploded through, face rosy red and strained, hair slicked back with too much product.

There was a strange light in his eyes. A mix of earnest anticipation and unthinkable strain. From the flight deck overhead the scream of a siren rang, matched by the continued blare of orders for four of the *Boxer*'s F-35B Joint Strike Fighters to be moved into position for immediate launch.

It was happening. Only a few thousand miles from the American homeland, the *Boxer* was preparing to go to war. Even after six hours of the vessel standing at general quarters, with every member of its twelve-hundred-person crew manning their battle stations while the United States Navy stood at white alert, the call for launch still felt sudden.

It still sent a cold chill racing through Laura's petite body and down to the tips of her fingers. When she blinked, she saw fire. She heard the scream of an F/A-18E Super Hornet's incoming weapon alert as an Iranian air-to-air missile raced toward her, high above the Persian Gulf.

She felt the bite of the ejection handle into her gloved hands as she pressed her helmet into the fighter's headrest . . . and pulled.

"Listen up!" the air boss shouted through the room, yanking her attention back to the present. Laura focused on him even as continued orders barked through the ship's intercom.

"We've got a target and we're cleared to fire. *Cartova*, Liberian flagged container ship steaming straight for the Panamanian coast, three-hundred forty-two miles distant. The vessel is believed to be carrying a WMD, likely a nuke, targeted at the Panama Canal."

The ice in Laura's gut turned sharp, and she swallowed before she could stop herself. Even with her eyes open, she could see the fire now. The thunder of wind blasting through her helmet as she exploded out of the Super Hornet and raced into the sky.

The missile detonated only seconds later, so close she could feel the heat wave. The world spun beneath. She vomited, body slamming against her ejection seat restraints.

The parachute launched. Her head snapped back. She raced for the ocean floor . . .

Laura blinked again, forcing the memory back. Focusing on the moment.

Zero in, Hutch. Pay attention!

"I'm authorizing a flight of four aircraft armed with AGM-158C cruise missiles," the air boss continued. "Your flight leader will radio the ship and attempt communication. After that, you're clear to engage with maximum force. Good luck."

He turned for the door, and the air wing commander took his place, a Navy O-6 wearing a sweat-stained shirt with deep creases lining his forehead. His gaze swept the small crowd of pilots, flicking from one eager face to the next, all ten of the Navy aviators packed into the small room silently pleading to be chosen.

Years of training. Thousands of flight hours. Peacetime drills and ages of monotonous classroom learning, all preparing them for this single moment. A moment that could easily pass them by.

But Laura didn't want it. Not because her transition from the USS *Reagan* and its wing of Super Hornets to the much smaller USS *Boxer* and its wing of F-35s had been a difficult one. She'd adapted to the advanced Joint Strike Fighter with ease, passing her coursework with the same flying colors that had landed her in the cockpit of a Navy fighter in the first place.

It wasn't the aircraft, or the mission, or even the prospect of a nuclear weapon detonating in her face that concerned Laura. The anxiety eating at the back of her mind was much deeper. Much more personal.

Laura no longer trusted herself.

"Packer, you'll take command," the air wing commander said. "Torch, Diamondback, Hutch. You're up!"

The O-6 jabbed a thumb over his shoulder, and Laura winced, but she didn't hesitate to scoop up her helmet and turn for the door. Metal steps pounded beneath her boots as she followed the other three pilots—all men—onto the flight deck. Her bird waited near the starboard side, fueled and armed, ready for a vertical takeoff.

It didn't surprise Laura that she'd been chosen. Of the ten aviators crowded in the ready room, all were expert fighter pilots, but only she had actual combat experience.

"Let's freakin' go!" Diamondback's voice burst through the intercom as Laura's canopy locked into place with a hiss of the airlock. Her mask snapped into place, then the heads-up display connected to the F-35's onboard computer system flashed on.

Everything was digital inside the Joint Strike Fighter. Touch screens and a lot of virtual reality displays, connecting her view to onboard cameras that allowed her to look straight through the floor at the ground far beneath.

Or the ocean.

Laura's heart rate accelerated as the F-35 lifted elegantly off the flight deck, rising straight up like a helicopter with its jet pipe pointed down and lift fans built beneath the cockpit generating forty thousand pounds of vertical thrust. Then she was banking, leaning into the turn. Gaining speed under afterburner and racing to fall into a diamond formation behind

Packer—Diamondback to her left, Torch taking tail. They were three of the *Boxer*'s best, Packer having flown the F-35 since its earliest integration into the Navy.

They all knew what buttons to push and what controls to leverage, but none of them knew what it *felt* like to be shot at. Not yet.

Laura focused on the display, orbiting quickly through menus to land on her navigation. The route from *Boxer* across three-hundred-plus miles of open ocean was translated by Packer's jet and loaded into her autopilot. The time to target was displayed as a slow countdown, seconds ticking by as miles evaporated.

Seventeen minutes.

71

Cartova
The Caribbean Sea

The captain could see the lights of Colón bright in the bridge windows as the container ship closed to within five miles of the Panamanian coast. It was fifteen minutes to midnight, and he couldn't help but appreciate the irony of the time. He certainly hadn't planned it this way, but as an amateur poet in his spare time, he appreciated the symmetry of the situation.

Of course he knew all about the famed "Doomsday Clock," originated and operated by the Bulletin of Atomic Scientists, a nonprofit founded by some of the same brilliant minds who originated the nuclear weapon in the first place. The clock wasn't actually a clock so much as a thermometer. It displayed an estimate of the temperature of global tensions, projecting the likelihood of a world-ending catastrophe, specifically a nuclear one.

The reading was expressed as "minutes to midnight." The closer the Bulletin of Atomic Scientists set the clock to midnight, the more imminent they considered a catastrophic event.

The captain had run a web search earlier that day and found that the clock was currently set to ninety seconds to midnight, an unprecedented adjustment triggered by the string of equally unprecedented events that had ravished the world's leading superpower. How those events linked to the plausible end of the world was, of course, undetermined.

But the captain of the *Cartova* knew how they linked to the first use of nuclear weapons in anger since the Second World War, and he didn't at all mind being an integral part of that, even if nobody would ever know.

Maybe especially because nobody would ever know. There was some poetry in that, also.

Boots struck the steel deck behind him, and the captain turned to see the specialist step in—the ostensible "cook" who was in fact responsible for readying the weapon. He nodded once, and the captain looked to the digital display built next to the throttle controls.

Cartova proceeded west at full speed, the autopilot routed for the entrance of the Panama Canal. All security controls and emergency protocols had been suspended. The engines wouldn't stop even as the bow rammed into the soft Panamanian mud.

But by then, there wouldn't be a bow. Or a town. Or any of the forty-thousand-odd residents who called Colón home. There would only be a mushroom cloud.

The time on the autopilot displayed the true doomsday clock—fourteen minutes to midnight.

"Head for the lifeboat," the captain said. "It's time to abandon ship."

72

The Caribbean Sea

"She's four miles off the coast!"

Packer's voice stormed over Laura's headset as her F-35 streaked through the air fifteen thousand feet off the torn salt water. She already had the ship on her scope, a targeting protocol locked onto the heat signature. The AGM-158C anti-ship cruise missile housed in her weapons bay was armed and ready for launch.

Laura likely wouldn't launch. Packer would deploy his weapon first—she would fire second if there were any error.

Cold sweat ran down her face, slipping behind her mask as Laura blinked hard and focused on the black sky ahead. The time to target clock spun down on her digital dash, and the Joint Strike Fighter hummed a steady roar as the afterburner kept her at maximum cruising speed.

She was blowing through fuel. She knew the Navy didn't care. Only one thing mattered—stopping that ship before the world changed forever.

"*Cartova*, *Cartova*, this is the United States Navy. We have weapons locked and are prepared to fire on your ship. Stop your engines and immediately state your intentions."

Packer's voice remained calm as he hailed the container ship. Laura licked her lips and wondered whether she hoped for a response. It would be reassuring to hear the *Cartova*'s skipper return the call, announcing himself as nothing more than a normal cargo freighter with a disabled transponder.

But seconds ticked by, and no response came. Packer radioed again.

"*Cartova, Cartova.* This is the United States Navy. We are seconds away from firing on you. Stop your engines and declare your intentions!"

Again the radio went silent, and Laura measured her breathing. Her palms felt cold, but still somehow she sweated. She kept one hand on the stick and the other free in her lap, fingers stretching and flexing.

Stay in the fight. Stay in the fight.

"Viper One, sitrep, over."

Boxer called from three-hundred-plus miles behind, and Laura recognized the air boss's voice. Packer didn't leave him hanging.

"We're radio silent, *Boxer*. No word from *Cartova*. She's proceeding at present course and speed."

"Copy that, Viper One. You are cleared to engage. Sink that sucker!"

"Cleared in hot," Packer replied. "AGM, fifteen thousand feet."

A dull whoop rang through the pilot-to-pilot intercom. It was Diamondback, ready for action. Laura's fingers played across the digital screen as she gave her F-35 the order to open its weapons bay. She felt none of Diamondback's enthusiasm. Only burning anxiety as memories of the last time she had readied weapons in combat stormed through her mind.

The sweat redoubled. She blinked it away and zeroed in on the canopy ahead. Her body tensed, but her hand remained loose over the stick, finger curled a half inch over the trigger. Targeting solution locked. A breath away from blowing *Cartova* into a billion burning fragments.

"Viper One, going hot." A hint of excitement edged into Packer's voice. Laura swallowed once and glanced left, ready to see the nearly three-thousand-pound AGM-158C missile drop from Packer's open weapons bay.

But nothing happened. A moment that felt like a minute passed. Packer repeated his intention to fire. Still, the weapon wouldn't release.

"I'm locked up, Hutch. Something's wrong. Go hot!"

Laura's mind skipped. She inhaled sharply, currents of sweat now draining down her face. She turned forward, looking automatically to her targeting display. *Cartova* lay less than three miles ahead, and only half a mile from the Panamanian coast. It would take the AGM seconds to close that distance. She had only to press the trigger.

"Hutch? Go hot!"

Packer's command crackled through the radio again, but Laura couldn't move. Her fingers went rigid. She tried to swallow to jar herself out of it, but her throat wouldn't work. Her chest tightened.

It was like telling herself to jump off the side of a building. Her mind screamed the order but her body wouldn't respond.

"*Fire*, Hutch!" Packer's voice snapped now, finally sharp enough to break the trance. Laura's mind clicked into gear, and her finger clamped down.

"Viper Two, fox three. Weapon away!"

The F-35 bounced upward a little as the hefty cruise missile deployed. A vibration shook her seat, then the orange glow of the missile's engine lit the night sky as the weapon raced away.

"Diamondback, go ahead. Let's give 'em two!"

Packer didn't need to say it twice. Diamondback's matching cruise missile flashed into the night before his voice even crackled over the intercom.

"Viper Three, fox three. Weapon away!"

"Break out!" Packer ordered.

Laura pulled on her stick, rolling the fighter right and lifting the nose to bring the jet into a turn away from Panama. She added afterburner as Diamondback completed a mirror version of her turn and Packer and Torch both swept directly up and over. The four jets settled into the same diamond formation while the clock continued to count down on Laura's targeting display.

Time to impact: Forty-eight seconds. Forty-seven. Forty-six.

Suddenly, all the mental deadlock evaporated, replaced by instantaneous anxiety of a new sort. Laura fixated on the targeting system and willed the missile ahead.

Faster. Faster. Hit it now!

And then came the blast. Not the crack of a cruise missile, or even the twin flashes of two. Laura saw the light first, blazing past the tail of her jet and illuminating the eastern sky as bright as midday. Her night vision flooded with the glare, instantly blinding her as heat sensors buzzed from the dash. Fresh oxygen surged into her mask, and Packer's voice crackled over the intercom.

"Al—ude. Thirty—and—feet."

Laura yanked back on the stick even as the bright light continued to blind her. The F-35 nosed up. The glare intensified.

Then came the concussion—a mass shockwave that grabbed her little plane and shook it like a leaf in a thunderstorm. Worse than any turbulence she'd ever experienced, almost enough to knock her sideways like a drifting car. Her heart hammered and she clung to the stick by sheer willpower, working the plane slowly out of the sideways slide even as garbled bits of communication chirped through her headset. The displays flickered. Warning lights built into a crescendo. The F-35 continued to glide sideways, spinning in midair even as the displays cut off, terminated by a massive electromagnetic pulse.

The breath stuck in Laura's throat. She saw the mushroom cloud rising high over Panama. Her brain descended into panic.

And for the second time in less than two years, she yanked the ejection handle.

73

The Situation Room
The White House

From the leather chair halfway down the length of the conference table, Acting President Jordan Stratton watched the world go nuclear.

The blast illuminated the feed of the CIA's overhead spy satellite, flooding the screen with bright orange and yellow and red—so much light that the entire Panamanian coast was illumined like day. The city of Colón sat at the heart of the blast, and it simply vanished amid the light. Smoke erupted upward. Tall swells of water ran against the tide, blasting out to sea like a reverse tsunami.

The *Cartova* was gone in the blink of an eye, and with it more than forty thousand souls. Stratton didn't need to be told that the blast exceeded that of the Hiroshima bomb. That much was evident by the sheer size of the cloud alone. Something truly unthinkable had been unleashed in quiet little Panama, and he already knew the world would never again be the same.

"A moment of silence," Stratton said softly. It was a needless comment. Everybody was already silent. But he wanted to voice it anyway—not just because the vaporized Panamanians deserved it, but because he never wanted to forget the utter dread and complete defeat that radiated through his body in red-hot misery.

He would remember this for the rest of his life. Whatever happened next. Whatever the world came to. If this was the beginning of the end—he would never forgive himself for this failure.

"General, did your aircraft survive?"

Yellin blinked from the end of the table. He tore his gaze away from the screen with an effort, his eyes rimmed red. He cleared his throat aggressively.

"I don't know, sir."

"Get them back to safety, then notify the Navy to begin shifting resources into the Caribbean. I want an aid plan put together by morning. Madam Secretary, connect with Panama City and commit our support. Jill, put together a conference call with London, Paris, Berlin, and Tokyo. I want everybody on the same page. We're remaining at DEFCON 1 until further notice."

The room remained quiet as everyone went to work. Stratton never looked away from the screen. He watched as the column of fire slowly faded, the light dimming a little but not disappearing. The jungle around the former city of Colón was on fire.

Just like Stratton.

74

Vauxhall, London
England

The largest display in the SIS operations center depicted the blast in vivid detail. A spot of white fire, rapidly developing into every hot color on the spectrum, ripping across the coast and wiping a city from existence in the blink of an eye.

The Prosecution Force remained behind their desks, staring dumbfounded as the room went silent. For a brief moment, not even a breath was heard. Dozens of faces fixated on the display in transfixed horror.

Then the gasps began. The subdued sobs. The muttered curses.

Wolfgang's body went rigid as fire ripped across the screen, but by the time many of the others were finding their voices, he'd already found his phone. He dialed the only number he'd spoken with in the past two days—an international area code. It rang only twice before former SVR officer Ivan Sidorov answered.

"It happened," Wolfgang said, simply.

"Where?"

"Panama. At the canal."

Silence filled the line. Wolfgang thought that Ivan was probably surprised by the target, but momentary confusion would quickly be replaced by the cold calculation of Abdel Ibrahim's final attack. It was a blow that would rock the American economy to its core. Shut down shipping. Throttle the movements of the United States Navy. Put global trade in a tailspin.

Dozens of countries would be impacted, but save for Panama itself, none would be more wounded than America.

"I think you should come in," Wolfgang said. "The agency will want to speak with you. We'll need to know everything."

A long pause. A weary sigh.

"Yes," Ivan said.

75

The Oval Office
The White House

It was almost dawn before Stratton ascended from the White House bunker and turned for the Oval. Jim Dorsey hadn't wanted to let him out of the armored box, but Stratton hadn't been asking. He needed fresh air, and he needed a calm place from which to work.

There was still so much to be done. He had to coordinate with allied powers—especially the nuclear ones—all around the globe. He had to touch base with Moscow and Beijing and ensure everybody who was both nuclear and *not* an ally were keeping cooler heads. He had to address the nation. He had to formulate a military response plan.

He had to be the president of the Free World, even if he'd never been elected as such. He would begin with a hot cup of coffee and a call to Britain. As the allied power that had most directly contributed to the chase for Ibrahim, the authorities in London were his first priority to coordinate with. A discussion needed to be had on what level of detail would be released to the public. On which cards to play, and which to hold.

Stratton pushed through the heavy door and stopped for a moment just inside. The Oval was dark and desolate. The bourbon cart remained, but the empty glass he'd drank from while speaking to Victor O'Brien had been cleared away by a steward. The room smelled like peaches, the couch cushions freshly fluffed and the rug freshly vacuumed.

Stratton let the door ease closed behind him, enveloped for a moment in the surreal. He'd stepped through that door hundreds of times since joining the Trousdale administration, but none of those trips felt like this one. Even when he assumed the role of acting president for the second time in his life and met with O'Brien in this room as a show of power, it felt superficial. Like it wasn't really his. Like it was rented space.

For the first time, a new thought settled into his brain and sank into his very bones. This could be it. Maggie might not recover. He might not just be the president for today, or for a month . . . but for the rest of her term. The crisis facing the nation now was more absolute than anything Maggie had confronted in her tumultuous tenure as leader of the Free World, and there was nobody to share that responsibility with. It was solely on his own two shoulders, whether he was ready for it or not.

Jordan Stratton was president of the United States. Acting or permanent, it didn't much matter. Everything that happened from this moment forward would go down in history as *his* responsibility.

A dryness crept into Stratton's throat, but he bypassed the bourbon cart and headed straight for the Resolute desk. He didn't want to dull any of his mental faculties with alcohol. If anything, he needed an energy drink. He likely wouldn't sleep until the following night. He had to work now. To focus.

Jill Easterling had already assembled a punch list of phone calls to make. A report waited on the desk with initial estimations of the economic and military consequences of a complete loss of the Panama Canal. They couldn't know for certain, of course, that the canal was lost . . . but it didn't take a genius to assume that it was. That much radiation would not only have vaporized Colón, but also poisoned the area for decades to come. It would be a permanent problem, something both the U.S. Navy and the U.S. economy needed answers for, immediately.

Stratton eased into his chair and reached for the telephone, ready to ring up a steward and request the coffee. Then he stopped, his eye caught on a small envelope resting on the desktop. It was made of cream-colored paper, resting face up. Scrawled on the face in blue ink were two simple words: *Mr. President*.

Stratton's blood pressure spiked. He ignored the phone and used Maggie's letter opener to slice the envelope open. A single card fell out, a bright blue seal emblazoned on one side—the seal of the Central Intelligence Agency.

And on the other side? Five more words, written in the same ink and the same hand.

I'm going to enjoy this.

No signature.

Stratton gazed at the card for a long moment, his mind skipping back to the meeting with O'Brien, now feeling like an age away. He thought of his threats, and O'Brien's flushed face. His wounded pride. Stratton had hoped that intimidation would generate results that bribery had failed to.

Apparently, both methods had failed. Victor O'Brien was no longer a capitalist, and he clearly wasn't afraid. Much like Ibrahim, O'Brien was waging a holy war. A campaign against injustice, perceived or otherwise.

And just like Ibrahim, there was only one way to stop such a jihad.

Stratton's shoulders fell and he tossed the card down. For a long moment he sat alone in the darkness of the Oval Office, sucking his teeth and contemplating the weight of the moment. Feeling the pressure, and owning it. Measuring the threat of a rogue former director of the CIA hell-bent on tearing down the Trousdale administration right in the middle of the nation's worst crisis since . . . the Second World War? The Civil War?

What kind of president will you be, Jordan?

The thought rang through his head in his father's voice. Barrett Stratton had never actually posed the question, but years of pressure under his father's demanding method of parenting made it easy for Stratton to hear the challenge in that familiar voice. It spiked his heart rate up another notch. His blood ran hot. He pictured O'Brien again, and disgust flooded his mind.

No way in hell.

Scooping the phone up, Stratton rang the operator.

"Yes, sir?"

"Can you find out if James O'Dell is still in the building?"

"Mr. O'Dell?"

"The president's special advisor."

"Yes, sir. I'll check."

Long pause. Stratton waited.

"He's in the Residence, sir."

"Send him to the Oval."

Stratton hung up, tapping one finger slowly on the table as he stared at the card. It was just like the card Maggie had received, the one inscribed with the word *Karma*. The one that had finally pushed her failing liver over the edge with a surge of mental and physical stress.

It was a blow the nation couldn't afford. Not now. Not when the integrity and unity of the executive branch needed to be absolute.

The door opened and James O'Dell rushed in, dressed in the same jeans and tight t-shirt Stratton had seen him in before. Stress illuminated his handsome face. He stopped just on the other side of the couch.

"Is she dying?" O'Dell asked.

Stratton didn't answer. He kept tapping slowly with one finger, then tilted his head toward the door. O'Dell frowned in confusion, but he closed it. Stratton tilted his head again to indicate that he should sit. O'Dell chose the chair Stratton had most often used while meeting with the president.

Stratton kept tapping with his finger, that one question on repeat in his brain. All the frustration and suppression of a career of feeling inadequate and underpowered came crashing in at once.

What kind of president will you be, Jordan?

"What is it, sir?" The stress in O'Dell's voice renewed. He leaned close. "Is she dying?"

Stratton stopped tapping with his finger. He sat rigid. Then his gaze pivoted to lock with O'Dell's.

"No," he said. "But she's under attack."

O'Dell's frown intensified, and a flash of hot anger radiated behind his dark eyes. Stratton caught it, and he knew. He'd found his man.

"How far would you go to protect the president, Mr. O'Dell?"

76

Leiper's Fork, Tennessee

The Gulfstream V touched down on the private airfield with the same gentle kiss of tires on pavement that Reed had come to expect from Strickland. Even Corbyn was impressed, offering a slap on her co-pilot's shoulder and an "Attaboy!" that Strickland didn't seem to appreciate.

Reed blocked them out, simply grabbing his bag and walking down the steps without a word to any of the others. It was hot in Tennessee, as it had been hot all summer, but he barely noticed. Turk said something to him about dinner and beers and Reed just kept walking, head down, circling the nose of the jet and routing for the hangar.

It had been thirty-six hours since London and the bomb blast, and the numbness in his mind had returned with a vengeance. He felt so flat and lifeless, he didn't even notice the sweat draining down his neck, or the warmth of the asphalt under his feet. His chest felt like a cavity. His mind like an abyss. When he'd tried to sleep on the flight, the dreams had returned. Stronger even than before, and more cutting.

The fire. The screams. His daughter, yanked away under the demon laugh of Ibrahim—a man who was now apparently immortal, a permanent fixture of Reed's subconscious. He longed to see April in that open golden field, like he had before. He longed to hold her, to touch her. To cling to her.

He couldn't. He could only feel the pain, and yet even the pain barely registered. He just knew he wanted to collapse, to drink half a bottle of whiskey by himself and pass out.

"Reed."

The voice was soft to his left as Reed reached for the hangar's door. He stopped and pivoted, squinting at the sunlight. He'd walked right past the bright red Volkswagen SUV parked in front of the hangar, and the beautiful blonde standing slumped over next to it, one arm wrapped around her still-healing midsection. She held car keys in one hand, the other braced against the doorjamb to keep herself upright. Her face was pale and tinged a little yellow, her eyes washed out. Despite a careful application of makeup, the scars still healing on her neck were visible. The bags beneath her eyes still defined.

She stared, and Reed stared back, and neither of them spoke. Then Reed simply turned away from the hangar and joined her at the SUV. Banks wrapped him in a hug, pulling him close and sniffing. He detected tears joining the sweat on his neck, and he gave her a squeeze. She felt weak in his arms, slouching against him. He knew he should fuss at her for driving out of Nashville—something she wasn't supposed to do for at least another couple of months.

Somehow, Reed couldn't find the words. He didn't argue as she beckoned for him to help her back into the driver's seat. He closed her door and threw his backpack into the back seat, then he walked around the hood and took shotgun. The Volkswagen rumbled to life under the pressure of the start button, and the radio clicked on.

Reed recognized Vice President Jordan Stratton's voice. The acting president was delivering an address to the nation. His voice was stiff and focused, as though he was forcibly containing his own emotion. He talked about pain, and loss. He empathized with a terrified nation. He detailed what he called an "unprecedented act of wickedness" in the bombing of Panama and the closure of the Panama Canal. He promised immediate and absolute retribution—a storm of vengeance unseen in the history of the world.

Banks tapped a button and shut the radio off. Reed didn't complain. Rolling Tennessee hills passed on either side, sparse traffic breezing by every few seconds on the two-lane. Banks was pointed north, Back toward Nashville. Reed didn't look at her, but he could tell by her irregular sniff that she was holding back tears.

"Did you get him?" Banks asked at last, voice raspy and dry.

Reed looked at his hands. He still hadn't scrubbed Ibrahim's blood away. It stained his fingers, and a part of him hoped it always would. He never wanted to forget.

"Yes," Reed said, simply.

Banks nodded a couple times. She rolled to a stop at a traffic light, and the sun baked down. It was hot, even in the car. Reed didn't care.

"So it's over?" Banks asked. Her voice was timid.

Reed pivoted to face her, staring into deep blue eyes clouded by tears. She blinked to drive them back, but they slipped out anyway. They dripped onto her lap. The pain in her face was absolute, consuming.

And Reed still couldn't feel a thing.

"No," he said. "And it never will be."

Banks swallowed. Her breath hitched. She looked ahead and mashed the gas.

Reed's face pivoted slowly toward the trees, hands lying palms up in his lap, trembling a little. He thought of Ibrahim. He thought of his daughter, and the bomb, and all the meaningless death.

And the only thing he wanted to know was who he would kill next.

77

Arlington, Virginia

The house sat by itself at the end of a cul-de-sac. A very nice place, but by metro DC standards it was far from a mansion. Maybe six or seven hundred thousand dollars, with a two-car garage and a yard. O'Dell already knew by looking at a satellite image that there was a pool out back. He knew Victor O'Brien was home because he'd watched his silver Mercedes pull into the garage. He waited two hours afterward, until it was full dark and the former head of the Central Intelligence Agency hadn't left.

Then O'Dell abandoned the rental car with stolen license plates and walked through the park, across the golf course, through the trees, and to O'Brien's side yard. There was a door to that side of the house, standing right next to a pair of trash cans and a gate in the privacy fence that surrounded the backyard. A small duffel bag swung from O'Dell's right hand as he approached the gate. He could already hear O'Brien in the backyard, talking on a cell phone. The conversation was loud and spirited. O'Brien cursed a lot amid an impassioned tirade.

From what O'Dell could hear, he was speaking to Senator Roper. Apparently, O'Brien's testimony had been canceled. As chairman of the

Senate Intelligence Committee, Roper was now between a rock and a hard place. The bomb in Panama had escalated everything, forcing him to reevaluate his intentions to roadblock Aimes's confirmation.

In fact, Roper had already decided to push the confirmation through. There was no longer any political hay to be made in grandstanding while the nation stood on the brink of apparent nuclear war. O'Dell knew, because he'd seen all the news reports. Aimes would be the bona fide director of the nation's intelligence service by the end of the week, which was good news for the nation, but failed to solve Muddy Maggie's Victor O'Brien problem.

The president hung to life by a thread. Without a liver, she would be dead within the month. That was a problem O'Dell didn't yet know how to solve, but the more immediate threat was the man sitting beyond the privacy fence. With or without the confirmation hearings, O'Brien had made it clear that the stories he would tell about Muddy Maggie would put her in her political grave. Senator Roper might not be able to stall the confirmation any longer, but that didn't make him the administration's friend.

When Maggie returned to the world of the living, she needed to *not* be in prison. O'Dell knew personally that there was an abundance of things Maggie had done for which she could be locked away for the rest of her life. He'd been there for many of them. Maybe he could even be locked away himself.

O'Dell didn't care about that. He had only ever cared about Maggie, and there was no way he would let her be stabbed in the back while she wasn't even conscious. She was an American hero. An icon of hope for a broken nation.

She deserved to be protected.

O'Brien hung up the phone just as O'Dell lifted the unlocked gate latch with a gloved hand and slipped inside. He closed it behind him and crept without a sound over smooth, manicured grass. He saw O'Brien sitting next to the pool, a drink in hand, his face fixated on his phone. O'Dell approached from the side, dipping his hand into the bag to retrieve the Smith and Wesson M&P chambered in .40 caliber that he'd bought off a street dealer in Baltimore the previous day.

The weapon was dirty—not physically, but certainly metaphorically. Who knew where it had been, or what it had done. It would be at the bottom of the Potomac River before the night was over, but nobody would go looking for it.

If things went according to plan, O'Dell would never squeeze the trigger.

He waited until he was five yards from the former intelligence director before he spoke. When he did his voice was soft, the Cajun drawl just loud enough to draw attention.

"Have a nice phone call?"

O'Brien sat bolt upright, dropping the phone and nearly spilling the drink as he pivoted toward O'Dell. The muzzle of the Smith covered him, and O'Brien's face blanched.

Then it turned rosy red.

"You—"

"Relax, O'Brien. If I wanted to shoot you, you'd already be dead."

It was a half truth, but it was enough to derail O'Brien's panic train. His owl eyes fixated on O'Dell, gleaming behind his trademark round glasses. O'Dell circled him, still keeping the pistol trained on his chest. Then he used the toe of his boot to flip the fallen cell phone neatly into the pool.

"What the—"

"Shut up, O'Brien. You come out of that chair and it'll be the last thing you do."

The crimson of O'Brien's cheeks darkened. O'Dell backed up and hooked his boot around the leg of a patio chair, dragging it into position behind him. He sat, resting the bag on the concrete next to him. A glass bottle clinked softly as it settled onto the concrete, and O'Brien's gaze darted from the pistol to the bag. He swallowed, despite himself.

"You won't get away with this, you swamp rat."

"Get away with what?"

Despite his calm voice, O'Dell's heart thundered. He'd learned in the Navy how to be calm under pressure, and had put that into practice as a Louisiana state cop. He'd been under fire and he'd been under plenty of stress.

But this was different. This was new . . . and much harder.

"What do you want?" O'Brien said, declining to answer O'Dell's question. O'Dell adjusted his grip on the pistol and looked to the glass in O'Brien's right hand. It trembled slightly—he could see it in a little ripple that shot across the surface of clear liquid.

"What are you drinking?" O'Dell demanded.

"What?"

"*What are you drinking?*"

O'Brien glanced to the glass as though he'd forgotten. His lips tightened.

"Bourbon. *You want some?*" The question was sarcastic. O'Dell didn't answer. Instead, he dug into the duffel bag, quickly locating the premium bottle of Kentucky bourbon he'd bought at a Virginia liquor store. O'Dell knew little about fancy liquor and he didn't recognize the brand, he only knew that it cost nearly two hundred bucks. Stratton told him not to cheap out—that O'Brien was a bourbon man and that it would be suspect if cheap liquor was found in his stomach.

The two hundred dollars was a price O'Dell was perfectly willing to pay.

"Here," he said. "Let me top you off."

O'Brien's gaze flicked to the bottle as O'Dell stood. Another wave of uncertainty rushed across his face, followed by sudden disgust.

"What do you take me for, you—"

"Drink," O'Dell said, flatly, stepping to O'Brien's side and upending the bottle to flood O'Brien's glass. Bourbon spilled out of his hand and O'Brien recoiled.

"What the—"

"*Drink*," O'Dell snapped.

O'Brien made as if to stand. O'Dell's right arm twitched, ramming the muzzle of his Smith against O'Brien's temple. Not hard enough to leave a mark, just hard enough to startle him.

O'Brien held up a hand. "Okay, okay! Geez. Relax."

He drank. O'Dell kept the gun against his temple until the glass was empty. Then he poured another.

"Drink."

"W-what?" O'Brien stuttered a little, his eyes rimming red. "What are you doing?"

"What should have been done a long time ago."

O'Brien stiffened. He gritted his teeth and again he attempted to stand.

O'Dell didn't bother with the gun this time. He stepped quickly behind O'Brien, encircling his throat with his pistol arm while he held the bourbon bottle with the other. O'Brien thrashed, sudden understanding flashing across his face. He reached for the gun, but O'Dell's iron grip held it fast. He pressed against O'Brien's windpipe, just strong enough to force him to gasp.

Then he rammed the bottle's neck between O'Brien's lips and poured.

The former intelligence director choked a lot. He spilled bourbon down his shirt. He spat up some, and some exploded out of his nose. But he drank a lot more—fully two-thirds of the bottle before O'Dell finally released him.

O'Brien heaved, gasping for air and falling out of the chair. His knees struck the concrete, and his hands followed. He choked, almost as though he were going to vomit.

O'Dell put the gun to the base of his neck. "You puke, you die."

O'Brien closed his mouth, still heaving through his nose. His glasses fell off and struck the concrete. A guttural growl erupted from his chest.

O'Dell stepped away, resuming his seat. He checked his watch and decided to wait fifteen minutes. The Smith remained pointed at O'Brien as the former director of the CIA slowly dragged himself to his feet, wiping his mouth and stumbling.

However much bourbon O'Brien had consumed prior to O'Dell's arrival, the onslaught of the better part of a bottle was leaving its mark quickly. O'Brien slurred a curse and stumbled, catching himself on the chair.

"You dumb . . . fool," O'Brien choked. "Whaddaya want?"

O'Dell just stared, body relaxed even if his mind couldn't be. He blinked back a blur and licked his lips.

"I was in the Navy, O'Brien. Of course you know that. You were only too happy to remind me."

O'Brien leaned on the back of the chair, still breathing like a winded dog. He laughed.

"That's r-right. You washed out, didn't you? Of . . . BUDS!" He spat the word after a drunken hesitation. O'Dell actually smiled.

"I sure did. I guess I wasn't up to the cut."

O'Brien's grin turned cold. "And you still aren't. You ignorant n—"

O'Brien hiccupped. O'Dell cocked an eyebrow.

"What's that, O'Brien?"

The drunken man stumbled, catching himself. O'Dell rose slowly out of his chair.

"Finish your sentence, O'Brien. What did you call me?"

O'Brien looked up. Drool slipped out of his jaw. He smiled again.

"You heard me."

O'Dell had heard him—and he didn't particularly care. He was Black and he was from a poor state. He'd been called every name in the book before he was in high school. He'd learned to ignore it.

But what he couldn't ignore was a direct threat to the only thing he had left to love. Bigger than the country he'd failed to serve or the daughter he'd failed to parent or the ex-wife he'd failed to cherish.

Maggie was all that remained. James O'Dell was done losing things.

He pocketed the handgun as O'Brien lifted a finger and inhaled to launch another insult. He stepped behind the spook and grabbed him by the collar. Sudden panic washed through O'Brien's body, and he thrashed desperately. But in addition to being a relatively small guy, the alcohol had muted all his motor skills. He couldn't reach O'Dell. He couldn't stop the president's lover from dragging him all the way to the edge of the pool, and kicking his feet in.

O'Brien descended into the water with a splash. O'Dell yanked his head backward on the way down, smacking his head against the pool's concrete edge hard enough to draw blood and stun him. O'Brien's desperate thrashes grew weak.

O'Dell held him down. Twenty seconds. Then sixty.

Two minutes.

When he released the body, it floated slowly to the surface, face down. The arms splayed outward. O'Dell removed his gloved hand slowly and stood, his eyes still blurred. His heart hammering. His body alive with tension.

But no regret. He took the bag and the bourbon bottle and left everything else as a disorganized mess. He returned to the rental, and drove it all the way to Baltimore. He left it in a bad neighborhood where it was certain to be jacked. He took the train back to DC.

Thinking of Maggie the entire way.

78

The Kremlin
Moscow, Russia

President Makar Nikitin was in his office. Not the fancy one with all the expensive gold trim and antique furniture. This was the real office—the working place deep inside the heart of Russian power where he was joined by his closest confidants and deepest supporters.

Not his full Russian cabinet. These were only a select few—men he could trust implicitly. Men who knew of each of the chess moves made over the last eighteen months, and what they all led to. Men who were prepared to assist him in the next big step.

The step that would change the world forever.

Spread across the screens lining the walls were reports out of Panama. The bomb—a small, Russian-built uranium device constructed to look and operate like an outdated Soviet RDS-4—produced a blast yield of right at thirty kilotons. Twice the size of the bomb that leveled Hiroshima and more than enough to decimate Colón and close off the eastern mouth of the Panama Canal for decades to come.

The economic impacts would be swift and ruthless. Forty percent of U.S. trade passed through that narrow stretch of water annually, and that said nothing of its strategic value to the U.S. military. With the canal out of operation, the world's most powerful navy wasn't technically cut in two . . . but it might as well be. Sailing around Cape Horn took weeks longer, and burned valuable resources. The throttled trade route would hamper the American war machine just as it would hamper their economy.

And that was *after* the terrorist attacks that had blanketed the nation in fear. *After* the attempted assassination that might still throw America's executive leadership into chaos. *After* the inflation, and the congressional squabbling about President Trousdale's use of executive authority that had further deepened the political rift running through the country.

Oh yes. The first moves in this chess game had been marvelously effective, even if Nikitin's attempt to establish a Russian foothold in South America had backfired magnificently. The world's greatest superpower was reeling, engulfed in woes of her own that not only hampered her ability to maintain global control . . .

But also distracted her. Just like the modified bunker buster that blew a hole in the Channel Tunnel and claimed a paltry three hundred and twelve lives had distracted from the real threat.

The Americans would blame Ibrahim. They would blame radical Islam. They would panic and rage and Russia would rage with them. Answers must be found. Those guilty must be punished.

How could a Soviet-era nuke fall into the hands of a peasant radical? Where had it come from?

It had come from Georgia, of course. It had come from the Caucasus. That oil-rich Soviet holding that had been one of the first to declare liberation from the faltering union.

Nikitin overlooked the table laden with charts and tablet computers, many depicting battle lines and routes of incursion. The air hung thick with Turkish cigar smoke, and on a lefthand screen a chart displayed the result of a military muster. A preparation for emergency action.

He looked to Golubev, his trusted number two. The ghost of the Kremlin who made all the dirtiest of tricks possible. The man's teeth were clamped around a cigar. He nodded once.

Nikitin smiled. "Let us begin."

NUCLEAR NATION
THE PROSECUTION FORCE THRILLERS Book 7

In a world on the brink of nuclear war, one man stands between peace and global chaos.

Following the devastating aftermath of a nuclear detonation in the Panama Canal, the world teeters on the edge of war. The Russian president's claims about a hidden Soviet weapons depot in Georgia escalate tensions, pushing the globe closer to the abyss of conflict.

Acting U.S. President Jordan Stratton faces a nation in turmoil, grappling with the shadows of recent terrorist attacks and the critical condition of President Maggie Trousdale. Amidst this chaos, Reed Montgomery, the leader of a covert black ops team, is thrust into the heart of the storm. Challenged by personal demons and the weight of national security on his shoulders, Reed is sent on a critical mission to uncover the truth behind the Russian allegations.

But in Georgia, Reed and his team's quest quickly spirals into a deadly game of cat and mouse with heavily armed Russian forces. When the team discovers that yet another weapon of mass destruction is already en route to slaughter tens of thousands, the only path forward is to throw themselves right into the jaws of disaster...or risk the next world war.

ABOUT THE AUTHOR

Logan Ryles was born in small town USA and knew from an early age he wanted to be a writer. After working as a pizza delivery driver, sawmill operator, and banker, he finally embraced the dream and has been writing ever since. With a passion for action-packed and mystery-laced stories, Logan's work has ranged from global-scale political thrillers to small town vigilante hero fiction.

Beyond writing, Logan enjoys saltwater fishing, road trips, sports, and fast cars. He lives with his wife and three fun-loving dogs in Alabama.

Sign up for Logan Ryles's reader list at
severnriverbooks.com